What early readers are saying about *One Moment*

'I tore through it, alternating between rage and pain. In
particular, Kaz (and Terry's) situation is explored with
forensic authenticity – Linda has centred the experience
of people so often treated as marginal in fiction'
Shelley Harris, author of *Vigilante*

'Up there with the very best. I sobbed big fat tears and at
one point I was inconsolable. Truly a classic of our time'

'WOW! I've read hundreds of books and never
has one touched me like this one'

'Oh, how I loved this book. It had me in the depths
of sadness and the heights of joy. Beautifully written.
This is one story that will stay with me'

'Someone point me in the direction of all her other
books because I need to make a start now!'

'This book is just beautiful. I loved every page. I'd go so
far as to say, one of the best books I've ever read'

'Buy it, you will not be disappointed. I laughed and
cried the whole way through in equal measures'

'Linda Green is an incredibly talented author and this book is
crafted in such a special and clever way. I absolutely LOVED IT'

'I feel like I've experienced something very special.
Linda Green has woven an incredibly compelling and
timely story which made me laugh, cry, fume with
anger and nod in agreement so many times'

'One of the most uplifting yet heart-breaking novels
you will ever read'

'... ng just
s'

one moment

LINDA GREEN

Quercus

First published in Great Britain in 2019 by Quercus
This paperback edition published in 2020 by

Quercus Editions Ltd
Carmelite House
50 Victoria Embankment
London EC4Y 0DZ

An Hachette UK company

A CIP catalogue record for this book is available
from the British Library

PB ISBN 978 1 78747 874 9
EB ISBN 978 1 78747 876 3

10 9 8 7 6 5 4 3

Typeset by CC Book Production
Printed and bound in Great Britain by Clays Ltd, Elcograf S.p.A.

MIX
Paper from
responsible sources
FSC® C104740
FSC
www.fsc.org

Papers used by Quercus are from well-managed forests and other responsible sources.

Linda Green is the bestselling author of nine novels. Her latest novel, *The Last Thing She Told Me*, was a Richard & Judy Book Club pick, a top twenty *Sunday Times* bestseller and a top five Amazon Kindle bestseller. Her previous novel, *While My Eyes Were Closed*, was the fourth bestselling novel on Amazon Kindle in 2016, selling more than 450,000 copies across all editions. She lives in West Yorkshire with her husband and son. Visit Linda on Twitter at @LindaGreenisms and on Facebook at Fans of Author Linda Green.

Also by Linda Green

For Rohan

And all the boys who dare to be different

BEFORE
1

FINN

My name is Finn, as in Huckleberry, and there is nothing wrong with me. I know this because my dad has tried very hard to find something wrong with me, but I did OK in all the tests. It turns out I am just weird, and they don't have a test for that yet, or, if they do, my dad hasn't heard about it.

My surname is Rook-Carter, which also sounds weird because it is double-barrelled (which is the proper way to say it's two names stuck together). Mum said they did it so that my name had a bit of her and a bit of Dad in it. Only now they're getting divorced and they're fighting over who I'm going to live with, so I don't know what's going to happen to my name. Maybe I'll be Finn Rook on Mondays to Wednesdays, Finn Carter on Thursdays and Fridays and Finn Rook-Carter at the weekends when I switch between them.

When I say Mum and Dad are fighting over me, I don't

mean actual fighting, like a *Star Wars* battle, I mean they are arguing a lot and they both have solicitors who write letters to each other that make them angry. Jayden McGreevy in my class used to write notes to me, which made me angry when I was in year four, but my mum went in to school with one of them and he got in trouble and had to write another note saying he was sorry, even though I knew he didn't mean it.

Mum and Dad have both told me that the solicitors cost a lot of money, which seems stupid because if they asked Jayden, I'm pretty sure he'd write letters to make them angry for a bag of Haribos.

I can't eat Haribos because they've got gelatine in and me and Mum are vegetarians and the kids at school don't get that because you can't see bits of dead pigs or cows in sweets, so it's another thing that makes me weird.

I keep a list of things about me that they think are weird. There are actually loads of things, but people always do top-ten lists, so this is the top-ten list of the things they seem to think are most weird:

1. Not liking football or being able to name a single player
2. Not eating Haribos
3. Having curly, red hair and not normal straight, short brown hair like them
4. Not having a mobile phone
5. Not doing gaming
6. Never having been to a McDonald's

7. Liking gardening and my hero being Alan Titchmarsh
8. Playing the ukulele
9. Not liking football (they think it's so weird, I've put it in twice)
10. Having a bee rucksack

On the last one, I don't mean having a yellow and black rucksack in the shape of a bee. I had loads of those when I was little – Mum got me a different one every year – but on my tenth birthday she gave me a grey rucksack that had bees printed on. She said it was more grown up. Dad rolled his eyes when she said that, only he didn't let her see because they are still pretending to be nice to each other in front of me and especially on birthdays. I took it to school the next week and the kids still laughed at it, so I guess Dad was right.

Anyway, it doesn't matter. The way I see it, if you're going to be weird, you may as well be weird all over, rather than think there's a little bit of you that's not weird, because they'll still laugh at you anyway.

And when I go to secondary school in September, it's going to be a whole lot worse. Mum and Dad did a lot of arguing about that as well. Dad said I couldn't go to the school most of the other kids in my class are going to, because I would get 'eaten alive at a comprehensive in Halifax'. He didn't say that in front of me, he said it in one of the arguments I overheard. They thought I was practising my ukulele in my bedroom and I was but then I had to go for a wee and I heard them arguing in the kitchen (kitchens are rubbish for arguing secretly in because they haven't got a door and I don't get why they don't know that). When Dad said I would get 'eaten alive', Mum's voice went funny and at first I thought it was because she is a vegetarian and didn't approve of anyone being eaten but then she said sometimes it was like he was embarrassed to have me as a son and he said he wasn't embarrassed, just realistic about the fact that I wouldn't fit in and she said that was why she wanted to home-educate me and he did a snorty sort of laugh and said I needed to go to a good school, not have half-baked lessons with her at the kitchen table, and she started crying and I couldn't hear anything else, so I went back to playing 'You Are My Sunshine' on my ukulele.

A couple of weeks later I had to go and play my ukulele and the piano at a different, old-fashioned-looking school near Ilkley on a Saturday morning and not long after that, Mum and Dad sat me down and told me I had got a place at that school from September. Mum had her smiley face on and nodded a lot but didn't say anything, which I think meant it was Dad's idea. She said not to tell anyone the name of the school because not everyone could afford to go to a school like that and they might not understand how music scholarships work.

I did tell Lottie, who's my best friend at school, well, my only friend actually, and she googled the school and said the real reason they wanted to keep it a secret was because it was a private school for posho boys like Tory MPs' sons. She knows about things like that because her mum is a Labour councillor and once sat next to Jeremy Corbyn in a soup kitchen for the homeless (her mum had made the soup and Jeremy Corbyn was visiting. I thought it was wrong that Jeremy Corbyn ate the soup when she'd made it for homeless people, but I didn't tell Lottie that).

'Finn, do you want to come down and help me with the muffins?'

It is Mum's voice calling up the stairs. She thinks baking is a 'fun thing to do together' after I've come home from school. To be honest, pretty much anything is fun compared to school and if it gets me out of having to do homework, I don't mind.

When I get downstairs, I see that the ingredients are already out on the kitchen table. We are making the apricot, orange and bran muffins as usual. That is another weird thing about me. When they have charity bake sales at school, the cakes I take in don't look like the other kids' cakes. Mine are a sort of orangey-brown colour, instead of being chocolatey, and they don't have icing on or sprinkles or anything like that. I suppose that's why none of the other kids ever buy them. Mine are always the ones left at the end. Sometimes my teacher buys one, probably because she feels sorry for me, and sometimes we've even bought our own ones back at the end of the day, to save them being wasted.

Mum smiles at me. 'Right, are you being the Honey Monster as usual?' she says as she pops an apron over my head. Sometimes she talks to me like I'm still nine. I don't think she realises she's doing it.

'Yeah,' I say, smiling at her as she hands me the jar of honey from the table.

We have made these muffins together so many times that

we both know exactly what to do without looking at the recipe or anything. I do all the measuring of the ingredients because otherwise Mum just guesses, and I don't like that.

'So, how was school today?' asks Mum as I tip the flour into the bowl.

'OK,' I reply. I have worked out that this is the best way of answering the question. If I say it was great, she knows I am lying. 'OK' is a way of saying I didn't enjoy it, but I wasn't beaten up or anything.

'What's your class reading at the moment?' Mum asks, as she tucks a long red curl behind her ear.

'Nothing. We're just doing English SATs practice papers,' I reply.

'What, all the time?'

'Yeah. Apart from when we're doing maths SATs practice papers.'

Mum shakes her head and does something funny with her lips. She doesn't agree with SATs. She told me at the beginning of year six that I didn't have to do them, but I knew I would be the only one who didn't, and I get fed up of being different from everyone else all the time. That's why I said I'd do them.

Mum lets me crack the eggs into the bowl. I make chicken noises as I do it. It always makes Mum laugh, which is why I do it. She starts doing chicken noises too and funny chicken arms as she dances around the kitchen. I like it when she is like this. She used to be like this a lot more than she is these days. I start doing the funny chicken dance too. We are both doing it and laughing so much that we don't hear Dad's key in the front door. We don't even realise he is home until we see him standing in the kitchen looking at us with one eyebrow slightly raised and a kind of half-smile on his face.

'Hello, what's all this then?' he says, ruffling my hair (everyone ruffles my hair, there is something about curly hair that seems to work like a magnet to people's hands). He is looking at me. He doesn't really look at Mum when he says anything, even if he is partly talking to her.

'We're doing the crazy chicken dance,' I say.

'Any particular reason?' he asks.

'Because it's funny,' I reply.

Me and Mum do it some more. Dad looks like he feels a little bit left out of the whole thing. He has never joined in with the baking, but he has always eaten what we made and when I was little, he used to take my muffins or cookies to work and take photos of them before he ate them to show me when he came home. I can't remember the last time he did that.

'Right. And have you done your revision yet or are you doing it later?'

Mum stops dancing and stares at him. It's like someone has stuck a big pin in our happiness bubble and made it go pop.

'We're having a bit of fun, Martin. If that's still allowed.'

'Of course it is.'

'Right. Well please don't spoil everything by mentioning revision the second you walk through the door? It's like you don't want to see that he's been having fun when you're not here.'

They have gone into the talking-about-me-like-I'm-not-here

thing they do. I don't know if I actually become invisible to them or if they think my ears stop working when they argue or what.

'You know that's not true.'

'So why bring up revision? He gets enough pressure about the stupid SATs at school, he doesn't need it here.'

I wipe my hands on my apron, even though they aren't actually messy. I cough as I do it to remind them that I'm still here. They both look at me, then look down at their feet.

'Right, well I'll leave you to get on with it then,' says Dad, putting a made-up smile on his face. For a moment, I think he is going to ruffle my hair again, so I step forward and pick up the wooden spoon. Dad leaves the kitchen without saying anything else.

'He didn't even ask if he could have one later,' I say.

'No,' replies Mum. 'He didn't.'

We go back to the baking but neither of us do the crazy chicken dance or the laughing again. When we put the muffins in the oven, I stare at them for a bit and wonder whether the arguing will have knocked all the air and laughter out of them, and they won't taste as good as usual. But later, when they have cooled down and Mum brings one up to my room on a plate, I find out they taste exactly the same as usual, which makes me feel a bit better.

I lie in bed that night, listening to them arguing downstairs. I can't hear the words, only the spikiness of their voices. They didn't always have spiky voices. I remember hearing sparkly voices and tinkly laughter. I don't know where they went.

Sometimes I feel like hunting around the house for them, in case they've left them in a cupboard or something and can't remember where they are. I wish I could find them again and give them back, so I don't need to listen to the spiky voices any more.

It never used to be like this. When I was little, we'd all go on walks together and Dad would tell jokes and Mum would groan, but be smiling at the same time, and we would stop and look at flowers and I would collect leaves and things and when we came home, Mum would help me make a collage and Dad would say nice things about it and everybody was smiley and there was no spikiness at all. At some point that I can't quite remember, it stopped being like that and started getting more like this and now it's a lot like this and I don't like it at all.

I turn over in bed and bang my head down on the pillow. The spiky voices have stopped, and they are back to the spiky silence now. Sometimes the silence is worse because, whatever they might think, you can still hear it. And what I want more than anything else in the world is to stop the arguing and the silences and make it go back to how it used to be: Mum's laughter tinkling about the house, her singing coming from whatever room she was in. I can even remember my giggles when I snuggled in between Mum and Dad in bed in the mornings when I was little and they started tickling me. I am very ticklish – just like Dad. Me and Mum used to tickle him to make him giggle. I want us to go back to being a family that make happy sounds again, but I don't know how to make that happen. I know how to make apricot, orange and bran muffins and how to play the ukulele and stupid stuff like that, but I don't know how to do the one thing I really want to do.

I arrive in the playground at school. No one runs over to say hello, but no one runs over to call me a freak or kick me in the shins either, so I suppose that is an OK start to the day. Mum is hovering by the school gate with a weird look on her face, the same look she used to give our cat Atticus when we left him in the cattery before we went on holiday. I don't know why; I mean it's not like she's going to come back and find me all meowing and skinny because I haven't eaten for a week. She's only actually leaving me for ten minutes because she is coming to our celebration assembly. We have one every Friday morning and the parents get invited and Mum usually comes because she is self-employed, and people don't tend to book appointments for this early on a Friday morning. Mum is a homeopath and aromatherapist, which means she makes people feel better without them having to take drugs or go to hospital. I am not supposed to talk about it because some people don't believe in it. I wonder if it's a bit like God. We don't believe in God but I still have to sing about him in assembly and yet we've never once sung about a homeopath, which doesn't seem fair.

Mum doesn't agree with some bits of the celebration assemblies, like when Olivia Worthington was presented with her certificate for going scuba diving in the Maldives during the Easter holidays, and she doesn't like that they play 'Simply the Best' by Tina Turner at the start of it, because she says 'it shouldn't be about being better than all the rest' (she sent an email to Mrs Ratcliffe suggesting they use 'Proud' by Heather Small instead but she never got a reply).

Anyway, Mum said she wouldn't miss this particular celebration assembly for the world because I am going to be playing the ukulele. I passed my Grade Three in music last week with a distinction and Mum told Mrs Kerrigan, my teacher, and she said I could play in assembly as 'an inspiration to others'. I don't think Mrs Kerrigan went to a school like ours because if she had done, she would have known that none of the other kids are going to be even the tiniest bit inspired by me playing the ukulele. I thought it would be rude to tell her that though, which is why I have my ukulele over my shoulder and am feeling slightly sick.

I wish I had someone to talk to, but Lottie never arrives until the last second before the bell goes and sometimes quite a few seconds afterwards. She's only ever had a mum to look after her, and Lottie's mum Rachel is also a health visitor, a member of Calderdale Council and volunteers at the soup kitchen, which Lottie says is why she is always late and in a rush and they have rubbish food at home. Lottie doesn't seem to mind but I would. I don't like being late. And I like Mum's cooking. I hope my mum won't get like that after the divorce. I glance over at her. She is still standing on her own near the gate. It always looks like the other mums have chats that she doesn't know the words to. She doesn't look like the other mums either. It's not just her red hair, it's kind of everything, all the way down to the wrong shoes (Mum doesn't wear shoes, she wears boots all the year round, even in the summer). I often wonder if that is why I'm not like the other boys, because my mum is not like the other mums, but maybe it doesn't work like that. Even if it does, I'm not mad at her for it. She probably can't help it any more than I can. I watch as she follows the other mums into school. She is wearing her favourite green cardigan and I remember for a moment how soft and snuggly it is.

Miss Dye rings the bell and we all line up in our classes. I try to be the last one – that way I only have one boy to bother me instead of two – but it doesn't work today because Ryan Dangerfield is late, so he has to go behind me.

'Ginger minger,' he says into my left ear. He says it loud enough that the other boys near me can hear but quiet enough that our teacher Mrs Kerrigan can't.

Lewis R (everyone calls him Lewis R because there is a Lewis B, so it's become like part of his name) starts laughing and says, 'Don't touch tree boy or you'll get Dutch Finn disease,' and they do some more laughing. Mrs Kerrigan smiles like she thinks we're all having fun together. Maybe school was different all those years ago when she went and kids were nice to each other, which is why she always thinks they're being nice when they're not.

Lottie runs onto the end of the girls' queue as we start walking in. Lottie doesn't look like the other girls because she has short hair, and all the other girls have long straight hair, like it's the law for girls or something. Lottie calls hers a pixie cut but I have never seen a pixie's hair, so I wouldn't know.

It's weird because everyone says I look like a girl and that Lottie looks like a boy, so maybe if we swapped heads we'd look right. I think that's why me and Lottie are friends, because we've both got the wrong hair. Well, she has the wrong hair, I have the wrong everything. I didn't know I had the wrong trousers until we were changing after PE once and Ibrahim picked up mine by mistake and started showing the other boys the label. They all started laughing because they said they were from the wrong shop, but they didn't tell me what the right shop was, so I didn't bother telling Mum. And anyway, I knew she still might not get them from the right shop if they didn't pay their taxes or used child labour. It turns out buying trousers can be a tricky thing.

I sit down next to Lottie. 'Hi Finn,' she says, 'will you sign my petition?' Lottie does petitions about everything. She also goes on protest marches with her mum. She thinks she might be a protestor when she's older, but I didn't even know that was an actual job.

I sign the petition without even looking to see what it is about. When you only have one friend there is no point in asking because you are going to sign it anyway. Lottie says something about being a friend of the badgers and I smile at her. I need all the friends I can get right now – even badgers.

When we get down to the hall for assembly, Mum is sitting on one of the benches at the back. She does a little smile, which makes me feel even more nervous than I already am. She thinks this is going to be one of those 'proud moments'. She has no idea.

I sit there with my ukulele in my lap, not really listening to what the head teacher Mrs Ratcliffe is saying until the bit when she says my name. I look up and she is holding my certificate and smiling at me. I stand up and pick my way through the legs of the other kids on my row and walk out to the front. Mrs Ratcliffe shakes my hand and gives me my Grade Three certificate and people clap, though Mum does it louder than everyone else. I start unzipping my ukulele case, while Mrs Ratcliffe explains that I'm going to play for them. My ukulele is yellow and has a big smile painted on the front. Mum got it for me when I learnt to play 'You Are My Sunshine'. I can see some of the kids laughing at it. Mrs Ratcliffe asks me to play the piece I did for my Grade Three exam. She asks me to tell everyone what it's called. I freeze for a moment, desperately hoping that the fire alarm will go off and save me, but there is silence. Mrs Ratcliffe is still smiling and waiting. Everyone is looking at me. I mumble '"Fanlight Fanny" by George Formby.' All I hear is the laughter from the boys in my class coming back at me. Like a massive wave of laughter getting louder and louder until it crashes over me. I can feel the tears coming and I don't want this to get any worse than it already is, so I do the only thing I can think of. I start playing my ukulele. Even though at that moment, I really hate George Formby.

BEFORE

2

KAZ

I sit next to the sniffing bloke on the bus. It's the beginning of May but is warm enough to be July. People are wearing sun tops and have bare legs and I manage to find the only person in Halifax with a cold.

It's my own fault; I should have walked, but it's always my treat on a Friday; a bus ride home. Not that it's the start of a weekend off; I'll be back in tomorrow at 7 a.m. It's simply that sometimes it's nice to pretend that I have an end to the working week like other people do.

I fish in my bag to see if I've got a tissue to give to sniffing man but all I have is a rolled-up bit of bog roll that looks like it's been in there for weeks. He sniffs again. It sounds like some annoying kid sucking up the last bit of his milkshake with a straw.

'You can use your sleeve if you like, pet, it won't bother me,' I say.

He looks at me, says nothing and goes back to staring out of the window.

'Suit yourself,' I say, glad there are only three more stops. I'd get my own back by taking my feet out of my Crocs, but I think they might be stuck in there due to the heat. They're not real Crocs, just those fake ones from the market. Yellow they are. Brighten the place up a bit, that's what I tell Bridget at work when I catch her giving them a look. She said staff in the catering trade are supposed to wear the proper covered bistro Crocs. I told her if she wanted to buy them for me, I'd be happy to wear them. Bloody full of it she is. Calls herself an entrepreneur just because she owns one lousy café. It might be called Teapots and Teacakes but it's nothing more than a jumped-up greasy spoon.

The man does one last almighty sniff as I ring the bell. I take the bog roll out of my bag and put it on his lap as I stand up.

'Do the next poor bugger who sits next to you a favour and use this,' I say. He ignores me. The bus pulls up at the stop and the door hisses back.

'Thanks, love,' I call out to the driver.

My feet squeak inside my Crocs as I step onto the pavement. There are still a few stragglers on their way home from school. I used to make the journey last four times as long as it should do when I was their age. Anything to avoid going home. And then when our Terry started school, I had a good excuse because I could take him to the park on the way home. I used to kill hours in that park, pushing him on the swings. He always loved the swings. Hated the bloody roundabout though. Especially if another kid got on and made it go fast.

I turn the corner. Ours are the first flats you come to. It's not a big block, just three storeys high, and we're on the ground floor so it doesn't really feel like living in flats. Not unless Joe upstairs has got his music on loud and the kids next door are playing up, anyway.

I do my special knock on the door, so Terry knows it's me, before putting my key in the lock. It's a while now since he's talked about MI5 having the keys to our flat but that doesn't mean he's not still worried about it.

'Hi, it's me,' I call out, as I dump my bag on the floor. I can hear the sound of the TV in the living room, which means Terry is out of bed, at least. I go in. He is lying on the sofa, his ridiculously long legs spilling over the far end.

'Hi,' he replies, not even looking up. He's watching *Stars in Their Eyes* on video. 'It's Freddie Mercury.'

I nod and smile as I watch an overweight bloke in his forties prancing around the stage in a white vest, too-tight trousers and a stick-on moustache.

'Hardly,' I say. 'He doesn't look or sound owt like him.'

Terry doesn't say anything, simply carries on watching. He has seen it before, of course. More times than I care to think about. He videoed pretty much every episode of *Stars in Their Eyes* during what he calls the Matthew Kelly years. He never took to any of the other presenters who took over after he left; still won't watch anything on TV with Davina McCall or any of the other presenters who came after him. They don't compare to Matthew, that's what he always says.

'You wanting a brew?' I ask. He nods, still without looking up. I go into the kitchen. An upside-down mug and cereal bowl are on the draining board, so he has at least had breakfast. He probably started watching *Stars in Their Eyes* before lunch-time, which explains why there's no evidence that he's eaten anything else since.

I put the kettle on and pop a couple of pieces of bread in the toaster. It worries me; how he'd survive if I wasn't here to look after him. Fifty-one years old and he's every bit as much my kid brother as he ever was. I don't resent it, not for one moment. But it does make me think about the Terrys of this world who don't have any family to look after them.

I open a can of beans and warm half in a pan, popping the rest back in the fridge. I butter the toast and pour the beans on top. It may not be the grandest meal in the world but it's still one of Terry's favourites.

'Here you are, then,' I say, taking it into the living room. Terry holds his hand out for the mug.

'You'll have to shift your arse and sit up,' I say. 'I've done some grub.'

Terry finally looks up. A smile spreads over his face. Terry's face looks permanently mardy when it's in neutral, but he makes up for it with a smile that could power the national grid.

'Thanks, Sis,' he says, sitting up and taking the plate from me. 'You're a star and Madonna's on next.'

I put his cup of tea down on the floor and plonk myself

next to him on the sofa. It is only then that I see the envelope sticking up from between the cushions.

'What's that?' I ask.

'Came this morning,' Terry replies.

'Have you opened it?'

He shakes his head as Madonna breaks into the first notes of 'Into the Groove'.

'Do you want me to?'

He shrugs. We both know what it is, we have been waiting for it long enough. But now it's here it seems neither of us wants to open it.

I pick up the envelope. She's good, the Madonna woman. Wipes the floor with Freddie Mercury anyway. I tear it open and pull the letter out.

It is headed: 'Your Employment and Support Allowance Work Capability Assessment'.

There is lots of stuff at the beginning explaining what it was, as if we are thick and might not remember. And then at the bottom of the page, a section that says, 'Our Decision'. Underneath it says: 'Your Work Capability Assessment shows that although you may have an illness, health condition or disability, you are now capable of doing some work. We realise this may not be the same type of work you have done before. We can help you identify types of work you can do, taking into consideration any illness, health condition or disability you may have.'

I shake my head as I blow out. It is what I had feared but didn't think could actually happen.

The Madonna woman finishes and gets a huge cheer from the audience.

'What's it say?' asks Terry, turning to me.

'They say you're fit for work,' I reply.

'That's bollocks,' says Terry.

'Yeah. I know.'

'He weren't listening, were he? That man who were asking me all those questions. I told him what had happened to me all those times I tried to work before, but he weren't even fucking listening.'

There's nothing I can say because he's right. They haven't taken a blind bit of notice of what Terry said. As far as they are concerned, he's some bloody scrounger and all they're interested in is getting him off benefits. They don't give a toss about what that will do to him. Why should they? They won't be there to pick up the pieces. That'll be my job.

'I'll go and ring them,' I say. 'Tell them there's been a mistake. I've heard about cases like this on radio. Where they've copied and pasted points from one assessment on to next one. Maybe that's what happened here.'

Terry nods at me. I don't think he holds out any more hope than I do but I've got to try. I've got to do anything I can to make this go away. Because I know exactly where Terry's going to end up if they make him go out to work. And I do not want him anywhere near a psychiatric unit again.

I take the letter through to the kitchen and shut the door so they won't hear Tina bloody Turner in the background.

I call the number at the top of the letter. It's not a proper number for the job centre in Halifax, because nobody there is capable of picking up the phone, apparently. It's one of those 0345 numbers where you have no idea where the person you're calling is and they've probably never been to Halifax in their lives. When I get through there's a recording of a posh bird telling me she's going to give me some options. There isn't one for 'I want to wring the neck of the arse-head assessor', so I press the one for 'something else'. She then asks what I'm calling about. I say, 'You've got me brother's assessment wrong and I need to speak to someone about it.'

She says, 'I'm sorry, I don't understand what you're saying, please select one of the following options.'

None of the options are for things I want. I press one of them anyway and I'm asked what I want again.

'Rhubarb and custard,' I reply. It seems to work because I get put through to the next bit, so I say 'rhubarb and custard' again. I keep saying it, trying not to think about how much credit this is using up on my phone, until there is a ringing tone on the other end and a real woman, not quite as posh as the recorded one but not far off, answers. She catches me singing the theme tune to the *Roobarb and Custard* cartoon that Richard Briers used to do, but she is probably too young to know what it is, so I don't bother trying to explain.

'Hello, love, I'm ringing about me brother. His name's Terry Allen and he's had a letter about his work capability assessment, and I think you've got it wrong.'

'I'm afraid I can't speak to you about someone else's case. You'll need to ask Mr Allen to give us a call if he's got a query.'

'Yeah, well he's got schizophrenia, see. That's why he's on Employment Support Allowance. And when he gets stressed it can lead to psychotic episodes, so last thing he needs to be doing is phoning you and having to press a dozen buttons to hear a posh bird say she can't understand what he's saying because he hasn't got a southern accent.'

There is a pause before she asks me for his National Insurance number and his date of birth and to confirm our address. She says she's going to get his case up on her screen.

'So, he's been found fit for work,' she says.

'Aye, he has, but that's why I'm calling because you've got it wrong, see. Last time he worked he ended up in a psychiatric unit. And twice before that, too. He can't cope being with lots of other people. If you force him to work, he'll get ill again. That's why I need to talk to someone about this.'

'He has the right to ask for a mandatory reconsideration,' she says. 'He'll have to do that in writing by submitting a CRMR1 form.'

'We'll do that, then. Can you pop form in post, pet?'

'You just print it out from our website.'

I sigh. They never get this bit.

'We haven't got a computer, let alone a printer.'

'OK. If you go along to the job centre, they'll be able to print one out for you there. Just fill it in, explaining why you think the decision is wrong.'

'Right. And once we've sent that off, how long until we hear?'

'It will be a minimum of fourteen working days, but it could be considerably longer. If they confirm the original decision, you do have the right to appeal to a tribunal, but that will all take several months.'

'You're kidding me. What's our Terry supposed to do for money until then?'

'Mr Allen will have to apply for Universal Credit and go to the job centre for a meeting, as advised in the letter.'

'But he can't work, it'll make him ill.'

'He's been found fit for work so I'm sure the job centre will be able to find something suitable for him. I can make him an appointment for an interview. You can pick up the form you need at the same time.'

This is stupid. She's not getting it. But at least if they meet him in person, they might understand what I'm talking about.

'OK,' I say.

'Right. So it looks like you're in luck. Halifax have had a cancellation and can fit him in on Monday at three forty-five. Is that any good to you?'

If I get the bus home from work, we should just be able to make it in time.

'Yes,' I reply.

'Great. He's all booked in. He'll need to take three items of ID with him, including proof of address. All the information can be found on our website. Is there anything else I can help you with today?'

'No, pet,' I say with a sigh. 'Not unless you can do owt for tired, swollen feet.'

I go back into the living room. I think there's a different

episode of *Stars in Their Eyes* on now because it looks like Matthew is wearing a different suit.

'Were it a mistake?' asks Terry.

'We know it were,' I say. 'It's getting them to see that. We've got to fill in a form asking them to reconsider decision, but that'll take a few weeks. In meantime, they want you to go to job centre and sign on.'

'When?' Terry asks.

'Monday afternoon,' I say.

'I won't have to get a job, will I? Not before we hear back from them?'

'Let's hope not, eh?'

He nods and says nothing. I can see his jaw tense. I hate it when he is like this because I know where it is heading. He goes back to watching *Stars in Their Eyes*. Elton John is on now. He is singing 'Sorry Seems to Be the Hardest Word'.

AFTER

1

FINN

I lie on my bed, staring up at the bee lampshade that Dad got me. It is blue, which is a bit stupid because bees aren't blue, but Dad said they only had it in blue or pink. Mum wouldn't like it because she always gets cross when she sees blue things for boys and pink for girls because she says colours are for everyone and years ago boys used to be dressed in pink and it's all marketing nonsense designed to get more money out of parents.

I couldn't say that when Dad got it for me though, because he was trying to be nice and Mum also says that we should be grateful for presents and it's the thought that counts.

Anyway, I suppose it doesn't matter because Mum won't see it, but I still think of how much she wouldn't like it every time I look at it.

My uniform is hanging up on the door of my wardrobe,

ready for tomorrow. It is neatly ironed, and the trousers have creases in them that they never used to. It turns out Dad is better at ironing than Mum, but he just kept quiet about it.

I have a bit of a tummy ache. I expect it will be worse by tomorrow morning. I don't want to see any of them apart from Lottie but I saw her the week after and I went round to her house for tea in half-term, so I've only just seen her anyway.

There is a knock on the door and Dad calls out, 'Hi Finn, it's me.' I know it's him anyway because no one else lives in our house now but maybe he sometimes forgets this like I do.

'Hi,' I say back. Dad opens the door. I'm sure his beard is getting greyer. It's probably because of everything that has happened. He steps inside my room and shuts the door behind him. He looks like he's worried I am still mad at him and he is right, I am. I am not going to shout and scream any more, but that doesn't mean I am any less mad, just that the mad bit is stuck inside somewhere and won't come out.

It's only as I sit up that I see he is carrying something.

'I got this for you,' he says, holding out a large carrier bag. I take it and look inside. It is a rucksack. It is black with a few blue flames and lines on it. There are no bees.

'I hope it's OK. It's hard to get something without football on, to be honest.'

I nod. I want to say thank you, but I am trying too hard not to cry to be able to open my mouth.

'It should do for your new school in September too. I just thought you'd want something a bit more grown-up for big school.'

My eyes give up the battle and start to let the tears out. I had been trying so hard not to think about what happened to the old rucksack. Mum was right. Dad never did know when to stop talking. He reaches out and rubs my shoulder.

'Hey, I'm sorry,' he says. 'I didn't mean to upset you.'

If he was paying attention, he would know that I haven't stopped being upset for the past three weeks. That I miss Mum so much it's like I've had my leg cut off or something. That I don't want him to keep buying me stuff, as if that will make everything all right. I just want it to go back to how it was before. The three of us here together. And I would put up with the arguing. I really would.

He keeps his hand on my shoulder until I stop crying a few minutes later and wipe my tears away with my fingers.

'Are you worried about going back to school?' he asks.

I nod and sniff at the same time.

'I've spoken to Mrs Ratcliffe and Mrs Kerrigan. I've asked them to do what you said and not mention it. And the other kids have been told you were on a special holiday before half-term.'

'But they'll all know,' I say. 'And they'll be staring and whispering stuff about me.'

Dad has got the frown on his face again. It's pretty much there all the time now. If I had to draw a picture of Dad, it would be one of him frowning and with an expression like he didn't know what to say. That's if I could draw, but I can't. So, my picture of Dad wouldn't look like Dad at all. Just a man, if I was lucky. I haven't got any better at drawing since

I was five. Mum said that wasn't true when I said it once. She pointed to the self-portrait I did a couple of years ago, which was made out of food, which was still stuck to the fridge. I did my hair with macaroni painted orange and she said it was great. It wasn't drawing, though. It was just a load of macaroni painted orange. And you can't go on making pictures from macaroni forever.

'Come on,' says Dad. 'It will be nice for you to see your friends again.'

'I haven't got any friends.'

'Yes you have. What about Lottie?'

'Yeah, Lottie but that's it. And I saw Lottie last week. I don't have to go back to school to see her. It's the rest of them I hate.'

Dad moves his hand down from my shoulder and rubs my arm instead.

'Come on, you're just upset.'

'I am upset but I didn't say it because I'm upset, I said it because it's true.'

Dad sighs and puts his head in his hands. He has been doing a lot of that lately.

'Look, I know this has been so tough for you, but you have to trust me that going back to school is the best thing to do now. You'll feel better once the first day is over.'

This is another stupid thing grown-ups say. I won't feel better after the first day, I'll feel worse because I'll have had a horrible day and I'll know I'll have to go through it all over again the next day and the one after that. I think of the school in the woods that Mum made me. It was the best school ever and she was the best teacher ever. She made it so special for me. What I really want is to go back to that school in the tent with Mum, but there's no point saying that because it can't happen now.

'I'd feel better if I never had to go to school again,' I say instead.

'Come on, Finn, we've been through all this. There's only one half-term left and then you'll be done. And Mrs Kerrigan said she's got lots of fun things planned for you all.'

'They're the reward things for doing well in your SATs. I won't be allowed to do them.'

'Of course you will. Mrs Kerrigan's not going to leave you out, is she?'

'Mrs Ratcliffe might make her. She's still mad at me because of what Mum said and did.'

Dad sighs and shakes his head. I know he is trying hard, but he is not good at this stuff. Not compared to Mum.

'Finn, no one at school's mad at you. They want to help you, that's all.'

'You're only saying that to make me go. Mum wouldn't make me go. Mum knew how much I hated it.'

I watch Dad blink hard and turn his head away. I feel a bit mean, but I am only speaking the truth. He's never done this. Mum always dealt with this sort of stuff. Dad is good at mending stuff and riding a bike and knowing about law. He is not good at making me feel better. Which is a shame really, because that's exactly what I need right now.

'I'm trying my best, Finn,' he says, still not looking at me. 'We've just got to try to get through it together the best we can.'

He turns round to face me. His eyes are glistening. I think for a moment he is going to hug me, but he doesn't, he just ruffles my hair and walks out of the room.

Dad drops me at Lottie's house the next morning. This was arranged with Lottie's mum Rachel last week. Rachel is still mad at Dad too, I know that from Lottie. But she is pretending not to be mad at him in front of me, for my sake. I think it was Lottie's mum who arranged to take me into school today, not Dad, but Dad seems very happy with it, probably because it means he hasn't got to take me himself and I suspect he thinks I'll have a massive meltdown if he does that.

Dad puts his hand on my shoulder.

'It'll be fine,' he says.

That is easy for him to say. He's going to work after this with people he likes, not being forced to go to a school he hates with a bunch of people he doesn't like and have everyone stare at him and say stuff behind his back.

Lottie's mum opens the door and waves. I think she is waving at me rather than Dad because she never really liked Dad very much, even before it happened. I know this because Mum used to talk about Dad to her in a quiet voice sometimes when she thought I wasn't listening and she often nodded and looked sympathetic and said things in a quiet voice back that I couldn't hear.

Dad raises his hand at her from the car and I unfasten my belt.

'Have a good day,' he says. His voice is a bit wobbly and I know that's because he doesn't think I will but can't say that to me. I pick up my book bag and my rucksack, which has my PE kit in, and get out.

'Hello, Finn,' Rachel says. 'How are you doing?' She gives me such a big hug that I can't actually breathe for a moment, let alone reply, which is probably just as well as I haven't worked out what to say to that question yet.

'Come inside a sec,' she says. 'Lottie's not quite ready yet, you know what she's like. Can't think where she gets it from.'

She smiles as she says this like she knows it's funny and leads me into the house. It's what they call a two-up, two-down, which means there are four rooms if you don't count the bathroom and it's such a small bathroom that you really don't need to count it.

Lottie comes charging downstairs.

'Hi Finn,' she says. 'Rachel, I've got toothpaste down my school trousers.'

Lottie calls her mum by her first name. She started it when she was seven and wanted to be more grown-up. I don't think it sounds grown-up, just weird. Like she's forgotten who she is. But, for the first time ever, I am glad of it today because the word 'Mum' makes me feel sad.

'Well, no time to change them now,' Rachel replies. 'We're not going to make Finn late.'

Lottie looks at me and it's like she suddenly remembers

why I am there, and she looks down again and picks up her book bag.

'OK, let's go,' she says, wiping the still-wet toothpaste stain with her hand, which smears it and makes it look worse.

I look down at her empty hand. 'PE kit,' I say.

'Oh yeah,' says Lottie and runs back upstairs.

Rachel smiles at me. 'What would she do without you?' she says. And that makes me feel sad too because Lottie will be going to a different school to me in September and that will mean I will have no friends at all. Dad says I will make new ones but he doesn't realise that I won't because I am not the sort of boy other boys want to be friends with and Lottie is only my friend because she is not like the other girls and what are the chances of there being a girl who isn't like the other girls at my new school? Probably zero.

Lottie runs back down with her PE bag and we pile into the back seat of her mum's car.

'I like your new backpack,' says Lottie.

'I don't,' I reply. 'Dad got it for me.'

I see Rachel glance at me in the rear-view mirror.

'Oh well,' says Lottie. 'You hate PE so you may as well have a backpack you hate for your PE kit.'

I give her a little smile. It is the first smile I can remember doing in a long time.

We get to the playground just before the bell rings. Mrs Kerrigan is standing by the gate and she smiles at me and says, 'Morning, Finn, it's lovely to see you,' only her voice goes a bit funny at the end so I don't actually hear the word 'you', but I think that is what she tried to say.

All the other kids stare at me, just how I knew they would, but the weird thing is that no one says anything mean to me like they usually do. Ryan Dangerfield looks at me, then looks away again. Jayden McGreevy doesn't have the usual smirk on his face. Even Tyler Johnson can't seem to think of something horrible to say to me. That is the thing that gets to me. That is why everything in front of me starts to go blurry. Lottie is standing next to me at the back of the girls' queue. She takes my arm and pulls me along in the right direction. Like I am blind but still waiting for a *Blue Peter* fundraising campaign to raise enough to get me a guide dog.

It is like that all morning. No one saying anything mean to me or making faces at me when Miss isn't looking. And I hate it because all it does is remind me all the time of why they are not being horrible to me.

Mrs Ratcliffe comes up to me in the playground at break time, all smiley and her bangles jangling like normal.

'Hello, Finn, Mrs Kerrigan says you've done so well this morning. I think there might be a star of the week award coming your way.'

I look at her and she is still smiling and jangling because she is so stupid, she doesn't even realise that the worst thing that could happen to me this week would be to have my name called out in the celebration assembly.

*

After lunch we get changed ready for PE. No one even teases me about my skinny white legs or tells me I should be getting changed with the girls because I am one. All the times I wished the teasing would stop and now it has, and I hate it.

We start playing invasion games in the hall. I hate invasion games because I am no good at running or jumping or kicking a ball or catching a ball or pretty much anything you have to do in invasion games. Usually the others all groan if I am on their team but nobody says anything today.

But a few minutes after we start playing, I am on the floor in no-man's-land and the others are on the benches and Lewis R forgets for a second and throws the ball straight at me deliberately. It hits me hard on the arm and really stings and a few people start laughing but then they remember and stop, without Mrs Kerrigan even saying anything. And I hate the sound of them not laughing even more than I used to hate the sound of them laughing.

I ask Dad pretty much as soon as we get home. I have been thinking about her a lot. About how nice she was to me. Sometimes I think I can still feel her arms round me.

'I want to see the sheep apron lady,' I say.

Dad looks at me, frowning.

'Who?'

'The sheep apron lady. The one who looked after me until you got there.'

Dad's frown clears as he realises who I mean.

'Really? Are you sure?'

'Yes,' I say. 'Can we ask her round for tea? She gave you her number in case she could help in any way.'

Dad thinks for a moment. Normally he would say no. But nothing's normal any more. We both know that.

'Let me ask her and see what she says,' he says.

AFTER

2

KAZ

The noise of someone shouting in the room next door wakes me up. I'm used to having neighbours in the flat above and next to the kitchen but not used to being surrounded by noise twenty-four hours a day in a hostel.

Still, beggars can't be choosers and as it was either this or roughing it in a shop doorway, I suppose I should consider myself lucky. And it could have been a whole lot worse, too. I haven't forgotten that. How can I, when I look in the bathroom mirror every morning? The shame doesn't wash off, it still stares straight back at me. I've told no one, of course. Certainly not Terry. But it's enough that I know.

At least I managed to get some sleep last night. The recurring nightmare I have had since childhood has receded in recent weeks, to be replaced by a new one, with new faces and new horrors. A new scream at the end. But last night it didn't visit me, although I am not naïve enough to think that it won't be back.

I get up and squeeze past Terry's TV and video player and his boxes of videos to get to the window to open the flimsy curtains. My neighbour Mark was good enough to bring them here in his van, along with my clothes. The other bits and bobs got shared out among my neighbours. Mark took the kettle and toaster to a mate he knew who had just come out of prison and was setting up in his own flat. I feel a bit like one of those organ donors who may have lost their life but at least were able to help other people to have a better one. Not that it will be much consolation when Terry is well enough to leave hospital and finds that he hasn't got a home to go to.

I haven't told him yet. How could I? It will only worry him at a time when he's got enough on his plate. What I need to do is concentrate on getting myself a job so we can get somewhere of our own to live again. Not that I'm any nearer to doing that than I was four weeks ago.

I haven't heard a dickie bird from any of the cafés I've been to. The Post-it notes with my number on have probably fallen off the fridges by now anyway. They weren't proper Post-its, only cheap copies from the market. And as I haven't had a sniff at an interview, Denise from the job centre is sending me on a 'work-ready' training course today. Because someone who has grafted every day of her life since she was sixteen, before losing her job a month ago, clearly hasn't got a fucking clue what work is.

I pull my dressing gown on, pick up my shower gel and shampoo and head across the corridor to the bathroom. The door is locked. I can hear someone singing in the shower. It's the one thing I can't get used to, not having my own bathroom. I go back to my room and sit on the bed. At least Terry has his own bathroom and gets fed where he is. I never thought I'd be grateful that he'd be in a psychiatric unit again, but then I never thought I'd be in a mess like this.

Ten minutes pass. I sit there looking at my watch, listening for the sound of the bathroom door opening. I think about the boy, Finn. Not a day has gone past since when I haven't. Nor a night either. I think of Terry at the same age, of everything he had to deal with, and I worry that Finn could struggle to cope, just like he did. Most of all, I hope he is being loved and cared for by his father. That he has someone fighting his corner. Because he will need it, I know that much.

By the time the bathroom door finally opens, I haven't got time for a shower, just to wash my face, brush my teeth and throw on some clothes.

The bus into town is late as well. A good fifteen minutes. I know I'll be cutting it fine, now. The last thing I need is to get a bollocking for being late from some kid in their twenties. The bus is packed and hot. We're all so used to the heat now that no one even talks about it any more. Apart from the occasional person who says something about their garden needing a bit of rain.

With two stops to go, the traffic is so bad I decide to get off early and walk. It's going to be a complete waste of time. I told Denise that last week and she trotted out the usual crap about me being sanctioned if I refuse to go on a course. Which is a bloody cheek when I'm still being sanctioned for having been sacked, but there you go. At this rate, I won't get my full benefits till Christmas.

I arrive five minutes late and have to press a buzzer and wait for someone to let me in. She looks pissed off when she opens the door.

'Hello, you must be Karen,' she says, smiling but clearly not meaning it. 'I'm Billie-Jo.' She holds out her hand. I shake it, deciding against asking if I've come to a country and western party by mistake. She doesn't look like the sort who would appreciate my humour.

'We have just started, and I would remind you how important it is to ensure you are punctual for all training courses and work programmes in future.' Billie-Jo is smiling as she says it. I think I'd rather have got a bollocking.

I follow her into a room where a dozen other people are sitting at desks with computers on. They all look at least twenty years younger than me. Billie-Jo stands in front of a big screen with a pointer thing in her hand.

'Right, Karen, if you could take a seat at the spare screen there, please,' she says, indicating with the pointer to a desk at the back. 'We haven't got time to do the icebreaker again but if you could just tell everyone who you are?'

'Morning all, I'm your Grandma Kaz,' I say. A couple of the others smile half-heartedly. Most simply carry on staring at their screens. Billie-Jo does a false laugh.

'Great. Let's get back to where we were then. I was talking about the importance of creating a strong first impression and how crucial your CV is in that. Today we're going to get your CVs up to date and ensure that you're all workplace-ready!'

She raises her left arm with a clenched fist as she says the last bit. Everybody else continues staring at their screens. It's going to be a long morning.

Half an hour later, Billie-Jo is standing next to me, looking at my blank screen.

'How are we getting on, Karen?' she asks.

'Haven't got a clue, Billie-Jo,' I reply. 'Never been on a computer before.'

Billie-Jo laughs, looks at me, realises I am not joking and appears horrified.

'Oh, right,' she says. 'Do you need any support to use a keyboard?'

'No, pet. There's nowt wrong with me. Just can't afford a computer and have never needed a CV to work in a café. As long as you can make a good builder's brew and a mean bacon butty, you're considered qualified.'

'I see,' she replies. She will tell her colleagues about me later, I am sure of it. If I had any colleagues, I would tell them about Billie-Jo too.

'Well, let's get you logged in and we can get you started,' she says, pressing a few buttons. 'You can start by listing your qualifications.'

'I've only got one O level,' I say. 'But it were an A I got in Art, so maybe we could put that in big letters. Or I could do some drawings on it, brighten it up a bit. I'm good at art, see. Art and making bacon butties.'

Billy-Jo gives me a very weak smile that she has probably been on a training course to work on.

Later that afternoon I come out with a dozen copies of a one-page CV, which Billie-Jo has emailed to Denise, as she couldn't email it to me. There's nothing important on it that you couldn't have fitted on a Post-it note, to be honest, but if it gets Denise off my back for a bit, it will be worth it.

There's no time for me to take the CVs in anywhere now though, because I want to get to the unit before teatime to see Terry. I walk across town. If I'm not careful, I'll get fit at this rate, all the walking back and forth I'm doing. I must have lost quite a few pounds with all the meals I've been missing over the past month too. They should do a programme about it on Channel Four: The 'Sanctions Diet', they could call it. I should get in quick before some stick-thin celebrity comes up with it and tries to make out that living on hardship payments is in any way glamorous.

The nurse on the front desk smiles at me when I arrive. They all know me now, which at least means I haven't got to explain that I'm Terry's sister, not his wife, for the hundredth time.

'I think he's having a nap,' she says.

I nod. Terry is always having a nap these days. He could nap for bloody England. It's his meds. They always do this to him. That's why he doesn't like taking them.

I walk down the corridor to Nightingale ward. I know the way to his room now with my eyes shut. I don't like it, though.

The fact that it has become so familiar. Terry shouldn't be here, he should be at home with me. If I still had a home, that is.

Terry is still asleep when I go in. He has at least got dressed today, or someone has dressed him, more like. If it was up to him, he'd probably stay in his T-shirt and boxers all the time.

I sit down on the chair next to the bed. He's put on a lot of weight since they started him on the antipsychotics. That's another thing he doesn't like about taking them. Not that it's a problem – there was nothing of him to start with – but it's still weird seeing him like this. He doesn't look like our Terry, my kid brother. Mam used to call him the runt of the litter. That was on her good days, when she was able to call him anything.

I haven't had the heart to tell him that the Department of Work and Pensions have reconsidered the decision that he was fit for work and found it was right. Bloody bastards. Still, no point in upsetting him over it. They said we could appeal to a tribunal, so I've sent off the form for that. They'll only find against him as well, but I've got to keep fighting for Terry. I'm the only one on his side.

After about ten minutes of shuffling around and doing little coughs, I decide to wake him up. It's not like he needs the sleep and they'll be waking him for his tea in an hour, so he may as well at least see me while I'm here.

I go over and shake his arm gently. 'Afternoon, our Terry,' I say. He stirs and opens his eyes. It seems to take a while for them to focus on me and for his brain to send the correct message about who I am.

'All right, Kaz,' he says, sleepily.

He doesn't try to sit up or even to say anything more. It's as if he'd be quite content just to lie there like the Queen of bloody Sheba.

'Let's get you up, then,' I say. 'Come and sit in chair for a bit. Just till it's teatime.'

He shrugs. I take it as a yes, because that's the most I can get out of him at the moment. I take his arm and help him up, even though there's nothing physically wrong with him. He's like an overgrown teenager who can't be arsed to move. I have to keep telling myself that it's not his fault, in order to stop myself from giving him a bollocking.

He sits down heavily in the chair. Scratches his head and stares blankly at me.

'What did you have for lunch?' I ask.

'Sandwich,' he replies.

'I've been on a course today,' I tell him. 'Some girl in her twenties trying to tell me how to use a computer so I can get a job.'

Terry goes back to staring.

'Printed me out a fancy CV, she did. Reckons that will get me a job. I bet she's never been out of work in her life.'

Terry stares at me some more and yawns. I sigh and look out of the window. I know it's wrong but right now I wish he'd ask for his torch or start hunting for rats. Because as much as Terry was a pain in the arse when he was psychotic, he did at least seem more alive than this version.

*

It's just gone eight that evening when my mobile rings. My first thought is that something has happened to Terry.

'Hello, is that Karen Allen?' a man's voice asks.

'Yes,' I say. 'Is it about our Terry?'

'Er, no. It's Martin Carter. I'm not sure if you'll remember me. I'm Finn's dad. You know, the boy from – '

'Of course, I remember,' I say. 'I've been thinking about him a lot. Is he OK?'

'Yeah,' says Martin. 'Well, you know. Still finding things tough. He asked after you, actually. That's why I'm ringing. He'd like to see you. He wondered if you might like to come to ours for tea.'

I wasn't expecting that at all. I don't know what to say.

'Are you sure? I meant it when I said to call me if I could help with owt, but I wouldn't want to come if it'll upset him, seeing me again.'

'That's OK,' says Martin. 'I was concerned about that too and I've explained to him that you won't be able to talk about what happened but he's adamant that he'd like to see you. Of course, I completely understand if you'd rather not meet up. Please don't feel at all obliged.'

'No,' I say. 'I'd like to. I really would. Tell him I'll come. It's right nice of him to ask.'

'Thank you. That's great. How about Saturday at five? Unless you're busy that is?'

I try not to laugh down the phone.

'Saturday would be fine. Where are you?'

'Not far from Manor Heath Park. I'll text you our address. Will you be coming by car?'

'No. Bus.'

'Oh, we can come and pick you up. It would be no trouble.'

'No, thanks,' I say quickly, realising I do not want the lad to see where I live. 'I'll make me own way.'

'OK, if you're sure. Thanks very much. Finn will be so glad you can come. We'll see you then. Any problems, just give me a call.'

I say goodbye and put down the phone. It's only then I realise that my hand is shaking.

BEFORE

3

FINN

They are still laughing at lunchtime and making fanny jokes. They will probably make fanny jokes for the rest of year six. If I wasn't going to a secondary school that none of them are going to, they would be making fanny jokes for years. When we were in reception and the teacher asked us to get undressed for PE for the first time, Lewis B took off his pants and everyone still goes on about that, even now.

'Just ignore them,' says Lottie. 'They're all idiots.'

'Yeah,' I reply. She's right but it doesn't make it any easier. Lottie's great but she doesn't really understand because no one laughs at her or calls her names, not since year five when Jayden said she looked like a boy and she kneed him in the balls.

At that moment, Riley comes up and shouts, 'Fanny face' at me before running away.

'Do you want me to do him?' she asks.

'No thanks, you'll only get into trouble.'

'Well, you should tell someone, he shouldn't be allowed to get away with it.'

'Yeah but if I do, he'll call me a grass and probably thump me and there's only the dinner lady around and I've told her about things before and all she says is not to tell tales.'

'So, what are you going to do about it?'

'Nothing,' I reply. 'Mum says if I ignore them, they might stop.'

Lottie nods although we both know that I have been ignoring them for nearly seven years now and it is showing no sign of stopping.

'Dad says it will be better at my next school,' I add.

'What, because they're posh?'

'I guess so.'

'Posh people do mean things too.'

'Do they?'

'Yeah. My mum said David Cameron who used to be Prime Minister was posh and he did really mean things.'

'Oh well,' I say with a shrug. 'At least he won't be going to my new school.'

I survive until the end of the day. I always feel a bit like that by Friday afternoon, that I should get a badge, or at least a certificate, for having survived the week.

Before we go, Mrs Kerrigan says she is going to have a chat with us about our SATs. She says that with only a week to go before they start, we need to do some revision over the weekend but make time to 'have fun too'. I wonder if Mum has talked to her about this or maybe given her one of our apricot, orange and bran muffins to show her what 'fun' tastes like.

'And next week,' she continues, 'we're going to have a special breakfast club for year six where you get to come in early and have toast and juice while we all do some revision together. There's a letter in your book bags explaining all about it.'

She says it like it's an exciting adventure and we should all be pleased. I look around the classroom. Only Caitlin Gilbody looks pleased and that's probably because she doesn't get any breakfast at home and is always saying she's starving. I'm definitely not pleased because I don't want to be at school one second longer than I have to be.

I put up my hand. 'Do we have to come to the breakfast club, Miss?' I ask.

Mrs Kerrigan, who hasn't stopped smiling the whole time, turns her smile up a little bit higher.

'Well, you're all invited, and we really wouldn't want any of you to miss out, as it's such an important time for you.'

I look at Lottie. 'That means yes,' she whispers. I nod. I know Mum won't want me to go but that means she will come into school and there will be a 'big scene' and I don't like 'big scenes' and there are enough of them at home and I wish it would all go away. I feel the tears gathering and trying to force their way out and I try to think about the time I met Alan Titchmarsh at Tong Garden Centre, to make them stop.

The bell rings and everybody puts their stuff away. Lottie looks at me and shakes her head.

'Don't worry,' she says, as she pulls on her rucksack. 'I'm going to start a petition.'

'Good,' I reply. 'I'll sign it.'

Mum is waiting outside the playground. She has that pretending smile on again. She doesn't even ask me how my day has been because she was there in assembly and you don't have to be a genius to work it out. She gives my shoulder a little squeeze and I try hard not to cry. I manage to hold it in all the way home but as soon as we get inside the door, it bursts out.

'Hey, come here,' says Mum, holding her arms out wide. I step towards her and let her hug me. My face is pressing against her green cardigan and it is soft and feels like a giant sponge for my tears.

'I'm sorry,' Mum says. She doesn't say what she's sorry for and I wonder if it's the divorce, me being different, buying me the George Formby songbook or simply because of them laughing at me in assembly. Maybe it's for all of them. I wish I never had to go back to school – any school. But I do. I have to go back on Monday for the stupid breakfast club.

'We've got to go in early every day next week for extra SATs revision,' I blurt out, when I eventually manage to stop crying.

'Who told you that?' Mum says, pulling away and looking down at me.

'Mrs Kerrigan. There's a letter in my book bag. They're calling it a breakfast club but really it's just extra revision.'

'You don't have to go.'

'She says I do.'

'Well, you don't. I'll email Mrs Ratcliffe now and tell her. I'm not having you put under any more pressure than you already are.'

It's like my whole life is turning into a series of big scenes when what I really want is to tiptoe around unnoticed by anyone.

'Lottie's going to start a petition,' I say.

'Good for her,' says Mum with a smile. Mum loves Lottie. She always tells me having one good friend like her is worth a million rubbish ones. She's probably right, it just doesn't feel like that when everyone apart from Lottie is laughing at you in assembly.

'I'm going to my room,' I say. Mum looks disappointed. I wonder if she was going to suggest we do something 'fun' together.

'OK,' she says. 'I'll go and write that email.'

I am still in my room when Dad comes home later. I hear Mum's voice coming up from the hallway. I can't hear exactly what she is saying, but it doesn't matter because I know that in a few moments, I will hear Dad's angry voice and they will be having the 'I know what's best for him' argument. Normally I would start playing my ukulele, but I don't feel like it right now, so I pick up my copy of Alan Titchmarsh's *Growing Roses* book and start looking through it. I know lots of things about growing roses. If there was a Top Trumps game about roses, I would be very good at it and if you could talk to other boys about the best varieties to grow, I would be very good at that too, but there's not and you can't. When I met Alan Titchmarsh, I wanted to have a long conversation with him about roses but there was a massive queue and the lady from the garden centre said we had to move on once I had got my copy of *Love Your Garden* signed and had my photo taken with him, which was a shame, as I think the smile he gave me meant he would have liked to have that conversation about roses too.

I try very hard to concentrate on the best ways to train climbing roses but the 'I know what's best for him' argument is getting very loud, so I decide to go downstairs, as sometimes it's the only way to get them to stop.

I walk into the kitchen just as Mum is saying, 'You didn't hear them, Martin, you didn't see his face –' They both stop and look down at me.

'Hi,' says Dad. He opens his mouth to say something else but shuts it without saying anything.

'Tea will be ready soon,' says Mum. 'We're having tofu vegetable stir-fry.'

I don't tell her that no one else in my class has tofu vegetable stir-fry for tea. I nod and smile like she wants me to and secretly wish I was having tea with Alan Titchmarsh instead. I wouldn't care what we ate, as long as we talked about roses.

I get up the next morning just as Dad is leaving for his bike ride. I stand at my bedroom window and watch him ride off.

When I was very little, he had a special trailer on the back of his bike that I went in. Mum says I used to like it; that I would get excited about going in it and that sometimes she would run behind us just to watch me laughing. Later, when I got too big for it, he tried to get me to ride my own bike, but I wasn't very good and kept falling off. Dad thought maybe I had dyspraxia, but I had the test for that, and I didn't, so when he realised it was just because I didn't like riding a bike and was rubbish at it, he kind of gave up asking. At first, he went out for a bike ride on his own on Sunday mornings, while me and Mum did some baking. But then he started going on Saturday mornings too. And now his bike rides seem to have got much longer.

I usually have my ukulele lesson on a Saturday morning, but my teacher Julian is away today because his daughter is getting married. He said I could practise extra hard, but I don't feel like practising this morning. My ukulele is still in its case after yesterday and I know if I unzip it, all the laughter will come out as well, so I am not going anywhere near it.

Mum looks up from her newspaper as I walk into the kitchen. She has her 'pretending to be happy' smile on again.

'Morning, lovely,' she says. How about some Millet Bran?'

Millet Bran is an organic cereal nobody else at school has even heard of, but I am not allowed the cereals they have because of all the sugar and rubbish in them. I open my mouth to say 'OK,' but nothing comes out and I can feel the tears coming again.

'Tell you what,' says Mum, quickly folding the newspaper

and standing up, 'let's go out for breakfast this morning. It's a lovely day and it would be nice to go for a walk first. I'm not that hungry either.'

I nod. I can't remember the last time we went out for breakfast, apart from when we were on holiday, but anything has to be better than sitting here and feeling sad. Even sitting somewhere else and feeling sad.

'Right, better go and get dressed then,' she says. 'Unless you're planning to go out in your PJs'.

I look down at my PJs, which have stars on, even though I told Mum on my tenth birthday that I didn't want to wear anything with stars or rockets on from now on. Mum tried to get bee pyjamas, but she couldn't find any for my age and the only flower pyjamas she could find were pink and although Mum said it didn't matter and pink wasn't just for girls and no one would see them, I said no thank you. If there was a fire in the middle of the night, or a terrorist bomb in our road, and we all had to be evacuated, people would come and take photos and film it and I could end up on the news in my pink flower pyjamas and I would never hear the end of it at school.

I go upstairs and put on a pair of jeans that are the wrong sort and a T-shirt that is probably the wrong sort too. I don't suit clothes. I look wrong in everything I put on.

When I come back downstairs, Mum is ready and standing by the back door.

'Are we going far?' I ask, looking at her walking boots.

'I don't know,' she says. 'I just thought I'd be prepared. You'll be fine in your trainers.'

She opens the back door and the smell of outside rushes in. I pull on my trainers (which are also the wrong sort) without undoing the laces, which usually annoys Mum but she either doesn't notice or, if she does, decides not to say anything.

The first thing I see as I step outside is the 'For Sale' sign. It has been there for months now and it never lets me forget. When it went up, some of the other parents and kids at school asked where we were moving to. Even Mrs Kerrigan saw it, because she drives past our house on her way to school and asked if I was off to 'pastures new'. I had to tell her my mum and dad were splitting up and I started to cry, and everyone saw, so that was another big scene. The good thing is that only three people have been to view it and one was a time-waster (I don't really know what this means, but I would quite like to be one because I am good at day-dreaming, which I think is similar), one didn't like it and the other one did but their house sale fell through, so I keep hoping that if no one ever buys it, Mum and Dad might have to find their happy voices and real smiles again and not actually split up.

The sun hits my face as I get to the front gate. My face doesn't really suit the sun because my skin is pale and I have freckles and, like Mum, burn very easily.

'You'll be fine,' says Mum, presumably guessing that I am about to ask if she's got any sun cream.

'But what if I burn?'

'You won't. It's only nine o'clock and we'll keep under the trees as much as we can.'

She gives me what is supposed to be her reassuring smile,

but it doesn't stop me worrying. Dad says I worry too much but that's easy for him to say because he doesn't have to go to school or have red hair or skin that burns easily and his parents, Grandma and Grandad, are still together, even though they have retired to Devon and we hardly ever see them. It must be easy not to worry when you don't have anything to worry about. I think the only thing he worries about is me not being normal, which is a bit stupid because I do enough worrying about that without everyone else having to join in.

We walk along the road that leads down to the park. It is nice, this bit of Halifax. In early spring there are loads of daffodils along the wide verge. They have died down now and been mown over, but I like knowing that the bulbs are still there, underneath, and the flowers will be back next year. We have lots of bulbs in our garden too. We planted loads the autumn I started school. Mum made holes with a dibber for me to put them in. The next spring, Mum used to help me count how many were out when I came home from school and when Dad came home from work, I used to run out and tell him how many daffodils and tulips there were. He seemed excited when I told him, I remember that much. What I can't remember is when I stopped counting daffodils.

'What will happen to the bulbs in our garden when you sell the house?' I ask Mum.

Mum doesn't answer straight away, even though I know she heard me. This means she is thinking very carefully about her answer.

'Well,' she says after a while, 'we'll leave them for the next people to enjoy.'

'But they're ours. I planted them. Can't we dig them up and take them with us?'

'No, love, it doesn't work like that.'

'Why not? I could replant them in our new garden.'

It is only as I say it that I realise we will have two new gardens, not one. 'I could divide them equally between the gardens at your house and Dad's house. It would all be done fairly; you wouldn't need to tell the solicitor about them.'

I see Mum bite her bottom lip and look away. She doesn't like talking about what will happen after the divorce, but I need to know about important things like this.

'The thing is,' she says quietly, still not looking at me, 'I can't guarantee that we'll both have gardens.'

'But we've always had a garden.'

'I know, love. But everything's going to be different. We'll only have half as much money each and we might not be able to find places with gardens.'

I look up at her, unable to believe what I have just heard.

'Where will I grow flowers then?'

'Maybe we can sort out some patio containers or window boxes. There are a lot of houses without gardens in Hebden Bridge, but people still manage to grow things.'

She says it in the sort of cheery voice grown-ups use to children when they are trying to pretend things are not as bad as they sound. But things are really bad if we are only going to have a patio container for a garden. I wonder, if I write to Alan

Titchmarsh at *Love Your Garden*, whether he and his team could somehow turn our patio containers into a proper garden, but I know that not even he is that clever. Besides, all the people who get to be on *Love Your Garden* have a disease or are in a wheelchair or have had something horrible happen to them. And even though Mum and Dad divorcing and making me leave all my plants and bulbs behind is pretty horrible, I don't think it is bad enough for them to make us a new garden.

I look up at Mum. I am about to say I don't think it's fair when I see that she has tears at the corners of her eyes and it is not windy or cold enough for the weather to have made them, so I don't say anything, and we walk on in silence for a bit.

'Mrs Ratcliffe got back to me about the breakfast club next week,' Mum says as we reach the park.

'Oh,' I reply.

'We're going to have a meeting with her before school on Monday.'

'But that's when I'm supposed to be in breakfast club.'

'I know. I told her you're not going to be there, so she asked us to come in before school to explain.'

'But I don't want to explain. Why can't you have a meeting with her on your own?'

'Because the only way we could do that is if you went to breakfast club.'

'I could just sit outside her office and read.'

'She said she wants to see us both together, Finn, so that's what we're going to do.'

'Is there going to be a big argument?'

'No, love,' she says. 'But I am going to tell her that we don't like the school putting this much pressure on you over the SATs.'

When she says 'we' I am not sure who she is talking about because I don't think Dad minds it at all. Sometimes it's like she forgets that they are getting divorced and that he doesn't seem to agree with anything she says or does.

'What if I get a detention for not going to the breakfast club?'

'You won't.'

'But they're going to be mad at me. I'll be the only one who doesn't go.'

'I thought you said Lottie was starting a petition?'

'She is but no one apart from me will sign it and she'll probably have to go anyway because it will help her mum get to work on time for a change.'

Mum gives a little smile. Rachel is her friend and she knows how busy she is. 'Well, that doesn't stop us taking a stand. You know what I always tell you, I don't care about what everyone else does, all I care about is what's best for you.'

Grown-ups say this when they want you to stop arguing with them. Mum says it, Dad says it, Mrs Ratcliffe will probably say it and the thing is they can't all be right because they all think different things are best for me.

We walk on through the park. There are little kids in the playground, and I can see Mum looking at me out of the corner of her eye and can almost hear her wondering whether to ask if I want to go on anything, but she guesses right and says nothing. I am getting a bit too old for playgrounds now and even if I wasn't, I do not feel in a playground kind of mood. I do not feel in the mood for anything really, apart from hibernating like a hedgehog until all this is over, and I can't even do that because it's May, and everyone knows it is the wrong season for hibernating.

We go out of the park and carry on towards the not-so-nice bit of Halifax where most of the other kids in my class live.

'Look, Teapots and Teacakes, that sounds nice,' Mum says, pointing to a café at the end of the road. I shrug because it is easier than arguing with her and I am getting a bit hungry now.

We have never been to this place before and when we arrive outside, I can see that it does not look like the sort of café we usually go to. There are checked plastic tablecloths, red and brown sauce bottles and lots of sachets of sugar on the tables and there is a grey-haired man sitting at the table nearest us in the window eating bacon and eggs and reading one of the small newspapers Mum doesn't like.

Mum smiles down at me even though I suspect she can see it's not our sort of café either. She opens the door and I follow her inside. I smell the bacon straight away and screw up my nose, but Mum is not looking. She has gone straight up to the counter and is reading the menu on the wall behind it, which is chalked on the board in fancy writing with little pictures of teapots and teacakes in each corner. I walk over to join her. I am not feeling hungry at all now.

'You can have beans on toast, Finn,' she says brightly, 'or scrambled eggs on toast.'

I shake my head. Normally either of them would be fine but I still have the bacon smell up my nose and I don't really fancy anything now. The lady behind the counter is smiling at me. She has a yellow and grey sheep apron on. They are fat, jolly sheep with funny faces, not normal-looking sheep. Her long hair is in plaits, but she is way older than Mum. I have never seen an older lady with plaits before.

Mum is still staring hard at the menu, like she is trying to magic something else we can have onto it. There is another lady standing behind us now. She is tall and smells of smoke and she does a big sigh like she is fed up waiting.

'Could you do a veggie version of the cooked breakfast?' Mum asks. 'Without the bacon and sausage, I mean.'

'We can do that for you,' replies sheep apron lady. 'Would you like fried bread or toast with it?'

Mum looks down at me. I don't think I have ever had fried bread, so I don't know if I will like it. I also wonder if the reason we've never had it before is because Mum doesn't approve of it, in which case she won't want me to have it now. I shift from one foot to the other, trying to decide.

'Toast please but I don't want the mushrooms, thank you,' I say. 'I don't like mushrooms.'

'Right you are,' says sheep apron lady, writing on her little notepad. 'No bacon, sausage or mushrooms. Would you like summat else instead? I can do you some hash browns if you like?'

I don't know what hash browns are, but I don't want to admit this.

'I don't like hash browns, thank you,' I say.

'They're just potatoes Finn,' says Mum. I wish I'd said yes now but I am not going to change my mind, because it would be too embarrassing.

'Is there owt else you do like?' asks sheep apron lady. She says it with a smiley voice, not a nasty one.

'I like your sheep apron,' I say, trying to be polite.

'Thank you,' she says, looking down at it for a second, 'they say sheep all look the same, but they don't, not really. People just don't look closely enough.'

I want to tell her about Dolly the sheep who was cloned, who I read about in my science magazine, but the smoky lady behind us coughs loudly.

'OK,' says Mum, 'so that's this one sorted and I'll have the same but with the mushrooms, please.'

'Okey dokey and what about drinks?' asks sheep apron lady.

I look again at the menu. I don't like tea or coffee and all the other drinks are fizzy ones that come in cans and I am not allowed cans.

I shrug and make fists with my hands. I don't want to make any more decisions because I keep getting them wrong.

'Do you have orange juice?' asks Mum.

'Only Tango, love.'

'One tea then and just a glass of tap water, please,' says Mum. I think she wishes we had gone somewhere else now, but she is not going to admit it because grown-ups don't like saying they were wrong. I turn my head and look back towards the door. That's when I notice the hygiene rating sticker. I usually look at them before I go in because I don't like eating anywhere that doesn't have a five-star one, but I forgot to look this time. I go over to the door to inspect it while Mum is getting out her purse. It's only got three stars. Three means satisfactory, which is like a polite way of saying it's not very good at all. I look back at sheep apron lady behind the counter. It might not be her fault, it might be her boss who doesn't wash their hands properly, but I can't eat here now. Mum is holding out her hand with the money for breakfast. She is going to pay for it, but I don't want to eat it and now there is going to be another big scene and I hate it before it has even happened.

I hurry over to Mum and tug her arm. She is too busy talking to sheep apron lady to take any notice.

'I don't want to eat here,' I say as quietly as I can. Mum looks down at me with a frown. I beckon her to come closer because I don't want to say it loudly because I know it will sound rude.

'It's only got three stars,' I whisper into Mum's ear.

'What has?'

'This café, it's only got a three-star hygiene rating.'

Mum's face does a weird expression. I'm not sure if she's angry or sad or a mixture of things all at the same time.

'Please Finn, couldn't you try to ignore it just this once?' she asks.

I shake my head. I have never eaten somewhere with three-stars, she knows that. It is one of the things about me that Dad thinks is weird. He laughed when I first said it and told me it was not like Michelin stars, where it's about how good the food is, and then he had to explain what Michelin stars were and a few days later we went to the garage to get his tyres mended and there was a big cardboard cut-out of the Michelin man and it all got really confusing.

'But Finn, it doesn't mean anything and you're only having egg, toast and beans.'

I shake my head again. Smoky lady behind us tuts.

'Are you getting owt or not?' she says.

Mum turns round to her. 'We're just sorting that out,' she replies. Her voice is a bit shaky and that makes me feel shaky. Sheep apron lady is looking like she feels sorry for us.

'Sorry,' Mum says.

'It's OK, love,' she says, smiling at me. 'You take your time and let me know if there's owt I can do to help.'

Smoky lady groans.

'For Christ's sake, hurry up, will you? If he's having a strop, let someone else go first,' she says.

'Hey, there's no need for that,' says sheep apron lady. For the first time, the smile has gone from her face and her voice is spiky.

'I think there is,' says smoky lady. 'I've got somewhere to be, and this spoilt brat is stopping me getting there. In my day you ate what you were given, and you were grateful for it.'

I start crying. I can't help it. The tears just sort of burst out. And now everyone is looking and it's a big scene and I don't want to be here. I want to run away and never see any of these people again.

'Now look what you've done,' says sheep apron lady to smoky lady. 'Apologise to him.'

'I'm not apologising to anyone,' says smoky lady.

Mum is standing there looking like she is going to start crying at any moment too. I tug her arm.

'I want to go,' I say. Mum nods and turns to mouth 'sorry' to sheep apron lady. I run to the door and pull it open, looking through blurry eyes at the hygiene rating sticker and wondering why it is so hard being me.

BEFORE

4

KAZ

'Proud of yoursen, are you?' I say to Fag-ash Lil. I have no idea of her real name but that's what I call her. Comes in here every Saturday and Sunday, always with a mardy look on her face and stinking of smoke. Right rude as well; we never get a thank you out of her.

'Like I said, he were a spoilt brat.'

My skin prickles. I've dealt with enough people like her mouthing off at Terry without knowing what they were talking about. Never once stopped to ask if they could help, even when he was in a bad way.

'You shouldn't judge people like that. He might have had summat wrong with him.'

'Oh, they've all got summat wrong with them these days. Learning difficulties, ADHD, allergies. Nowt wrong with any of them that a clip round the earhole wouldn't put right. Just stupid mums like her who indulge their little brats.'

'Or maybe bloody ignorant cows like you who make them cry and run out of cafés.'

I know as soon as it comes out that I shouldn't have said it. I'm glad I did, mind. She deserved every word of it and more.

'What did you just call me?' says Fag-ash Lil.

'A bloody ignorant cow. Now do you want owt or not?'

'I want to speak to your manager.'

'Well, you're out of luck because she doesn't work weekends.'

'And is that how you speak to all your customers when she's not here?'

'No, only those who make little boys cry.'

A young man comes in and hovers by the counter.

'Yes, pet, what can I get you?' I ask. He looks at Fag-ash Lil as if concerned he might be jumping the queue.

'It's OK, she's just leaving,' I say.

Fag-ash Lil scowls at me.

'I'll be contacting your manager,' she says. 'Don't think you're going to get away with this.'

'Fine,' I say, 'Please don't make any more customers cry on way out.'

I'm still het-up about it all when Danny arrives for his lunchtime shift.

'What's up with you? he asks, as I bang a saucepan down on the hob louder than I meant to.

'Bloody Fag-ash Lil,' I say. 'Came in here this morning and had a right go at little lad in front of her. Made him cry, she did.'

'What for?' he asks, as he puts his apron on.

'He wasn't sure what he wanted. He seemed a bit anxious or summat but Fag-ash Lil called him a spoilt brat. Ran out in tears, he did.'

'Stupid fucking cow,' he replies.

'That's what I called her.'

'You didn't?'

'No, a bloody ignorant cow is what I actually said.'

Danny grins as he picks up the frying pan. 'Jeez, Kaz, I wish I'd come in early now. I bet she kicked-off at that.'

'Said she were going to complain to my manager and not to think I'd get away with it.'

'She won't, will she?'

'Nah. And even if she does, she were one who upset one of our customers. It's her in wrong, not me.'

Danny shrugs and makes a face that suggests he's not so sure about that. I'm not bothered about getting a bollocking from Bridget, though. It was worth it to put Fag-ash Lil in her place. No one should speak to kids like that. I still can't stop thinking about the little red-haired lad. He looked like a rabbit caught in the headlights, poor sod. I've seen it so many times on Terry's face. When everything gets too much for him and people are staring, and he doesn't know the right thing to say or do.

And now he's got to try to cope with people like that again.

He won't be able to, of course. Terry explained that during his assessment. He was right, though. The bloke wasn't listening. Probably on a bonus for every person he found fit for work.

I bang the coffee filter out into the bin. Danny turns round from the cooker, where he is starting a fry-up, and gives me a look.

'Don't let her get to you,' he says.

'It's not just her. Our Terry's had a letter saying they're stopping his benefits and he's got to get a job.'

'But he can't, can he? I thought you said he couldn't cope with working?'

'Aye. But they don't want to know. Rather treat him like he's a scrounger. Some lazy, work-shy fop who can't get off his arse.'

'What you gonna do?'

'I've got to take him to job centre on Monday, try to sort it out.'

'Can I come and watch?' he says with a smile. 'It'll be like Fag-ash Lil round two.'

'Maybe I should sell tickets,' I say. 'Might get more than I do working in this place.'

I turn back to the counter as Joan comes in. Another one of our regulars but one I'm always happy to see. Despite the heat, she's still got her coat on. I don't think I've ever seen her without it.

'Hello, love,' I say, 'how you keeping?'

'Oh, you know,' she says, 'mustn't grumble.' The creases around her mouth push upwards into a smile. Her cheeks look even hollower than usual. Her lips are cracked and dry.

'You have a sit-down and I'll bring you your usual.'

I watch her walk unsteadily to the nearest table and lower herself into the chair. It's always the same; the ones who don't grumble are the ones who actually have the most to grumble about. I turn round to Danny.

'Rustle me up summat quick for Joan, will you? She looks fit to drop.' Danny glances over and nods. A few minutes later, I take her up a cup of strong tea and a special breakfast.

'What's this?' she asks, looking at the plate. I know she's worried that she can't pay for it.

'Compliments of chef. One we had left over. Lad ordered it earlier on and had to dash off before it were ready. Been keeping it warm for you.'

Joan reaches out and squeezes my hand.

'Thank you, lovey,' she says. I wink at her. For every Fag-ash Lil in this world, there's a Joan. That's what I have to keep reminding myself.

I'm mopping the floor later after Danny's gone home when I hear the bell go. I turn round to tell whoever has just come in that we're closed and see Bridget standing there. The look on her face suggests I am in for a bollocking. But what I can't work out is how she can have found out about what's happened already.

She takes her mobile out of her handbag, presses a couple of buttons and holds it up towards me.

'Have you seen this?' she practically spits at me. Her big, black bob makes it look like there's a panther curled up on her head scowling at me and about to pounce.

I put the mop down, step forward and squint at the screen. It's not easy to read the small writing without my reading glasses but I can see the name of the café with a single star under it and the words 'Rude waitress swore at me'. I didn't even think about Fag-ash Lil putting it on the internet. That's how old and out of it I am.

'I have now. What is it?'

'A review on TripAdvisor.'

'Never heard of it.'

Bridget raises one eyebrow at me. 'Don't play silly games with me.'

'I haven't got internet.'

'You've got a phone, haven't you?'

'Yeah, one with buttons that you can call people on.'

She frowns as if she didn't realise people like me still existed.

'Well, it doesn't matter whether you know what it is or not. The fact is, we've got a one-star review on TripAdvisor thanks to you and we'll probably be out of business by the summer.'

'Don't be daft. Nobody who comes here is going to take any notice of that rubbish.'

'Are you denying you called her a bloody ignorant cow?'

'No. I said it all right. She deserved a lot worse, to be honest. I don't suppose she mentioned she'd just made a little lad cry and run out.'

Bridget is still frowning at me.

'No, I thought not. She were right rude to him. Called him

a spoilt brat in front of his mum. I told her to apologise but she refused.'

'Was he playing up or bothering her?'

'No. Just took his time to order and got a bit anxious. She were one who were rude to him.'

'I don't care what she said, you should not have spoken to her like that. You've broken my golden rule of being polite to customers and you're going to pay for it.'

She's going to dock my wages. I can feel it coming. She pulls herself up to something approaching five foot two.

'I'm sacking you.'

'You what?'

'You heard me. You're fired, as Mr Sugar would say.'

I stare at her, unable to believe what I'm hearing.

'That's ridiculous. You're overreacting.'

'I am not,' she says, jabbing her finger at me. 'I've built up this business from scratch and I'll be damned if I'm going to stand by and let you ruin it. Get your things and get out.'

I shake my head. Inside, I am trembling, but I don't want her to see what this is doing to me. I turn my back on her and walk over to the counter, take off my apron and stuff it in my bag. I fiddle around for a moment before I compose myself enough to turn round to face her.

'When am I going to get paid?' I ask.

'You'll not be getting a penny from me for this week. Do you have any idea how much that review is going to cost my business?'

'You can't do that.'

'I can. And you can think yourself lucky I'm not taking you to court for my lost earnings.'

I pick up my bag, grab hold of the mop and shove it towards her.

'Well you can stick this where sun don't shine. And for your information, it's not a business, it's a crappy greasy spoon, only you're so far up your own arse you can't see it.'

I walk out of the café without looking back and giving her the satisfaction of seeing how much that hurt. Stupid fucking cow. Her and Fag-ash Lil deserve each other. It's Danny I feel sorry for now, having to work with Bridget until she gets a replacement.

I bite my bottom lip as I think about Joan. Danny won't be able to smuggle her any free meals with Bridget's beady eyes on him. I shake my head, still struggling to take in the fact that I am out of a job. I'm going to have to find another one pretty sharpish, too, what with Terry's benefits being stopped.

Shit. This is a nightmare. I should have kept my big mouth shut. It's not like it's the first time I've talked myself into trouble. But there again, the Fag-ash Lils of this world should not be allowed to get away with it. Poor little kid. I wonder what he's doing now. Whether his mum took him anywhere else or they just went home and got their own breakfast.

I think back over all the times Terry has had meltdowns in public. When people have looked at me as if it is all my fault. Maybe sometimes they thought he was my kid instead of my little brother. They didn't stop to think, see. They certainly never thought about how tough it must be to care for someone like that. Especially when no one had ever cared for you.

I'm so lost in my own thoughts I almost walk past the end of our road. Or maybe it's because I don't want to go home and tell Terry that I've lost my job. I stand on the corner for a bit, trying to work out what to say. I don't want to lie to him, but I don't want to worry him too much, either. Not with him already in a state about this appointment on Monday.

I knock on the door, then let myself in. I can hear noises but it's not the TV. They're coming from the kitchen.

'Terry, it's me,' I call out, before pushing open the kitchen door. He is lying on the floor with my Marigolds on and the rolling pin in one hand.

'Rats,' he says, looking up at me. 'Matthew says they've come back. They live behind cooker. I can hear them and I'm waiting for when they come out.'

I nod slowly while counting to ten.

'OK,' I say. 'How about you leave them to me now?'

'They're in water pipes too,' he says, getting up off the floor. 'I can hear them all over flat. I've blocked loo up with paper so they can't get out.'

'Right,' I reply. 'I know you've been trying to help but you need to let me deal with them now, OK?'

He shrugs. 'Matthew says there will be rats at job centre too.'

'No, they won't have rats there. Government wouldn't allow it.'

'Government know all about them. Matthew says they sent them there.'

I sigh. This has been brought on just by the prospect of having to sign on. God knows what he'll be like if they make him go to work. I put my arm round his shoulders.

'I'll be going there with you, so you mustn't worry about it.'

'Are you coming to kill rats?'

I sigh. 'I'll be going to sign on as well, Terry. I lost my job today.'

Terry looks at me, frowning.

'Was it because of rats? Matthew says they're at café too. That's why it didn't get a good hygiene rating.'

'No, I told you. It were because Bridget were too tight to buy a big enough fridge so things got put together that shouldn't have been.'

Terry shakes his heads. 'No, there were rats too. That inspector saw them.'

There is no use arguing with him when he gets like this, I know that.

'Well, it wasn't because of owt to do with rats, but I don't work there any more, so let's not worry about it. Put kettle on for us, would you, love?'

I go into the bathroom to sort the loo out. He has stuffed two entire bog rolls down there. And my spare kitchen roll. I get a bucket from the cupboard, put it next to the loo and start picking it all out.

It's going to get worse, that's the most difficult thing about it. I know this is only the beginning. It always gets a lot worse before we can get any help for him. I'll call the mental health team on Monday, but I already know what they'll say. It's not an emergency. And there's a lot of people who need help more than he does. And they've got no money and no staff. It's not their fault, poor sods. It's just how it is.

I stand up and wash my hands. I'll need to pop to the corner shop and get some more bog roll. I'll have to try to hide it, mind, or he'll only do the same thing again.

I go back into the kitchen. Terry has emptied the entire contents of my bag into the kitchen sink and is scrubbing everything with a nailbrush.

'Because of rats,' he says, looking up at me. 'Matthew said they got into your bag at café.'

AFTER

3

FINN

The first thing I notice about sheep apron lady when she arrives is that she isn't wearing her sheep apron. I can't help feeling a bit disappointed. It's like Alan Titchmarsh coming for tea and not having his gardening gloves on. Although I don't suppose it's very easy to drink a cup of tea with gardening gloves on, but I'd like to think he'd try.

She stands there for a second looking at me. Her plaits look sad again, like they did that night, and I think she might be about to cry.

Dad asks her in, and she steps inside.

'Hello, Finn, love,' she says. She steps forward and gives me a hug. The second I feel her arms round me I start to cry. I do not even have time to try to stop the tears before they come out of my eyes. It's like she has just pushed a button and all these tears are coming and I don't know how to make them stop and the more I cry, the more she hugs me tightly and the more she hugs me, the more I keep crying. She is crying too, not as much as me but still quite a lot for a grown-up. I think we might end up standing in a big puddle in the hall if we can't stop soon. It will be like that story in *Winnie the Pooh* where it kept on raining and Piglet was entirely surrounded by water and had to be rescued by Pooh and Christopher Robin. Mum used to do the voices when she read *Winnie The Pooh* to me. She was good at all of them, but I think her Eeyore was the best. Dad read it to me once when Mum wasn't here, and it was like watching a film with the sound off, because he didn't do the voices. I think I actually fell asleep.

Finally, sheep apron lady loosens her grip on me and pulls back a little. I look at her through blurry eyes.

'I've been thinking about you so much,' she says. 'Thank you for inviting me for tea.'

I nod. I am still trying to stop crying enough to be able to speak. I wipe my eyes with my hands. Dad comes back from the kitchen with a couple of tissues and hands one to me and one to sheep apron lady. His eyes are red too.

'Can I get you a drink, Karen? Tea, coffee, something stronger?'

'Tea would be grand, thanks,' sheep apron lady replies. 'And please, call me Kaz, everyone else does.'

'Will do,' says Dad. 'Finn, why don't you take Kaz through to the lounge, while I get the drinks?'

Sheep apron lady finally lets go of me.

'Shall I call you Kaz too?' I ask, as she follows me through to the lounge. 'Only I've been calling you sheep apron lady up till now.'

She bursts into laughter, which, I suppose, is better than crying. It's not like she is laughing at me like the kids at school do, though. It's a nice laugh. We sit down next to each other on the sofa.

'You can call me whatever you like, pet. Sheep apron lady is a good one, though. I've been called a lot worse in my time.'

'So have I,' I say. 'At school, I mean.'

She screws up her nose. 'My little brother got called a lot of names at school. Kids can be cruel.'

'What did he get called?' I ask.

'Oh, smelly pants and stick-insect, because he were skinny, loads of stuff like that.'

'I get called weirdo and freak,' I say. 'And other ones I can't tell you because they're rude.'

Kaz smiles. 'Try not to let them get to you,' she says.

I nod, remembering how many times Mum said that to me.

'My friend Lottie says they're all sad losers.'

'Well, she's right,' says Kaz. 'Is Lottie your best friend?'

'Yes,' I say. 'She's actually my only friend but that doesn't matter because Mum says one good one is worth a million rubbish ones.'

Kaz looks down at her hands. We sit in silence for a few moments.

'I'm sorry,' I say.

She looks up quickly, a slight frown on her face. 'Whatever for?'

'Running out of your café,' I reply. 'It wasn't because of you. You were really nice to me; it was because you only had a hygiene rating of three.'

Kaz looks at me.

'Is that what were bothering you?'

'Yes. Because three is generally satisfactory, and Dad wouldn't let me go to a school that only had a satisfactory Ofsted. My school is good, so like a four hygiene rating, but there are still mean kids there and the head teacher thinks I'm weird, so that's why I only like eating in places that have a five, because that means they are very good.'

'Well, I reckon that's pretty smart, working all that out for yoursen. At least I know it weren't my sheep apron that scared you off.'

'No, I like that. Do you have other things with sheep on or is it just the apron?'

She thinks for a moment. 'I used to have a tea-towel, but I can't remember what happened to it. Our Terry got me one for Christmas and apron for my birthday.'

'Is Our Terry you son?' I ask.

Kaz smiles. 'No, he's my brother. He's one I told you about who got picked on at school.'

'Does he like sheep too?' I ask, as Dad comes in with the tea-tray.

'Not really,' she says. 'He likes eighties TV shows. Ones you'll not have heard of. What about you, Finn? What do you like?'

'Flowers,' I say, 'and Alan Titchmarsh.'

Kaz looks a bit surprised but she doesn't laugh. 'Right you are, into gardening, are you? I used to go down allotment when I were little.'

'There you go, Finn,' says Dad as he puts the tray down and hands Kaz her mug and me my glass of orange juice. 'Maybe Kaz can give you some gardening tips.'

'Oh, I don't know,' says Kaz. 'That were a good while ago now. I haven't grown owt for years.'

'Haven't you got the allotment any more?' I ask.

'No. Me mam had to give it up.'

'It's a lot to manage, from what I've heard,' says Dad, sitting down in the armchair opposite us.

Kaz looks down at her hands.

'Have you got a garden?' I ask.

She shakes her head. 'No, love. Never had one.'

I'd hate that. I remember how worried I was when Mum told me I might not have a garden after her and Dad got divorced.

'Whereabouts do you live, Kaz?' Dad asks.

'In town centre,' she replies.

'Not much space for gardens, then,' Dad says.

Kaz holds her mug and doesn't say anything.

'I was thinking of doing macaroni cheese for tea,' Dad says. 'Would that be OK with you, Kaz? Do say if you're a vegan or anything.'

Kaz smiles. 'I'll eat owt that's put in front of me, I will.'

'Great,' says Dad. 'That makes things easier. My cooking's not up to much, though, so you might regret saying that.'

I don't like him talking about Mum like this. He is talking about Mum, even though he isn't saying her name, because she is the reason his cooking isn't very good. Hers was so good he never did any. We are all quiet for a bit. Kaz drinks her tea. I take a sip of my orange juice.

'Tell you what, Finn,' says Dad. 'Why don't you take Kaz up to see your room while I start cooking? You'll have lots of things you can show her up there.'

I'm not sure what sort of things he means, but I suppose I can show her some of my Alan Titchmarsh gardening books and maybe talk about roses or allotments. I stand up. Kaz finishes her tea and stands up too.

'Right,' she says. 'Let's have a look, then.'

I push open the door of my bedroom. I am not used to having people I don't know in here. I think the only person apart from Mum and Dad who has ever been in my room is Lottie. I am not sure what Kaz will make of it because it is full of me and I know I am weird so I suppose my bedroom must be weird too.

Kaz walks in. The first thing she does is look up at the bee light on the ceiling.

'Hey, that's smashing, is that.'

I pull a face. 'I don't really like it,' I say, 'but don't tell Dad, because he got it for me.'

'Why don't you like it?' Kaz asks.

'Because bees aren't blue. And because Mum wouldn't like it.'

Kaz nods.

'Do you like bees, then?'

'Yeah. I've always liked them since I was a little kid.'

'How old are you, Finn?'

'Ten. Eleven in August.'

'So, you start big school in September?'

'Yeah.'

'You don't sound right keen.'

'I didn't really want to go there. It was Dad's idea. It's a posh school near Ilkley. I got a music scholarship.'

'Wow. You must be right good at music then. What do you play?'

'Ukulele and piano. But I haven't played for a while. Not since, you know.'

I walk over to the other side of the room so Kaz doesn't see that I'm trying not to cry.

'Why don't you want to go to your new school?' asks Kaz, sitting down on my bed.

'Because it's big so there'll be even more kids to be mean to me. I don't suit school. Not normal schools. Mum made a school in a tent for me once. On the day when . . .'

My voice trails off. I still don't think I am able to talk about what happened. I take a deep breath and try again.

'It was brilliant, her school. We went on a nature trail and I drew pictures of what I found. They weren't very good but it didn't matter and I wanted it to be like that forever.'

I stop talking again to concentrate on trying not to cry.

'What does your dad say?' asks Kaz after a bit. 'About you not wanting to go to this school?'

'He says it might not be as bad as I think. He said the same thing about my primary school and it's been horrible.'

Kaz scrunches up her face. 'Dads do talk rubbish some-times.'

'Did your dad talk rubbish?' I ask.

'Aye, whenever he opened his mouth.'

I do a little laugh. It turns out I don't mind Kaz being in my room at all. I show her some other stuff. Photos and music certificates and that. Then we come to my gardening books.

'That's a right lot you've got there,' Kaz says. 'You must be a bit of an expert if you've read all them.'

'I want to be a gardener when I'm older,' I say. 'That's another reason why I don't want to go to school. Everything I need to learn about is in these books. Being able to label a Viking longboat isn't going to be much help to a gardener.'

'I don't think it's much help to anyone. We don't get many Vikings in Halifax.'

I do another little laugh and take one of my books off the shelf.

'I met Alan Titchmarsh once. He was at Tong Garden Centre. He signed this book about climbing roses,' I say, holding it out with the page turned to his signature for her to see.

'That's smashing, that is. He's good on telly, too,' Kaz says. 'But then he's from Yorkshire. All the best people are.'

'I'm not,' I say. 'I was born in Manchester and Mum and Dad were born in Cheshire and we all came to live here when I was one.'

'Well, you're honorary Yorkshire then,' says Kaz.

'The kids at school say I talk funny because I don't sound like them.'

'It doesn't matter what you sound like, it's words that come out of your mouth and kindness in your heart what's important,' says Kaz.

For someone who doesn't use proper grammar and wouldn't do very well in her SATS, Kaz seems to talk a lot of sense. I show her a few more of my books and I tell her about the sort of garden I would like to have one day. And finally, just after Dad calls up that tea is ready, I pluck up the courage to ask her the thing that I wanted to ask. The thing that I know we shouldn't talk about, but I have to, because I have lain in bed worrying about it every night since.

'Do you think it was my fault?'

She hesitates and looks at me, but I can tell that she knows what I am talking about because of the sadness in her eyes.

'No, love,' she says. 'And you must never think that, because it's not true.'

'But if I hadn't –'

'Ssshhh,' she says, putting her hand on my shoulder and bending down to my level. 'I won't hear a word of it. None of it was your fault. You are the bravest boy I have ever known.'

I nod, even though I don't think I am, and wonder if she means that or, like everyone else, she's just being nice to me.

'You called me Terry that night,' I say.

'Did I?' she replies. 'Sorry. I wasn't really thinking straight.'

'I didn't mind,' I say. 'I was just glad you were there.'

AFTER

4

KAZ

I follow Finn downstairs for tea. I am still thinking about what he said. I wanted to give him another hug, but I was worried I'd set him off crying again and spoil his tea. His fault. As if any of it was his fault. Poor little mite.

They have a dining room. A room that isn't a kitchen and just has a big, wooden dining table and chairs in it and a window that looks out onto their back garden. I don't think I have ever been to the house of someone who has a dining room before.

Martin has laid the table. There are table mats and serviettes. Bloody serviettes. I think about what Terry will say when I tell him. When he's better mind. He won't say anything right now.

In the middle of the table is a jug of water on a mat (they have mats for everything, even the table mats), with ice and lemon slices in it. I think of my tea last night, which was a pot of noodles made in the shared kitchen downstairs and eaten sitting on my bed.

'Can I get you wine, Kaz?' asks Martin. 'We've got red or white.'

'Oh, no thanks. I'm fine with that,' I say, pointing to the water on the table. I'm worried now that it was rude not to have brought a bottle with me – not that I could have afforded one. I'd thought tea was just going to be a couple of sandwiches and a slice of cake. I wasn't expecting any of this fancy stuff.

I sit down next to Finn while Martin goes to fetch our food. Right on cue, as he comes back in, my stomach rumbles.

'Sounds like you're ready for this.' He smiles as he puts the plate down in front of me. I can't begin to tell him how right he is.

'Finn tells me you work at the café on the other side of the park. I imagine it must get pretty hectic on a day like this. I expect you're too busy serving other people to have a chance to eat.'

'Oh, I, er, don't work there any more,' I say.

'Right. Where are you now then?'

'I've got nowt at moment but I'm looking,' I reply.

'Well, I hope you find something soon,' says Martin.

I pick up my fork and try a mouthful of the macaroni cheese. It tastes fine to me. Although, to be honest, I am that hungry I would eat anything.

'Why did you leave the café?' Finn asks. 'Was it because of the hygiene rating?'

'Finn,' says Martin.

'It's OK,' I say, with a smile. 'It was more me and boss not exactly seeing eye-to-eye about summat.'

I can't tell them it was because of him. He blames himself enough already. I don't want to give him another thing to feel bad about. I carry on eating, trying to get enough into my stomach so that it doesn't embarrass me and rumble again.

'Are you planning to stay in the same line of work?' asks Martin, 'or do you fancy trying something different?'

I know he's trying to be nice, but he's got no fucking idea if he thinks that people like me have a choice in the matter. Or that one-O-level Kaz might have some nice savings in the bank to live off while I retrain as an architect.

'It's all I've ever done,' I reply. 'Best to stick to what you know.'

'Try to choose a café with a five for its hygiene rating though,' says Finn. 'Then I can come and visit you there.'

I look up and catch Martin shaking his head.

'I'm sure Kaz has got more important considerations than that,' he says. 'Do you have a family at all, Kaz?'

'Just a younger brother,' I reply.

'His name is Our Terry and the mean kids at school used to call him names,' says Finn.

'I can see Finn has been interrogating you,' Martin says.

'We were just getting to know each other, weren't we?' says Kaz.

Finn nods and takes his first mouthful of macaroni cheese.

'Oh, I forgot the garlic bread,' says Martin, jumping up and disappearing into the kitchen.

It's all I can do to stop myself shovelling the rest of the macaroni cheese down in the two minutes he is gone.

'Sorry,' Finn whispers to me.

'What for?'

'The sauce is a bit lumpy and the pasta is too squishy. Mum's is way better than this.'

I give him a little smile as Martin comes back in with the slightly burnt garlic bread.

As I am putting my jacket on in the hall later, Finn asks if I can come for tea again.

I look at Martin before answering. He gives a little nod.

'I'd love to, pet,' I say.

'You can come every Saturday, if you like,' says Finn. 'Or maybe sometimes on Wednesdays when *Love Your Garden* with Alan Titchmarsh is on TV.'

'Let's take things one step at a time,' I say. 'I'll sort summat out with your dad.'

'You can bring Our Terry, if you like,' Finn adds.

'Thank you, only he's not right well at moment. But it were very nice of you to ask.'

'Are you sure I can't give you a lift home?' asks Martin.

'No, don't you worry. I'm used to bus, and I'll be there in ten minutes.'

Martin nods. 'Well, it's been lovely to meet you properly.'

There is an awkward silence for a moment. I don't really

remember him from before, to be honest. I think I was too busy concentrating on Finn to take much notice of him.

'You too,' I reply.

I turn to Finn and give him a big hug. I think for a moment he is going to start crying again but he doesn't. We hold each other for a long time. I know that he is thinking about exactly the same thing as me but neither of us says a word. We don't need to. Because we went through it together. And neither of us will ever forget.

'Thanks for inviting me,' I say. 'I'll see you soon. Just remember what I said.'

He nods, his red curls bobbing as he does so. And I realise that it's not just my stomach that is full, but my heart too.

I spot the sign on my way to see Terry the next day. It's on an 'A' board outside the garden centre on the way out of town. I've seen them advertise jobs there before; usually just for gardeners and sales assistants, although there was a sign up for a 'portly gentleman with white hair and a fondness for reindeer', last November. It made me laugh because it said those applying shouldn't be allergic to fake beards or children. It's a different sign I see today, though. One that says, 'Part-time catering assistant required for café. Apply within.'

I stop dead next to it. I haven't got my CV on me, but it doesn't matter, I have to go in. It may only be a part-time job, but some money is better than no money. I head across the car park, past the rows of trolleys and a stand full of bedding plants. Once inside, I go up to the nearest till.

'Hello,' I say to the woman serving. 'I'm interested in job advertised for café.'

'Right,' she replies. 'You need to talk to Marje. If you turn right and go through indoor plant section, café's on your right. That's where you'll find her.'

I thank her and follow her directions. When I get to the café it's busy. There's only one person serving, an older woman, not far off my age. I hang back for a second, not wanting to jump the queue, until she finally looks up and says, 'Yes, love, what can I get you?'

'I'm here about your job,' I say. 'I've been told to ask for Marje.'

'That were quick,' she says. 'We only put it up this morning. If you give me a few minutes until rush dies down, I'll be right with you. Have a seat at table in corner.'

I do as she says and look around me. Most of the customers are middle-aged or older couples, as you'd expect in a garden centre. The menu is mainly toasties, butties and jacket potatoes, with some cakes and pastries on the counter. All fairly run-of-the-mill stuff.

After about five minutes, Marje comes and sits down opposite me, still in her apron.

'Excuse state of this,' she says, wiping sugar from the table with her hand. 'As you can see, we're a bit short-staffed. Lass that worked here weekends has jacked it in. Too much like hard work. Don't know they're born, kids today. Anyway, here's me gabbing and I haven't even asked your name.'

'Karen Allen,' I say. 'Kaz to my friends. I've been working in cafés since I were sixteen, so I know what I'm doing.'

'Well, job's part-time, ten while four Thursdays to Sundays. I'm here whole bloody time and I sing while I work even though I've got a voice like a strangled cat, but if you don't mind that, we'll be all right. Have you got any references or owt?'

'No.' I hesitate, not sure whether to be honest or not but I have a good feeling about Marje.

'I had a bit of a falling-out with my boss at last place I worked. She blamed me for a one-star review some rude customer wrote online after I told her off for making a little lad cry.'

'Seems a bit harsh,' Marje says.

'That's what I thought. I'd worked there for years without a single complaint. I'm a hard worker, not afraid to get my hands dirty. Haven't had a day off sick in years.'

'When could you start?' Marje asks.

'Soon as you want. I've got nowt on.'

'How does Thursday sound to you?'

'Really?' I say. 'I've got job?'

'Well, I reckon you've got more chance of sticking it out than any of youngsters we'll get, and I don't suppose you'll be on your phone every two minutes either.'

'You're right there,' I say, smiling. 'Thank you.'

'I'll see you Thursday then, Kaz,' she says, standing up.

As I get up to leave, I notice the hygiene rating sticker behind the counter. It's a five. In a café at a garden centre. The smile on my face gets a bit broader. I suspect Finn might be paying me a visit sometime soon.

*

'I've got a job,' I say to Terry, as soon as I arrive. He looks at me blankly from his chair.

'At café in garden centre. They had an advert up on board outside, so I went in on my way here, was interviewed and they said I could start on Thursday. Four days a week, it is and woman in charge seems right nice. A lot better than bloody Bridget, although that's not hard.'

Terry nods. 'Great,' he says, his voice flat, his face expressionless. I try not to take it personally. I know this is what the meds do to him, but I still find it hard.

'So, how's you?' I ask.

He shrugs.

'Why don't you try sitting in main room and watching telly,' I say.

'Nowt good on,' he replies.

'Maybe I could ask them if they could get hold of a video player, so I can bring your tapes in.'

'Nah,' he says. 'They won't do that.'

'We need to get you better, Terry. That's only way you're going to get out of here. You know how it works.'

He shrugs again and starts picking at a button on his cardigan. It feels like I've lost my brother. That's what I hate about it. I know he couldn't go on like he was, but this doesn't seem like much of a life either. Somehow, I've got to try to rebuild his life, as well as my own.

When my name is called at the job centre the next morning, I sit down opposite Denise and make no attempt to hide the grin on my face.

'I've got a job,' I say.

'Really?' I wish she wouldn't sound so surprised.

'Yep. Had an interview and was taken on yesterday. It's at café at garden centre. Four days a week but it's better than nowt. I start on Thursday.'

'That's great. Well done. I wasn't aware you'd applied for that.'

'I hadn't. Just saw sign up outside yesterday as I were walking past and went in and asked. Old-fashioned way of doing it. Still bloody works sometimes, though. She didn't ask for my CV or an email address. Just when I could start.'

Denise smiles, obviously trying to hide her irritation at my dig, and a tiny bit of me admires her for it. Only a tiny bit, mind. The rest of me is enjoying sticking my two fingers up at her.

BEFORE

5

FINN

I have to get up earlier than usual on Monday morning because of the meeting with Mrs Ratcliffe, which means we all have breakfast together (usually I don't see Dad in the mornings because he's gone to catch his train to Leeds). Mum and Dad sit opposite each other across the round kitchen table, and I sit between them, trying to pretend I don't realise they are not speaking.

'Can you pass the butter, please?' says Mum. She doesn't say who she wants to pass it to her, but it is in front of Dad. He doesn't move, so I pick it up and pass it to Mum and she smiles at me and says 'Thank you, Finn,' and looks at Dad, who doesn't say anything, just makes loud noises with his spoon scraping the cereal bowl and stands up as soon as he is finished.

'Have a good day at school, Finn,' he says. This is such a

stupid thing to say as I have never had a good day at school in my life and he knows that today is not likely to be the day that happens. I don't say that, though. I just nod and he ruffles my hair and looks at Mum and says nothing and she looks down at her toast and says nothing and I want to scream at them to stop it with all the saying nothing, but if I do that, it will only create a noisier scene, so I settle for the quiet one.

'Right,' says Mum a few minutes later, once we've heard the front gate click shut behind him and she has finished her last mouthful of toast, 'have you had enough?'

I nod.

'Not hungry?' she asks, looking at the soggy mush of Millet Bran left in my bowl.

'Not really,' I reply.

'Remember, you're not in trouble at school. Mrs Ratcliffe has agreed to see me because I'm cross at the school. None of this is about you.'

It is a weird thing to say because, as far as I can see, all of it is about me.

As we arrive in the school playground, the other kids in my class are going in for the breakfast club. They all look at me because Mum is with me and that makes it weird.

'Why's your mum here?' asks Daniel Williams.

I freeze. Whatever I say, it's going to sound wrong, so I decide to say nothing.

I follow Mum into school, past my classroom and down the corridor towards Mrs Ratcliffe's office. I imagine the other kids all talking about me; some saying I'm in trouble, others saying I'm going to grass them up. Or simply that I'm the weird kid being weird again.

The school secretary's door is open, and Mrs Ravani smiles at us both.

'Good morning, she's expecting you. Please go through.'

Mum knocks on the door and Mrs Ratcliffe's voice calls out, 'Come in'.

I follow Mum inside. Mrs Ratcliffe is tall because she used to be a policewoman and she wears big dangly earrings and bangles. I hope she didn't wear them when she was a police-woman because the thieves and robbers would have heard her coming and got away. She stands up and jangles towards us.

'Hello Finn. Hello Mrs Rook-Carter.' I look at Mum, but she doesn't say anything about the fact that her name is Ms Hannah Rook and you would think Mrs Ratcliffe would know that by now.

She shakes Mum's hand and smiles at me and tells us to sit down.

'Now, Finn,' she says. 'Your mum contacted me about the breakfast club, and I asked you to come and see me with her today so I can put your mind at rest that it's nothing to worry about.

'All we're doing is giving our year sixes a chance to get together over breakfast and do a little bit of extra revision with their friends.'

I want to tell her that I've only got one friend and she's started a petition against it and the others are only going because they think there might be jam or Nutella, but I don't say that in case it sounds rude.

'The thing is,' says Mum, 'Finn, as you know, is a sensitive boy and he's feeling under enough pressure about the SATs already, without the school adding to it like this.'

Mrs Ratcliffe smiles but still looks at me, rather than Mum.

'What you need to understand, Finn, is that we want to give all our year sixes the best possible chance in their SATs. It's about doing what's best for you.'

I can see Mum getting super-angry. I hope she isn't going to say anything bad, but I think she probably is.

'And what you need to understand,' says Mum, in a higher-pitched voice than usual, 'is that I am quite capable of deciding what's best for my son and this isn't really about him at all. It's about school league tables. And I won't have my son used in this way.'

I don't really listen to the words after that, just the voices. When people are trying not to argue in front of children, they talk in very strange voices and have expressions on their faces that don't match what they are saying. Mrs Ratcliffe does lots of smiling and Mum does lots of nodding, but they don't seem to be agreeing with each other about anything. I know they are talking about me, but I try to drown out what they are saying by doing bee noises in my head. It works until I notice they are both staring at me and the bee noises obviously aren't in my head any more.

'Is there something you'd like to say, Finn?' Mrs Ratcliffe asks, looking concerned.

'I don't want to do the SATs and I don't want to do the breakfast clubs and I don't want to come to school any more.'

For a second, I wonder if I just said it in my head, instead of out loud, but the look on Mrs Ratcliffe's face suggests not. Mum looks like she might start crying but stands up instead.

'Right. You heard him. He won't be attending the breakfast club or sitting the SATs next week. I'll send you confirmation of that in writing later. Thank you for your time.'

Mum strides out of Mrs Ratcliffe's office, with me trailing behind her. I have never stormed out of anywhere before and part of me thinks it needs some sort of sound effect to go with it, like they'd have in the movies, but as I've already been doing weird noises out loud, I decide to go silently.

When we get to the end of the corridor, Mum turns round and looks at me.

'Are you OK?' she asks.

'I'm better now I've got a week off school.'

'You'll probably still have to come to school.'

'Why?'

'Because it's the law, Finn.'

'But what will I do?'

'I expect you'll go in with the year fives instead. You liked Mr Mukhtar, didn't you?'

'Yes, but I'm a year six and they'll all ask me why I'm in with them and I won't know what to say.'

I can hear my voice trembling as it comes out. Mum bends down and puts her hand on my shoulder.

'It'll be fine. Let's talk about this at home later, love.'

She gives me one of her reassuring smiles, but I do not feel reassured.

'Dad will be really cross.'

'I'll explain everything to him.'

'But he'll still be mad and there'll be a big argument.'

'Try not to worry, eh? We'll get it all sorted out later.'

Mum's eyes are watery. At that point my classroom door opens, and Mrs Kerrigan comes out.

'Hello, Finn,' she says. 'Are you ready to join us now?'

I'm not. What I really want is to run away and never come back but then I'd be in even more trouble than I already am. So, I nod, turn round, give Mum a little smile and follow Mrs Kerrigan into the classroom.

'Wow, a boycott, that's awesome,' says Lottie at break when I tell her I'm not doing the SATs. She is looking at me as if I have just conquered Mount Everest. Up until this point, I haven't even thought of it as something to be proud of, but now I suppose I ought to act that way, even if I don't feel it.

'Yeah, Mrs Ratcliffe is pretty mad about it.'

'Are you going to stand outside with a placard? You might get on the news.'

'No,' I reply. 'Mum thinks they'll make me go in with year five for the week.'

'Oh well, maybe you'll get a blue plaque on your house when you die.'

'Really?'

'Yeah, if your protest starts a national boycott and it ends SATs forever.'

'I don't think that will actually happen, will it?'

'I don't know. I would join you, but Mum says she's got some early starts at work next week, and it might be easier if I just go in for the breakfasts and not bother much with the revision. Like sort of fighting it from within.'

'Right,' I say.

'I'm still doing the petition, though,' she says, fishing in her bag and pulling out a piece of A4 paper.

'I'll sign it then,' I say.

'Great,' she says with a smile. 'You can be the first.'

Mum doesn't suggest baking or going for a 'nice long walk' when we get home from school later. It's like she knows that this is so serious, even muffins won't distract me from it.

'Are we going to get into big trouble?' I ask.

'No,' says Mum. 'Mrs Ratcliffe says she's disappointed and we can still change our minds, but I've told her that we won't.'

'But Dad will still be mad, won't he?'

'Let me handle him,' she says. 'I don't want you to have to worry about it.'

I wonder if I should point out to her that I will worry about it because her and Dad are getting divorced and whenever they speak to each other, it ends up in an argument and there was a bad enough one about me not going to breakfast club, let alone her pulling me out of the SATs altogether. I don't say anything, though. I nod and go upstairs to my room and watch YouTube videos about bee-keepers.

I want to keep bees one day when I am older. I would like to keep them now but when I asked Mum if we could get a hive about a year ago, she said it was a big commitment and she wasn't sure it was the right time. I think she must have known they were going to get divorced even then, because when I said that if we had bees, we could use our own honey for the muffins, she got upset and I didn't mention getting bees to her again. I suppose she was right because I'd hate to have to leave the bees behind and I couldn't hide them in my pockets and take them with me, like I can with the bulbs from the garden.

They have the big argument as soon as Dad gets home. Maybe Mum thought it was best to get it over with or maybe Dad asked her about the meeting, and she didn't want to lie to him.

As soon as I hear it start, I go and sit on the stairs. Usually, when they argue about things that aren't important, I play my ukulele or put my headphones on and listen to music turned up loud to try to drown it out. But this is an argument about me doing the tests and I want to know what Dad says and if I ask Mum afterwards, she will try to make it sound better than it really was, and I want to know the truth.

The first thing I hear is Dad's angry voice. If you gave voices numbers, like they do with the Richter Scale for earthquakes, I would say it's a nine on the anger scale (which for earthquakes would mean it only happens every 300 years), and although there are quite a lot of fours and fives in our house, and a fair few sixes and sevens, I don't think I have ever heard a nine before.

'You cannot make major decisions about our son's education without consulting me,' is what Dad shouts.

Mum's voice isn't as loud and I can't hear it so clearly, but I hear the 'it's making him anxious, Martin, I told you what happened in the café. If we're not careful, this is going to push him over the edge,' and then they have a sort of mini-argument within the argument about whether I should be wrapped in cotton wool or not (really, I think they should say bubble-wrap, because everything comes wrapped in bubble-wrap these days, I have never seen anything arrive wrapped in cotton wool) and Mum says he was the one who didn't want me to go to the high school in Halifax and he says that was different and it goes a bit quieter.

Just when I think the worst is over, Mum says something about me being used for league table results and Dad goes back to a full-on nine and shouts, 'You are jeopardising our son's future for your political beliefs and I will not have it,' at which point Mum's voice goes up to at least a seven, and Mum never normally goes above a five, and shouts, 'It will have no impact on his future whatsoever and you know that, you're trying to emotionally blackmail me.'

I sit a little bit longer on the stairs while they have another mini-argument about who is emotionally blackmailing who and then Dad says he won't let her get away with it and I hear the back door slam and when I run back to my bedroom and look out of the window, Dad is standing in the garden with his head down kicking the apple tree, which seems a bit mean because the apple tree has nothing to do with SATs whatsoever.

I pick up my ukulele and try to play but it doesn't sound right so I stop and lay on my bed and read for a while, trying not to think about my rumbly tummy, and by the time Mum calls up that tea is ready, I have a tummy ache and don't really feel like eating any more.

I go downstairs and hover in the hallway. Dad is already sitting at the dining room table. Mum is getting the macaroni cheese out of the oven. We haven't had macaroni cheese for ages. Mum always says it is a comfort food so maybe she has made it as a kind of medicine.

Dad looks up and manages a smile as I sit down next to him. 'Your sunflowers are doing well, aren't they?'

I nod. I know he is trying to be nice, but I can't help thinking about having to leave them behind when they sell the house.

Mum comes in and puts a plate of macaroni cheese down in front of me. She has put broccoli on the plate too. This is fine because I like broccoli, but I know Dad doesn't. He still says thank you when she puts his plate down, even though there is broccoli on it too. We sit there and eat, and no one says anything much, but the macaroni cheese is very nice and I can't help thinking we should have comfort food more often. Even if Dad has left his broccoli.

BEFORE

6

KAZ

'Matthew says not to trust them,' Terry tells me as I put my shoes on.

'You don't have to trust them. You just need to get what you're entitled to.'

'They'll take all my details and send them to MI5. Then they'll start watching me again.'

I've heard all this before. It's like the first sneeze when you know a cold is on its way. The difference being, a cold is over in a few days and having a runny nose isn't much of a problem. Not compared to what he's going to have to deal with.

I know there's nothing I can do about it. All I can do is be here with him and watch him struggle until it gets so bad, they'll have to do something.

'I'm going to be with you, Terry. You don't have to worry about owt. Now, have you got your earphones?'

He nods, puts them in and threads the wires down under his cagoule like I've told him to.

'Right,' I say, hoping I don't look as nervous as I feel. 'Let's go.'

When we arrive at the bus stop there are three other people there; two lads who look like they're not long out of school and a pensioner with a shopping trolley. Terry is shifting from foot to foot. He is already muttering under his breath and he hasn't even got on the bus yet.

When it arrives, I pay while Terry makes for a seat near the back, opposite the teenage lads.

'I can see them, Matthew. I know which ones are spies,' he says.

I look out of the window, trying to keep up the pretence that Terry is talking to someone on his phone. That was the whole idea of getting the earphones for him. To make him look normal. Get him to blend in. Number of times I've turned round thinking someone was speaking to me, only to realise they were talking into a microphone on their headphones.

'Snake eyes and baseball cap, that's what I'm calling them.'

I see him glance sideways as he says it. The lad in the baseball cap looks across.

'You got a problem?' he asks. Terry ignores him and carries on talking.

'Yeah, they're following me. They were watching my house last night with binoculars. I saw them.'

'What's his problem?' the lad in the baseball cap asks me.

I shrug and gesture that he's on the phone. Terry continues talking.

'I were listening to Pet Shop Boys singing "It's a Sin", that's how I knew. Neil Tennant sends me signs sometimes.'

I am willing the bus to go faster. I don't know how this is going to end and I don't like it.

'What's wrong with him? Fucking fruit-loop,' the lad with the baseball cap says. I want to shout at him; tell him to piss off and mind his own business. But I know from experience that if I do, it will only make things worse. And my mouth has already got me into enough trouble. So, I ignore him. Although I hate myself for doing it.

'I think they're going to try to tail me,' Terry continues. 'No, it's OK, Matthew, I can deal with it. I don't need you to do that. I can handle this.'

There is a pause while he is listening to Matthew. It does sound like one end of a phone conversation. Which is good, because it means sometimes, he can go unnoticed. But not always.

'I don't think there's anyone there,' baseball cap lad says to his mate. 'He's fucking talking to himself.' They both start laughing loudly and pointing. Other people are looking now. Terry starts singing 'It's a Sin'. He is doing it to try to cover up the laughter, I know that, but he is making things worse. I reach up and ring the bell. We are still two stops before the job centre, but I don't care. I want to get off before this gets out of hand.

I stand up. Terry looks across at me with a frown. I gesture to him to get up. He does so and starts to follow me towards the doors, still singing. As we get off, he looks up at the lads, who are sticking their middle fingers up at him from the bus.

'It's OK, I've given them the slip,' he says to Matthew. 'Yeah, I know there'll be others. I'm looking out for them, don't worry.'

I'm used to it now. I've been hearing him say stuff like this since he was a teenager. But it doesn't get any easier. I always wish I could comfort him in some way. When he was little and Dad was hitting Mam or throwing stuff, I'd get him out of the way and sit holding his hand or cuddling him until it was over. But you can't hold the hand of a fifty-one-year-old man in public. Not without pretending he's your husband, and I don't want to go there.

There's nothing I can do for him; enough doctors have explained that to me over the years. But I still hate feeling so helpless. Feeling like I've failed him. 'Good-for-nothing waste of space,' I hear Mam's voice calling again. 'What kind of big sister are you?'

I try to shut her voice out. We're a right pair, we are. Him talking to Matthew Kelly and me with me mam's voice permanently goading me.

Terry is still talking to Matthew. They're not going to get any sense out of him at the job centre, I know that. It's a shame he wasn't like this when he went for the work capability assessment, they might have come to a different decision. But I'd kept the appointment from him until the last minute, so he didn't get in a state. Because who in their right mind would try to make their brother have a psychotic episode just so he would be believed? I'd stupidly thought they'd listen to him and read about what had happened before and understand that just because he didn't seem crazy at the time, it didn't mean he couldn't get that way again very quickly. That's how bloody naïve I was.

We reach the door of the job centre. It's a new place, I've never been here before. I take Terry to one side and remove the earphones.

'We've got to go in now,' I say. 'Try not to worry. I'll get it all sorted for you. Let me deal with everything and just answer truthfully when they ask you questions.'

'I don't trust them, Kaz. They'll pass it all on to MI5, I know what they're up to.'

'Just trust me,' I say. 'That's all you have to do.'

We go inside. It's all modern and done up in purple and grey. It doesn't look a bit like job centres as I remember them. I go up to a man with a clipboard and give him Terry's name and he tells us to take a seat and wait.

'It's like being in a bloody doctor's waiting room,' I say to Terry as I sit down.

'Matthew says you shouldn't have given them my name.'

'I had to let them know you were here. You might not have been called otherwise.'

Terry goes quiet for a bit. I can feel his leg trembling against mine. I hate them for doing this to him. I look at the other people waiting. They all have the same look on their face. Like they're about to be processed in a sausage-making factory. None of us matter. That's what it feels like. They can do what they want to us, and we can do fuck-all about it.

Terry starts talking to Matthew again. I reach over and put

the earphones back in for him. When his name is called, he is busy telling Matthew about something he saw in a James Bond film.

'Come on,' I say, standing up. 'It's your turn.'

The man with the clipboard points us to a desk, where a middle-aged woman with the name 'Denise Donaldson' pinned to her chest is sitting.

'How can I help you?' she says, gesturing for us to sit down.

'I've been told me brother Terry here needs a form for this mandatory reconsideration thing of his work capability assessment because he's been found fit for work and told he's got to sign on for Universal Credit in meantime, though he can't work because he's got schizophrenia, see.'

'Right,' says Denise, turning to look at Terry. 'Let's take one thing at a time. We'll do your claim for Universal Credit first. Have you got your form?'

'No. We haven't got internet, love,' I say. 'The woman I spoke to on phone said you'd be able to give us one.'

She nods and does something on her computer.

'Her name's Denise Donaldson. Is she on your list Matthew?'

Denise looks up as Terry speaks. 'Sorry, were you talking to me?'

'No, he's talking to Matthew Kelly from *Stars in Their Eyes*,' I reply.

'Mrs Allen, as you can see, there are a lot of people waiting to be seen and I don't appreciate time-wasters.'

'No, I'm serious. He hears Matthew Kelly's voice. If you're in luck, you might get a bit of Cilla Black and Jim Bowen thrown in for good measure. And it's Miss Allen, but you're welcome to call me Kaz, like everyone else does. I haven't got a husband and I don't suppose I ever will but, as you can see, it's pretty crowded in our flat already, what with Matthew and that.'

Denise looks like she wishes she had been dealing with any case other than Terry's. She walks over to the printer and comes back with a form, sitting down heavily on her chair.

'Right, let's get this filled in. Can he read and write?'

'He's not stupid,' I say. 'He's got schizophrenia. And he is still here.'

I slide the form across to Terry.

'Fill this in, love,' I say.

'Matthew says they're collecting information about me.'

'Would you like to see our data protection agreement?' asks Denise.

'No, you're all right, pet,' I reply.

'Terry, it's just so you can get your money,' I say.

Terry picks up the pen and starts filling in the form.

'Has Mr Allen brought his ID with him?' Denise asks.

'Yep,' I say, reaching into my bag and pulling out a bundle of papers. 'I've got his birth certificate here and gas and leccy bills.'

Terry looks up from the form and grabs my hand as I pass them to Denise.

'You're giving them what they want. They'll send them to MI5.'

'No, Terry, she's going to give them back when she's looked at them.'

'I need his passport or driving licence,' Denise says.

'He hasn't got owt like that.'

'They're the primary forms of identity we use.'

'Sorry, love but he's never been out of Yorkshire. He's not even got a bus pass.'

Denise frowns and looks through the rest of the papers.

'Marriage certificate?' she asks.

I raise my eyebrows at her.

Terry looks at her and says, 'I know you have rats here. Matthew told me. He said they were sent by government.'

Denise looks at Terry and back down to the papers.

'Er, right. I'll show these to my supervisor,' she says before going off with the papers.

'This is how they do it,' says Terry. 'She'll be passing information on now. She's one of them.'

'How are you getting on with form?' I ask him. Terry lets me look. 'Put my mobile down for contact number,' I tell him.

Terry couldn't have his own phone even if we could afford it. He'd get himself in too much trouble trying to call Matthew and ringing MI5 all the time to report stuff. That's why I never let my phone out of my sight.

Denise returns and hands the papers back.

'We'll be able to accept those on this occasion,' she says. Terry hands her his form, which she starts to read.

'Do you not have an email address?' she asks him.

'No because MI5 would hack it if I did,' he replies. Denise sighs. 'You'll need to set up a free one for online job applications.'

'What's the point when he can't work?' I ask. 'He's only filling this in so he can get his benefits.'

Denise pulls herself upright.

'You need to understand that this is a claimant contract and Mr Allen's part of the agreement is that he actively looks for work in return for his benefits.'

'But he's not fit for work,' I reply. 'You know that, I know that, he knows that. So why do we have to go through this whole stupid process? Why can't you just admit they've messed up and sort it out? If you force him to work, it's only going to get worse. He'll end up in psychiatric unit again. Do you really want that to happen?'

She looks down and for a moment, I think I have got through to her. Maybe I have but she can't admit it because it's more than her job's worth. So, she does what they all do, trots out the rules and regulations line.

'The DWP have found him fit for work and therefore we must treat him as such while he goes through the mandatory reconsideration process.'

I shake my head. The only thing in our favour is that I can't imagine anyone giving him a job when he's in this state.

'Fine' I say. 'He'll look for work. When is he going to get his money?'

'It takes five weeks for Universal Credit applications to be processed and the first payment made.'

I stare at her.

'You're having a laugh, aren't you? What's he supposed to live off during that time?'

'It is possible to apply for an advance if you're struggling to cover basic needs, but that has to be paid back out of your benefits, so you'll need to ensure you can live on reduced benefits in future weeks.'

'Well that's no good, is it? You're giving him a choice of being skint now or skint later.'

Denise sighs. 'I'll print you out the form for an advance payment. It's up to you whether you apply or not. What other household income do you have?'

'We haven't got owt now. I lost my job on Friday. I need to sign on while I'm here, too.'

'I'm afraid you can only do that if you've made an appointment.'

'I thought I could do it at same time as our Terry.'

Denise shakes her head. 'No. The next available slot is on Friday afternoon at four thirty. I can book you in for that if you'd like?'

I shrug. It doesn't look like I have any option.

'Fine. We're screwed, whenever it is.'

Denise ignores me and looks back down at the form.

'I see your last job was as a cleaner, Mr Allen.'

'Yeah, in a restaurant,' says Terry. 'I didn't like it because there were rats. I could hear them running across floor in kitchen.'

Terry starts singing 'Rat in Mi Kitchen' by UB40 under his breath. It makes a welcome change from the Pet Shop Boys, to be honest. Denise looks at me.

'I'll go and get those forms,' she says.

*

Terry is quiet on the bus home. It's all still going on in his head, though. I can see it from the expression on his face. He leaves me when he gets like this. It's like he's gone to another place where I can't reach him. That's what worries me most. Not being able to help him. It's the one job I have as his big sister; to protect him. After what happened when he was little, I vowed I'd never let another person hurt him again. I managed to keep that promise but what I couldn't do is protect him from himself. I cried the first time he was sectioned, because I knew I'd failed him. I've cried every time since. And every time I hear her voice, cackling with cruelty and alcohol. 'What kind of big sister are you?' She said sorry afterwards, when she was sober. More times that I care to remember. But I never hear that voice. Only the mocking one. 'What's he done to deserve a big sister like you?'

Denise rings the following morning when Terry is still in bed. She seems surprised when I answer.

'Can I speak to Mr Allen?' she says.

'It's Kaz, his sister. I met you yesterday. He's still asleep so you'll have to make do with me.'

'It is Mr Allen I need to speak to. Is it possible to wake him up, please?'

'No,' I reply. 'I'm not going to do that because he hardly got any sleep last night. Spent most of it walking round flat with a torch looking for rats. I know because he weren't quiet about it and light kept coming under my door. You'll have to talk to me, and I'll pass it on.'

She hesitates, seemingly still reluctant.

'Well, it's good news. We've found a position for him.'

'You what?'

'A job. As a toilet attendant in the shopping centre.'

'Is this some kind of joke?'

'No. I didn't expect to find anything so quickly but it's a work programme for the long-term unemployed. Sometimes these things fall into place.'

'But he's not long-term unemployed.'

'He hasn't worked for five years.'

'Because he hasn't been able to, not because he's a lazy scrounger.'

'Well, it'll be difficult for him to find work without recent experience, so it's ideal for him.'

'Yeah, it's perfect for someone who hallucinates about rats to be working in public toilets.'

'They've always been very clean whenever I've been in.'

'Jesus, he's mentally ill. It's not about reality. It's what's in his head that matters. He hears rats. Voices tell him that there are rats. It doesn't matter that there aren't really any rats there. He can't do it. He can't work there.'

'I'm afraid he will be sanctioned if he turns down a work programme placement. It would be a minimum of four weeks without benefits.'

'You can't do that to him. He needs that money. He's already got to wait five weeks to get it. What's he supposed to live on for nine weeks?'

'Please understand that it's not my decision. The government sets the rules and we merely apply them.'

I sigh. 'Well, doesn't he need to go to an interview or owt?'

'No, we're placing him there. It's all been agreed.'

'Not with him, it hasn't. You saw what he were like yesterday, he's not fit for work.'

'As I explained, you can still request the mandatory reconsideration, but in the meantime, Mr Allen has entered into a contract with us in order to receive his benefits. If he breaks his contract, he loses his benefits. It's as simple as that.'

I don't know what to say. This wasn't supposed to happen. He was only signing on to get some money while we appealed against the assessment.

'Well, it's not going to work out, I can tell you that now. And they'll see that on his first day, so you'd better be prepared for phone call. When is he supposed to start?'

'Thursday.'

I snort down the phone. 'You really are having a laugh, aren't you?'

Denise is having none of it. 'There's a letter in the post with the full details. If he has any queries, he's welcome to call me. I'd be grateful if you could pass that on to him. Goodbye.'

She hangs up. I can imagine her at the job centre, complaining to her colleagues that nobody wants to work these days. She has no idea. No fucking idea at all.

I wait until the following morning when the letter arrives before I say anything to Terry. Partly because I need to see it in black and white myself before I believe it, and partly because

I know it will send him into a hell of a state and I want to put that off as long as possible.

I open the letter and read through the details, hoping to discover they've somehow muddled him up with someone else. They haven't though. Terry Allen, my kid brother, is supposed to be turning up for work tomorrow. It really is happening.

Terry is in the living room watching *Bullseye*. It's his second favourite TV show. He cried when Jim Bowen died, said it was like losing his father. To be fair, he'd seen a lot more of him than his actual father.

Terry turns to me. 'Can't beat a bit of Bully,' he says. Normally it would make me smile but not today. I feel like such a cow, breaking into his safe little haven to throw him kicking and screaming out into the real world.

'Denise from job centre sent this,' I say, holding out the letter.

Terry frowns.

'Have they admitted they cocked up?'

'No love. She's found a job for you. Some work programme thing that you have to go on to get your benefits. It starts tomorrow.'

Jim Bowen is unveiling the star prize of a caravan. No one would want a caravan these days. They probably wouldn't play for anything less than a Porsche, but back then, caravans always got a big ooohhh from the audience.

Terry looks up at me.

'Where?'

'At shopping centre in town. As a toilet attendant.'

I brace myself for what is to come. I wouldn't blame him if he threw something or burst into tears. He doesn't do either of those things, though. That's what makes it so awful. He simply goes back to watching *Bullseye* without a word. Fiddling with the buttons on his cardigan.

AFTER

5

FINN

As soon as I wake up, I check the Gardener's Year calendar opposite my bed and see that as well as being a good time for dead-heading, it's also finally the day I have been waiting for. The last day of the summer term, and therefore my last day at primary school.

The trouble is, now it is here, I don't want it to be, because I have to get through the Year Six Leavers Assembly before it is over. We all have to sit at the front of the hall and go up in turn as they show old photos of us when we were in reception and wearing silly costumes in nativities, and they say nice things about us and everyone is supposed to clap at how wonderful we are, including all the kids who have been mean to me all the way through school (apart from the last half-term when they had not been mean to me and that's actually been almost as bad as them being mean, because I know why they have done it).

The other thing that happens at the Year Six Leavers Assembly is that all the mums cry and talk about how it doesn't seem five minutes since we were in reception. They only say that because they have not actually been to school during that time; just dropped us off and collected us and been to a few celebration assemblies. To me, it feels like I've been here about fifty years.

Dad was going to come. He tried to get the time off work but then an important meeting came up that he couldn't get out of and he was very sorry, but it was just one of those things. When I told Kaz, she offered to come instead. I was pleased about that because quite a few grandmas come and Kaz looks a bit like a grandma, apart from the plaits. I have never seen a grandma with plaits.

'Is she your real grandma?' asks Lottie, when I tell her I have someone coming.

'No. But my real grandma lives in Devon, and that's too far to come and my other real grandma died when I was seven.'

'My mum's coming,' says Lottie.

'Is she?' Lottie's mum has only been to a celebration assembly twice as far as I can remember, and both times she had to leave early to get to work and waved to Lottie as she left, which embarrassed her, and Lottie didn't mind her not coming after that.

'Yeah, she says it's a rite-of-passage thing, so she's not going to miss it.'

'A passage where?' I ask.

'I don't know. She didn't say that.'

'What do you think Mrs Ratcliffe will say about me?' I ask.

'She'll probably talk about your ukulele-playing.'

I think Lottie is right. At least I won't have to play it this time. It's bad enough that everyone still remembers the last time I played it.

'Yeah. That's sort of like the polite way of saying I'm weird.'

Lottie smiles. 'You're a good weird, though.'

'Am I?'

'Yes. You're only weird compared to that bunch of idiots. Actually, they're the weird ones but because there are loads more of them than you, they can make out you're weird and get away with it.'

'Right,' I say. 'So, what I really need is to find loads of good weird boys like me, so that none of us are weird any more.'

'Yeah,' replies Lottie.

'But have you ever met any other boys like me?'

'No.'

'So, I'm always going to be the weird kid and it doesn't matter that I'm good weird because I'll always still be weird.'

'I suppose so. But at least you know.'

I am still trying to work out if that is a good thing or not as our class walk into the hall. They are playing 'Simply the Best' and I try not to think about how much Mum would hate it and how rude it was of Mrs Ratcliffe never to reply to her email. Instead of sitting at the back of the hall as usual, they have put benches for us at the front facing everyone. Me and Lottie sit in the back row, but it still feels like everyone is staring at me. Lottie's mum is crying already and a couple of the other mums are passing tissues along the row to her. It is not Lottie she is looking at, though. It is me.

Kaz is sitting in the back row of the mums. I think we are both back-row kind of people. She gives me a little smile but doesn't wave or do anything embarrassing. I am trying very hard not to think about the person who is missing. The trouble is I can still see her smiling at me. I can feel her green cardigan soft against my face and hear her clapping louder than anyone when they call my name. Lottie gives my hand a little squeeze, but she makes sure that no one else sees it.

Mrs Ratcliffe stands up and starts jingling and jangling as she waves her hands about. She is acting like she's very excited, but I don't know why, unless she is that pleased to be getting rid of me. She talks about what a wonderful year group we have been, which is a lie because half of the boys have been dead annoying and spent most of their time messing about and getting into trouble.

And then she gets her little controller for the PowerPoint out and presses the button and the embarrassing photos start and everyone is laughing. I look a bit sad in all the photos, probably because I have pretty much hated every minute of it.

The next thing is that we are all called out to stand at the front one at a time while Mrs Ratcliffe says nice things about us and our achievements. It must have been hard to think of them for some of the boys. She says Jayden is 'popular and a valuable member of the school football team', but she doesn't mention the time he threw a burger at my face or pulled my hair until he made me cry.

When Tyler goes up, she says he is 'fun-loving and always the first to finish his lunch'. I don't really understand how that is supposed to be an achievement, because it means he gulps his food down without chewing properly, but his mum is crying so I suppose she must think it is.

And when it comes to my turn, I stand there and stare straight out at Kaz, while Mrs Ratcliffe says I have 'demonstrated courage and resilience and am also a talented musician', and for some reason all the other mums are crying and all the other kids, even the ones that hate me, are clapping. I stand there not knowing what to do. What I want to do is shout at them to stop because it is all my fault and if they knew that, they wouldn't be clapping. But I can't do that, so I just stand there and count in my head until it finishes.

Afterwards, when it is all over, there is a little sort of tea party where the mums and grandmas and the one dad who came stay in the hall and there is tea and biscuits and we are allowed to have one biscuit each.

Kaz comes up to me and gives me a hug. 'I don't think you liked that one little bit, did you, pet?'

I shake my head.

'What's up with your head teacher? Does she think she's auditioning for children's TV or summat?'

For the first time that morning, I manage a smile.

'She used to be a policewoman,' I say, 'she jangles too much and thinks I'm weird and Mum had quite a few arguments with her.'

'I'm not surprised. How does a policewoman end up as a head teacher?'

'Well, we have got a lot of naughty boys, so maybe that's why they gave her a job.'

Kaz looks around at the other children. 'So which ones give you bother?' she asks.

'All the boys have been mean to me, but Jayden, Ryan and Tyler are the worst,' I whisper, pointing them out.

'Do you want me to tread on their toes on my way out?' she asks.

I do a little laugh.

'Well, at least one good thing about going to your posh new school is that you won't have them to deal with any more.'

'I suppose not.'

'And is that your friend Lottie?' she asks, nodding towards where she is standing with Rachel, both of them still wiping away tears.

'Yes. How did you guess?'

'Because she were sitting next to you and she looks different to other lasses. Got a bit about her, I'd say.'

I realise as she says it that it's the last day I'm going to be at school with Lottie and I'll really, really miss her. I am trying hard not cry again when Mrs Ratcliffe comes over.

'Hello,' she says to Kaz. 'Are you one of Finn's relatives?'

'No, I'm a friend,' says Kaz. 'His dad couldn't make it because of work.'

'Well, we're all very proud of how he's coped with . . . everything,' she says, avoiding looking at me and continuing jangling and trying to smile, although her face doesn't look very smiley.

'Just a shame it's taken something like this for most of the kids to stop being mean to him,' replies Kaz.

Mrs Ratcliffe pulls a weird face and shifts her feet before turning to me. 'And you must be looking forward to going to your new school, Finn.'

I don't know what to say. I don't think it would be polite to say no. I look to Kaz for help.

'I tell you one thing,' Kaz says, turning to Mrs Ratcliffe. 'He can't wait to get out of this dump.'

Mrs Ratcliffe stares at Kaz, opens her mouth and shuts it again before walking away without a word or a jangle.

'Should I have not said that?' asks Kaz.

'I don't know,' I reply with a little smile. 'But I'm glad you did.'

I walk back to Lottie's house with her after school. Her mum is looking after me until Dad gets home from work. Our polo shirts have been signed by everyone in our class. I ask Lottie to check that no one has written 'weirdo' or 'fanny boy' on mine but she says they haven't.

'It feels weird, doesn't it?' I say.

Lottie nods. 'At least you won't have to see them again. I've got five more years of putting up with them.'

'I wish you were coming to my school,' I say.

'You'll make new friends there.'

'I won't though, will I?'

Lottie shrugs. 'There might be some decent kids.'

'Good weird ones, you mean?'

'Yeah,' she replies with a smile.

When Dad arrives to pick me up later, I know that this is the last time I will get picked up from Lottie's house after school. Her mum has already told me that we'll still see each other lots in the holidays and maybe we will, but it won't be the same as going to school together.

'Hey, school's out,' says Dad, ruffling my hair. He seems to think I will be happy about this, but I don't feel happy about anything right now.

'How did it go?' he asks, smiling.

'Fine,' I say. I catch Rachel looking daggers at Dad. It's like sometimes she gives him the looks he needs on Mum's behalf.

'Right, better get you home then,' he says. 'I've got celebration pizzas in the car.'

I manage a little smile. I hope he has got the one I like. Mum knows the one I like but I'm not sure Dad does.

Rachel comes up to me and gives me a big hug.

'You did so well, today,' she says. I'm right proud of you. I'll be in touch with your dad to sort out the first summer holiday meet-up.'

I nod because I still haven't got any words. Lottie is standing there. She doesn't seem to have any words either. I think for a moment I am going to leave without us saying anything but at the last second, she throws her arms round me and says, 'See you soon, good weird boy.'

*

Dad hasn't got me the pizza I like, but I eat it anyway because it is supposed to be a celebration pizza, so it seems rude not to. I don't say much but he talks about stuff, I am not sure what, as I am not really listening. I only start listening when he mentions the holiday club.

'I've got you booked on this for three days next week,' he says, sliding a leaflet onto the table. It says 'Halifax Holiday Club. Fun activities for school-age children' and underneath it lists lots of activities, like football and gaming and other things I hate.

I look up at him. 'But I don't want to do this,' I say.

'You'll enjoy it when you get there.'

'I won't. I don't enjoy things other kids think are fun.'

'Come on, Finn. It says you can do baking.'

'Yeah, that will be for little kids and they'll all be girls.'

'And you get on well with girls.'

'Not girls I don't know. Anyway, I don't like baking.'

'You used to love making those muffins.'

'That was because it was with Mum.'

Dad sighs. He stares out of the window and doesn't say anything for a minute before he turns to look at me. 'I'm sorry, Finn. I can only work from home two days a week. I had to find something for you to do for the other three days and this is the only one that had places. It might be better than you think. There might be kids you know there.'

'That's what I'm worried about.'

'Well, let's just give it a try. You never know, you might enjoy it.'

I look at Dad. He really doesn't get it. I think he must have been a pretty normal kid at school. He's good at sport too. Being a boy is easy when you're good at sport.

'I won't,' I say. 'But I'll go as long as you tell them it's OK for me to read by myself and I don't have to join in with things.'

Dad shuts his eyes for a second.

'I'm sorry, Finn,' he says. 'I'm doing my best but I'm struggling a bit, just like you are.'

I finish the last piece of my pizza in silence.

In the morning, when I come downstairs, Dad is in the kitchen cooking breakfast.

'Hey,' he says. 'Just in time.'

'What are we having?'

'Your favourite; veggie sausages,' he says, putting a plate down in front of me. There are beans and toast on the plate too, but I don't see them. I just see the sausages. They are the same ones we never got to eat on our camping trip.

'No!'

Dad looks at me, frowning.

'What?'

'I'm not eating them.'

'Why? I thought they were your favourite?'

I think about telling him, but I can't get the words out. They are stuck in the place where all the hurt is.

'Not any more,' I say, standing up and running upstairs to my room.

AFTER

6

KAZ

'What are you clock-watching for?' asks Marje, as I glance at my watch again during a quiet spell at the café. 'Anyone would think you were waiting for a hot date to turn up.'

'Maybe I am,' I say, smiling as I give the counter a quick going-over with the dishcloth.

'Oh, aye. It's a young man you're expecting is it?'

'It is, as it happens. A lot younger than me.'

'Blimey, am I supposed to think there's life in an old girl yet?' asks Marje.

'Just you wait and see, if you don't believe me.'

I serve an elderly couple who want a pot of tea and one scone to share between them, then busy myself drying some cutlery, before finally looking up to see Finn standing on the other side of the counter smiling at me.

'You've got your sheep apron on,' he says.

'Yep. Different café, same apron. I've washed and ironed it specially for you, mind.'

Martin, who is standing behind Finn, nods at me. 'Hi Kaz, good to see you. I'll have a coffee, please. Finn, what about you?'

Finn looks along the counter, contemplating the options. I point to the hygiene rating sticker on the wall behind me.

'Proof of the five-star rating,' I say.

'I know. I wouldn't be getting anything otherwise.'

I laugh because I know it's true.

Someone joins the queue behind Martin. I am momentarily reminded of Fag-ash Lil.

'Take all the time you need, Finn,' I say.

'I'm between the chocolate brownie, the millionaire short-bread and the carrot cake,' he says.

'Well, if you're looking for a recommendation, I'd go for the brownie.'

'OK,' he says. 'Can I have an orange juice too, please?'

'Coming right up.' I turn round to see Marje looking at me. She shakes her head.

'Told you,' I say.

'Yeah, you didn't say how young, though. That's a bit of a cheat.'

'Had you going though, didn't I?' I reply with a smile.

I pop the chocolate brownie on a plate and pour the orange juice while Marje makes the coffee.

'Is he family?' asks Marje.

'No, just a friend. His name is Finn. We met a few months

ago. He's been through a tough time. Needs all the friends he can get right now.'

I haven't told her about what happened. As much as I get on well with her, it still feels like too big a thing to share. Besides, I don't want to be talking about it here. It's bad enough that it keeps me awake at night sometimes, I don't want to be thinking about it when I'm supposed to be serving customers as well.

Martin pays me and carries the tray over to an empty table, with Finn following him. Marje looks at me.

'What you waiting for?'

'I don't knock off for another twenty minutes.'

'Don't be daft. You were in early this morning. You're all done for day. Go and sit down with lad.'

I take my apron off and go and join Finn and Martin at the table.

'How's the chocolate brownie?' I ask.

'Good,' says Finn, wiping the crumbs from his mouth and looking around. 'It's a nice café.'

'Thank you. Glad it meets with your approval. Haven't you ever been here before?' I ask.

'No, not to the café, only to the garden centre with Mum. We used to come at weekends sometimes when Dad was on his bike rides.'

Martin shifts in his chair.

'So, how's the first week of your summer holidays been?' I ask, sensing that the subject needs changing. 'What have you been up to?'

'Not much,' replies Finn.

'You've been to holiday club, haven't you?' says Martin.

Finn nods.

'Right, what did you get up to there?'

'The other kids mostly played football and computer games and I did some reading.'

He falls silent again and eats the rest of his brownie while scuffing his shoe on the leg of the table. I look at Martin. He is drinking his coffee and staring down at the table.

'Kaz,' he says, as he puts his mug down. 'I need to get some wood stain for the garden fence and a few other bits and bobs. Are you OK staying here with Finn for a few minutes?'

'Course I am,' I say. 'We can have a good natter, can't we, Finn?'

Finn nods and Martin stands up. I get the idea he can't get away quickly enough.

'So,' I say as Martin disappears round the corner. 'On a scale of one to ten, how bad were holiday club?'

'An eleven,' replies Finn.

'Oh dear.'

'Ryan Dangerfield from school was there. I thought I'd got rid of him.'

'Was he one of mean kids?'

'Yeah.'

'Did he say owt to you at holiday club?'

'Not to my face but he was whispering things about me to the other kids. I think he told them about, you know.'

'Oh.'

'Yeah. And I've got to go there three days a week for the rest of the summer. Apart from the week when we're on holiday.'

'Have you tried talking to your dad about it?'

'There's no point. He said it was the only holiday club that had places and there's no one else to look after me.'

'What about your friend Lottie?'

'Her mum's working most of the holidays so her auntie's looking after her and she's already got three kids.'

I screw up my face. 'What would you like to be doing instead of holiday club?'

Finn answers without a moment's hesitation.

'A gardening club.'

'Now there's a surprise,' I say, with a smile.

'I've got a newspaper supplement from the *Mail on Sunday* called "Create Your Dream Garden in Just 4 Weeks" by Alan Titchmarsh. I asked Mum if we could buy it when I saw it in the newsagents and she said usually she wouldn't buy that newspaper because it wrote nasty things about some people, so I asked if we could pay for it and just take the supplement and leave the newspaper as a protest and she said that was a good compromise.'

I nod. Life sounded complicated in Finn's household.

'And is that what you want to do? One of those garden makeover things?'

'Yes. And I'd like to do a trip out to another garden for inspiration, because that's what Alan does. I have his book *Alan Titchmarsh's Favourite Gardens*, but I have only ever been to two of them and there are a lot more to go to.'

'Right,' I say. 'Only problem is, I don't suppose Alan Titchmarsh is available to do all that with you.'

'No but you could help me. Your mum used to have an allotment.'

I look at him. He means it too. That's why I'm struggling to know what to say in response.

'You don't want to be spending your summer holidays with an old codger like me, pottering around in back garden.'

'I do. It's why I'm weird.'

I smile at him. I can't help thinking how much he reminds me of Terry at his age.

'What days do you go to holiday club?' I ask.

'Mondays to Wednesdays. And when Dad works from home on Thursdays and Fridays, I could just carry on doing jobs in the garden, which would mean he'd get more work done.'

I nod. It would fit in with my work and I could still go and see Terry in the evenings, as usual. I can't think of anything I'd rather do than be with Finn all day, to be honest.

'You'd be a good lawyer, Finn,' I say. 'You're very good at persuading people.'

'I don't want to be a lawyer, though, because there are only nasty ones who send people letters that make them cry, or boring ones like my dad, who have to do lots of searches of old documents so people can sell their houses.'

'I didn't know that's what your dad does.'

'It's called conveyancing and I don't think it sounds very interesting. You have to work in an office.'

'I wouldn't like that, either,' I say. 'I can't sit down for five minutes, me.'

'I can,' says Finn, 'but only if I'm reading a book by Alan Titchmarsh.'

I am still laughing at this when Martin returns, carrying a bag of things.

'Right, that's me done,' he says.

I look up at him. I have no idea if he'll go for it, but I owe it to Finn to try.

'Finn would like a little look around outdoor plant section,' I say.

'Sure,' he replies. 'Have you finished work now, Kaz?'

'Boss says so,' I reply, nodding towards Marje.

'Great. Shall we all have a look around together then, before we take you home for some tea?'

'Sounds good to me,' I say.

I wave goodbye to Marje, and we head off, Finn leading the way. When we get there, Barry, who is in charge of the outdoor plant section, is putting out some more hanging baskets.

'Hiya, Kaz, are you coming to give us a hand?' he says with a smile.

'Just having a look around with my young friend here,' I reply, putting my hand on Finn's shoulder. 'He's a budding Alan Titchmarsh.'

'Is that so?' says Barry, wiping the sweat from his bald head with his arm as he turns to Finn. 'What's your favourite flower?'

'Roses,' he replies.

'Right, well would you like to come and have a look at ours and I'll give you a few tips while you're at it.'

Finn looks round at Martin, who nods.

'Thanks Barry,' I say, as he heads off with Finn.

I glance across at Martin.

'Seems like you've got friends in all the right places,' he says.

'It's least I can do for him,' I reply.

'Seriously, I can't thank you enough, Kaz,' says Martin. 'Finn looks forward to seeing you so much. It really is the highlight of his week. Certainly much better than being with boring old me.'

I look across at Martin. His face suggests he knows he's making a pig's ear of parenting but doesn't want to admit it. Which is something I can relate to.

'It's not easy,' I say, 'looking after a lad that age on your own. I remember how hard it were with our Terry.'

'Was your mum a single parent?'

'She weren't really any kind of parent. Too busy drinking herself into an early grave once me dad had buggered off. It were me who brought him up.'

'I'm sorry,' says Martin, his brow furrowed. 'I hadn't realised.'

'It's OK,' I say. 'It were easier once she'd gone, to be honest. Terry were certainly safer without her.'

I notice Martin glancing at me out of the corner of his eye, but he obviously decides not to probe any further on that one. Which is good, because I'm not sure I'm ready to talk about what happened.

'So how old were you then?'

'Eighteen and our Terry were ten. Same age as Finn. That's why I know how tough a job it is, raising a lad that age on your own.'

'Well, it sounds like you've done a very good job of it.'

I smile but don't say anything. Perhaps if I told him I'm still waiting to hear from the police if Terry is going to be taken to court, he'd think differently about that.

Martin says nothing for a moment. I can see Finn in the far aisle with Barry; peering closely at some rose bushes, reading the labels, writing things down in a little notebook he produces from his pocket.

'The thing is,' says Martin. 'Everything I do seems to be wrong.'

'I got plenty wrong,' I said. 'I still do but you learn from every mistake.'

'It's difficult because Finn's nothing like I was at his age. I was always on bike rides or fishing trips with my brothers but everything I suggest to Finn is wrong. He's so different to me and I feel so bloody clueless.'

'He's been through an incredibly tough time,' I say. 'He misses his mam. You must miss her too.'

Martin stares into the distance. His eyes are glistening.

'I do but I know it's nothing compared to what Finn's feeling. He was always so close to her. And he's still mad at me about what happened. He blames me, I know that. And he's got every right to, of course.'

He looks down and wipes at the corners of his eyes. I read

what they said in the papers about the background to what happened, just like everyone else did, I expect. I'm not going to judge him, though. Enough people have done that to me. And I know how much that hurts. I put my hand on his shoulder.

'Hey, come on. You mustn't blame yoursen. Believe me, I know what that's like, and it's a mug's game.'

'I can never take back what happened, though, can I? It hangs over us the whole time. I simply want to make him happy, even if it's for one day, but I don't know how.'

'Look,' I say, stopping and turning to face him as we reach a big display of geraniums. 'He's been talking to me, telling me what sort of holiday club he'd like to go to.'

'Has he?'

'Yeah. He wants to do a gardening club at home. Do one of those makeovers, like they do on telly.'

'But how could he do that? I looked into getting a child-minder, but they work from their own home and look after several children at once. He wouldn't like that. He's not good with other kids. And I don't suppose you can get a nanny for three days a week in the school holidays. And certainly not one that gardens.'

'Well,' I say, seeing that I am going to have to spell it out to him. 'I'm not Mary bloody Poppins but I'd be happy to look after him, help him do his gardening club.'

Martin's face visibly brightens. 'Would you? I mean I'd pay you the going rate and everything.'

'Don't be daft. You don't need to pay me.'

'Well, I wouldn't let you do it otherwise. I'd be employing

you. And I'd much rather pay you than the holiday club he hates. Would it fit in with your hours at the garden centre? '

'Yeah. I only work Thursday to Sunday so I could do Monday to Wednesday fine.'

'But that would mean you wouldn't have any days off.'

'I don't need days off. Days off don't pay rent. Anyway, I can't think of owt I'd rather do than be with Finn, to be honest. It would certainly beat making teas and washing up all day.'

Finn is on his way back to us with Barry, a small rose bush tucked under his arm.

'Tell him,' I say. 'You'll put a smile on his face and right now you both need that.'

'Look,' says Finn, holding out the rose bush. 'Barry said I can have this one for free as long as I look after it for him.'

'That's very kind of you,' Martin says to Barry.

'He's very welcome. Lovely to see a young lad taking an interest in gardening. He knows a fair thing or two about roses, too.'

Barry winks at Finn and goes back to his hanging basket display. I gesture to Martin to spill the good news.

'Finn,' Martin says, 'Kaz tells me you'd like to do a gardening club at home.'

'Yes,' he says. 'I've got a four-week plan from Alan Titchmarsh on how to do it and we'd have exactly four weeks taking away the one when we're on holiday.'

Finn looks from Martin's smiling face to mine and back to Martin.

'Can we do it?' he asks. 'Can Kaz look after me and can we do the gardening club together?'

Martin nods.

'We'd need to buy some plants and things,' continues Finn, talking so fast I can barely make out what he's saying, 'but Alan tells you how to do it on a budget and you can use lots of things you've already got. And I've got this one to start with,' he says, holding his rose bush aloft.

'Sounds like you've got it all worked out already,' says Martin.

'And I don't have to go back to the holiday club?' asks Finn.

'No.'

Finn throws himself at Martin, who appears so taken aback he doesn't know what to do for a moment. But then he wraps his arms round Finn and holds him, looks across at me and mouths the words, 'thank you'.

BEFORE

7

FINN

By the third day of the SATs breakfast club, when I catch Lottie wiping a bit of strawberry jam from the corner of her mouth as I sit down next to her, I am starting to feel she might not be hating it any longer, but doesn't want to let on in case it makes me feel bad.

'Hi Finn,' she says. We're more than halfway through the week but I don't think she's given the petition in yet, probably because my name is the only one on it.

'What did you revise this morning?' I ask.

'Spelling, punctuation and grammar but I couldn't remember what a fronted adverbial is. Are you really not going to do the SATs?'

I have only told Lottie so far, because I know if I tell the others they will ask loads of questions and go on about it all the time and it will be another thing to have a go at me about.

'I don't know,' I reply. 'Mum's told Mrs Ratcliffe I'm not doing them, but Dad is still mad about it.'

I scuff the toes of my shoes on the floor under the desk. What I really want is for this whole thing to go away and not to feel like I'm caught in a massive tug-of-war. I have never seen a tug-of-war where the rope snaps, but I am starting to feel that's what might happen here.

Tyler Johnson kicks the back of my chair.

'You're late, fanny face,' he says and a few of the other boys start laughing. Mrs Kerrigan looks up and smiles, clearly not having heard what was said, before starting to do the register. When she says my name, the boys all pull faces and hold their noses. She never sees it because she is looking down. One day I'm going to come to school with a secret spy camera and film all the stuff the teachers don't see.

'Finn, will you take the register down to Mrs Ravani, please.'

I wish she had asked anyone but me. I stand up and go to the front of the class to get it from her. I can hear sniggering from behind my back. I head back up the aisle with the register and am nearly at the door when Tyler sticks his foot out and trips me up. I put my hand on Grace Miller's desk to stop me falling and I accidentally knock her unicorn pencil case onto the floor and all the pens and pencils come out.

'Goodness Finn, you're all fingers and thumbs this morning,' says Mrs Kerrigan, looking up from her desk. I kneel to start picking everything up. I can see Lottie with her hand up and I know that she is going to tell Miss about Tyler, so I give her a look and shake my head and Lottie puts her hand down. I will only get called a grass and get more hassle, so it's best to forget it.

I give the pencil case back to Grace.

'Sorry,' I say. She pulls a face at me.

I step out of the classroom into the corridor. As soon as I am there, I think about carrying on walking out of the school and never coming back. That's what I would like to do. I don't though. I knock on Mrs Ravani's door and give her the register and she thanks me and asks how I am and I say, 'Fine, thank you,' because that is what you're supposed to say, and go back to our classroom.

Mrs Kerrigan has given out a grammar worksheet. I look at it but all I can think of is that I wish I was outside in our garden. Because what I really want to be doing right now is planting out some of our summer bedding lobelias and begonias.

Someone kicks me under the desk. I look up. Lottie is making a face at me. I am suddenly aware that the other kids are staring at me and laughing.

'You were doing the buzzing noise again,' she whispers.

As soon as I get to Mum outside the gate, I can see that she has been crying. Her eyes are puffy and a bit red. She has tried to put eyeshadow over the red bits, but it only makes me notice it more, because she doesn't usually wear eyeshadow.

I don't know what to say so I just give her a little smile. She does a little smile too and asks how my day has been and I say 'OK' and we go home without saying anything about her having been crying.

It is only when we get to the kitchen and I put my book bag on the table and see the letter there that I think I might know why she has been crying. The letter is from Dad's solicitor. I know this because I recognise the name and logo on the top of the piece of paper and the scribbly signature at the bottom of the page. I think the solicitor has been writing letters to make her angry again, only this time she is more upset than angry. I am very glad I want to be a gardener when I grow up, not a solicitor. Gardeners make beautiful gardens that make people happy. They do not write letters that make people cry. Dad is a solicitor, but he is not the type of solicitor who sends out letters like that. He is the type who helps people when they need to sell their houses, but his solicitor's letter has made Mum cry and that's nearly as bad.

'Are you divorced now?' I ask. The 'getting divorced' thing has been going on a while and I don't know how long it takes but I can't help thinking it must be nearly finished and that might be why she's been crying.

Mum sits down at the table and reaches out for my hand.

'No, love,' she says. 'Not yet. We're still sorting out the arrangements.'

'So why are you upset?'

Mum looks up at the ceiling and shuts her eyes for a second before answering. 'The letter says that if I don't let you sit the SATs, Dad will ask the court for an order that would mean you would live with him all of the time after we get divorced.'

'But I thought you were going to share me?'

'So did I. But the solicitor says that because I acted without

Dad's permission and pulled you out of the SATs, they will be claiming I'm an unfit mother.'

'But that's not fair. You don't like going to the gym and someone has to look after me when Dad goes for his bike rides.'

Mum does a little smile.

'It doesn't mean that sort of unfit,' she says. 'It means not good enough to look after you.'

I frown at her. 'Of course you're good enough to look after me. Why would Dad let you look after me all the time if you weren't good enough?'

'I wish it were that simple, Finn.'

'I'll tell Dad to tear up the letter and say he's sorry when he gets home.'

'No, love. I don't want you taking sides. It's not right.'

'But it's not right to send letters that make people cry.'

Mum looks down and sighs before pulling me closer to her.

'You,' she says, 'are wise way beyond your years.'

I know she is trying to say something nice, but I don't understand that saying because the way I see it, people get less wise as they get older. I mean, children don't start wars or kill people or get divorced, do they?

'So have I got to do the SATs now?'

'I don't know,' says Mum, her voice trembling. 'I don't know what to do for the best. Maybe your father's right. Maybe I am being unreasonable.'

She starts crying. Big proper-tears crying that grown-ups aren't supposed to do. It makes me start crying too and I stand up and go and give her a big hug.

'I'm so sorry,' she says, holding my face close to hers. 'I hate what this is doing to you. It's not your fault, I want you to understand that. He's mad at me because I didn't ask his permission before I told school you weren't doing the SATs.'

'But if you'd have asked him, he'd have said I had to do them, wouldn't he?'

'Yes.'

'So even if you had asked, there would still have been a big argument.'

Mum nods and looks down. She doesn't seem to be saying much and I am doing all the talking. It's like I'm her parent and she's just a big kid who doesn't know the answers. Which means I should probably come up with them.

'What about if I did the maths SATs to make Dad happy and didn't do the English SATs to make you happy?'

Mum bursts into a fresh round of tears. I don't think that was the right answer. I don't know what to do. Maybe I should make a cup of tea. That's what the adults seem to do on television when something bad happens.

'Would you like a cup of tea?' I ask. Mum looks up and gives me a watery smile.

'Thank you, Finn. You deserve so much better than this,' she says.

'Do I?'

'It wasn't ever supposed to turn out this way, you know. We were so happy once.'

'I remember,' I say.

'Do you?'

'I remember you laughing and singing all the time and me snuggling in bed with you and Dad and you both tickling me to make me giggle and us tickling Dad to make him giggle. You used to have happy voices then.'

She strokes my hair and screws her eyes up tightly.

'I wish that you could get them back,' I say.

'So do I,' she whispers.

When I've made Mum the cup of tea, I go to my bedroom and start googling 'Alan Titchmarsh gardening books' (I had to change the search to 'gardening books' because he has written love stories too and they do not look like the sort of books I would want to read). I am collecting the Alan Titchmarsh How to Garden series. There are twenty-three of them and I have six, but I have just found out there is a container-gardening one, so I am saving up my pocket money for that because I will need that if we only have a patio container. I would like to get all twenty-three of them one day, although I am not that bothered about Pests and Problems because I don't want to kill anything.

When I hear Dad coming up the garden path, I know I should probably stay in my room because there will be a big row and it might go very high on the Richter Scale, but instead, for some reason I don't really understand, I go out and sit on the landing with my head pressed against the wooden bars.

The first thing I hear Dad say as he comes in is, 'I know what you're going to say,' but Mum cuts in and says what she was going to say anyway, only she says it in such a high-pitched voice and speaking so quickly and with so much crying in between that I have trouble picking out any words apart from, 'not what we agreed', 'acting like it's a war' and 'how could you do this to him, when you know it's not what he wants?'

Dad's voice goes very low and he speaks slowly. 'You forced me into this. I did not want to do it, but your behaviour gave me no option.'

'Don't talk to me like I'm a child,' screams Mum. 'I did not force you to do anything. We'd agreed to share custody because it's the best thing for Finn and it still is, you know that.'

'Well, if you want me to stop treating you like a child, perhaps you should start acting responsibly like a parent.'

'What's that supposed to mean?'

'You never want to take the tough decisions, do you? If it was up to you, Finn wouldn't even go to school. At some point, Hannah, you have got to stop being so fucking idealistic and start living in the real world.'

I have to clap my hand over my mouth to stop myself gasping out loud because Dad has used the f-word.

'That is bang out of order and you know it,' says Mum. Her voice is small and hurt, not shouty any more. I find myself scrambling to my feet.

'It's the truth, Hannah. And sometimes it has to be spoken.'

My feet are on the first step of the stairs and I don't seem to have any control over them.

'You're prepared to take Finn away from me to teach me some kind of lesson, is that it? Christ, how can you do that to him?' Mum starts to cry.

My feet are on the fifth step now and they are running. They run so fast that I seem to explode off the bottom step and into the hallway before Mum and Dad even realise I am there.

'Stop it,' I shout at Dad. 'Stop making Mum cry.'

'Finn, love. It's OK, go back upstairs,' says Mum.

'No. He's being mean to you and he's got to stop it.' I turn to face Dad, who looks a bit like I do when I've been told off.

'I'm sorry, Finn. I didn't know –' he starts, but I do not let him finish.

'Stop sending horrible letters to Mum and stop saying you're going to make me live with you because I don't want to and I'm not going to and stop arguing with her every time you come home because I can hear it and I hate it and I just want it to go back to how it used to be.'

I'm not sure if he hears the last bit because I am crying as I say it and I turn to run back upstairs, slamming my bedroom door behind me.

I listen hard but it is silent downstairs. I listen for a long time and the silence gets louder and louder. I start making the buzzing sound again. It is OK to do it in my bedroom because there is no one to hear it and I wonder if that is what bees are doing all the time – trying to hide the silence.

BEFORE

8

KAZ

It feels like Terry's first day at school all over again. I have made him a packed lunch – although this time I did find one slice of ham left in the fridge to put in his sandwiches. I'm pretty sure back then it was nothing but Marmite. Mam never did have anything in the fridge – apart from cans of Strongbow, that is.

I've washed and ironed his clothes too. He may only be a toilet attendant (glorified bog cleaner to you and me), but I'm not having people think he's scruffy.

And he's standing here in front of me now looking scared and completely unready for this and what I want more than anything else in the world is to give him a hug and tell him not to worry, it will all be fine. But I can't do that because it won't. He knows that and I know that. I may as well be sending him off to war. The chances of him surviving intact feel about as optimistic.

'Right,' I say. 'I'll come on bus with you. Make sure you get there OK.'

'You don't need to,' says Terry.

'I know, but I want to.'

He shrugs and pulls on his cagoule and pops in his earphones. He looks tired. He barely slept again last night. I saw the torchlight flickering under my door more times than I care to remember. Even when he was in his room, I suspect he wouldn't have been sleeping. The voices keep him awake sometimes. I know that. He told me last night that Matthew is very worried about the rats.

'MI5 will be watching me,' he says. 'There are security cameras there. They have all my details on file now.'

'All you have to do,' I say, as I open the door and step outside, 'is keep your head down and do as you're told. Other people might not understand what you're saying, so best not to talk to them.'

'I can talk to Matthew, though,' he says. 'Matthew always understands.'

I nod and we walk silently to the bus stop. When the bus arrives, it is, at least, too early for it to be busy and the few people who are onboard have their heads down looking at their phones.

Terry sits fiddling with the wires of his earphones. He hasn't said he's worried. He doesn't have to. I wish I could go to work with him, stand watch over him. Maybe I could ask Denise if there are any other jobs going there. I'd be happy to clean up other people's shit if it meant I could keep an eye on him.

We get off at the bus station and start to walk towards the shopping centre. It's a nice day again but I don't care about the weather. All I can think about is the assessor who passed Terry as being fit for work. This is his fault. Only he won't be around to help when it all goes arse-over-tits.

The loos are on the ground floor of the shopping centre. Tucked away on the left just past Poundland. There is a little office at the side.

'That's where you need to go,' I say to Terry, pointing.

Terry nods. He takes the torch out of his carrier bag. I hadn't even seen him put it in.

'You don't need that,' I say. 'Let me take it home for you.'

Terry shakes his head. 'Matthew says I need to check for rats.'

'No. There aren't any, I told you that. They wouldn't allow it in a place like this.'

Terry shrugs and puts the torch back in his carrier bag. 'I'm keeping it with me, just in case,' he replies.

'OK but you don't need to get it out again. I'll meet you back here at four when you're finished. My appointment at job centre is at half four, so we'll need to go straight there after.'

'They're watching me. They'll be watching you too. They'll find you a job where they have cameras. That's what they do.'

'Everywhere has cameras now, Terry, but no one's watching us. It's just to keep people safe.'

'Keep 'em peeled,' he says, pointing to his eyes and then at me, like Shaw Taylor used to do at the end of *Police 5*. He hasn't done that for years. I give him an uncertain smile and turn to walk away. Just like the day he started school, I have to bite my lip very hard. I remember then hoping that Mam would make it out of bed to bring him the next day. She did manage it for a bit. She went to an assembly once, told me all about it when I came home that night. Right proud of our Terry, she was. It didn't last, though. It never lasted. Dad may have walked out on us but the marks he left behind on her were enough to ensure she never forgot him.

As soon as I get home, I start cleaning the kitchen. Maybe it's because it seems the best thing to do to try to take my mind off Terry. Or maybe I've got withdrawal symptoms from cleaning the café. I wonder how Danny's been getting on with Bridget, poor sod. He texted me earlier, saying how sorry he was I'd lost my job and how he'd told Bridget she was out of order. He said there was a card up in the window advertising for my replacement already too. They'll be no shortage of people applying either, even on those crappy wages.

I know I should probably go to all the cafés in town to see if they've got any work going, but right now I'm too worried about Terry to concentrate on anything else.

When I go to the job centre later, they'll probably tell me I should have got off my fat arse and found something already. They don't know what it's like, though, to have someone like Terry to look out for. I feel sick inside just thinking about what state he'll be in by the end of the day.

By lunchtime there's nothing left to clean. As I gave Terry the last bit of ham, I have cheese spread in my sandwich instead. I remember making cheese spread and crisp sand-wiches for Terry when he was a kid. I'd only put a couple of crisps in each half, so I could make a packet last as long as possible. Terry used to love them, though. Thought it made him right special. He offered me a bite once, but I said no, I'd already had one. It's the only time I've ever lied to him, to stop him feeling bad about having things I didn't have.

I start getting ready at quarter to three. Not that it is going to take me more than a few minutes. You hear these women saying it takes them an hour to get out the house in the morn-ings. I've got no idea what they find to do in that time. I'm never more than five minutes in the shower and the only other thing I do that takes more than two minutes is my plaits. I suppose it's a bit strange, a woman of my age still wearing her hair in plaits. I can't remember a time when I didn't have them. Mam used to do them for me when I was little. It is one of my earliest memories. Her telling me to stand still and stop fidgeting while she separated my hair into sections. My plaits were always neat back then too, which suggests that if she was drinking, it wasn't too much. She even put red bows on if she were having a good day. I've seen them in a couple of old Polaroids. I wish I could remember more about the good days. Sometimes I think I can recall a slight trace of her perfume, a smile when she picked me up from school, maybe the softness of her hand in mine. But I have probably made that up. Because the next thing I can clearly remember is Dad hitting her and sending her flying across the room into the electric heater. I didn't make that up. He hit her lots of times but that was the first one in front of me. My plaits weren't always so neat after that. And by the time Dad left, I was doing them by myself. She was too drunk to get out of bed, most of the time, let alone manage plaits.

I stick a bit of deodorant on and change into different clothes. Not that I've got anything fancy to wear but I'm not turning up at the job centre in my cleaning rags. I have got some standards. I pick up my bag and check my phone is inside. I'm surprised I haven't had a call, to be honest. I hadn't really expected Terry to last the morning. Maybe he will be OK. Maybe if he keeps his head down, stays quiet and gets on with the cleaning, he'll be able to cope. I know this will not be the case, but it would be nice to believe it, even if it is just for a little while.

I arrive outside the shopping centre quarter of an hour before Terry is due to finish. There is a police car parked outside. They are often called to deal with rival gangs of school kids in there. I hope there hasn't been any trouble. Terry would hate it if a fight had broken out.

As soon as I step inside, I realise that there is a commotion in the far corner by the toilets. A small crowd has gathered. I hurry towards them. I see a flash of a police uniform through a gap and I can hear a lot of shouting. I know instantly that one of the voices shouting is Terry's. I break into a run. A run I didn't realise I was even still capable of until that moment. As I approach the edge of the crowd, I can hear Terry shouting, 'Get off me, leave me alone!'

'Terry, it's Kaz,' I call out. 'It's OK, I'm here.'

The crowd turn and look at me as I push my way through.

'I'm his sister,' I say. 'I need to get to him. He's mentally ill.'

'He's a fucking paedophile,' a woman's voice calls out.

I freeze, wondering what on earth has happened. The crowd parts to reveal Terry lying on the floor outside the toilets, his head to one side and his arms handcuffed behind his back. A bearded policeman is crouched over him.

'What the hell do you think you're doing?' I shout at him. He turns to face me.

'Are you a relative?' he asks.

'Kaz, they're MI5,' shouts Terry, still struggling on the floor. 'Don't talk to them.'

'I'm his sister. You can't do that to him. He's got schizophrenia.'

The policeman looks at me, as if working out if he can trust me.

'I had to because he was resisting arrest.'

'Why have you arrested him?'

'He's been accused of a serious crime.'

'Shit,' I say, quietly, wondering what the hell has happened. I look down at Terry, hoping he'll be able to tell me something.

'Kaz, they think I'm a spy,' he says. 'I wasn't spying on her. I were trying to save her from rats.'

'Pervert. Lock him up!' a woman with a scraped-back pony-tail shouts. I notice a group of schoolgirls nearby, probably twelve or thirteen years old. Three of them are crying. I am starting to feel incredibly uneasy.

I turn back to the policeman. 'Please get him away from these people,' I say. 'Somewhere quiet to help him calm down.'

The policeman tries to help Terry up. I go over and put my arm round him. I can feel his shoulders shaking. His eyes are wild and staring.

'It's OK,' I say. 'Whatever's happened, we're going to get it sorted out.'

'They were everywhere Kaz,' Terry says.

'Who were?'

'Rats. Dozens of them. I could hear them in cubicles of ladies' loos. That's why I were shining torch under door and went under to look for them.'

I shut my eyes for a second. Not wanting to believe what I am hearing.

'Can we get him in there?' I ask the policeman, nodding towards the little office at the side of the toilets.

'No,' he says. 'My colleague's in there with the girl.'

'What girl?'

He shakes his head, his face suggesting that now is not the time to discuss it. I am starting to feel sick. I think I know what's happened. Terry's slid under a cubicle looking for rats while a girl was in there. That's what he's fucking gone and done.

'As soon as my colleagues arrive,' the policeman continues. 'I'll be taking him down to the station.'

'I'm coming with him, then,' I say. 'I can't leave him, not in this state.'

The policeman nods. I get the impression he is glad to have

me because Terry has calmed down slightly since I arrived. He is still shaking and muttering about the rats, but he is not struggling now. I stroke his hair. It is flecked with grey at the sides, but I do not see that. I see the scared little boy standing there. The little boy I should have protected from everything bad that was happening around him. The little boy I have let down so badly. I hear Mam's voice mocking, taunting: 'waste of fucking space you are. So much for looking after your brother.'

I whisper in Terry's ear. 'You're going for a ride in a police car, Terry.' He would have loved that when he was a kid. He used to make the siren noise all the time. Drove me up the bloody wall, it did. I wish he wasn't going in one now, though. This is not how it was supposed to be. This is so fucking messed up.

I look up as I hear another commotion. A policeman and policewoman are coming through the crowd. They are with a woman, probably in her late thirties. Her long brown hair is tucked behind her ears. As soon as she sees the group of schoolgirls she bursts into tears. One of them runs up and gives her a hug. I think she is the mum of the girl in there. The girl that Terry must have scared half to death. The policewoman starts to lead her towards the office next to the toilets but Terry mutters something out loud and the woman looks over at us. She sees Terry and lets out something that sounds like a howl.

'You bastard,' she screams. 'You filthy, dirty bastard.' She starts to make a rush for him, but the policewoman grabs her arm. The other policeman joins ours and together they bundle Terry forward through the crowd. People are calling out, hurling abuse at him. Terry puts his head down. If his arms were free, I know he would be covering his ears, but he can't because of the handcuffs.

'Make them stop, Matthew!' he shouts. 'Make them stop.'

We cannot get out of the shopping centre and into the police car fast enough. Terry struggles to sit down with his arms behind his back.

'Can't you take those handcuffs off?' I ask the bearded policeman. 'He's not going anywhere, not with me here.'

'Not till we get to the station,' he replies.

'They're taking us to be interrogated, Kaz,' Terry says. 'They know all our secrets. They've caught us on camera. They were watching us. It were a trap.'

Terry starts singing 'Trapped' by Colonel Abrams. I catch the policeman raising an eyebrow in the rear-view mirror. He clearly thinks Terry's a nut-job. I'm not bothered about that, though. All I can think about is the mum of that girl in the shopping centre. I can still see the anger in her eyes. I would be like that if anyone ever hurt Terry. But it's Terry she's mad at. Terry who has done something to her daughter that he can't take back. Terry, who they have arrested and who's in such deep shit.

I sit quietly next to him in the back of the car. One hand on his still-trembling leg. The other brushing away the tears from my eyes.

*

I've never been inside Halifax nick before. It looks a bit like all the police stations on telly, only maybe a bit smaller and shabbier. The bearded copper takes Terry up to the desk and talks to the white-haired policeman behind it. A few moments later he nods towards me to come forward.

'I'm going to leave you both with Sergeant Hopkins now,' he says. 'He's the custody sergeant and will explain what's going to happen next.'

I nod. Terry has at least stopped singing but is muttering to Matthew under his breath. Sgt Hopkins looks at Terry.

'Right, I need to book you in, first,' he says. 'Name?'

'Don't tell them, Kaz,' says Terry. 'Matthew says they've already got a file on me. We're not to tell them anything else.'

I sigh and turn to Sgt Hopkins. 'Terry Allen.'

Terry glares at me and goes back to talking to Matthew.

'Has Mr Allen ever been in custody before?' Sgt Hopkins asks.

'No,' I say. 'And he's got schizophrenia. He also needs those handcuffs taken off because they're not helping.'

Sgt Hopkins turns to Terry. 'Would you like to be seen by a mental health professional?' he asks.

'Matthew says not to tell you anything because you can't be trusted.'

'Yes, he would,' I say quickly. 'This whole thing is a mess and whatever he's done, he meant no harm. It's his first day in job. He shouldn't even be working but they found him fit for work and made him do this. I told woman at job centre he couldn't cope but she wouldn't listen.'

As I say it, I remember that I should be at the job centre for my appointment. I ought to ring them to let them know I can't make it. Not now, though. I need to get Terry sorted out first. Sgt Hopkins picks up the phone and makes a call.

'Someone from mental health team will be with you shortly,' he says, when he puts the receiver down. 'Do you have a solicitor you'd like to contact, or should I call duty solicitor?'

'Call Matthew,' Terry says. 'Matthew will know how to get me out of here.'

'Who's Matthew?' Sgt Hopkins asks.

'He means Matthew Kelly, him off telly,' I say, relieved he is at least old enough to remember.

Sgt Hopkins nods slowly. Terry starts laughing. 'That rhymes,' he says. 'I never realised before.'

He's nice, the psychiatric nurse who comes to see Terry. His name is Michael and he has a hint of an Irish accent, several piercings and smiling eyes. He also gets the police to take the handcuffs off Terry before we go into a little room together.

'Michael's here to help you,' I tell Terry as he sits down. 'We need to tell him everything that's happened.'

'Is he one of them?' Terry asks.

'I'm independent of the police,' Michael replies. 'My job is to make sure you get the care and support you need.'

Terry sits down and starts singing, *'What have I done to deserve this?'*

'He's a big fan of Pet Shop Boys,' I say to Michael.

'And Dusty,' says Terry. 'Dusty Springfield and Dusty Bin.'

He starts doing the 3–2–1 thing with his fingers that Ted Rogers used to do.

Michael gives us both a wee smile and gets out a big notebook.

'Terry, when were you first diagnosed with schizophrenia?' Terry is still doing the Ted Rogers impression, so Michael turns to me.

'When he were eighteen,' I say. 'Though I think he had it before that. He's been hearing voices since he were about thirteen. Matthew Kelly from *Stars in Their Eyes* mainly, but we've had Cilla Black, Jim Bowen and Ted Rogers at various points.'

'Matthew's my friend,' says Terry.

'Aye, I know, love,' I reply.

'Is there any history of mental health issues in the family?' asks Michael.

'Our dad were a fucking psycho, if that's what you mean. Knocked our mum about a lot. And our mam were an alcoholic and suffered with depression.'

'Are they not around any longer?'

'No. Our mam's dead and our dad pissed off years ago, so he may as well be. I'm his next of kin. It's just two of us.'

Michael nods and makes some notes.

'And how old was Terry when his mother died?'

'Ten,' I reply.

Usually at this point people make sympathetic noises and tell us how sorry they are to hear that, but Michael doesn't give me any of that crap and I like him for it.

'Who looked after him after that?'

'Me,' I reply. 'Though I pretty much looked after him from when he were a toddler. Mam wasn't up to much most of the time.'

'And is he on any medication?'

'No. It don't agree with him. He were dosed up on all sorts last time he were in psychiatric unit but he put on weight and slept whole weeks away. Like a zombie, he were. He came off everything when he got out and he hasn't been on owt for years. He doesn't need it, see. Not when he's just at home with me.'

'And how many times has he been admitted to a psychiatric unit?'

'Three. Always because of work. He can't cope with being out somewhere unfamiliar with people he doesn't know. He goes downhill fast and ends up being sectioned.'

'When was the last time that happened?'

'Back in 2013. He were in there for six months.'

'And when did these latest episodes start?'

'Only last few days, since he got letter saying his benefits were being stopped and he'd been found fit for work. He started talking about MI5 again and hearing rats.'

Michael turns to Terry.

'Tell me about the rats, Terry. What do you hear?'

'Feet,' says Terry. 'I hear their feet. They're everywhere see, but most people can't hear them. I heard them today in ladies' loos. Dozens of them, scurrying about, there were. I got my torch out to find them and got down on floor on my back. I had to go under door because I could hear them, and Matthew said they were attacking whoever were in there.

'I didn't know it were a girl, not until she screamed. I didn't see owt. I weren't looking at her. I were only looking for rats.'

Michael makes some more notes. I wipe my eyes with a scrunched-up tissue from my pocket.

'And the other girls were screaming,' continues Terry. 'Because of all them rats. I were trying to catch them so I could stop girls screaming. That's what I were still trying to do when policeman came in. That's why I wouldn't let him grab hold of me, because I were still trying to grab hold of rats.'

Terry goes back to singing Dusty's bit from 'What Have I Done To Deserve This?', even though he struggles with the high notes. And all I can think of as I sit there feeling sick inside is how I wish the assessor who found him fit for work and Denise from job centre could be in the room with us now to see what a massive fuck-up they have made.

Sgt Hopkins comes over to me later that evening while Terry is being interviewed and hands me a cup of coffee from the machine.

'Thanks,' I say. 'Any idea how long it will take?'

Sgt Hopkins shakes his head.

'No. Try not to worry, though. Michael will see he's OK.'

'He's never been in trouble before,' I tell him. 'Not even at school. He'll be mortified when he realises what he's done. When he's better, like. Whenever that is.'

Sgt Hopkins starts to walk away.

'Is she OK?' I ask. 'That wee lass, I mean.'

He turns back to me and nods. 'Her mum took her home.'

'Poor kid,' I say. 'Must have scared her half to death.'

'We can contact you when he's all done, if you need to get off home,' he says.

'No, thanks,' I reply. 'I'm not leaving him. I'm all he's got.'

It's a policewoman who comes out to talk to me half an hour later. Introduces herself as DC Hoyle.

'We're detaining your brother under the Mental Health Act,' she says, sitting down on the bench next to me. 'Obviously, this was a serious offence, but our mental health team have asked for a full assessment under the Act, so he's being sent to the psychiatric unit in Halifax.'

I nod. Terry will hate it, but I know it's probably the best we could have hoped for.

'Is he going to be charged?' I ask.

'It's still too early to say. The Crown Prosecution Service will decide that, once we have the full psychiatric assessment.'

I try to steady my voice before I speak again.

'When is he going?' I ask. 'Only he hasn't got any pyjamas or owt and I need to get bus home to pick them up for him.'

'He'll be ready to go in about ten minutes. You can go with him, if you like. I'll ask the officer to stop off at your place on the way so you can pick up what he needs.'

'Thank you,' I say. 'Will you be speaking to that little girl's mam? Only if you do, I'd like you to tell her sorry from me. I know she won't want to hear it and I can't say I blame her, but I want her to know he never meant her wee lass any harm.'

She nods, gives me a little smile with her mouth shut and walks away.

AFTER

7

FINN

I put the 'Create Your Dream Garden in Just 4 Weeks' Alan Titchmarsh supplement in a plastic folder, so it keeps clean and dry when I take it out into the garden.

Dad has given me a budget of two hundred and fifty pounds for the whole project, which, when he first told me, I thought was enough money to make our garden look like the Chelsea Flower Show but, having researched online to see how much the things I need cost, I now know is actually only enough to buy four climbing roses and a garden arch (Alan is a big fan of garden arches).

I am a bit worried about that, but I have decided that I will just have to budget very carefully and maybe try to make my own garden arch out of bamboo canes, so I can get some more flowers instead.

I have drawn out my garden design and put that in a plastic

folder to keep it nice too. Although it turns out that even with a very good set of felt-tip pens, I still can't get my plan to look anything like the picture I have of it in my head. Of course, on *Love Your Garden*, Alan has 3D computer graphics, but Dad said the software for that would blow my entire budget before I started, so I suppose my rubbish felt-tip pen design will have to do.

I don't mind, though. I still can't believe that this is actually happening. The only thing I am a bit worried about is the party they have on *Love Your Garden* when they reveal the finished garden, because, apart from Dad and Kaz, I can only think of two people I want to invite and one of them can't come.

I'm pretty sure Lottie will come, though. And Rachel will bring her, so that's one more. And I'll have to try very hard not to think about who won't be there. That's the only thing that is making me a bit sad. I'm mainly excited, though. The last time I was as excited about something as this was when I was with Mum doing the school in the woods, and to be honest, I was more scared than excited then. This is different. I will be safe because I will be at home with Kaz and Dad will know where we are. The only places we will go will be to the garden centre and on a trip to one of Alan Titchmarsh's favourite gardens.

I have been looking through Alan's book and there are none in West Yorkshire, which seems a bit strange because he was born in West Yorkshire but maybe it's because there are too many hills and too much rain here. He has three favourite gardens in North Yorkshire, though, so perhaps we can go to one of those. Although I'll have to ask Kaz because she hasn't got a car and goes everywhere by bus and I'm not sure if you can get to North Yorkshire on the bus.

I hear a knock at the front door and run downstairs. I get there as Dad opens the door. Kaz is standing there in some old jeans and a sweatshirt. She has her hair in plaits as normal and I realise that is very sensible for gardening. She is also holding a big carrier bag with plants sticking out the top.

'Your friend Barry from garden centre said you can have these because they're not good enough to sell but will be fine with a little TLC.'

'Thanks, Kaz,' I say, beaming. Alan said some plants needed some TLC once on *Love Your Garden* and I asked Mum if you could get that at Homebase, which is why I know what it means.

'You're a complete star, Kaz,' says Dad. 'Finn's been busy planning it all since you left. I think you're going to have a busy day. There's plenty of food in the fridge and I've left some bread out for sandwiches, so please just help yourself.'

'Thanks. Will do,' says Kaz.

'Right,' says Dad, ruffling my hair. 'I'll be off then. Have fun.'

I don't even mind him ruffling my hair today. I'm too keen to get going.

Kaz comes in and puts the bag of plants down in the hallway.

'Would you like to see my plans before we go out?' I ask.

'Wow, you don't waste any time, do you?' she says.

'Alan never starts work without proper planning,' I say. 'Though I'm afraid my plans aren't very good because I'm rubbish at drawing.'

'I'm sure you're not,' she says. 'Let's go and have a look.'

We go upstairs and I hand her the plans. I can tell by her face that she is trying to think of something nice to say.

'I really am rubbish at drawing, aren't I?'

Kaz grins at me. 'It's not your strongest point, is it, pet? Don't worry, I'm rubbish at lots of things but weirdly, drawing isn't one of them. Do you want me to have a go?'

'Yes, please,' I say, rushing to get some more paper and my best felt tips from my desk.

'Have you got a pencil?' she says. 'I only draw in pencil.'

'Don't you like felt tips?' I ask, handing her a pencil.

'We didn't have none at home,' she says. 'I like to stick to pencil, because that's what I know best.'

'Why didn't you have felt tips?'

'We didn't have lots of things. A car, a home phone. Not much money around and what little there were went on drink.'

'The drinks you had must have been very expensive then. Did you have lots of fizzy drinks? I'm not allowed fizzy drinks because they rot your teeth and they're expensive.'

Kaz smiles at me. It's a sad sort of smile. 'Let me draw these plans for you. You tell me what you'd like it to look like and I'll see what I can do.'

I stand at my bedroom window so I can see the garden and start telling Kaz about my design. I don't stop talking for ages and I don't look back to see what Kaz is drawing until I run out of words. When I go back to my desk and look, I can't believe it.

'Wow, that's amazing. Everything looks like the thing it's supposed to be. It's almost as good as Alan's and they do his on computer. How did you do that?'

Kaz shrugs. 'Just summat I can do. I don't know how.'

'Did you go to art college?'

She laughs. 'No, pet. But I got an A in O level Art. Proud of that, I am. Only qualification I did get at school, mind.'

'So why didn't you become an artist?'

Kaz laughs again. She seems to find a lot of things I say funny. 'Because being an artist doesn't pay rent and someone had to.'

'Why couldn't your mum pay the rent?'

Kaz hesitates before replying. 'She wasn't up to working, see. And someone had to put food on table and new shoes on our Terry's feet. He were going to school in his slippers by that time because he didn't have owt else to wear.'

I look down at my shoes. The kids at school used to say I had the wrong shoes and the wrong trainers, like I had the wrong trousers. I wonder what they'd have said if I'd have turned up in my slippers.

'Did he like them?' I ask. 'His shoes, I mean.'

'Oh, aye. Right proud of them, he were. I used to think of smile on his face when I gave them to him when I were doing a massive pile of washing up at café.'

'I still think you would have been a very good artist,' I say.

Kaz grins. 'Thank you, pet.'

'Did you draw the pictures at the old café where you worked?' I asked, suddenly remembering. 'There were pictures of teapots and teacakes on the blackboard and they were really good.'

'Yeah, I did, thanks.'

'So you were a sort of an artist. Just for a bit.'

'Come on,' she says. 'Let's get to work on this garden of yours.'

We start digging in the bottom corner, where there aren't any bulbs. Sometimes, *Love Your Garden* get a proper big digger in but I didn't even ask Dad how much that would cost because they would need to lift it by crane over the back fence and, if I have learnt anything, it is that real life isn't actually like the *Bob the Builder* episodes I used to watch when I was little.

'How old were you when you started gardening?' Kaz asks.

'About three,' I reply. 'Mum says I always liked gardening, but I didn't like getting my hands dirty.'

'Is that why you wear them?' she asks, nodding towards my gardening gloves.

'Yes.'

'I'm complete opposite, I am. I used to love getting right filthy when I went down allotment with me mam.'

'What did you grow there?' I ask.

'All sorts. Tatties, peas, beans, carrots, sprouts. If it grew in Yorkshire, we grew it. There were plenty of stuff we went without but at least we didn't go without veg, not for most of year, at any rate.'

'Why did your mum give up the allotment?' I ask.

Kaz pauses for a moment before replying. 'It were too much for her. She weren't right well for a long time, before she died.'

'Did she have cancer?' I ask.

'No. She drunk too much, sweetheart. It's not good for you, drinking alcohol. You want to stay well clear of it.'

I frown because I remember on the night that we are not supposed to talk about, she bought a bottle of alcohol just before it all happened.

'Is that why you left it?' I ask.

'Sorry?'

'The bottle you bought from the probably-a-student-man behind the counter. You left it on the floor afterwards, even though you'd paid for it.'

Kaz seems to work out what I am talking about because she shuts her eyes for a moment.

'I realised I hadn't been thinking straight,' she says. 'I'd let everything get on top of me and done summat stupid. Only sometimes things have to happen to make you see that.'

I nod, even though I don't understand what she just said, and we both go back to digging in silence for a bit.

'Why did your mum drink?' I ask.

Kaz carries on digging and says, 'Me dad weren't right nice to her before he left.'

'Did they argue a lot? I ask. 'My mum and dad used to argue a lot.'

Kaz puts her fork down and looks at me.

'Did they, sweetheart?'

'Yes. I used the Richter Scale to measure their arguments. They had a lot of sevens and eights and once, they had a nine.'

Kaz nods slowly.

LINDA GREEN | 173

'It's not nice when your parents argue, is it? I used to hate listening to mine. Dad used to gamble his money on horses. He didn't have much to start off with and what he did have were supposed to pay for food and rent and clothes for me and our Terry. That's why we often had to do without, even when he were living with us.'

'Is that what your mum was cross at him about?'

'Yeah. Only when she got cross at him, he used to get nasty and hit her. That's why she started drinking.'

'My mum and dad never did that,' I say.

'I'm glad to hear it,' says Kaz, giving me a little smile. 'What did they argue about?'

'Me,' I say. 'About what was best for me. Only they could never agree on it.'

'At least they loved you enough to argue about you.'

'I never thought of it like that,' I say. 'I just wanted it to stop and now it has stopped, I wish that it could start again. The thing I hate most of all is the silence of them not arguing.'

Kaz comes over and gives me a hug. Her hands are a bit dirty, but I don't mind.

'How's it going with your dad?'

'It's OK. He doesn't really know me, though. He doesn't know all the stuff I like and the things I don't like. And I'm mad at him for arguing with Mum, because if he hadn't, maybe none of that stuff would have happened and she'd still be here.'

Kaz gives me a squeeze and takes hold of my shoulders, so I look up at her.

'Thing is, Finn, we can't change what's already happened.

Even when it were horrible, and we wish we could. All we can change is how we respond to it and what happens in future. That's what you've got to think of now.'

'Like finishing the garden,' I say.

'Exactly,' she says, giving me another smile as she picks up the fork. 'We'd better get our arses in gear, then.'

It's my turn to do a smile.

'What?' she asks.

'Dad doesn't let me say that word.'

'Well, I shan't tell him,' she replies.

'Arse,' I say, trying not to giggle. 'Arse, arse, arse, arse, arse.'

Kaz makes sandwiches for us at lunchtime. I'm a little bit disappointed she hasn't brought her sheep apron with her to do it, but I don't say anything. I have cheese and tomato because it's the best sandwich in the world and Kaz just has cheese. I am happy when I see that Dad has bought white bread, because Mum always bought brown, but then I feel bad for feeling happy and I try not to feel anything.

We sit on the picnic bench in the garden to eat them and I bring out my Alan Titchmarsh *Favourite Gardens* book, to show Kaz some of my ideas.

'Some of them are quite tricky to do,' I say, 'because they have got castles, palaces, Japanese pagodas, bridges and palm trees, and Dad says palm trees only grow in certain climates in this country, like Cornwall, and definitely not in Yorkshire.'

'He's not wrong there.'

'But I like this one,' I say, turning the page to Castle Howard in North Yorkshire, 'because it's got roses and delphiniums and we've got those already, so that's a good start, and I know we can't get a big fountain like that, but maybe we could get a little water feature.'

'It's lovely, is that.'

'Have you ever been there?' I ask.

'No, pet. I haven't been anywhere like that.'

'Could you take me on Wednesday, please? Dad says I can choose one garden to visit and he'll pay for us and won't take it out of the budget.'

'Trouble is, I haven't got a car, see.'

'I know, but I looked at their website and we can get the train to Malton and catch the number 181 bus from there, and they will give us twenty per cent off the entrance fee for helping to save the planet.'

'That does sound like a good deal,' says Kaz, after finishing the last mouthful of her sandwich. I haven't even started mine yet, because I've been too busy talking, but I have noticed that Kaz does eat fast.

'So, can we go?'

'As long as your dad says so.'

'OK. I'll check with him tonight, but it will have to be this week because I've got to go on holiday with Dad next week.'

'You don't sound too pleased about that. Where are you going?'

'The Lake District.'

'That's nice.'

'Mum booked it.'

'Oh.'

'Dad says we still have to go because the campsite's paid for and it would be a shame to waste it and anyway, it will do both of us good.'

'But you don't want to?'

I shake my head.

'It won't be the same without her. I'll be sad she's not there all the time and it'll be boring just with Dad.'

'But Lake District's supposed to be lovely. I've seen it on TV and it always looks nice.'

'Haven't you ever been?'

'No.'

'Not even to the Beatrix Potter Museum?'

'Nope.'

'I've been to the Beatrix Potter Museum at least five times that I can remember, and I probably went before that too. I thought everyone had been there. Where do you go for your holidays, then?'

'I don't,' she says. 'I've never been on holiday.'

I stare at her, wondering if she's joking, but she hasn't got a joking face on.

'Never?'

'Holidays cost money,' she says. 'Money we've never had.'

'Oh.'

I feel a bit bad now for saying I didn't want to go to the Lake District. I look up at Kaz as the thought comes to me.

'You can come with us,' I say. 'I'll ask Dad. I'm sure he won't mind.'

Kaz looks down at her empty plate. She looks a bit sad.

'Thanks, pet,' she says. 'It's right nice of you to ask but I can't go.'

'We'll pay,' I say. 'It won't cost you anything.'

'I can't leave our Terry, see,' she says.

'But I thought he was in hospital.'

'He is, but I still visit him every day.'

'Isn't there anyone else who can visit him?'

'No, pet. I'm only visitor he gets.'

I'm surprised to find there is anyone with fewer friends than me. Terry must be very weird indeed.

'Oh, right. I could send you a postcard.'

'That'd be nice,' she says, before she stops for a moment and looks a bit serious. 'Actually, don't worry with that, you'll be too busy for postcards. Just tell me all about it when you get back. I'll look forward to that.'

I nod, still trying to get my head round the fact that there are people who have never been to the Beatrix Potter Museum.

On Wednesday morning, the day we are supposed to be going to Castle Howard, Lottie gets dumped at our door. It's not like I didn't want to see her or anything. Just that it is unexpected.

Dad opens the door and I rush out, thinking it will be Kaz, but it's not, it's Rachel and Lottie.

'Hi Finn, hi Martin,' says Rachel. 'Unexpected emergency. Two of Lottie's cousins have come out in chickenpox this morning, which means she can't go to my sister's because she's never had it. And we're already two down at work and I'm chairing an important case meeting at nine thirty so although I wouldn't normally do this to you, I hope you don't mind . . .'

'No, it's fine,' says Dad.

'Brilliant,' says Rachel, kissing Lottie, pushing her towards us and already heading for the car.

'Kaz is looking after me and we're going to Castle Howard. Can Lottie come too?' I ask.

'Yes,' yells Rachel, fishing in her handbag before running back to us and thrusting a twenty-pound note into my hand.

'Is that enough?' she asks.

'Yes,' I say.

'Brilliant. She's got fig rolls in her bag. You like fig rolls don't you, Finn?'

'I think so.'

'Fantastic, have a great time,' she says, dashing back to the car. 'Martin, please say thank you to Kaz. I owe you both a massive favour. Sorry to dump her on you like this.'

She jumps in her car, gives a quick wave and is gone.

'Hi Lottie,' I say, grinning at her.

Lottie shakes her head. 'I can't believe I've just been dumped on your doorstep.'

'I don't mind,' I say.

'It's no problem Lottie,' says Dad. 'I'll go and do some extra sandwiches.'

Lottie groans as he leaves. 'Mums can be so embarrassing.'

She appears to realise as soon as she says it.

'Sorry,' she says. 'Wasn't thinking. Shall we start again and pretend it was all arranged?'

'We can do, if you like.'

Lottie ushers me inside. I shut the door and she waits a second before ringing the bell.

'Hi Finn,' she says when I open it. 'I'm looking forward to our trip to . . .' She frowns as she tries to remember.

'Castle Howard,' I whisper.

'Yes, Castle Howard. Why are we going there again?'

'Because it's one of Alan Titchmarsh's favourite gardens.'

'You really are weird, aren't you?' says Lottie, shaking her head.

'Yep. Good weird, though.'

'Absolutely,' she says with a smile.

I am just about to finally let Lottie in when Kaz arrives.

'Hi Kaz,' I say. 'Lottie's coming with us too because her cousins have got chickenpox. Her mum says she owes you a massive favour.'

'Nonsense,' says Kaz. 'It's no problem. Just means we'll have an extra lass to keep you in check.'

She pulls a face at me. Lottie laughs.

'I've got fig rolls with me,' she tells Kaz.

'Even better. Are we off then?'

'You just need these,' says Dad, coming to the door and handing Kaz the packed lunches. 'Should be enough in there to keep you all going. Are you sure you're OK with this, Kaz?'

'Aye, it'll be fun. You get off to work.'

'Have a good trip then,' he says. 'And don't steal any of their roses.'

I smile at him. That was almost funny. I'd forgotten he could almost be funny.

Dad has given me the Family and Friends Railcard to look after. It is weird, because I have only ever used it before with Mum. It feels kind of wrong to be using it without her. But I try to think that, as Kaz and Lottie are friends not family, I am using a different part of it.

I've packed a big notebook and pencils for drawing, in the hope that Kaz will draw me some pictures, and the train and bus times, which Dad printed off the internet for me, because it turns out Kaz hasn't got the internet. She hasn't got a computer and she hasn't even got a smartphone. I thought I was the only person in the country without a smartphone, so I am glad to have found someone else. I wonder if that is why Kaz and I get on so well, because she is a bit weird like me.

'Do you mind not having a computer?' I ask Kaz, as we all sit in the waiting room at Halifax station.

'You don't miss what you've never had,' she replies.

'Don't you?' I ask.

'No,' says Lottie. 'I've never missed having a dad because I don't know what it's like to have one.'

'There you go, see,' says Kaz.

'But how do people send you emails?'

'They don't but I have got an email address now. Woman at library set one up for me. They're good there. Right patient with folk like me who don't know what they're doing.'

'Can I have your email address, please?' I ask. 'So I can email you a photo from my holidays.'

'That'll be nice,' says Kaz. 'Let me see if I can find it for you.'

She rummages in her purse and pulls out a crumpled slip of paper with it written down on.

'Here you go,' she says, handing it to me. I take my note-book out and carefully copy it down and hand her the piece of paper back.

'Go to the library and check your email next week,' I say. I'll send you a photo every day, then it will be like you're on holiday with us.'

'Thank you,' she says. 'That'll be grand.'

'Are you going to send me photos too?' asks Lottie.

'If you like. What do you want photos of?'

'Anything but gardens,' she says.

The number 181 bus to Castle Howard from Malton train station is a single-decker. Kaz gets on first and pays for all of us. She passes the bus ticket to me for safe keeping for our discount. Lottie leads us straight to the long seat at the back, like we are on a school trip.

'I've never been to North Yorkshire before,' Kaz says, as she sits down next to us.

'Not even for a day trip?' I ask.

'Nope. Never been outside West Yorkshire. Surprised they didn't ask for a passport.'

She smiles as she says it, so this must be a joke.

'The kids at school thought I was weird because I've never been on a plane,' I say. 'But I have been abroad. We've been to

France four times on camping holidays, but we always went by car because it was easier for Dad to take his bike.'

'Have I missed much in France, then?' asks Kaz.

'Not really. It didn't rain as much but their shop on the campsite didn't have very good food. Not unless you like smelly cheese.'

'Don't suppose they had Yorkshire Tea either.'

'No. Mum took our own teabags.'

'There you go then,' says Kaz. 'Better off staying at home. Have you been abroad Lottie?'

'Only twice to France with my mum. We went on the Eurotunnel.'

'Is that good?' asks Kaz.

'Yes but the sandwiches are rubbish.'

'See,' says Kaz. 'I really am better off at home.'

A little bit later we are standing looking at the massive house at Castle Howard, which looks like a palace to me.

'Tell you summat,' says Kaz. 'I wouldn't fancy cleaning all them windows.'

'No and there's a lot of lawn to mow,' I say, looking across the grass. 'I know we can't afford a sit-on lawnmower for our garden, but I bet they have one here.'

'I'm not stealing a sit-on lawnmower for you,' says Lottie.

Kaz laughs. 'Come on,' she says. 'Before you two get me into trouble. Where do you want to go first?'

'I think we should go and find the delphiniums, because Alan says in his book that they are at their best in July.'

Alan is right; the delphiniums are very pretty. There are loads of them in the borders, every colour you can think of. We find the rose garden too. Only it isn't just one; there are four of them and they have more varieties of roses in them than I have ever seen in my life. I start writing down the names of the ones I like best in my notebook. That's when I see it.

'Look,' I call over to Kaz, pointing at the large pink rose bush in front of me.

'What is it?'

'It's the Alan Titchmarsh rose. I've never seen it before. Isn't it beautiful?'

'It is,' she says. 'Lovely colour. If they named one after me, it would have to be all pale and droopy and past its best.'

I laugh. 'No, it wouldn't,' I say.

'What would it look like then?'

'It would be yellow and have petals you could plait.'

Kaz is laughing now. We both laugh together. It feels like a very long time since I last laughed.

Lottie comes over to us from the far end of the rose garden.

'Can we have our lunch now?' she asks. 'I'm starving.'

So we sit in the rose garden next to the Alan Titchmarsh rose to eat our sandwiches and I can't help thinking it's the next best thing to meeting the real Alan. And if he was here, we wouldn't have enough fig rolls for two each, so maybe it's just as well he's not.

When we have finished eating, I get out my sketch pad and pencil and hand it to Kaz.

'Can you draw me a picture of the rose garden, please?' I ask. I want to remember exactly what it looks like.

'But you've got a picture in guidebook.'

'I know but I want this one to go on my wall.'

I stand with Lottie behind Kaz and we watch as she draws. Lottie turns to me and whispers, 'She's brilliant.'

'I know. I told her she should have been an artist, but she said she couldn't because being an artist doesn't pay the rent.'

'It does if you're Banksy,' Lottie replies.

'Who's Banksy?'

'He does secret street art. People wake up in the morning and find he's drawn a massive picture on their garage.'

'Doesn't he get in trouble for that?' I ask.

'No, because he's famous.'

'So how does he make money from drawing on people's walls?'

'I don't know,' she says. 'But he does.'

Kaz turns round and hands me the finished picture.

'Will that do you?' she asks.

'Thank you, it's even better than a photograph. I think I'll get a frame for it.'

'It's only a rough sketch,' she says.

'I know, but you did it.'

She bends over and kisses me on top of my head.

'I think that's the nicest thing anyone's ever said to me.'

I smile at her and can't help thinking that she can't have had a very nice life.

AFTER

8

KAZ

By Wednesday the following week I am missing the boy so much it is ridiculous. I can't even take my mind off it by cleaning the flat, as I only have a room to clean now and it's a pretty small room at that. Hopefully it won't be for much longer, though. I've given up on getting anything from the council. I'm on waiting list but I'm not a priority and there are loads of families with kiddies in front of me. But now I've got two jobs, I'm trying to cobble together enough money for the rent deposit I'll need to get a new place. It won't be much, but I need somewhere for Terry to come home to. I'll pretend we had to move out of our old flat because the landlord put up the rent. I can't bring myself to tell him the truth. I'm still too ashamed of what happened. He won't like the fact that we've moved, I know that. He's never been good with change. But I'm hoping having his old TV and video player back will help soften the blow. I may not be able to win him over, but I can usually rely on Matthew Kelly to do the job.

I go downstairs to wash out the cleaning things I've been using. It's on my way back that I see the little pile of post on the table by the front door. A letter addressed to Terry is on the top. I know straight away it is either from the police or the DWP. I had to give them both my new address for Terry, because I couldn't afford to have post redirected.

I pick it up and see the West Yorkshire Police logo. I have been dreading this moment. As much as I've tried to push it from my mind, I've had nightmares about visiting Terry behind bars. About him going into prison and never coming out again. Because he wouldn't survive in there. I'm pretty sure of that.

I take the envelope straight back up to my room and close the door before sitting down on my bed and opening it. My hands are already shaking. I start reading. There is a lot of stuff about the Mental Health Act and detailed psychiatric reports. And then I get to the important bit. The part where they say the Crown Prosecution Service have decided that in light of the psychiatric report they have received, it is not in the public interest to press charges and therefore no further action will be taken.

I collapse down on the bed, a jibbering mess. Terry's not going to prison. He's not even going to court. He hasn't got to go through that, and I haven't got to watch him suffer. I shake my head over and over again, unable to believe that something has finally gone right. I'm still fucking furious because it should never have happened in the first place, but at least it stops here. All I need to do now is try to undo all the damage it's caused. Terry's got to get well enough to come home. And I've got to get him one.

Doctor Khalil is in reception when I arrive at the hospital.

'Can I see you for a minute, please?' I ask.

He nods and leads me through to his office. We both sit down.

'I just want to say thank you,' I say. 'Terry's had a letter from police and they're not going to take him to court because of psychiatric report you did.'

'Well, that is good news. Are you going to tell him now?'

'Yeah, he hasn't said owt about it lately but that doesn't mean he's not been worrying about it. He's good at keeping his worries to himself, is our Terry.'

'I've noticed,' Doctor Khalil says with a smile. 'Although there is some other good news. He asked me if we could start to reduce his medication this morning.'

'Did he? That's a good sign, for him to be thinking positive like that. What did you tell him?'

'His condition has stabilised and his responses in the Cognitive Behaviour Therapy sessions have been much more positive of late, so I said that if we continued to see an improvement this week, we'll start a gradual reduction from Monday. And we'll be looking to move him to Kingfisher ward as well.'

I smile. It's what I've wanted to hear for so long.

'Thank you,' I say. 'I just want him to get back to normal now. His normal, not everyone else's normal.'

Terry is sitting in his chair when I go into his room. He looks up at me. Gives a glimmer of a smile. Even manages a quietly muttered, 'Hiya, Sis.'

I sit down on his bed.

'I hear you've been talking to Doctor Khalil,' I say.

'I don't want to carry on like this,' he replies, 'I'm like living dead.'

'He says he'll let you cut down meds, as long as you do it carefully.'

'Yeah. It'll take longer than I want, mind.'

'I know, love. But at least you're on right road. That's most important thing. And he says they're looking at moving you to Kingfisher ward.'

'Good,' he says. 'I hope I get a room with a view of car park.'

I smile and shake my head. 'Anyway, love, I've got some more good news for you today.'

Terry looks up at me, waiting for me to go on.

'Police have been in touch. You know, about what happened. They're not going to take you to court. Doctor Khalil told them it were because of your schizophrenia and they understand that. They're not going to press charges.'

Terry puts his head down. I can see his shoulders shaking. I stand up and go over to him. Pull his head towards me like I used to do when he was a kid.

'It's OK,' I say, holding him as he sobs. 'It's over now.'

'But I scared that girl, Kaz. I feel right bad about that.'

'You weren't thinking straight. That's what Doctor Khalil told them.'

'I did hear rats.'

'I know you did.'

'And Matthew told me it were rats that were scaring her. I didn't know it were me.'

'I tried to tell you at time, but you thought I were lying to you. You always think that when you're poorly.'

'Is she OK, that girl?'

'The policeman at station told me she'd be all right. Her mam were looking after her.'

Terry takes a deep breath, wipes the snot from his nose.

'I want to write to her mam, tell her how sorry I am.'

'That'd be nice, love. Maybe police could pass letter on for you.'

'Not now. When I'm properly better. When I can think and feel a bit more clearly.'

'OK.'

Terry goes quiet for a moment and then looks up at me.

'You don't hate me do you, Kaz?'

I look at him and shake my head. 'I could never hate you, Terry. Anyway, it's not you that does it. It's your illness. That's what you've got to keep telling yoursen. I don't want you to worry about all that now. All you've got to concentrate on is getting better.'

*

I don't even realise I'm humming as I walk through the garden centre next morning on my way to the café until a voice calls out.

'Someone's in a good mood this morning.' I turn round and see Barry grinning at me from behind a display of fuchsias.

'Sorry,' I say. 'Didn't realise you were there.'

'Don't apologise for being happy,' he says. 'We could do with a bit more of it in world. Have you won lottery or owt, because if you have, I'd like a share.'

''Fraid not,' I say, smiling at him. 'But me brother's turned a bit of a corner. He might be coming home from hospital soon.'

'That is good news,' he says, stepping out and coming over to me. 'What's he been in for?'

I hesitate before replying but Barry has kind eyes and I feel I can tell him.

'He's in psychiatric unit. He's got schizophrenia. He's OK most of the time when he's at home with me, like, but they made him go out to work when he wasn't up to it and he ended up in a bit of a state.'

'Sorry to hear that,' he says. 'Has he not got anyone else to look after him?'

'No, it's just me.'

'Bloody hard, isn't it?' says Barry. 'I cared for my wife for nine years before she died. Toughest job in the world.'

'It is,' I reply. 'And I'm sorry to hear that about your wife.'

'She had early-onset dementia. Went from being life and soul of party to someone I didn't recognise in a few short years. Bloody horrible it were.'

I nod, knowing exactly what he means. 'You feel so helpless, don't you?'

'Yep. Devoted my life to her, I did, but still never felt I were doing enough.'

His eyes are glistening. I reach out my hand and put it on his shoulder.

'I'm sure you did,' I reply. 'I'm sure you were a huge help to her.'

'I hope so,' he says. 'Anyway, there's me making us both sad when you were in such a good mood.'

'It's OK,' I say. 'It's good to find someone who understands what it's like.'

'And how's your young friend getting on with his garden makeover?' Barry asks.

'He's doing right well with it, in his element, he is.'

'Good, well hang on a sec and I'll get you some more plants. I've been saving some out the back for him.'

When I arrive at the café with Barry, both of us carrying a boxful of plants, Marje looks up from behind the tea urn.

'What are you two up to?' she asks. 'Clearing out half our stock?'

'Barry's donating them to my little friend Finn. I'm helping him with a garden makeover.'

'There you go, Kaz,' he says, putting the heaviest box down and rubbing his back as he stands up. 'I'll have some more for you next week. Just let me know when you need them.'

'Thanks Barry, you're a star,' I reply. He smiles at me.

'Delighted to be of service,' he says, before walking off,

whistling. I catch Marje looking at me with a huge grin on her face.

'What?' I say.

'I think our Barry's got a soft spot for you.'

'Don't be daft. He's just helping Finn out.'

'It's not Finn who's put that sparkle in his eye, though. I can see it now, you and him driving off into the sunset in his old Ford Cortina with a "Baz and Kaz" sticker across windscreen.'

'Behave, you daft bat,' I say, shaking my head at her. But later, when I'm cleaning the tables, I can't help thinking about the tears in those kind eyes of his. And how good it is to have someone I can talk to who knows what it's like to care for a loved one.

I go to the library on my way home from work. It's a new library, spread over three floors. More books than you could ever imagine. And computers too. Which is where I'm heading now. The librarian who helped me set up the email address told me you could look for flats on the internet, because that's how everybody does it nowadays.

It's a different lady to the one I saw last time, but she stands next to me and makes sure I've logged in properly before typing in 'Rightmove' on the screen, and a different site comes up.

'So if you type in Halifax and click here,' she says, showing me, 'you can say how many bedrooms you want and how much rent you can afford, then it will search for you on a map, or just list them from the cheapest to the most expensive. And the phone numbers to call are all listed for you.'

'Thanks,' I say. 'That's a lot bloody easier than it used to be.'

'I know. Just as long as you don't get distracted looking at one-million-pound homes the way everyone else does.'

'Believe me, there's no chance of that,' I tell her.

I click to search for the lowest prices. The first one that comes up is seventy pounds a week. It would be a stretch, but I reckon I might be able to manage that. The one three places underneath it is walking distance from the hospital and the garden centre. It's a house, too. A tiny two-bedroom one that you couldn't swing a cat in but an actual house. I've never lived in a house before. I read what it says underneath and gasp out loud when I see the 'zero deposit required' line. I scribble down the phone number and am about to go outside to make a call when I remember the other reason I came in here.

I get the piece of paper out of my purse and log in to my email. It says there are four new messages. All of them from Finn. I click on the first one. There is a photo attached of him standing, looking rather glum, outside the World of Beatrix Potter. Underneath it he has written, 'wish you were here'.

BEFORE

9

FINN

When I come out of my bedroom on Friday morning, I see that Mum has left the spare room door open by mistake. I know she has been sleeping in the spare room for a while because I hear her crying in there sometimes, like she did last night. But she has been trying to hide it by not taking any of her things in there and keeping the door shut.

I put my head round the door. It smells of Mum, even though she has opened the window. It's a nice smell, the Mum smell. It's warm and fuzzy and fun, even though she doesn't seem like that any more. I wonder if her smell will change soon, if it will stop being her, just like she has. I wonder what sad smells like.

Mum has made the bed, so the room looks like it does when Grandma and Grandad come to stay, although she usually puts some flowers in the room for them and she hasn't put any there for herself. I don't understand why it's Mum who has moved out of their bedroom, not Dad, because he is the one whose solicitor sent her a letter that made her cry. Maybe Dad cried about her pulling me out of the SATs, but I didn't see him. I have never seen him cry about anything.

I go to the toilet and think about what Mum said about Dad wanting me to live just with him now. It still doesn't seem right because Mum is the one who has always looked after me. Dad only does some looking-after bits in the evenings and at weekends when he comes back from his bike rides. And even then, Mum is usually still around and helps when he doesn't know where things are or if he's not understanding something that's bothering me. I don't know if Dad is any good at the important bits, like finding clean school uniform for me and remembering to sign the forms for visits and knowing what I like if I need a packed lunch.

And he wouldn't be able to come to celebration assemblies because he never has done and even if I get the bus to my new secondary school, like he says I'll have to, he still wouldn't be back from work when I got home so I'd have to be home alone like that kid in the old film I watched on TV last Christmas, the one Dad told me was funny but was actually really scary and kept me awake at nights worrying about burglars. I don't think I'd be very good at making traps if there were burglars. I'd probably just play my ukulele in the hope it would make them go away because all the kids at school say no one normal likes ukulele music.

And I don't know when I'd get to see Mum, apart from at

celebration assemblies, and I don't think Dad knows the recipe for apricot, orange and bran muffins and I don't think Dad would know what to make instead for bake sales and he would probably get mini-doughnuts from Tesco like Lottie's mum sometimes does and you are not really supposed to do that, even though everyone likes them a lot more than my muffins.

I wash my hands and start to go downstairs but I stop before the creaky step because I can hear Mum talking in the kitchen. It's not to Dad because he has already gone to work, so she must be on the phone. I sit down on the stairs, so I can listen.

'I'm scared I'm going to lose him, Rachel,' she says, her voice shaking. She is on the phone to Lottie's mum. I wonder if Lottie is listening to the other end of the conversation, because if she is, I can ask her what her mum said and we'll be able to piece all of it together, like a big jigsaw.

There is a gap and I hear Mum sniff and then she says: 'It doesn't matter what I've done for Finn, though. Martin's a solicitor. He'll know how to do this. He'll get them to twist it, make it sound like I haven't got his best interests at heart. He's already emailed school and told them he wants Finn to sit the SATs and asked for a meeting on Monday. He's building a case against me.'

I sit and fiddle with my fingers during the next gap. I don't think Dad has ever emailed my school before. Mrs Ratcliffe must have wondered who he was. I shift position on the stairs. Mum starts talking again.

'It's not a case of picking my battles, though. Our whole relationship has become a battleground ever since Finn was born. Since before he was born, for that matter. I didn't even get the home birth I wanted, because Martin insisted that a hospital birth would be safer.'

I didn't know that, and I wonder why Dad thought a hospital birth would be safer. Maybe we didn't have enough towels and soft things for me to land on at home.

Rachel is saying something on the other end. If I had a phone I could text Lottie now and ask her what it was.

'The thing is,' Mum continues, 'if I back down over the SATs, the next thing will be just round the corner. Look how he got his own way with the private school too. At some point I have to stand up to him or the Finn I love will disappear and I couldn't bear that either.'

There is another sniff. I wonder exactly how I would disappear and whether an invisibility cloak could be part of it. I would sit here and listen to more, but I am worried I am going to be late for school. And if I am late, Lottie will be even later than usual. I stand up and go downstairs, making extra-loud footsteps, so Mum will hear me coming and it will not look like I have been listening.

'Anyway,' she says, wiping her nose as I come through the hall, 'I've got to go. Thanks for listening, I'll catch you later.' She puts the phone down and does a little smile at me, even though there is nothing else about her face that is smiley at all.

'Morning, love,' she says. 'Sit yourself down and I'll get your breakfast.'

She walks to the other side of the kitchen and puts the radio on. The floaty lady with long red hair is singing the song about the dark days being over. I have heard it before, but I don't know her name because I am not very good at pop singers. Mum likes her though, I know that. She usually sings along to it and dances around the kitchen, but she doesn't this morning. She just brings me over my bowl of Millet Bran and goes to get the milk out of the fridge, only she drops it and it spills all over the floor and she bursts into tears.

I don't know whether to go to Mum first or pick up the milk bottle, so I sort of hover in the middle. There is a saying about not crying over spilt milk, but I decide not to say it in case it makes her cry more instead of laugh. In the end, because my shoe is in the middle of the milk and I do not want to make milky footprints, I take my foot out of it and hop over to put my arm round Mum.

'I'm sorry,' Mum says.

'What for? You said never to cry over spilt milk.'

Mum reaches out, squeezes my hand and gives me a watery smile.

'None of this is your fault, Finn. Always remember that.' I nod and go and get some kitchen roll to mop up the milk. Afterwards I have apple juice on my Millet Bran because there is no milk left and it is pretty disgusting, but I don't say anything.

Lottie is later than usual. She only just makes it in time for us to go down for the celebration assembly.

'I know why you're late,' I whisper, as we walk down the corridor. 'My mum was talking to your mum on the phone. She was crying and saying I might disappear.'

'Why?'

I haven't told Lottie about the solicitor's letter yet, partly because if I do, it will make it seem real and I don't want it to be real. But I think I'll have to tell her now, otherwise none of it will make sense.

'My dad is going to ask the court to let me live with him instead of sharing me with Mum.'

'That's horrible,' says Lottie. 'Grown-ups always tell us to share things, then they won't share us.'

'He's mad at Mum because of the SATs thing.'

'That's such a stupid reason. What did my mum tell your mum to do?'

'I don't know. I was hoping you could tell me that.'

'I was upstairs reading a book about a boy whose mum has got cancer and who has nightmares about monsters but then the monster, which is really a tree, comes to life and tries to help him.'

'Oh. That's not much help then.'

'It was a big help to the boy, actually.'

'I meant to me. I want to know what my mum's going to do to try to stop it.'

'Does your mum do kick-boxing or anything like that? Because if she does, she could use that on your dad.'

'She does yoga. But that's all peaceful and gentle and some-times she falls asleep during the relaxation bit.'

'That won't work then,' says Lottie. 'Maybe I could start a petition for you?'

'Yeah,' I say, knowing already that she would only get one signature. 'Maybe.'

The celebration assembly is bearable because my name is not mentioned, and I do not have to go out to the front. Tyler Johnson gets the 'star of the week' award for our class and even though this is not right because he has been so mean to me and he lifted Caitlin's skirt up in the playground so everyone could see her knickers, I do a pretend clap when everyone else does.

Mum sits at the back and tries to pretend everything is OK. She gives me a little wave before she goes. I wonder if she is going to go home and cry some more or if she has got some appointments and is going to try to help people feel better. I'm not sure she will be very good at that right now and I am a bit worried she might start crying in front of them and make them feel a whole lot worse.

As we go back to our classroom, Lewis R elbows me hard in the ribs and says, 'Out of my way, Little Red Riding Hood.' They call me this sometimes; I think it is something to do with me having red hair and looking like a girl, but I don't really get it. I look around to see if Mrs Kerrigan has seen what he did, but it looks like she was too busy trying to stop Lewis B and Kian having a fight.

Lottie saw it though.

'Tell Miss what he just did,' she says.

'No,' I say. 'It's not worth it.'

'Well, I'll tell her then,' she says and marches off to Mrs Kerrigan before I can stop her. She comes back a few moments later looking cross.

'What did she say?' I ask.

'That she was busy, and I shouldn't tell tales.'

I nod. That is what they always say.

When we get back to the classroom, Mrs Kerrigan gives out another SATs practice paper. I look up at her and whisper, 'Have I got to do it too, Miss?' and she nods and says, 'Yes, just in case.' I wonder if Mrs Ratcliffe has shown her the email from Dad. Maybe they think there will be a tug-of-war with me in the playground and Dad will win. Maybe they're right.

I try to concentrate on the English paper, but I keep thinking about Mum crying and about what's going to happen on Monday morning, and I start getting even more worried about it all than I was before. When Mrs Kerrigan collects the papers at the end, she can see that I haven't written very much, and she looks down at me and says, 'I do hope you're trying your best, Finn. This classwork is important, even if you aren't going to do the tests.' And I know that she thinks I have done badly on purpose and I want to tell her I haven't, but I can also feel the tears coming and I don't want to cry in front of everyone, so I put my head down and don't say anything.

Lewis R is sitting behind me and he obviously heard what she said because as soon as she has gone, he kicks my chair and says 'Why aren't you doing the tests? Everyone has got to do the tests, it's the law.' And other kids hear him, and they start talking about me and why I'm not doing the tests and I want to disappear so badly that it starts to hurt.

They are all still looking at me and talking about me as we

go out into the playground. Ryan comes up to me and says, 'I know why you're not doing the tests. It's because you're a girl.'

Tyler says: 'No, it's because his mum complained and he's a little mummy's boy,' and everyone starts laughing and I am looking around for Lottie but I can't see her and everything is going blurry and then they start laughing at me because I am crying and I shout something very loudly but I am not sure what it is, and Miss Dye comes up and puts her hand on my shoulder and leads me back into school.

She takes me to the welfare room. It is a small room that used to be a sort of cupboard and they keep the first aid kit in there and there are two big beanbags on the floor and kids come here sometimes if they are feeling poorly or need a time-out. When I was little, I used to call it the farewell room and that always made Mum and Dad laugh. I don't know if they'd laugh about it any more.

Miss Dye hands me a tissue and I dab at my eyes, then screw it up in my hand.

'What's the matter, Finn?' she asks.

She asks it nicely but I want to ask her if she hasn't been paying attention because my mum and dad are getting a divorce and fighting over me and I don't even know if I am doing the tests on Monday and I only have one friend in the whole world and all the other kids hate me and make fun of me all the time and I would have thought the answer was pretty obvious.

'Nothing,' I reply.

'Why did you just swear at the other children?'

'Did I?'

'Yes.'

I wonder what word I said but I don't think I should ask that.

'Oh. Sorry, Miss. I was getting very cross with them.'

'Were they bothering you?'

'They always bother me.'

'What were they saying to you?'

'Just stuff.'

'What sort of stuff?'

'About me not doing the tests, about me being a girl and a mummy's boy.'

Miss Dye looks sad. She was my teacher in year four and I liked her.

'Would you like me to have a chat with Mrs Kerrigan or Mrs Ratcliffe about this?'

I shake my head. That will only make it worse and I want it to get better, not worse. I see Miss Dye glance at the clock on the wall. Break will be over in a few minutes and she will have to go and teach her class.

'Are you going to be OK to go back to your lessons now, Finn?' she asks. 'I can phone your mum if not.'

I don't want her to say anything to Mum because she is sad enough as it is, without this making her even sadder.

'I'll be fine,' I say. 'Does it look like I've been crying?'

I know it does because even if I cry for five minutes, you can tell I've been crying for about the next five hours. Mum is the same. She says it's something to do with having pale skin and red hair. Dad has got different skin and brown hair, so he doesn't have that problem. I don't think I've ever seen him looking like he's been crying but maybe that's because he's never cried. I certainly can't remember him ever doing it.

'You look fine,' Miss Dye lies, and pats me on the shoulder.

I hear the bell being rung and I go back to my classroom. Mrs Kerrigan looks up and smiles at me.

'Are you OK, Finn?' she asks, even though she must be able to see that I am clearly not OK.

I nod because that seems less of a lie than lying out loud. I sit down and a moment later Lottie comes in and sits down next to me.

'What happened?' she whispers. 'They're saying you went crazy and shouted at everyone to piss off.'

I am a bit disappointed I didn't say a ruder word than that but try not to let it show.

'Yeah,' I say. 'I did.'

'I can't believe I missed it,' says Lottie.

'Where were you?'

'In the loo. Will you do it again at lunchtime so I can hear?'

I shrug. I don't want to do it again but I'm not sure I'll be able to stop myself. It's like all the anger is overflowing and I don't know how to stuff it back in. The others come in and sit down at their desks. Everyone is looking at me again and whispering and I am wondering if it will ever get any better, but I am pretty sure it won't.

*

I am expecting trouble at lunchtime, but I am not expecting it the second I step out into the playground. Which is a shame, because Tyler is lying in wait for me behind the door and punches me in the side of my face.

'That's for telling me to piss off,' he says.

His fist feels like it has gone right through my cheek but when I touch it, the skin is still there. All the other kids are staring, and Lottie has her arm round me and is shouting at the dinner lady to come over, but it seems to be ages before she does. Then Mrs Ratcliffe comes out and it all gets noisy as everyone tries to tell her what happened at the same time and she tells Tyler to go and stand outside her office and asks me to come inside with her.

Lottie comes with me because she is my friend and that's the sort of thing friends do. Well, girls do, I don't think boys would bother. Mrs Ratcliffe takes me to the welfare room and asks to look inside my mouth to make sure I'm not bleeding, and I still have all my teeth. I'm not and I do, which is good because I don't want to tell Mum about this in case it makes her cry even more.

'Now, Finn, I need to go and deal with Tyler. Will you be OK sitting here with Lottie for a minute until I get a member of staff to come and take over?'

I nod. I wonder what's going to happen to Tyler. If he was a grown-up and she was still a policewoman she would probably get him locked up in jail but because he's a kid and she's a head teacher he'll probably just get a detention.

'Tyler's going to get in such massive trouble,' Lottie says, as soon as Mrs Ratcliffe has gone.

'He'll probably blame me for that.'

'Ignore him, he's an idiot.'

'Yeah,' I say. And then I think that the one good thing about being hit is that I haven't thought about all the bad stuff with Mum and Dad for at least ten minutes.

Mum is waiting for me outside the school gates at the end of the day, all bright and smiley as usual, as if this morning never happened.

'Hi, love,' she says. 'Everything OK?'

I nod. I am hoping she will leave it at that and I won't have a bruise on my cheek in the morning and can pretend it never happened but then she sees Lottie and waves to her and Lottie comes over and before I can give her a look, Lottie tells her.

Mum frowns at me.

'A boy punched you?' she says.

'Yeah. I'm OK, though,' I reply.

'You were punched, Finn. There is nothing OK about that. Why didn't you tell me?'

I shrug. I feel a scene coming on.

'Lottie told you before I could,' I reply.

'Well, a member of staff should have phoned me. Or at least come out with you to tell me now. I'm going to go and see Mrs Ratcliffe.'

I look at Lottie. She mouths 'Sorry' to me and I follow Mum back into school. She walks down the corridor like there is a massive wind blowing her from behind and goes straight to the secretary's office.

'Hello Mrs Ravani. I'd like to see Mrs Ratcliffe please.'

'Is she expecting you?'

'No but I'd like to see her straight away.'

Mrs Ravani looks at Mum, then at me, and picks up the phone. A moment later Mrs Ratcliffe comes out of her office. Although she hasn't been a policewoman for quite a few years now, sometimes she still does what Mum calls her 'dealing with the troublemakers' look. She is doing it right now.

'Hello Mrs Rook-Carter,' she says.

'It's Ms Rook, actually. Always has been, always will. I'd like to speak to you about what happened to Finn today.'

'Oh, right. Come through to my office,' she says with one of her 'not really a smile' smiles. We follow her through. She offers Mum a seat, but Mum shakes her head.

'First of all, I'd like to know why I wasn't told that Finn had been hit today.'

'There was no need to trouble you,' says Mrs Ratcliffe. 'We dealt with it all ourselves.'

'He's my son! I have a right to know if he's been physically attacked at school.'

'I'm afraid we don't have time to ring parents every time there's a minor incident in the playground. We'd never be off the phone. It's like *The Jeremy Kyle Show* out there some days.'

Mum stares at Mrs Ratcliffe. I don't know who Jeremy Kyle is, but the mention of his name seems to have made Mum even angrier.

'Well it shouldn't be! And I do not consider this a minor incident. I send my son to school every day and I expect you to keep him safe and if you don't manage that, I expect to be told.'

Mrs Ratcliffe takes a deep breath and glances up at the ceiling for a moment before looking back at Mum.

'I can assure you that we do our utmost to keep children safe and incidents like these are very rare but obviously in a busy school like ours, they do occur from time to time.'

'Well, which is it? You said it was like *The Jeremy Kyle Show* out there a moment ago.'

I don't think I'd like to watch *The Jeremy Kyle Show*. It doesn't sound very nice at all.

'The important thing,' continues Mrs Ratcliffe, 'is that we are quite capable of dealing with whatever happens in the playground ourselves and, in our experience, telling parents about every incident tends to inflame the situation for all those concerned.'

She looks at me as she says it and I think, if I was giving marks for this argument, that I'd probably have to give her one for that.

'And what about the boy who did this to Finn?' asks Mum.

'He has been dealt with and I do not think he'll be bothering Finn again.'

I do. I think he'll probably whack me as soon as I step into the playground on Monday morning.

'Why did he hit him?' asks Mum.

Mrs Ratcliffe glances at me before answering.

'There was an incident in the playground this morning where Finn swore at him and other pupils.'

Mum looks down at me with a frown.

'Is that true, Finn?'

I nod.

'Why did you swear at him?'

'He said mean things to me.'

'What sort of things?'

'About me being a girl and a mummy's boy.'

Mum shakes her head and looks back at Mrs Ratcliffe.

'And is that going to be dealt with as well or is it going to carry on like this for the rest of his time here?'

'The boy has been spoken to and, as far as I'm concerned, that's the end of the matter.'

'Not for Finn, it isn't,' says Mum. 'He's the one on the receiving end.'

'We've spoken to Finn and checked him over,' replies Mrs Ratcliffe, 'there are no injuries, which is why we didn't call you. He's absolutely fine, aren't you, Finn?'

She looks down at me. Mum is looking at me too. I don't know what to do because if I nod it will make it look like Mrs Ratcliffe has won, but if I don't, it will look like I'm being rude. I start humming inside my head. Hoping I am not doing it out loud.

'I think I'll be the judge of that,' says Mum. She turns and marches out of Mrs Ratcliffe's office. I think I would give Mum a mark for that one too, so maybe it was a draw, I'm not sure.

'You didn't ask about what's going to happen to me on Monday,' I say, as I catch up with Mum in the corridor.

'I'm trying to deal with one thing at a time.'

'What is going to happen on Monday?'

'I don't know, Finn.' Mum's voice is a bit snappy. She never does snappy.

We go back outside. The other kids have gone home now, so the playground is quiet. School is OK when the other kids aren't here. Mum said to me once that home education would be a bit like school but without the other kids. Only it would be more fun. I think that means we would do a lot of baking muffins, but we would have to eat them all ourselves because there wouldn't be other kids to try to sell them to or teachers to buy them because they feel sorry for me. I like the sound of home education. But Dad thinks it's not proper education at all, which is why it's not going to happen.

Mum doesn't say much on the way home. She has got her worried face on. Dad told me once that I should give as good as I got at school, and Mum got very cross with him. She said if anyone hit me, I should walk away and tell a teacher, but I think she has just realised that it doesn't work very well.

When we get home, I see that there is another letter on the kitchen table. It looks like it's from Mum's solicitor.

'What does it say?' I ask.

'Nothing important,' Mum says, picking it up and putting it in her bag. This means it is important and she is trying to hide it. I don't know why grown-ups think we don't understand things like that.

Mum fills the kettle and flicks the switch. She stands there with her back to me until it boils and then turns round.

'How many times have you been hit since I last had to go

in?' she asks. I don't know what to say because I don't want to lie to her, but I don't want to get her cross and upset either.

'A few,' I reply.

'Why haven't you told me?'

'I didn't want to upset you. Anyway, there's no point saying anything because nothing's going to change. It's just what school's like.'

'Do other boys get hit or just you?'

'Some other boys,' I say, 'but mainly me.'

Mum shuts her eyes for a second.

'Why do you think that is?'

'Because I'm weird and I don't thump them back.'

'Who says you're weird?'

'Everyone apart from Lottie.'

Mum shakes her head.

'You're not weird, Finn. You're just different, unique.'

'It's the same thing,' I reply with a shrug.

'It's not,' says Mum, walking up to me and putting her hands on my face. 'I love how you know the name of virtually every variety of rose, I love how you think about things more deeply than other kids, I love how you can play more than a hundred different tunes on your ukulele. None of that is weird – it's wonderful.'

'Yeah but only because you're my mum. To the other kids, it's weird, which is why they keep picking on me.'

Mum sighs.

'Well, I shall email Mrs Ratcliffe and tell her that we won't allow this bullying to continue.'

'But it will, the only way it will stop is if I stop being different.'

Mum closes her eyes for a second before grasping me by the shoulders. When she speaks, her voice is all wobbly. 'You must promise me you will never do that, Finn. Never stop being you. You're worth a million of them.'

I frown. I don't think that could possibly be true, but I am quite tempted to put myself on eBay to see how much I would sell for. Maybe whoever buys me would have a big garden and I could give the money to Mum to pay for the solicitor's letters.

'Promise me,' she says, squeezing my shoulders tighter.

'I promise.'

Mum pulls me into her and starts crying again.

I am in the downstairs toilet when Dad gets home. I didn't plan it that way, it just turned out to be a longer poo than I thought. Neither of them realise it, so I just sit there and listen. It's a much better place than the landing to hear things and it turns out it's a bit of luck I am trapped in there because it doesn't start off like a shouty argument. Just a quiet one with sad voices.

'Finn was punched in the face at school today,' Mum tells Dad.

'Jesus. Is he OK?'

Dad sounds worried. I had no idea he would be that worried about me.

'No physical damage. But he's obviously upset.'

'What did school say?'

'Didn't even tell me about it. I only found out through Lottie. And when I went to see Mrs Ratcliffe, she tried to brush it off and made some crack about it being like *Jeremy Kyle* in the school playground.'

'That's not good.'

'No, maybe you can ask her about it on Monday when you have your meeting with her.'

'You and Finn are supposed to be there too.'

'Yeah. That's such a great idea. Us having a domestic in front of our son and his head teacher.'

My poo is finished but the last bit fell quietly into the rest, so I don't think they heard it. I sit there without moving. I think I would be a good spy. I can sit really quietly when I need to.

'I'm trying to find a way forward, Hannah,' says Dad.

'No, you're not. You're trying to get your own way as usual. And you're using Finn to try to break me. I got the letter from my solicitor.'

'You're not giving me any choice.'

'I can't believe you're actually going to go through with this. Not after what happened on Wednesday. You saw how upset he was.'

'I don't want to do it, Hannah. I'm still hoping you'll see sense and change your mind.'

'What and be blackmailed by you into sending our son to do his SATs against his will, in a school where he clearly isn't safe.'

I have heard about blackmail before and I know it's serious.

You can get sent to prison for it. I am still mad at Dad for all of this, but I don't think I want him to go to prison.

'You're twisting things again, Hannah.'

'I don't think so. Finn told me today that the only way the bullying will stop is if he starts acting like the rest of them.'

'Well, maybe that's not such a bad thing.'

'Are you serious?'

'It's a survival tactic, that's all. You won't let him hit them back, so maybe if he blended in a bit more, they'd leave him alone.'

Mum does something that sounds like a cross between a laugh and a snort.

'So basically, you're forcing me to choose between watching my son disappear to save himself being bullied at school, or having you tell the court I'm an unfit mother so you can take him away from me permanently.'

'Now you're being ridiculous.'

'Am I? I don't think so.'

There is a silence for a moment. I imagine Mum standing there trying not to cry. I want to go out there and give her a hug but I think it will make things worse if they realise I have been listening to all of this, so I just stay quiet. When Mum finally speaks, her voice is so soft, I can barely hear it.

'I don't understand how you could do this to him,' she says. 'How the man I married could do this to our precious boy.'

There is a noise that sounds a bit like a dog whimpering, then I hear footsteps across the tiles in the hall and above me up the stairs (the downstairs loo used to be a cupboard under the stairs, like the one Harry Potter lived in, but they had it turned into a toilet when we moved here). I stay in the toilet for a long time before I flush and creep back upstairs.

When Mum calls me down for tea, our plates have been put on trays and she tells me I can take it through to the front room and watch TV. I am never usually allowed to sit on the sofa and eat my tea while watching TV (it's another thing that makes me weird, as all the other kids at school do it, even Lottie).

I want to give Mum a hug, but her face makes me think she might break in half if I do that.

'Where's Dad?' I ask instead.

'He's in the study. He's got some work to do. He's already had his.'

I know this is a lie, but I nod anyway, pick up my tray and follow her through to the living room.

'Can we watch *Love Your Garden*?' I ask. We have this week's episode recorded and I haven't seen it yet.

She nods and does a little smile. We sit down and I pick up the remote and put the TV on. As soon as I see Alan Titchmarsh, I feel a bit better. I hope Mum does too. Alan Titchmarsh is better than antiseptic when you're hurt, because he doesn't even sting when you put him on. We eat our tea in silence while watching. My favourite bit is where they build a little bridge over the pond. At the end, when the old lady who nursed her husband until he died and now spends all her time helping others opens her eyes and sees the garden, she bursts into tears and can't speak. When I glance at Mum, she is crying too.

'It's a lovely garden, isn't it?' I say, stroking her on the soft bit on her arm.

'Yes,' she says. 'It is.'

I wait until Mum is having a bath later and I can hear Dad watching the news on TV before creeping into the kitchen. Mum's bag is still exactly where she left it when we came in from school. I stick my hand in and find the letter straight away. I don't understand why grown-ups are so rubbish at hiding things. They are the same with Christmas presents. Nearly everyone in my class finds their presents before Christmas Day because their mum or dad hide them in the same place every year. Even squirrels know to hide their acorns in different places to stop them getting found. Humans ought to be ruled by squirrels really, because they know more about hiding things. I think I would like to live in the world ruled by squirrels because, unlike grown-ups, I am good at hiding things.

I take out the letter and lay it on the kitchen table to read it. There are a lot of long words that I don't understand, and it keeps mentioning Child Arrangement Orders and then says, 'I have been informed by your husband's solicitor that his client will be applying for full residency and for a Prohibited Steps Order to prevent you from making future decisions relating to the child's education without his consent.'

He is actually going to do this. He is going to ask the court for me to live with him all the time, even though I told him I didn't want to. I don't understand why Dad is doing this because he has a proper job in an office in Leeds, so he can't look after me all the time and, even if he could, I don't think he would be very good at it because he doesn't know how to have fun like Mum does and he doesn't know where everything is.

And then I get to the end of the letter and I see it. The thing that must have upset Mum earlier. A date for the divorce proceedings to be heard. Thursday 18 July. We have PE on Thursdays. I've always said it's a bad day.

I still have the letter in my hand when Dad comes into the kitchen. I look up at him, he looks down at his feet.

'I said I don't want to live with you,' I say.

'Finn, please, let me try to explain,' says Dad, stepping towards me.

'There's nothing to explain. You just need to stop it and stop making Mum cry and go back to having happy voices again.'

Dad shakes his head. 'I'm afraid it's not that easy,' he says.

'Well you tell me that when things aren't easy, you just have to try harder.'

Dad's face looks like I've stood on his toe and it really hurt. I am not going to say sorry though, because I meant it. I drop the letter on the table and run upstairs.

When I get to my room, I get out Alan Titchmarsh's book on perennials and start reading. It is hard to concentrate, though, and when I am on page twelve, I hear the water draining out of the bath. I don't want to tell Mum that I read the letter and what I said to Dad, because I think she is sad enough already and that is why she had a very long bath. I have a bath twice a week to keep clean and because Mum tells me to. Mum has a shower every day, but she still has very long baths sometimes and no one tells her to, and I don't think she does it to keep clean. I think she has one when she is sad because when she comes out, she always smells of the oils that she uses to try to make people happy. I don't think they last very long, though, otherwise, she wouldn't need so many baths.

I wake up. It is dark. I wonder for a second if Mum's crying has woken me again, but it is perfectly quiet. A moment later I realise that I woke up because I feel sick. Worse than that, I am actually going to be sick. I sit up in bed and my feet somehow find my slippers in the dark. I stand up and start to hurry to the bathroom. I've only got as far as the landing when the vomit overtakes my legs. I throw up right outside the spare room. It is still coming out of my mouth when Mum opens her door.

'Oh, Finn, love,' she says. She puts her arms round me, even though I am covered in sick. I start crying. I hate the taste of sick in my mouth. I hate even thinking about the way it has come up through my body. And most of all I hate it in my hair. And somehow it is in my hair, even though I was sick downwards, not upwards. It's like vomit hasn't learnt the laws of gravity.

'Let's go and get you cleaned up,' Mum says. She says it in her mum voice. The warm and gentle one that is like the softest towel wrapping itself round you. She leads me to the bathroom, unbuttons my pyjama top and peels it off. Some of the sick nearly falls off but she catches it with her hand. I don't know how mums can do things like that and not mind. I could never be a mum. I would run away screaming if my kid was sick. She lets me hold her shoulders while I step out of my pyjama bottoms and she puts them in the bath with the top.

She runs some water into the beaker on the sink and hands it to me.

'Swish your mouth out with this,' she says.

I do it and spit into the sink. She hands me my toothbrush with the toothpaste already on it. I brush hard and spit and repeat until I can't taste it any longer.

'It's in my hair,' I say, with a little sob. 'I can feel it in my hair.'

'I know, that's why we're going to give you a very quick shower,' she says. I don't know why she is saying we because Dad isn't here. Dad has never cleaned up my sick as far as I can remember. I have no idea what will happen if I am sick when I am living with him. Maybe I will have to clean myself up.

Mum turns the shower on and gets it to the right temperature and I step inside. I've been showering on my own since I was nine, but Mum doesn't move, and I don't protest. She keeps the door open a little and takes the shower attachment and rinses all the sick out of my hair first, before putting it back on the wall. Then she takes the shampoo bottle and squirts some into her hand and starts lathering it on my head. It feels nice, the way her fingers massage my scalp. I shut my eyes, partly to keep the shampoo out and partly because it's nice to think about nothing else apart from Mum massaging my head. I think I can hear her singing and humming while she is doing it but when I open my eyes for a second, I see that she is not singing or humming, so it must just have been a memory. A nice one, though.

When she has finished and has rinsed it off, I step out the shower and she wraps me in a soft towel. I don't have to do anything; she rubs me dry, like a human version of one of those drying machines you can pay for at the swimming pool.

'There,' she says, when she has finished. 'We'll give your hair a quick whizz with the dryer, then we'll get you to bed.'

She guides me around the sick on the landing and back into my room. She hands me the hairdryer while she gets some clean pyjamas out for me. I step into the trousers, suddenly feeling sleepy again, and she buttons up the top for me, turns back the duvet and lays it down over me once I'm inside.

'I want you to get back to sleep now,' she says, sitting on the edge of the bed and stroking my head.

'I don't want to live with Dad,' I say.

'You won't have to. I won't let that happen.'

'Have you secretly been learning kick-boxing?' I ask.

Mum does a little smile. 'No but I'm going to sort it all out. I've got a plan, and everything will be fine. I love you.'

She kisses me on the forehead, turns off my light and shuts the door quietly behind her. I lie there, warm and clean and tired, and listen to the sound of her crying softly to herself as she scrubs the carpet on the landing. Wondering what her plan might be and hoping it doesn't involve yoga.

BEFORE

10

KAZ

When I arrive at the psychiatric unit the next morning, I'm told that Terry's been taken to Nightingale ward. It means he's not in a good way, I know that. He's been in there every other time when he's first been admitted. You don't go home from Nightingale or Swallow, though. You have to be well enough to be in Kingfisher or Goldfinch before they'll consider letting you out.

Terry looks like he hasn't had any sleep either when they show me to his room. He is sitting in the chair next to the bed and looks to have aged about ten years overnight. I try to give him a reassuring smile, but he stares straight through me.

'Hello, love,' I say, putting the holdall down on the floor. 'I've brought you some more clothes as I didn't have time to grab much last night.'

Terry looks at the bag then back at me.

'I can't find my torch,' he says.

'I know. Police are looking after it for you.'

'I want it back. I need to keep checking.'

'I'll bring it back when they're finished with it,' I reply.

'Are you working for them now?' he asks.

I sigh. I know I need to keep him onside but it's not easy.

I walk over to the window. 'At least you've got a better view, this time,' I say, looking out at the square of grass and flower borders below.

'I liked looking at car park,' says Terry.

I manage a smile. The boy who could name pretty much any vehicle he saw had never got tired of looking at cars. I turn back to Terry.

'When you see doctor later, you need to tell them about how you've been feeling.'

'How have I been feeling?' asks Terry.

I sigh and walk back over to him. 'You've got in a bit of a state. About rats and that.'

'Screaming girls and chocolate twirls,' he replies. He does remember, although I am not convinced that he understands.

I crouch down in front of him, so he can't avoid looking at me.

'They were screaming because of what you did, Terry.'

'I were saving them from rats.'

I shake my head. 'No, you weren't. There were no rats, Terry.'

'You're only saying that because you're one of them, now. Matthew says you've crossed to dark side. You don't give a toss about me.'

I feel the muscles in my neck tense. I put my face closer to his. 'You slid under cubicle door when a twelve-year-old girl were in there. You scared fucking life out of her and her friends. That's why they were screaming.'

I stand up and head back to the window, still shaking my head. It is quiet for a long time. I know I shouldn't have snapped. I know it was not his fault. I know he doesn't really hate me. I know all of these things, but sometimes it is so bloody hard to keep myself together.

I turn round. Terry is frowning. I am not stupid enough to think he is questioning what happened. He never does that until he starts to get well again. What he doesn't understand is why I got angry with him. I go back over and put my hand on his shoulder.

'I'm sorry,' I say. 'I know you had a scary day. It's just that I did too. That's why I lost it. I hate that I can't help you. It's like I've been given a really hard test and I don't know the answers. Sometimes I can't even understand the questions.'

Terry sits for a moment and then says, 'If you're at home having your tea and there's no one else around, do you and your husband use serviettes sometimes, always, never or occasionally?'

I shut my eyes for a second. We haven't had *Mr & Mrs* for ages. Not since they announced that Derek Batey had died. I lean over and kiss Terry on the forehead.

'Never. Who the fuck has serviettes in their house anyway?' I say.

I walk into town to the job centre after I've left Terry. I haven't bothered calling because there's no local number to call and I don't want to go through the whole palaver with some stranger in a call centre who won't know what I'm going on about or who Terry is. Anyway, I want to see Denise. I want to tell her what really happened before she hears a different story from the firm.

There are lots of people waiting when I get inside. I look around and spot Denise at her desk, talking to a young lad in a denim jacket.

A woman with the clipboard comes up to me.

'Do you have an appointment?' she asks.

'I had one Friday but I couldn't make it, so I've had to come today instead.'

'And did you phone us to let us know?'

'No, I couldn't. It were a family emergency and then you were closed.'

'But you haven't made a new appointment for today?'

'No. I just came as soon as I could.'

'I'm afraid that's not how it works,' she says. They all have this superior tone in their voice, these people with a little bit of power. They know it all right and they like to lord it over you with the whole, 'I'm better than you' thing. It makes me want to tell them that they could lose their job at any moment and then they'd be just like the rest of us. Maybe if that happened to them, they'd have a bit more human decency about them.

'And I'm afraid I couldn't help it. If you ask her,' I say,

pointing to Denise, 'she'll tell you that she sent my brother out to work, even though he has schizophrenia, and I told her he couldn't cope with it and she wouldn't listen and that is why I was at a police station on Friday afternoon instead of here and why I've just come from visiting him in psychiatric unit.'

The woman pulls a face like there's a bad smell in here.

'What's your name?' she asks.

'Kaz Allen and Terry Allen's my brother. If you have a word with your Denise, she'll be able to tell you all about him.'

I watch the woman go over to Denise and speak in her ear. They both glance over at me before the woman with the clipboard returns.

'She'll try to fit you in between appointments but it may be quite a wait.'

'That's OK. In case you haven't noticed, I've got no job to go to.'

I plonk myself down on one of the purple chairs. I wonder how much they spent doing this place out. We got two chairs for a tenner off some old boy who put a card in the corner shop window. Nothing wrong with them. Except that they're grubby beige, not designer fucking purple.

I'm almost nodding off sitting there, an hour or so later, when I hear my name called. I go over to Denise and sit down.

'Have you heard what's happened?' I ask.

'I had a call from your brother's employer first thing this morning,' she says, not looking me in the eye.

'I told you, didn't I? Said he wouldn't cope. Didn't listen though, did you?'

'I understand Mr Allen was arrested over an incident involving a young girl. Obviously, we had no reason to think something like that may happen.'

'Don't make him out to be some fucking paedophile,' I say.

Denise looks up at me. Her face hardens.

'Miss Allen, if you use language like that again, I'll have no option but to ask security to remove you from the premises.'

'And I'm telling you that reason he went under cubicle door were because he could hear rats, same rats he went on about when he were here. My brother is not a pervert or a criminal. He's just ill.'

She pauses.

'Well, there is a letter in the post to him, informing him that his work programme placement has been terminated.'

'Good. He won't have to work then.'

'But because he lost his position through gross misconduct, he will also be sanctioned for thirteen weeks for what is the former Jobseeker's Allowance part of his benefit when his money comes through.'

I start laughing. Other people look over, but I really don't care. They couldn't make this stuff up.

'So you find a man who hasn't worked for five years because of his schizophrenia fit for work, send him out to a job where his mental illness causes him to get arrested, be sectioned and lose his job and tell him that as a punishment, his money's being stopped?'

Denise looks down again. I know they're not her stupid rules, but she could at least apologise for them.

'What about his day's pay?' I ask. 'He did a full day's work, apart from last twenty minutes.'

'I don't think, in the circumstances, that any payment will be forthcoming.'

'Well, that went really well, didn't it? You got my brother landed in nuthouse, and while we wait to see if he's going to end up in prison, he gets his money stopped. Bit of luck I've got a well-paid job and all my life savings to keep us going. Oh, hang on a minute, I've remembered why I'm here.'

Denise shifts in her seat. I reach into my bag and pull out my completed Universal Credit application and slap it down on the desk.

'I need to ask you why you failed to turn up for your appointment on Friday.'

'Because I were tap-dancing in bloody bath.'

'There's no need to be sarcastic, Miss Allen.'

'And there's no need to ask stupid bloody questions, is there? Or have you not been listening to owt I've said for last five minutes?'

'Usually there is a four-week sanction applied where claimants have failed to turn up for their appointment and failed to notify us of the reason.'

'And at what point while me brother were being arrested and sectioned should I have given you a call and had a little chat?'

'However, on this occasion,' Denise continues, giving me a look, 'I will treat it as exceptional circumstances and not sanction you.'

I suppose I should say thank you, but I am not sure I can say it without sounding sarcastic, so I say nothing. Denise picks up my form and starts reading.

'You don't say why you left your job,' she says, looking up.

I roll my eyes. Now I'm the one in the dock.

'A woman complained about me on some website and gave our café a one-star review and my boss decided it were enough to sack me.'

'Were you dismissed for gross misconduct?' she asks. 'Because if so, you may be subject to a thirteen-week sanction on your payments. You should be aware that we will be contacting your former employer to ask the reason for your dismissal.'

I shake my head. It looks like I can either lie now and get found out later, because I have no doubt that Bridget, being a vindictive cow, will say I was dismissed for gross negligence, or I can fess up now and say goodbye to my money straight away.

'I were dismissed because a rude customer called a wee lad a spoilt brat and made him cry and I told her she were an ignorant cow when she refused to apologise. I have no idea if that's gross misconduct, you'll have to ask her. I didn't have a contract and she didn't give me any of wages I were owed, so maybe you can ask her about that at same time.'

Denise sighs. She's having a bit of a mare at work today, is our Denise.

'Miss Allen, I will process your application and it will be sent to our head office for a decision, but I need to inform you that if your former boss confirms this situation, you will be sanctioned for thirteen weeks for what is the former Jobseeker's Allowance part of Universal Credit.'

I stand up and cup my ear, beckoning to the young man at the desk next to ours. 'Can you hear that?' I say. 'Record's stuck over here. If I die while waiting for this money, they'll probably sanction me for that too.'

He grins back at me. Denise glares and gestures for me to sit down before continuing. 'However, in the meantime, you have signed a claimant contract and you will be expected to look for work or join a work programme. As for the remaining part of your Universal Credit claim, it takes five weeks for the first payment to be made. Do you understand?'

'Oh, I understand all right,' I say, 'Basically, I'm shafted. And what exactly am I supposed to live on and pay my rent with for next five weeks?'

'As I explained before, you can apply for an advance payment of Universal Credit to help you get by while you're waiting for your first payment. That can be up to one month of your Universal Credit entitlement. However, it is a loan and you'll have to pay it back out of your future payments when they commence.'

'No, I won't. I've never been in debt in my life and I'm not going to start now. That's how people end up using loan sharks.'

'I'm just saying it is an option. Though you will have to be assessed to see if you qualify for the advance payment, it's not automatic. However, if approved, it should come through to your bank within a couple of working days.'

'Have you thought about getting another job?' I ask.
'Because you'd be bloody good on radio reading out all those
terms and conditions as fast as you can.'

'Miss Allen, if you're quite finished.'

I look at her and shake my head. 'You don't get it, do you?
I've worked all my life to support our Terry and now, in the
space of a few days, because of one stupid decision by DWP, all
that's gone, he's locked up in a nuthouse facing police charges
and I'm also being made to feel like a criminal when all I did
were try to be kind to a little lad. You lot think it couldn't
happen to you, but it could. It can happen to anyone, at any
time. One little bit of bad luck and it can all come crashing
down. And that bunch of bastards in government who make
up these rules don't give a toss about any of us. Not me, not
you. We're on same side really, you know. You just haven't
realised it yet.'

Denise goes back to her form-filling. She is thinking about
what I said, though. I am sure of it.

I'm still fuming when I get home. I put the kettle on, checking
first that the bare minimum of water is in there, because
I know there's not much money left in the meter. All this
time I've muddled along the best I could. Always done what
I thought was best for our Terry. And yet somehow, my best
hasn't been good enough. We wouldn't be in this mess if it
was. I have no idea how we're going to survive, this time. All
I know is that I am not going to give up without a fight.

I sit down and pick up the mandatory reconsideration form

they gave Terry last week, which is still on the kitchen table. They ask for lots of evidence I haven't got and I'm pretty sure they won't take one blind bit of notice, but I have to keep fighting for Terry's sake. Because the one thing I do know is that no one else out there will.

AFTER

9

FINN

I thought Dad was joking when he said we were going to the Beatrix Potter Museum, but he wasn't. When we've visited other years, it's been on rainy days when there wasn't much else to do apart from get wet, but it's not even raining today. I suppose he couldn't think of anywhere to go or anything else to do because I don't like doing the things he likes or going to the places he does. Yesterday he suggested I try water sports. That wasn't a joke either.

Which is why I don't complain about going to the Beatrix Potter Museum in case he takes me kayaking instead. He has said the phrase, 'You never know, you might enjoy it,' quite a few times already this holiday. And I have given him lots of looks to let him know that at nearly eleven years old, I know exactly what I enjoy and it doesn't include doing sports on water.

As we queue up to go into the museum, I notice that it's

not actually called the Beatrix Potter Museum but the World of Beatrix Potter. I suppose they thought that would make it sound more exciting, but it only works if you haven't been five times before. I look around and see that I am the oldest kid going in, apart from a few who are only there because they have younger brothers or sisters. I look up at Dad. I think he has noticed this too, because he is avoiding looking at me.

When we get in, there is a five-minute introductory film. It is the same film I have seen all the other times, but I have to watch it again because the doors don't open until it finishes.

The first character I see is Jemima Puddleduck, and all I can think of is Mum reading her story in a funny duck voice that made me laugh. When we reach the Peter Rabbit bit, I remember that I always actually sided with Mr McGregor because you really shouldn't spoil people's gardens by stealing or eating things from them. I don't think you are supposed to think that, so it must just be me being weird again.

And then we get to Mrs Tiggy-Winkle. Me and Mum always liked her best. When I started at my Montessori nursery, I used to get upset about Mum leaving, so after she dropped me off, she would hide a little pocket handkerchief, like the ones Lucie kept losing, in the trees on the walk back to the main road, so when she came to collect me, I did a pocket-hand-kerchief hunt on the way home and we used to talk about all the different places Lucie had lost them.

There is a little boy having his photo taken next to Mrs Tiggy-Winkle and his mum is smiling and talking in that sing-song voice mums do and I want to get past really quickly but there is a queue in front of us, so we can't move and I clench my fists hard and Dad reaches down and takes my hand and even though he doesn't usually do that, I don't mind and I let him hold it until we get past.

'Would you like anything from the gift shop?' Dad asks at the end. I shake my head.

'What would you like to do now?'

'Go back to the campsite,' I reply.

Dad got us a new tent for this holiday. I know why and he knows that I know why, but neither of us have mentioned it. He didn't even ask if I liked the new tent when I saw it. He just put it up without saying a word. I don't like it, because it isn't the old one, but it is orange, which at least means it's easy to find at campsites. He had to get a new rucksack too. We never got the old one back afterwards. Both of us know what happened to it but neither of us mention that either. The new rucksack looks very different from his old one. I think he did that on purpose. But it still reminds me of why he hasn't got the old one.

Our tent is pitched at the far side of the site, in the corner. We walk back there together in silence. It is the worst thing about the holiday: camping without Mum. Every camping holiday I remember, and there have been a lot of them, Mum has been there; laughing while helping Dad put up the tent, singing while cooking our tea and snuggling next to me in the night (once she even zipped our sleeping bags together). When we were here last summer, I woke up on the first night and found her sitting outside looking at the stars. I asked her what she was doing, and she said you could never feel lonely when you knew the stars were watching over you. And then she gave my hand a squeeze and we both went back inside the tent.

This holiday, though, there is no Mum. And that is the weirdest thing ever. I keep expecting to hear her voice outside or see her coming back from the woods with an armful of things for my nature tray. She doesn't do any of those things, though. She just keeps on not being here. And her not being here is the loudest, hardest, saddest thing about this holiday.

'What do you fancy for tea?' Dad asks later, poking his head through into the tent as I am reading my book.

I shrug. I don't know because whatever he cooks it tastes of Mum not being here.

'Anything but sausages,' I say.

When I wake later that night, the first thing I remember is that Mum is not here. There is no one to snuggle up to. No one to whisper to or who can tell me stories to help me go back to sleep. I unzip my sleeping bag very quietly, so I don't wake Dad and crawl to the end of the tent. The zip on the flap is harder to do quietly because it is quite tight, so I just go very slowly. When I've done it far enough up, I crawl outside and look up at the sky. It was cloudy earlier, but the clouds have gone now. The stars are out. I sit looking at them for a long time before I hear Dad's voice next to me.

'They never stop being beautiful, do they?'

I look round. He has my sleeping bag in his hand, and he sits down next to me and wraps it round my shoulders.

'There's Ursa Major,' I say, pointing.

'Yes, well done. Ursa Minor's stronger though, at this time of year.' He traces the outline of the smaller bear in the night sky. I nod when I see it. Mum never knew the names as well as Dad, or how to find them. She was good at the stories behind them, though.

'Scorpius is very strong tonight,' Dad says pointing, 'and you should just be able to make out Lyra.'

'That's the one with the harp isn't it? I ask.

'That's right.'

'Tell me the story again.'

Dad hesitates before starting. 'Well, Orpheus was given the harp by Apollo and his music could soothe anger and bring joy. When his wife died, he wandered the land in depression, was killed and his harp thrown into the river and Zeus sent an eagle to retrieve the harp and put it in the night sky.'

Dad's voice is quiet as he finishes. He is still looking up at the stars.

'I didn't choose a very happy story, did I?'

'No,' Dad replies.

'Mum was good at stories to cheer me up.'

Dad looks down at me.

'It's not the same without her, is it?'

'No,' I say, shaking my head. 'I miss her all the time.'

'I know,' says Dad. 'So do I.'

We sit out there for a long time, not really saying much, just looking up at the sky. I think Dad is trying to do the same thing as me. Stay under the stars long enough so that he doesn't feel lonely.

When we arrive home on Saturday afternoon, I notice something as I go through the gate.

'When did the For Sale sign go?' I ask Dad.

'A couple of months ago,' he replies. 'After I told you we wouldn't be moving. Didn't you notice?'

I shake my head. I suppose I was too busy missing Mum to miss the For Sale sign.

'I'm glad we don't have to leave this house,' I say.

Dad shuts his eyes for a second and nods silently before we carry on up the path.

As soon as I hear the doorbell later, I run downstairs, because I know it is Kaz. I give her a great big hug and nearly knock her off her feet.

'Did you see my photos?' I ask.

'I did. Right good they were. Made me feel like I were there with you. How was your holiday, pet?'

'Fine, thank you.'

'You missed her, didn't you?'

I nod. It's weird how I have only known Kaz for a few months, but she already seems to understand me better than lots of other people who have known me for years.

'It felt wrong to be on holiday without her,' I say.

'I bet it did. Your dad tried his best, though, I expect.'

'He took me to lots of places and tried to get me to do lots of different things.'

'I could see that from photos.'

'It didn't make any difference, though, because whatever we did, it just reminded me that Mum wasn't there, and she should have been, and I kept thinking of our last holiday together and that made me sad.'

Kaz gives my arm a squeeze. 'You got through it, that's main thing. And you're back home now, so we can get on with that garden. Talking of which' – she points to two bags that are on the step next to her – 'Barry's sent you a few more plants that were going spare at garden centre.'

'Thank you,' I say, taking them from her. 'I've had a few more design ideas.'

'Great,' she says, stepping inside. 'You can tell me all about them, so we'll be ready to get cracking on Monday.'

We go through to the kitchen.

'Kaz has brought me some more plants,' I tell Dad. 'Barry sent them.'

'Wow, please say thank you to him, Kaz. It'll be like the Chelsea Flower Show out there soon.'

'Will do. How was your holiday?'

'Fine thanks,' says Dad. And I wonder if, like me, he says that when it's easier than saying the truth.

'Before I forget,' says Kaz. 'I'm afraid I can't come next Saturday. I'm moving into a new flat after work.'

'No problem,' says Dad. 'As long as you let us give you a hand with the move instead. I'd be more than happy to shift some boxes for you and Finn's good at packing.'

'Thanks,' says Kaz, 'but I really haven't got much.'

'Oh, we all think that until we come to move. It's amazing how much stuff you acquire over the years. Have you got a van booked? I've got a friend with one, if not. I'm sure he'd let me borrow it for a bit.'

Kaz does a little smile. 'Thanks, but I really haven't got enough stuff for a van. If you're able to take my things in your car, that would be grand.'

I see Dad frowning at Kaz. I don't understand either.

'But how are you moving your bed and all your furniture?'

'They're not mine, pet. I'm in a rented room.'

'What about all your other things?'

'I haven't got much. Main thing I need moving is our Terry's TV and video player.'

'Well, I could definitely fit them in the car,' says Dad, 'no trouble at all.'

'Thanks. That'll be a huge help.'

'Is Our Terry going to be living there with you?' I ask.

'He is,' says Kaz, 'just as soon as he's well enough.'

'He's been in hospital for a long time now,' I say. 'Can't the doctors make him better?'

'Finn,' says Dad.

'It's OK,' says Kaz, before turning to me.

'Thing is, Finn. It's not like he's got a broken leg or summat that they can put in plaster and mend. He's got schizophrenia. That means his mind doesn't work like yours or mine and he gets scared and upset and confused. Most of time it's OK and he can get by with a bit of help from me, but if he gets stressed about summat, it gets worse and he has to go in hospital so doctors can look after him.'

I think for a moment. I get scared and upset and confused. I wonder if I've got schizophrenia and Dad just hasn't found out about it yet. Maybe I never had the test for that.

'That must be a huge strain on you, Kaz,' says Dad.

'We muddle by best we can. We were fine until DWP found him fit for work. He got sectioned on his first day.'

I don't know what getting sectioned is, but it doesn't sound very nice. I wouldn't want anyone to try to split me up into sections.

'That's appalling,' says Dad. 'Have you appealed against the decision?'

'Yeah. They reconsidered and agreed with original decision, but I've got a tribunal hearing through for next month. Haven't got a clue what to say, though. It'll be all legal bods and me who don't know owt.'

'Well, I'd be very happy to help your brother, if you'd like me to?'

'But you only help people who are moving house,' I point out.

Dad looks at me. He seems a bit cross. 'I am still a solicitor, Finn. I used to do cases like this years ago.'

'Did you? Why did you stop then?'

Dad shakes his head. 'Because I had to earn more money when Mum was at home with you and conveyancing pays more than what I was doing before.'

'Oh,' I say, looking down at the mention of Mum's name.

'Thanks, Martin,' says Kaz. 'Thing is, I couldn't afford to pay you.'

'Don't be daft,' says Dad. 'I'd be doing it as a friend. You've done so much to help Finn. It's the least I can do.'

'If you're sure,' says Kaz, her face brightening.

'Absolutely,' replies Dad. 'Have you got a date for the tribunal?'

'September seventeenth,' says Kaz.

'Right. I'll get it booked off. And if you can give me any paperwork you've got next Saturday, I'll start going through it for you.'

'Thank you,' says Kaz. She looks happy about Dad helping Our Terry. I'm happy about it too. I had no idea Dad could be useful.

'Can I meet Our Terry when he comes home?' I ask.

'Course you can,' Kaz says with a smile. 'I reckon you two would get on a treat. Now, are you going to help me get these plants out in garden before tea's ready?'

I nod and follow Kaz outside, still wondering if I have schizophrenia.

AFTER

10

KAZ

I wait in the hall of the hostel for Martin to knock. I wish I hadn't told them now. They have no idea of how I have been living. Finn probably doesn't even know that places like this exist. What bothers me is that he might think I lived here by choice. That I've been scrounging off the state while he pays his taxes. I'd hate anyone to think that I'm not the sort to pay my own way.

There's a knock at the door. I can see two shadows behind it; one tall, one short. I wonder if Finn will be as tall as Martin one day. I remember how Terry shot up when he hit thirteen. Like a bloody beanpole he was, it was all I could do to keep up with him saying he was hungry every five minutes.

I open the door. Martin smiles at me.

'Hello, Kaz,' he says. 'I've managed to park almost outside, so we should be able to load up nice and easily.'

They step inside. Finn looks at the case and bags I have stacked up at the bottom of the stairs, then looks at me earnestly.

'Is that all you have in the world?' he asks.

'Yep,' I say. 'It may not be much to show for fifty-nine years, but at least I travel light.'

Martin looks embarrassed. 'Right, let me go and fetch your TV and video. Which room is it?'

'Let me show you.'

I lead them up the stairs and open the door. The TV and video are at the end of the bed, as they have been since I moved in.

'Is this where you've been living?' asks Finn.

'Yeah. It actually looks bigger without rest of my stuff.'

'You must have been like a little mouse burrowing in every night,' says Finn.

'I suppose I was.'

'Has your new place got more than one room?'

'It has. It's got a bedroom for our Terry too.'

'Do you think Our Terry will like it?'

'I hope so,' I say. 'Because as soon as he's better, it's going to be his new home.'

Martin carries the TV downstairs for me, while I carry the video player and Finn carries a bag of videos of *Stars in Their Eyes*. We load them up into Martin's car and set off.

'Do you feel sad to be leaving?' asks Finn.

'No. Not this time, because it never really felt like home.'

'Why did you live there then?'

'Finn,' says Martin from the front.

'No, it's OK,' I say, turning to face Finn, who is sitting next to me in the back. 'It was because I couldn't afford to stay at my last place after I lost my job, and sometimes, when you're in a tight spot, you have to make do with what you can.'

Finn nods, seemingly satisfied. We carry on, through the centre of Halifax and out the other side.

'Has your new place got a garden?' Finn asks.

'No, I'm afraid not. Is it OK if I carry on visiting yours?'

'That's fine,' says Finn. 'Even when it's finished, Alan says there's always work to do in a garden.'

I catch Martin smiling in the rear-view mirror. I thought he was a bit of a cold fish at first but I'm starting to see that he does appreciate Finn's funny ways. He just needs to get better at showing it.

We arrive outside my new house. I still can't get my head around it. That for the first time in my life, I am going to live in an actual house. It's also midway between the garden centre and the psychiatric unit, and not too far from Finn's house, which couldn't be better, really.

I open the front door and they follow me inside.

'Nice place this,' says Martin, as he carries the TV into the front room. I look around me and smile. It is nice. It's exactly what I need right now. 'I bet you can't wait to have your own space again,' Martin continues.

'I can't wait to clean it,' I say. 'No one else in hostel ever seemed to bother. I like a place to be squeaky clean, I do.'

'When you've finished, shall I come and inspect it?' asks Finn. 'If it's really clean, I'll give it a five-star hygiene rating.'

'Thank you, Finn,' I say, with a smile. 'That would be grand. Now, why don't I give you a quick guided tour while your dad sorts out the TV for me.'

I take him upstairs to see the tiny bathroom and two bedrooms.

'Which one is going to be yours?' he asks.

'This one,' I reply.

'It's the smallest.'

'I know, Terry's got more stuff than me. Anyway, I'll like being at back, should be nice and quiet.'

'Where are the duvets and pillows?'

'They're on my shopping list but I can't afford everything at once.'

We go back down to the kitchen. I can see that it really does need a good scrub.

'Where's the kettle and the toaster and the smoothie maker?' Finn says, looking at the bare surfaces.

'What would I be wanting with a smoothie maker?'

'You can make banana and blueberry smoothies with them.'

'Can you now. Well, I'll stick with a brew, if it's all the same to you.'

'When you've got your kettle.'

'Aye. It's next on my list, mind.'

We go back through to the front room.

'There,' says Martin, emerging from the back of the television. 'That's your TV and video player all set up.'

'You're a star,' I reply. 'That's first thing our Terry will ask about when he visits.'

'When's Our Terry going to come and see it?' Finn asks.

'In a fortnight's time. Just for the afternoon. Doctor says he'll be ready for a trip out by then.'

'That'll be lovely for you both,' says Martin.

'Yes,' I reply. 'Yes, it will.'

I don't tell them that I haven't told Terry yet. That I am dreading it. Dreading setting him off again.

Martin goes off to get takeaway pizza for us. He says it's what everyone has on moving day, although I wouldn't know about that, only having moved once before, when ordering pizza was the last thing on my mind.

'Come on then, Finn. Are you going to give me a hand with cleaning?'

'Have you got Marigolds?' he asks. 'Only I don't like getting my hands wet, as well as dirty.'

'You really are a funny onion,' I say with a smile, fishing my Marigolds out of the bag for him.

'Mum used to say that to me sometimes,' he says. 'Even though I don't think I look like an onion at all.'

I laugh, pass him a scouring pad and we make a start on the cleaning.

I don't realise how long Martin's been gone until he gets back when we're almost finished cleaning.

'Sorry,' he says. 'Took longer than I thought.'

He puts the pizza boxes down on the floor and goes back to the car. Finn runs out after him. They return a few minutes later, Finn almost entirely covered by a duvet and pillow.

'These are for you,' he says, dropping them on the floor. I look from Finn to Martin and back again.

'Where's this from?'

'Our spare room,' says Finn. 'Mum would want you to have it.'

I give him a hug. It lasts for quite a long time.

'Thank you,' I say. 'That is right kind of you.'

Martin puts down three boxes: a kettle, a toaster and a four-piece dinner set with cutlery.

'And this is a little housewarming gift for you,' he says. 'I'm told you didn't fancy a smoothie maker.'

I look at Finn and he grins back at me.

'You didn't have to do this, you know,' I say.

'We wanted to make it feel like home for you,' Finn says.

'Thank you,' I say, trying hard to keep my voice from breaking. 'You bring pizzas through and I'll christen kettle.'

The first thing Terry does when I arrive at his room in Kingfisher ward the next day is hand me a letter.

'What's this?' I ask.

'It's for mam of that lass, like I said.'

'Thank you,' I say. 'I'll ask police to pass it on to her.'

He nods and sits down again.

'I wish I knew,' he says. 'When I'm like that, I mean. I wish I knew it at the time, instead of thinking I'm fine and it's everyone else who's crazy.'

'It doesn't work like that, though.'

'I know. That's what makes it so bloody hard. Anyway, what you been up to?'

It takes me a moment to be able to reply. I can't remember the last time Terry asked after me. Certainly not since it all kicked off. I decide it's time.

'I've been a bit busy, actually,' I say. 'Only I've got some news for you. I had to move out of our old flat. Couldn't afford rent after I lost my job, see. Only now, what with me having two jobs and that, well, I've got us a new place. It's a proper house. Right nice it is. I've got your TV and video player all set up waiting for you.'

I smile at him, bracing myself for his response. It's a few moments before he says anything.

'What about my tapes?'

'I've got them as well. All your stuff is there. It's not far from here. Salterhebble, just behind primary school.'

He nods, seemingly trying to digest what I have told him.

'So I won't be going back to our old place?'

'No, love.'

'We lived there a long time, didn't we Kaz?'

'Yeah, we did. But they say a fresh start is good for people. I think it'll do us both good to be somewhere else.'

'When can I see it?'

'I've spoken to Doctor Khalil and he says you can visit in a fortnight. Once I've got it all nice for you.'

He nods.

'I'd like that.'

'Good,' I say. 'We can walk from here. Be nice for you to get a bit of fresh air.'

'Do you think Matthew will like it?' he asks.

I hesitate before replying.

'Yes. I do.'

'Here you are,' I say, handing Finn the box of plants I have brought, 'latest offerings from Barry.'

'Thank you,' says Finn. 'It's very nice of him to help me like this.'

'He's a lovely fella.'

'Do you think he'd like to come to the opening of my garden when it's finished? I want to invite all the people who have helped me.'

'I reckon he might do,' I say.

'Will you ask him for me?'

'Yeah,' I reply, feeling so daft because I know the colour is rising in my cheeks. 'Yes, I will.'

We go out into the garden.

'I can't believe it's our last week,' says Finn. 'We've still got so much to do, and I know Alan always says the same thing but then they have the adverts and by the time they go back they seem to have done an awful lot and have loads of people helping.'

'Well, let's see how much me and you can get done in three days, eh?'

Finn nods and puts his gardening gloves on.

'I'll get on with the planting out and maybe you can finish the rock garden?'

'That'd be grand,' I reply.

We go out into the garden. We've got into a real routine with it now. It will be strange not coming here next week. I don't think he's got any idea how much I'm going to miss him.

'What will you do next week?' Finn asks, as if reading my mind.

'Oh, I'll be busy getting house nice, I expect.'

'Will you get another job?'

'I don't know. I'm looking. It's hard to find summat that fits in with hours I'm doing at garden centre, mind.'

'I wish we didn't have to stop doing the garden club.'

'I know. But at least we got chance to do it.'

'That's what Dr Seuss says, don't cry because it's over, smile because it happened.'

'That's a good way to look at it. Who's Dr Seuss, someone you've been seeing?'

Finn gives me a funny look. 'No, the children's author. He wrote *Cat in the Hat* and the Grinch one and *Horton Hears a Who!* and loads of other stuff.'

'Right. I've obviously missed out on him.'

'You can get his books from the library. Mum used to read them with funny voices. She did a very good Horton. Horton's an elephant. He doesn't fit in either.'

He goes quiet for a bit. I watch him press down the ground firmly around each plant.

'You're not looking forward to starting your new school, are you?'

Finn shakes his head. 'Not one little bit.'

'Do you know any of the other kids?'

'No. They had a transition evening, but I didn't want to go because of, you know.'

I nod. 'Is that what's bothering you?'

'They'll all know about it.'

'I doubt it. Their parents might, but not kids. Kids don't watch news.'

'I do.'

'Yeah, but like you say, you're not like other kids your age, are you?'

'No. But if they don't know about it, they'll be mean to me, because I'll be the weird kid. And when I got the place, Mum said not to mention the bursary, which must mean they'll tease me about that if they find out.'

'So don't tell them. You don't need to tell them owt you don't want to.'

'I suppose not.'

He goes back to planting out. His eyes fixed intently on the plant, his little fingers, lost inside the gardening gloves, but pressing down hard on the soil. And I wish that I could do that first day of school for him. Or, better still, remove the need for him to go at all. Anything, to help take away his pain.

BEFORE

11

FINN

When Mum wakes me up the next morning, I am confused. She only usually wakes me up on school days, but I am pretty sure it is a Saturday.

'Finn, you need to get up, love.'

And then I remember that I was sick last night. I can't smell it, only taste it a little in my mouth.

'Have I been sick again?'

'No. We're going camping.'

I frown at her. Usually, when we are going camping, I know about it and we pack everything the day before.

'Are we?'

'Yes. Come on, I want to make an early start. It's a beautiful day out there.'

I sit up in bed and squint towards the window. Bits of

sunlight are coming through the gap where the curtains Mum made don't quite meet.

'Where's Dad?' I ask.

'He's gone out on his bike,' says Mum.

'Is he going to pack when he gets back?'

Mum looks down at her hands.

'Let's not worry about that now,' she says, 'we need to get packed.'

I get up and pull my dressing gown on and go to the bathroom for a wee. My pyjamas that were covered in sick have gone from the bath, but I still think I can smell them. When I get back to my room, Mum is making a pile of my clothes on my bed.

'I don't need all that,' I say. 'You usually tell me to make one T-shirt last two days.'

'I know,' she replies. 'But I'm packing a few more in case. You get yourself dressed and let me sort it out.'

Mum's voice is a bit snappy. She is normally excited when we are going camping, not snappy. She puts some separate clothes out on the bed for me to wear and picks up the other pile.

'Are you going to put them in the big rucksack?'

'Yes Finn. And I'll sort your toiletries. You get your bee rucksack packed with things you want to take.'

'OK,' I say. I still don't understand why we are doing this in a rush, but I get dressed and start to gather my things anyway. I put two Alan Titchmarsh books in and my wind-up torch, bug-collector, magnifying glass and compass. It doesn't fill up much of the rucksack but that is all I usually take.

Mum pops her head round the door.

'Maybe put in a couple of extra books and things to keep you occupied,' she says.

I'm not sure why because Mum usually says that nature provides everything you need when you go camping, but I get one of my bee-keeping books and my school pencil case and a wordsearch book and put them in too.

I take my rucksack downstairs. Dad's rucksack is in the hall. Our tent and sleeping bags are strapped to it and it looks very heavy. I am glad I don't have to carry it. I go into the kitchen to have my breakfast. The washing machine is on but Mum isn't there. I go back upstairs to the landing and call out: 'Mum, I'm ready.'

She comes out of the bathroom clutching a toiletry bag and looking a bit flustered.

'That's great,' she says, 'let's get our boots on.'

'But we haven't had our breakfast yet,' I point out.

'I've packed some breakfast. We'll have it when we get there.'

'And Dad's not back from his bike ride yet.'

Mum crouches down next to me. Her face is serious.

'Dad's not coming with us this time.'

'So why have you packed his rucksack?'

'I'm borrowing it. It's bigger than mine.'

'Have you asked him?'

'Sorry?'

'Have you asked him if you can borrow it because it's rude not to ask and he gets very cross when you don't ask him about things.'

'It'll be fine, Finn. It's only a rucksack.'

'Yeah but he won't see it like that, will he? His solicitor might send you another letter.'

Mum shuts her eyes and sighs.

'Just trust me on this one, Finn. We need to get going.'

She goes past me and hurries downstairs. I follow her and watch her put the toiletry bag in one of the side pockets of Dad's rucksack.

'Didn't Dad want to come with us?' I ask.

'He's busy. He's always got lots to do at weekends, hasn't he?'

'But he doesn't mind us going?'

Mum hands me my walking boots without answering. I suddenly realise that this is Mum's plan.

'He doesn't know we're going, does he?'

'I've left him a note,' she says, nodding towards the narrow windowsill next to the front door, where there is an envelope with 'Martin' written on it. 'Now put them on quickly.'

I sit down on the bottom step of the stairs and pull my boots on. Dad sometimes helps me with my boots. He is good at tying them not too tight and not too loose. There aren't many other things he is good at, apart from being a solicitor and cycling, but he is good at shoelaces.

'How is this going to help because he's going to be even crosser than he is already,' I say as I stand up.

Mum turns to me as she opens the front door and swings the rucksack onto her back.

'It'll do us all good,' she says. 'We need some time away to think things through. He could do with some time on his own thinking things through too.'

'There'll be a big argument when we come back tomorrow, though.'

'Let's not worry about that now, shall we?' says Mum. Her voice is wobbly, and her bottom lip is too. I put my bee rucksack on, hoping that I don't see any of the kids from school on the way.

'Are we going to the same campsite as usual?' I ask.

'No,' she says. 'We're going somewhere new.'

I follow her out of the house and watch as she pulls the front door hard behind us.

'Have you got your car keys?' I ask.

'We're not going by car.'

I frown at her. 'How are we going to get there, then?'

'By bus,' she replies, with a little smile.

I am still frowning at her, but she has set off down the road, all the things tied on to her rucksack bumping into each other and against her.

I hurry after her. I am going to say something but when I look up at her I see she is crying again, so I decide not to say anything. One of Mum's favourite things in the world is camping so the best thing is probably to get to the campsite as quickly as possible, because that will stop her crying and make her smile again.

'Can I carry anything for you?' I ask. Mum looks down and does a little smile.

'I love you, Finn Rook-Carter,' she replies, which is kind of a funny thing to say because there are no other Finns here, so she didn't have to use my surname.

'I love you too,' I reply, deciding not to add 'Hannah Rook' because there are definitely no other Hannahs or Rooks here and I'm absolutely certain she'll know I'm speaking to her.

Mum wipes her nose with her shirtsleeve (even though you're not supposed to) and carries on walking and crying a bit at the same time. She stops when she gets to the bus stop at the end of the road.

'Where are we going?' I ask.

'Not too far.'

'What does that mean?'

'Two bus rides.'

'Will we still be in West Yorkshire?'

'Yes.'

'OK,' I reply. I do not really want to leave West Yorkshire as we'll be coming home tomorrow so it would be silly to spend all our time getting there and back and not much time camping.

I have been camping just with Mum once before when I was little, and Dad had to go to a work thing, so Mum took me away for the weekend. I remember it was fun and we did some singing and there was more room in the tent, and she brought lots of food, including things I wasn't usually allowed to have.

'Have you packed nice food?' I ask.

'Just what we had in. I didn't have much time to prepare.'

'Why didn't you know we were going camping?'

'It was kind of a last-minute decision.'

'But you must have known when you booked the campsite?'

'Don't worry about it, Finn,' she says with a smile. 'Sometimes it's nice to be impulsive. This is a chance for you to leave all your cares behind and have some fun.'

I nod and don't say anything because I don't think Mum is in the mood for arguing. I start thinking about how big my pile of cares would be if I really had left them all behind. I think they would fill my room and most of the landing too. Some of them might even have to go in the loft. Maybe they could help to insulate it. I feel a bit better thinking that my cares could help to save the environment. I always knew they had to be good for something.

The bus comes and we get on and pay. Mum heaves her rucksack off and puts it in the luggage area. We sit down in the seats behind it.

'These are the priority seats,' I say to Mum.

'I know, love. It doesn't matter today though, does it? There's only one other person on the bus.'

I look around. She's right. There's just a man with earphones in sitting on the back seat looking at his phone. I turn back to Mum.

'When will Dad get home?' I ask.

Mum sighs.

'You don't need to worry about that,' she says. 'Just look forward to our camping trip, OK?'

I nod. But all I can think about is what Dad will say when he reads Mum's note and how long it will be before he phones her and there's another big argument. Though not as big as the argument that will happen when we get home tomorrow.

I start to get a tummy ache like I have on school days. I try to think about the campsite and whether I'll be able to stay up late enough to see the stars, which is one of my favourite things. I start to imagine star constellations in the sky but then I remember Dad pointing out Ursa Major to me for the first time and I feel bad because Dad taught me all the stars and he isn't going to see them with us.

Mum rings the bell and stands up as we go past the big Tesco. She hauls the rucksack back on and turns to look at me.

'OK,' she says, 'this is our stop.'

I follow her off the bus and we walk down the road and round the corner to another bus stop.

'Will Dad be home yet?' I ask.

'Finn, please don't.'

'Did you say that you'd taken his rucksack in the note? Only he might think that we've been burgled, and it's been stolen. The house was a bit of a mess when we left.'

Mum shakes her head and looks up at the sky.

'Please try to stop worrying,' she says.

'I didn't have time to unpack my worries from my head before we left.'

Mum manages a little smile.

'You are a funny one, Finn.'

'Where are we going next?'

'Triangle.'

I nod. For the first time this morning, I am smiling. Triangle is the best place name I have ever heard. The first time Mum took me there when I was little, I was expecting it to be an actual triangle and I cried when I got there and discovered it looked just like other places. I asked once if there were any other places that had the same names as shapes. Dad showed me a photo of the Pentagon on his computer, but it doesn't really count because it is a government building in America and not a town. I have decided to collect towns with the same names as shapes. So far, I have only got one but if I ever hear of a town called Rectangle or Rhombus, I will save up all my pocket money until I can afford to go there and I will take a photo of me in front of the name sign and add it to my collection.

The bus for Triangle arrives. It is a bit busier than the last one and we sit a few seats back from the front. I look out of the window as we go through Sowerby Bridge, which I still call Strawberry Bridge in my head because Lottie used to call it that when she was little and couldn't pronounce 'Sowerby'.

Mum lets me press the bell when we get to Triangle and it's time to get off. You can see the woods from the main road. Mum seems a bit happier now that we are here. I decide not to mention Dad again.

I follow Mum into the woods. We have been here several times to have picnics and go for walks, but we have never camped here before. I didn't even know you could.

'Where's the campsite?' I ask.

'Quite a way in. I've got a map if I need it. Don't worry.'

Her voice is lighter than it has been for a long time. But all

I can think is that if Dad was here, he would ruffle my hair at this point.

We carry on for another fifteen minutes or so. Mum gets a piece of paper out of her pocket and looks at it for a moment.

'Why don't you look it up on your phone?' I ask.

Mum ignores me. 'It's this way,' she says, heading off to the right. I follow her for another ten minutes or so until we get to a clearing. I can only see one other tent up but there is a tepee by the entrance and when Mum calls out hello, a man with grey hair comes out.

'Hello, we'd like a pitch, please,' she says. The man nods and smiles and beckons her to come inside the tepee.

'Just wait here a minute, Finn,' she says.

She hadn't even booked in advance. I start to fiddle with the cord on my rucksack.

'All sorted,' she says, coming out of the tepee a few minutes later.

'Where do we have to go?' I ask.

'Anywhere we like,' she replies. 'That's the beauty of making an early start. You get to choose.'

I lead the way over to a spot at the far edge of the clearing. Mum takes off her rucksack. There are red marks on her shoulders where the straps have rubbed but she doesn't say anything about them. She starts humming as she unpacks the tent. I can't remember when I last heard her hum. I wonder if maybe it will all be OK and Dad won't be as mad as I think and will miss us while we're away and actually, this is a really good plan on her part.

I help Mum with the tent. She is quite good at putting it up but she never follows instructions and that usually makes Dad cross, but he isn't here today, so I suppose it doesn't matter and I just fetch her the next bit she needs when she asks me to.

The sun has come out now, so I ask Mum for some sun cream. She rummages around in her rucksack for a bit and I start to worry that she has forgotten it, but she pulls out a tube and my legionnaire's hat. It doesn't really suit me, but no one is going to see me here, so I put it on and squirt some cream on my arms and rub it in.

'Ta-dah,' says Mum, eventually, turning round and smiling at me. The tent is up. It is a bit wonky, but it doesn't matter.

'Great,' I say.

'Let's try it out and cool down for a bit,' says Mum, who looks hot. I crouch down and follow her inside. It is a three-man tent. I don't know why they call it that because I have never seen three men sharing a tent but maybe they do if they are in the army or something.

Mum lies down and pats the ground sheet next to her and I join her for a cuddle. Mum's cuddles are pretty much the best things in the world, although I can't really tell anyone that because I am supposedly a bit old for cuddles now. It's OK here, though, because none of the idiots from school are here so I can do anything I want and not have to worry about what they will say.

'Sometimes, I wish it could be like this forever, just you and me in a tent.' At first, I think I have said what I was thinking out loud but then I realise it was Mum who said it.

'Me too.'

She smiles and brushes a strand of hair out of my eyes.

'We could just go for walks and sit round a campfire at night and we wouldn't have to worry about anything else.'

'Why don't we do it then?' I ask.

'I don't know, Finn. The trouble with being an adult is that you end up doing what is expected of you, not what you want to do.'

'I don't think I want to be an adult then.'

'I don't blame you,' she says. 'It's massively overrated. It's daft really, you spend the first eighteen years of your life wishing you were a grown-up and the rest of it wishing you were a kid again.'

'But we can be who we like here, can't we?'

'Yes,' she says, hugging me a bit tighter. 'We can be exactly who we are. That's why I wanted to come.'

'Have you got our breakfast?' I ask. 'Only I'm hungry now.' Mum smiles and sits up and starts rummaging through her rucksack again. She pulls out two chewy cereal bars and a banana each.

'Here,' she says, handing one to me. 'I've done us pack-ups for lunch too. Carrot and hummus sandwiches and cheese and tomato. You get first choice.'

I smile at her even though I know they will both have been made with brown bread with bits in. I prefer white bread, but I only get that when I go to other children's parties, which is not very often, as most of them don't invite me.

'Thanks,' I say, trying not to show that I was hoping she'd

only been pretending she hadn't brought any special food with her. We sit and eat our breakfast together. Mum has rolled up the end of the tent so we can look out on the trees beyond. It feels like we are the only people in the world right now and I like that. But I also know that Dad must be home from his bike ride by now and will have found out we have gone camping without him.

'What did you tell Dad in the note?' I ask.

Mum sighs before answering.

'Just that we had gone camping because we both needed a break.'

'A break from what?'

'Everything,' she replies.

'Did you tell him where we were going?'

'No,' she says, looking down at the ground.

'Why not?'

'Sometimes, Finn, it's good for people to have some time to themselves to try to sort everything out in their head.'

'You thought he'd follow us and try to bring me back, didn't you?'

Mum turns to look at me. 'The pressure of everything was making you ill, Finn. That's why you were sick last night. It's not fair for you to be in the middle of a tug-of-war like this. And the only way I could get you out of it was to bring you away somewhere we wouldn't be disturbed.'

'But why hasn't Dad rung you? He must be home by now.'

Mum does another big sigh.

'He hasn't rung me because I haven't brought my phone with me.'

I stare at Mum. The way she said it made it quite clear it was deliberate; not like she'd forgotten it or something. It's actually a much bigger plan than I'd realised.

'We've run away, haven't we?'

'I'm not thinking of it like that, Finn. I just tried to do what was best for you in a very tricky situation.'

'Am I going to school on Monday?'

'It's up to you. If you go, Dad had arranged a meeting with Mrs Ratcliffe, and I think they might send you straight from that to do your SATs. If that's OK with you, I'll take you back home tomorrow evening. If not, it will be Thursday evening, when they're over. It's your choice.'

I stare at Mum some more. I didn't think she was capable of coming up with a plan like this. I have never heard of a homeopath or an aromatherapist going on the run before. There are all sorts of weird things going on inside my stomach. It is like it doesn't know whether to be scared or excited. If I even think about what Dad and Mrs Ratcliffe will say if we don't turn up for school on Monday, I think my stomach might explode. So, I try to think about what Lottie will say when she finds out that I've run away to protest about the SATs. We may even get a blue plaque on our house, like she said. And if we do, we can't sell it, so maybe Mum and Dad will stay together.

'Thursday,' I whisper to Mum. 'We'll go home on Thursday.'

BEFORE

12

KAZ

I wake up at six thirty. I no longer have a job to go to on a Saturday morning, but you try telling my body-clock that. I am obviously primed to be making pots of tea and fry-ups at this time, whether I am needed to make them or not.

I had the nightmare again. The second night in a row. Mam stands in front of me, brandishing an iron. Her hair is black and white like Cruella de Vil. Terry is standing behind me crying, screaming for his mam. And she just stands there, pouring lager down her neck while the pan on the cooker behind her bubbles over. And as the water lands on the kitchen tiles, it spells out the word 'useless'.

I open my eyes wide, determined to get the images out of my head, and swing my legs out of bed. I may as well get up and make a brew for me, even if there's no one else to cater for. The flat feels incredibly empty without Terry. At least if

I still worked at the café it would take my mind off him a bit. Here, the emptiness just reminds me that we are a man overboard. There's no lifebelt either. I have no bloody idea how to rescue him. All I can do is try to keep my head above water in the hope that if he does surface, he'll still have a home to come back to. Because I am up shit creek without a twig, let alone a paddle.

I have a shower, being even quicker than usual, as I'm aware that it really is money down the drain. Money that I don't have. As if to illustrate this, the hairdryer cuts out only a few seconds after I turn it on. I go to the tin on the windowsill to get some pound coins for the meter. There are only six left. I think I've got a couple in my purse but that is it. I put three pounds in and give my hair another quick blast before plaiting it while still damp.

When I get downstairs, I take the last piece of bread from the bag, put the dial on the toaster to one and watch as it pops up barely having turned colour; what our Terry would call 'warm bread'. I take the spread from the fridge and put the thinnest possible covering on. There's no prospect of 'jam tomorrow' either. Not unless I get myself a job, and that's not going to be easy at my age and without any references. Five years I'd worked at that poxy place. The café I worked at before has long since shut and I've no idea how to get in touch with the bloke who owned it, even if he is still alive.

'You'll need to put together a CV with career history and full references.' That's what Denise at the job centre said. Like I've ever had a 'career' or a CV in my life. Silly cow. I'm going to have to do what I've always done: knock on doors, ask around, check for cards in windows, all the things people did before the internet.

I sit down at the kitchen table to eat my toast. About the only thing to be thankful for is that at least where Terry is, he will be getting properly fed.

When I've finished and washed up the pots, I rummage in the back of one of the kitchen drawers, trying to find a decent pen and the Post-it notes that I know are in there somewhere. Terry got them once. Something to do with making it easier to find the episodes of *Stars in Their Eyes* he wanted to watch.

When I find them, I sit back down at the kitchen table to write them. Just my name, phone number and 'Hard worker. Forty years experience in catering,' written on each one. It may not be as flashy as a business card but at least it'll be harder to lose, what with being neon-yellow and that.

The first café I go to in town has that familiar morning smell of bacon, coffee and stale breath. I approach the young woman behind the counter.

'Hello, pet. I'm on the lookout for any jobs going. Don't suppose you've got owt, have you?'

She shakes her head. 'Sorry, no. We've all been here a while and no one's leaving.'

'Thought as much. Can you pass this on to your boss, love? Just in case anything comes up in future.'

I hand her the Post-it note, hoping she's not going to laugh out loud at me.

'Yeah, OK,' she says, looking around for somewhere to put it, and sticks it on the fridge behind her. I may not get a job by the end of the day, but at least I'll give the fridge magnets a run for their money.

Seventeen cafés, I go to. Each one giving me the same response. Nothing doing. As I leave the last one on my list in the town centre, I see the McDonald's across the road. I could try there. I'm not too proud to serve burgers to teenagers. I cross over and go in. They have those screens now where you can order and everyone over fifty has to get a little kid to do it for them.

There's a long queue, so I look around for someone who works there and spot a young lad in uniform clearing a table. I go up to him.

'Hello, pet,' I say. 'I'm asking around about any jobs going. Is there a manager here I can speak to?'

'She's in the back on the phone,' he says. 'But I'm her deputy.'

'Oh, right,' I say, trying not to sound surprised. 'Would you be able to pass this on to her?'

I hold out the Post-it note. He looks down and reads it, a frown gathering across his face.

'What's this?' he says.

'Just my contact details, in case any jobs come up.'

He shakes his head and starts laughing. 'Nah,' he says, 'You have to apply online. All the jobs are on the website. You just attach your CV to the submission form.'

I stand there, not knowing what to say in response. He's

young enough to be my grandson and he's laughing at me like I'm some relic from the past, which I am, I suppose.

'Right. I'll, er, do that then, thanks,' I say, putting the Post-it note back into my bag. He looks at me and I see pity in his eyes. He'll be telling the others about it when I've gone, I know that. I turn and hurry away as quickly as I can, so I don't hear the laughter.

It is not like doing a normal hospital visit when you go to a psychiatric unit. We are not dealing with broken bones and minor operations and the like. You can't bandage broken brains. You can't say things like, 'the doctor says they'll have you up and about in no time'. Which is why all the visitors tend to look like me: empty-handed, serious faces and a complete lack of hope in their eyes.

When I sign in at Nightingale reception, the woman behind the desk says the doctor treating Terry would like to have a word with me. I'm not sure whether this is a good or bad thing, but at least I'll have the chance to ask some of the questions I have.

She points me down the corridor to a couple of seats outside a room and I wait there for a few minutes until a young man comes out. Not as young as the lad in McDonald's, which is something. Probably in his thirties, which is still young enough.

'Miss Allen?' he asks, holding out his hand and smiling.

'Kaz,' I reply, standing up and shaking it.

'I'm Doctor Khalil. Please come in and take a seat.'

I follow him into his office and sit down.

'I've carried out the detailed mental health assessment that was requested for your brother. I'll be preparing a full written assessment, which will be sent to all those involved, but I just wanted to let you know that I will be referencing a range of positive and negative symptoms of his schizophrenia and the fact that he has been suffering from psychotic episodes and auditory hallucinations.'

I nod. He's not telling me anything I don't already know but at least they are going to hear it from a doctor. That is the important thing.

'It's because he were made to work,' I say. 'He were all right before, but ever since he were found fit for work, he's been going downhill. Having to work in public toilets pushed him over edge. I told them it would, but they wouldn't listen.'

He nods. He has sympathetic eyes.

'Well, hopefully my report will help with his case.'

'Are you going to say that they shouldn't charge him?'

'That's not for me to tell them but I will certainly be making it clear that, in my view, your brother's schizophrenia and psychotic episodes caused him to behave as he did on the day in question.'

'Good. Thank you,' I say. 'I'm just relieved he stopped talking to Matthew Kelly long enough to speak to you,'

Dr Khalil smiles. 'I also wanted to let you know that I am proposing we start him on antipsychotic medication today.'

I shrug. 'That's what they always do,' I reply.

'I do appreciate that he has been able to function without

them for some years now, but due to the escalation of his condition, it really is the only way forward.'

'OK,' I say. 'He won't be happy about it, mind.'

'I know,' Dr Khalil replies, 'we've already had that conversation.'

'How long, do you reckon? Before he's well enough to come home.'

'I imagine it will be several months, I'm afraid.'

I sigh and look down at my hands.

'What may be quicker is if we manage to get him into supported housing in a therapeutic community.'

'What's that, when it's at home?'

'A sort of halfway house. He'd have his own room in a house where mental health professionals are on hand to support him.'

'We couldn't afford owt like that,' I say.

'They are mainly NHS or local authority-funded places, although vacancies don't come up that often and funding is very tight at the moment. But I could make an enquiry, if you like?'

'No. Don't worry, I'll look after him mesen,' I say. 'It's what I've always done, he's always better when he's at home.'

Dr Khalil looks at me and nods.

'It must be tough for you,' he continues, 'Caring for your brother on your own. Do you get any support?'

I feel my skin bristle. He thinks I can't cope, that I'm not up to it. That's what all of this is about. He thinks it's my fault Terry's ended up in this state.

'No,' I say. 'I've always managed fine, thank you. We're a

team, me and our Terry. We don't need anyone else sticking their nose in where they're not wanted.'

'I wasn't suggesting – '

'Good. And I'm just making it clear that he don't need any fancy place to go to when he's got family to look after him at home.'

I stand up. Dr Khalil does the same. I wonder if he's going to be laughing at me too, once I've left. Stupid Kaz who can't even look after her brother properly. Who can't stop bad things happening to him. Because she's such a fucking useless waste of space.

I stop for a minute in the corridor outside and try to compose myself. My heart is still beating ten to the dozen and I don't want Terry to see me like this. I want one of us, at least, to be on an even keel.

I knock on Terry's door before I go in.

'Hello, love,' I say. 'Only me.'

'Have you brought my torch?' he asks.

'No, they said not to. There's only certain things we can bring in.'

'They don't want us seeing what it's like in here,' he says.

'You've got a nice room, Terry. It's very clean too.'

'They're going to put me on medication.'

'I know. I just spoke to that Doctor Khalil.'

'They want to keep me quiet, see. They know I'm going to blow whistle on them. Tell everyone that this place is infested and then they'll get shut down.'

I walk over to Terry and put my hand on his shoulder.

'You're not well, Terry. Doctor Khalil is trying to help you. He's writing to police to say what happened weren't your fault. He's on your side.'

'Matthew says girls were screaming at rats, not me.'

I look up at the ceiling and try to count to ten. He does my head in when he's like this. But I also know that when he's better and realises what he did, he will beat himself up about it so badly that he will nearly make himself ill again. I wish there was some place in between those extremes but there's not. Not with Terry.

'Just remember they are trying to help you,' I say. 'So don't give nurses any hassle about taking tablets and don't pretend to take them and not swallow. Sooner you get better, sooner you can come home.'

Terry sits there and says nothing.

'You do want to come home, don't you, Terry? You know you can tell me if you're not happy living with me. If you think someone else could make a better job of it. I won't be offended, like.'

Terry looks up at me. 'Will you bring my torch tomorrow?' he asks.

I sit in the kitchen later, staring into my pot of chicken noodles. I found it at the back of the cupboard. It's out of date but I'm not fussed. I don't really see how dried stuff can go off and I've certainly never heard of anyone getting food poisoning from a Pot Noodle.

It's still bothering me, what Doctor Khalil said. To be fair, I don't really know what I'm doing. All I know is what doctors have told me over the years and what I've learnt from the books I've borrowed from the library. I muddle by as best I can, but maybe I have got it all wrong. Maybe if he was being looked after properly, none of this would have happened. I'd hate to think that. That I'd let him down so badly again.

Perhaps Terry would be better in a place like the one Doctor Khalil was talking about. Truth is, if they released Terry tomorrow, I couldn't have him back here. Two tins of beans, half a packet of crackers and two Cup-a-Soups are not going to last forever. We've never been in a position to put stuff by for a rainy day and now I'm paying for it. Fucking Old Mother Hubbard I am.

I wouldn't mind if having no food was all I had to deal with, but the rent is due and I've got nothing to pay it with. I've never missed a payment before. Always prided myself on it. Never been in debt, either. That's the good thing about not having a credit card. But now I need money quickly and I haven't got any. I'd sell my body if anyone would have it but I'm aware I'm well past my sell-by date. If I had one of those cards they used to put in phone boxes it would be 'Lard arse with a face like a wet dishcloth'. Not exactly one to bring in the punters.

I finish off my chicken noodles and start walking around the flat. I always used to joke that if burglars broke in here, they'd be bloody disappointed. No jewellery, no cash, no computers, no fancy gadgets. I don't suppose you'd get much for a crappy little telly and video player these days. Not when they've all got these massive smart TVs. And anyway, they're pretty much all Terry's got. I couldn't do that to him. I'd rather starve than sell his telly.

The ache of missing him hits again. I sit down on the sofa and turn the TV on. Press play on the video. Matthew is talking to a woman who is going to be Shirley Bassey. Only 'Hey Big Spender' is so far wide of the mark it's embarrassing. I wonder if the people who go on the show don't realise either that they are being laughed at. And that they are no good at the one thing they are supposed to be doing.

I go to bed early, to save electricity, as much as anything else. I know that if I am able to get to sleep at any point, she will be there waiting for me. Cruella de Vil. Only this time I will look in the mirror and see that I have black and white plaits. And I can be every bit as cruel as she can.

AFTER

11

FINN

I lie awake thinking about how Mum used to bring me a 'little something' on my birthday eve, because she knew I always found it hard to get to sleep. It was usually a book and she'd read it to me and do all the voices and she also used to make a photo book of all the things we'd done together the year before and talk about what I'd like to do the next year.

There is no 'little something' this year and no photo book. I don't think I have ever missed her so much. She would make everything better right now. She would stop the bad things happening and tell me about lots of good things to look forward to. And it's all my own stupid fault that she's not here. Everyone tries to be nice about it but that's the truth. I spoiled everything. She wouldn't have done what she did if it wasn't for me. And if I had kept quiet, none of this would have happened.

I sigh and turn over. I don't think I have ever not looked forward to a birthday so much. I don't even want to be eleven, because being eleven means going to my new school and I would like to stay 'between schools' forever. I want to do a sort of Peter Pan thing but instead of going to Neverland, I would just like to go to garden club with Kaz. Garden club suits me much more than school. Mainly because there are no other kids there.

Dad did ask me if I wanted a party. I think he meant a party like other kids have, where they go to Laser Quest and zap each other, or whatever they do at places like that (I don't know because no one has ever invited me to one of those sort of parties and if they did I wouldn't go anyway, because I am pretty sure I would hate it and they would only have invited me so that everyone could zap me and make fun of me). He seemed to have forgotten that I don't have any friends apart from Lottie. For the whole of primary school, the best thing about my birthday being on the last day of August was that none of the other kids knew when it was and I didn't have to take apricot, orange and bran muffins in for them and watch them all pull faces and throw them in the bin, and I didn't have to invite them to my parties when I knew that none of them would have come. My parties were not real parties anyway, they were just Lottie coming to my house for a birthday tea.

Anyway, I told Dad that I didn't want a proper party but would like to have Lottie, Kaz and Barry round for a birthday tea and to do a grand opening of the garden at the same time.

He seemed to be quite happy with that, probably because I don't think he'd be very good at organising one of those other sorts of parties. I really wanted to invite Alan Titchmarsh to the grand opening, but I knew he must be very busy in the garden at this time of year, so I didn't bother in the end. Instead of counting sheep, I try counting different varieties of roses.

When I wake up, the first thing I do is check my watch because I was born at seven fifty-nine in the morning and Mum said it was therefore not officially my birthday until eight o'clock. It is eight forty-seven, so I am eleven years old. I don't feel any different. I certainly don't feel happy or excited. I feel a bit numb, to be honest. I get up and put my dressing gown and slippers on and go downstairs.

'Hey,' says Dad as I enter the kitchen, 'here comes the birthday boy.'

I do a little smile and he comes over and gives me a hug. I find myself hanging on to him for quite a long time.

'You OK?' he asks when I finally let go.

'It feels weird without her,' I say.

'I know,' he replies. He goes over to the kitchen table and picks up a present from the table and hands it to me.

'Here you go,' he says. 'Happy Birthday.'

'Thank you.'

I have no idea what it is. Mum always seemed to work out what I wanted, even though she never asked me directly. She just kind of knew. I am not sure Dad is going to be so good at birthdays.

I open one end of the parcel and slide out the box inside. It is a mobile phone. A proper smartphone, like the kids at school have got.

'It's an iPhone 6S,' says Dad. 'It's still a good phone even though it's not the latest model. I figured now you're starting big school, it was time we got you one.'

'He says 'we' like he is talking about him and Mum. He is not though. It is just him who has got me this. I don't know if Mum would have agreed to it. She always used to say I couldn't have one until I was thirteen. If she was here, there would have been a big argument about it and I don't know who would have won, which is why I am all mixed up inside. I am pleased to have one, but it feels kind of wrong and like we are going behind Mum's back.

'Thanks,' I say.

'You did want one, didn't you?'

'Yeah.'

'Did you want a different model?'

'No, this is great, thanks. It's just . . . you know.'

Dad looks down. We both go quiet for a moment.

'I know it's tough for you today,' says Dad, eventually. 'But we've got to try to move on together. Me and you. We have to find our own way to do things.'

I nod, because I don't know what to say.

'Right,' says Dad. 'I'll get a birthday breakfast sorted. Are pancakes OK?'

'Yeah,' I reply. Hating that he has to ask me about everything now and doesn't understand that it's just sausages I don't want.

The party and grand opening is at six o'clock, so that Kaz and Barry can get here after work. I have opened my cards and put them up on the window ledge. I have never had one with Dad's writing on before. He has very neat handwriting, not like Mum's at all. Or mine.

I am in the kitchen, helping cut the carrot sticks for the hummus, when the doorbell rings. I hurry to the front door and open it. Alan Titchmarsh is standing there in a posh suit and bow tie. Not the real Alan Titchmarsh, but a cardboard cut-out of him. I don't know what to do for a moment; whether I should say anything or invite him in. Then Lottie's head pops out from round the corner.

'Surprise,' she says. 'Sorry we couldn't get the real one, but we hope he'll do.'

'Thank you,' I say. 'I can't believe you've got me Alan Titchmarsh.'

'Happy Birthday, Finn,' says Rachel, sticking her head out from the other side. She steps forward and gives me a big hug on the doorstep.

Lottie gives me a hug too. She is the only girl who I would let do that. 'Finally made it to eleven, then,' says Lottie. 'What took you so long?'

I smile back at her. Lottie can get away with being cheeky to me because she is my best friend.

Dad appears behind me. 'Hi, Lottie, Rachel. Come in. Oh, I see you've brought a friend,' he says, looking at Alan.

'Isn't he great?' I say, smiling.

'Yeah,' says Dad, looking at me with a weird expression on his face, as if I'm a member of an alien race or something, which I suppose I am to him.

'First time in years I've brought a plus-one,' says Rachel, 'but at least he won't drink too much or tell inappropriate jokes.'

Dad laughs as Lottie and Rachel follow him inside. I pick Alan up and carry him through to the kitchen.

'I'll put him in here for now,' I say. 'And then I'll bring him outside to do the grand opening.'

Dad is getting the drinks when the doorbell goes again.

I open the door to find Kaz standing there holding a bin bag. Barry is standing next to her. They both have big smiles on their faces. They remind me of a picture of a jolly farmer and his wife that was in one of my old nursery rhyme books. But I don't tell Kaz that, in case it's not a very nice thing to say.

'Happy Birthday, love,' she says, putting the bin bag down for a second to give me a hug. The sort of hug Mum would have given me if she'd been here.

'Tricky day?' asks Kaz, when she finally lets go.

I nod.

'Well, we've got summat for you here, but we'd best go through to garden to open it.'

'Happy Birthday young man,' says Barry, patting my shoulder as he steps inside.

'Thank you,' I reply. 'And thanks for all your plants. I should probably put a sign up saying my garden has been sponsored by you, like they say that *Love Your Garden* has been sponsored by the cruise people.'

Barry smiles. 'No need for that. Just happy to have been able to help. It's not often you see a young fella like you who's into gardening.'

'I know,' I say. 'It's one of the things that makes me weird.'

We go through to the kitchen, where Lottie is standing next to Alan Titchmarsh.

Barry bursts out laughing. 'Wow, I feel underdressed now,' he says, looking at Alan. 'I didn't know it were a posh do.'

'Lottie brought him for me,' I say. 'So he did come for the opening after all.'

'That's cracking, that is,' says Kaz. 'I didn't know our Finn were so well connected.'

I don't know if she realises it, but Kaz has just called me 'our Finn', like she calls Terry 'our Terry'. I think this must mean that we are sort of family now.

Lottie smiles back at her and Rachel goes over to introduce herself to Kaz.

'Thanks so much for all your plants,' Dad says to Barry. 'They've made such a difference.'

'He's very welcome,' Barry replies. 'And thanks for inviting me. It's not often I get asked to parties at my age. Especially not ones Alan Titchmarsh goes to.'

Kaz turns round and catches me looking at the bin bag, which she is still holding.

'Oh, we were on our way out to garden to open this, weren't we, Finn?'

I nod, pick up Alan and lead the way out. When we get to the lawn, Kaz hands me the bin bag.

'Here you go, then,' she says. 'Sorry it didn't come gift-wrapped.'

I open it up and look down into the bag. I know what it is straight away, but I lift it out just to be sure.

'It's an Alan Titchmarsh,' I say, holding up the rose bush. 'Thank you,' I say, putting it down and throwing my arms round Kaz.

'You're welcome, pet. You wait eleven years for Alan Titchmarsh and two come along at once.'

We are all still laughing when Dad comes out to join us, holding a tray of drinks.

'What have we got here, then?' he asks.

'It's an Alan Titchmarsh rose,' I say. 'Just like they've got at Castle Howard.'

Dad looks at me. I have a feeling he is thinking that it's not only Mum who does better birthdays than him, but Kaz and Lottie too.

'Fantastic,' he says. 'That'll just about finish off your garden.'

'I should hope so,' says Kaz. 'I don't think there's room for owt more.'

I look around. There are four little separate rose gardens, just like they have at Castle Howard. And a rock garden and a woodland area, which will look nice next spring. Kaz got me a staff discount on an archway from the garden centre, although it did mean we only had enough left over for a bird bath, rather than a proper water feature.

'You've done a great job with it, Finn,' says Barry. 'Are you going to say a few words, declare it open, like?'

I look at Kaz and Lottie and try not to think about the person who isn't here.

'I'd like to thank Kaz for doing the garden club with me and Barry for giving me lots of the plants, and Lottie, for bringing Alan Titchmarsh, who is now going to show you around.'

I pick up Alan and we lead the way down the garden. Everyone says nice things and smiles a lot, and I wish that the garden club didn't ever have to end. But as much as I try not to think about starting my new school on Monday, it is like a big, black cloud hanging over me and stopping the sun getting through to my garden.

I have a tummy ache when I wake up on Monday morning. That is before I open my eyes and see my uniform hanging up on the front of the wardrobe. It is a stupid uniform: grey blazer with a crest on the lapel and a burgundy and white striped shirt and burgundy tie with little crests all over it.

I hate it so much and I haven't even worn it yet. I wish Mum had won the school argument. I wish I was still sitting in the school tent with her. That was the best school ever. That's the school I want to go to, not this one.

I sit up in bed. Cardboard Alan Titchmarsh is in the other corner of the room, still looking very cheery. I would much rather stay home with him, but I suppose that isn't an option.

I get up and go to the toilet. I sit there for a long time while the world falls out of my bottom. I hear Dad call out from the landing. I tell him I'll be down in a minute. I don't say anything about my tummy ache.

When I go downstairs, I see my school bag packed and waiting for me. I want to throw it out of the window. I didn't need a school bag when we were camping. I didn't need a maths set with a compass and protractor. I didn't need any of that stuff and I don't want it now.

My toast is ready for me on the kitchen table. Dad has put Marmite on it without even asking me. I think this is because he hasn't got time for me to decide what I want.

'Morning, Finn. All set?'

I shrug and nibble at the edges of my toast and drink my orange juice.

'Come on,' says Dad, pointing at my plate, 'you need to have a bit more than that. You've got a long day ahead.'

He has talked to me all about this. How he has signed me up for extracurricular clubs after school and the bus won't get me home until quarter to five, when he will be waiting for me, because he has changed his hours to eight till four so he can get back from Leeds in time. He said it like I should be grateful. I felt like telling him that I didn't want any of this. It was his stupid idea to send me there. I didn't, though. I didn't say anything.

He is looking at me now and I know he is trying to work out what to say to try to make me feel better.

'What you've got to remember, Finn, is this is a new school.

The chance for you to make a fresh start. I know you don't want to go but I think it will be much better than your old school. That's why we chose it for you.'

'Mum didn't choose it,' I say. 'She didn't want me to go to this stupid school and you argued about it and you made her cry.'

Dad stares at me. I don't think he expected that. I don't think he even realised I'd overheard.

'Finn, it wasn't like that. Your mum was worried about you, that's all.'

'She didn't want me to go there. She had a pretend smile on when you told me, so don't make out she liked it, because I know she didn't.'

I push the chair back with my knees and run upstairs. I brush my teeth hard. So hard, my gums start to bleed, and I have to rinse my mouth out because I hate the taste of blood. I take my uniform down and put it on, trying not to look at it. The tie is a proper one and I still can't manage to do it on my own, even though Dad has shown me lots of times. I end up taking it downstairs and throwing it at him.

He doesn't say a word. Just picks it up, ties it round my neck and pulls the knot tight.

'There,' he says. 'You'll get used to it.'

That's what he says about everything and he's wrong, because I won't. You never get used to bad things. You just don't complain about them so much.

Dad waits at the bus stop with me, even though I don't really want him to. We don't say anything until the moment the bus pulls up and then he turns to me, squeezes my shoulder and says, 'It'll be fine, Finn. Try not to worry.'

I know as soon as I get to school that it is not going to be fine. It is a different school in a different building in a different town with different kids but in so many other ways it is still the same. It is a school where I don't look right or feel right, and other kids stare at me the moment I walk through the gate. Whatever it is that is wrong with me, they can sense it. I may as well have a flashing light on my head with a big sign on saying, 'pick on me'.

There are only year sevens and sixth-formers in school on the first day. They are trying to make it easier for us to settle in. It doesn't matter what they do though, I can't see me ever settling in here. I check my letter with my tutor group number on and the name of my tutor for the hundredth time and go and join the right line for Mr Makin.

No one kicks me or calls me names, but they turn to look at me and kind of turn their noses up, like I have a bad smell. I think it is the hair. No one likes red hair. Not unless you're Ron Weasley.

Mr Makin has short brown hair and is wearing tracksuit bottoms and a rugby shirt, which is a bad sign. Very bad indeed. He also has a whistle round his neck. I remember watching *The Sound of Music* with Mum and seeing how Captain von Trapp whistled commands to the children. Neither of us liked him at first. I do not think I am going to like Mr Makin. He raises his hand and waits for silence.

'Good morning, Year Sevens, and welcome to Ickfield. Can anyone tell me what the Latin motto on the school crest, which you are all wearing, translates as?'

A boy in front of me puts up his hand.

'Yes, your name is?'

'Edward Palmer, Sir.'

'Go on, Mr Palmer.'

'Faster, Higher, Stronger.'

'Excellent. A pretty good motto for life, I would say.'

I wouldn't. I'd say it's a pretty rubbish one. Mine would have to be 'slower, lower and weaker'. At least for sports, anyway. If the motto is anything to go by, I am going to hate it here.

Mr Makin walks along our line. He stops next to me.

'And you are?'

'Finn Rook-Carter, Sir,' I say, although it comes out in a squeaky voice and I can hear other kids laughing.

'Welcome, Mr Rook-Carter. You will find in the school rule book that it says boys' hair should not be touching their collar, so I think a trip to the barber is in order at the earliest available opportunity, unless you want to be joining the girls for netball.'

The whole line of kids is laughing at me now. I feel something burning up inside me, like it might explode. I have never been to a barber in my life. Mum has always cut my hair for me and she can't do it now, but I can't tell him that without everyone knowing.

'Yes, Sir,' I mumble.

When he has inspected everyone and told two girls off about wearing make-up and their hair not being tied back, we follow Mr Makin into the building. The entrance hall is dark, and the stone floor feels cold, even through my shoes. There are lots of photos on the walls of groups of children, most of them in sports kits, holding trophies aloft. There is even a trophy cabinet stuffed full of them. I am not the sort of kid who wins trophies. I really have come to the wrong school.

When we get to our classroom, there are rows of old-fashioned desks in twos. Mr Makin asks us to find a seat. Lots of the kids seem to know each other. They all sit down, and I am left standing there, not knowing who to sit next to. There are no spaces next to girls. Only two boys. I pick the one with glasses. He doesn't look very happy about it. I can see a couple of other boys looking at me and whispering. It is starting already. I have only been here five minutes and already I am the weird kid.

We have maths and science. I am quite good at science. Mum said once it was because I have an enquiring mind. But the lesson doesn't seem to be one where you have lots of enquiring to do, just things to read and write down. They have proper science labs and everything, but we don't actually get to use any of those things. I put my hand up to answer a couple of questions about the structure of leaves and photosynthesis. The teacher, who is called Miss Cahill, seems impressed. The boy with glasses I sat next to in tutor group, whose name I now know is Harrison, is not.

'What's wrong with you?' he asks, coming up to me at break time, with two other boys behind him.

'Nothing,' I say, although I know that is not going to stop him.

'You've got girl's hair and now it seems you're a girly swot.'

'I know about plants, that's all.'

The two boys standing with him both laugh.

'Why?'

'Because I like gardening.'

'Then there must be something wrong with you. What's your favourite sport?'

'I don't like sport.'

'Wrong answer,' he says. 'And you're the wrong sort of boy for Ickfield then, aren't you?'

'I like music. I came for the music.'

Harrison laughs. 'Good luck with that, Gay Lord.'

He walks off, the other two boys laughing with him. I so wish Mum had won the school argument.

When I get home that afternoon, I text Lottie on my new phone.

'*I hate it. Even more than I thought I would.*'

'*Are they all Tory posh boys?*' She replies.

'*I think so. There's a boy called Harrison who is dead mean and the PE teacher told me I have to get my hair cut.*'

'*Sexist pig. Don't listen to him. I'd start a petition if I was there with you.*'

I manage a little smile as I read it.

'*What's your school like?*' I ask.

'*It's OK. Missed you though.*'

The little smile turns into a wobbly lip and then proper tears. I put the phone down. I have no idea how I am going to get through this.

AFTER

12

KAZ

I can tell as soon as I arrive that Finn has had a bad week. One look at his face as he opens the door is enough for that. I step inside and he throws his arms round me and bursts into tears.

'Hello, pet. I've missed you so much. Were it that bad?' I ask, stroking his hair. What there is left of it, at any rate. He's had a trip to the barber, by the looks of it. And I can't imagine that was his idea. It is a few moments before he can answer.

'I hate it,' he says. 'I'm the wrong sort of boy for that school.'

'Who says that?'

'Harrison. A boy in my class. He's right, too. I'm not like the other boys. I don't play rugby and football and cricket like them. And I don't do gaming or mess about or tease the girls, which is why they don't want to be my friend.'

'So who have you been sitting with, at lunchtime and that?'

'No one. On the second day, I tried sitting at a table where some older kids were, and they told me to go away, only they said a rude word.'

'And did you tell a teacher?'

'No. Because then they'll call me a grass. That's how it works. Anyway, my tutor group teacher's horrible. He's called Mr Makin and he said my hair looked like a girl's and it was too long for a boy so I needed to get it cut. I didn't want to but Dad said it was best not to get off to a bad start, so he took me to his barber this morning and now I don't even look like me any more.'

He looks up and wipes his snotty nose on his sleeve as Martin comes into the hall.

'Finn, let Kaz come in, love. She probably needs a sit-down after being on her feet all day.'

'He's all right,' I say. 'I'm fine. A brew would be good, mind.'

Martin nods and goes back in the kitchen.

'Have you talked to your dad about how much you hate it?' I ask.

'Yeah but he just says I've got to give it a chance. That it will get better. It won't, though. I've had all this before. It only gets worse.'

I look at him and wipe the tears from his cheeks. I hate seeing him like this. He's done so well all summer and now to have to go through this, it's heartbreaking to watch.

'Have you been able to make any friends?'

'There's a boy called Mustafa and I sit next to him in tutor group now, because he hasn't got any friends either. He's OK but he doesn't talk much. He's only lived in this country a few years. He's never heard of Alan Titchmarsh.'

I pull Finn close to me and give him another hug.

'What we going to do, then?'

'I don't know. I want to leave but Dad won't let me. He says we'll talk again at half-term and it'll probably all seem better by then.'

I shake my head. I'm trying not to show how cross I am at Martin, but it's difficult to hide.

'Would you like me to talk to him for you?'

Finn nods.

'Please don't do noisy arguing, though. I don't like that.'

'I won't,' I say. 'You go upstairs to your room. I'll be up when we're done.'

Finn goes slowly up the stairs, his head bowed. I take a deep breath and go into the kitchen, where Martin has just poured the tea.

'Thanks,' I say, as he hands me a mug. 'Poor lamb. Sounds like he's had a tough week at school.'

'I knew it was going to be hard for him, but I think he'd made up his mind he was going to hate it before he started.'

'He said he never wanted to go there. That it wasn't right school for him.'

Martin sighs. 'He'd struggle at any school, to be honest. That's why we took the decision to send him there. We thought it was better than him being eaten alive at the local comp.'

'We?' I ask.

Martin looks at his feet. 'OK, so Hannah didn't want him to go there. But she didn't want him to go to the comp either. She had this crazy idea about home-educating him.'

'That's what Finn says he wanted.'

'Yeah, well, we can't always have what we want. We couldn't afford for her to give up work to home-educate him, for a start. And anyway, a few half-baked lessons around the kitchen table wouldn't have got him into college or uni. It's a tough world out there. They want people with good qualifications and a proper education.'

I look at Martin. He really doesn't seem to get it.

'But Finn wants to be a gardener.'

'He does now but he'll realise later on that he'll need a proper career to earn him enough to buy a decent house or provide for a family. That's why he needs a good education.'

'Alan Titchmarsh has done OK for himself.'

Martin snorts. 'There are plenty of kids who want to be the next David Beckham, but it doesn't mean they're all going to make it.'

I pick up my mug and walk to the other side of the kitchen.

'Are you happy, Martin?' I ask.

'What kind of question is that?'

'Most important one there is. You've got a degree and a well-paid job and a nice big house. Are you happy?'

Martin's eyes darken. His frown lines deepen.

'That's hardly the right question to ask, in the circumstances, is it?'

'It is, because life isn't about having a well-paid job and a nice house. Believe me, I'd like both of them, but I'm not daft enough to think they're more important than being happy.

ONE MOMENT | 296

And I'm trying to work out why you think things that haven't made you happy are worth making Finn miserable for.'

'He's had a tough week, that's all. He'll get used to it. He'll make friends.'

'Like he did at his last school, you mean?'

Martin spins round to face me. 'That's not fair.'

'It's true, though. He only survived there because of Lottie, from what he's told me. Other kids were horrible to him. And now you're sending him to a school where kids are already picking on him and his teacher's publicly humiliated him and made him have a haircut.'

'You make it sound awful.'

'It is awful for him. And he's got no one fighting his corner this time, like his mum used to.'

'That was uncalled for,' says Martin, raising his voice and jabbing his finger at me. 'You've only known him five minutes and now you're telling me you know better than me how to bring up my own son.'

I can feel the heat coming to the surface. All the things I've held back for so long. It's a struggle to keep my voice low.

'I were with him for toughest hour of his life, remember. I were one who held him when you weren't there because your wife thought it best to take him away from you. And unlike you I am listening to him and hearing his pain, when you refuse to accept it, because that would mean you admitting you were wrong. Wrong about everything.'

I turn and walk out of the kitchen before Martin shouts at me and Finn has to cover his ears. I go straight up to Finn's room. He is lying on his bed, reading a gardening book. He looks up at me.

'He won't listen, will he?'

I sigh and sit down on his bed. 'No, not at moment. I gave him a bit of an ear-bashing, though, in hope it'll get through to him.'

'Is he mad at you now, then?'

'Probably a bit.'

'Will he still give you macaroni cheese for tea?'

'I don't know,' I say with a smile. 'But I hope so, because I'm bloody starving.'

'Maybe he'll just put lots of broccoli on it,' says Finn. 'Dad doesn't like broccoli.'

We go downstairs when Martin calls up that tea is ready. You can hardly see the macaroni cheese on my plate, for the great big pile of broccoli.

My alarm goes off at seven the next morning. I want to get a few hours of cleaning in before I start work, so it's ready for Terry when I bring him home later.

If I'm honest, it doesn't feel like home, yet. I've scrubbed it from top to bottom. Put in a few pot plants, which they gave me at work, and even put up a couple of photos; one of Terry and one of Finn in his garden at the grand opening, which he printed off for me. But I think that, despite all my efforts, the reason it doesn't feel like home is because Terry isn't here. That's what it's waiting for and what I'm waiting for.

As soon as I've had my breakfast, I get to work on the

kitchen. The best thing about the kettle and toaster is that they remind me of Finn. Although they also remind me of the kindness Martin showed me, and I'm feeling a bit bad about having a go at him.

He needed it; I haven't changed my mind about that. But I also know that the truth can hurt and he's probably still smarting from what I said. He was certainly quiet for the rest of Saturday evening. It was pretty stupid too, seeing as he's representing Terry at his appeal tribunal in a week's time. I should have thought of that before I opened my gob. Story of my life.

When I've finished in the kitchen, I go upstairs to Terry's room. I've got him a new duvet and pillow. Not that he's staying over tonight, but I wanted it to look ready. Wanted him to see that he's got a proper place to come home to when he's ready. Doctor Khalil says it won't be long now. They're still reducing his meds, but he's been doing fine on a low dose and he'll be able to come off them completely once he's home. I've told Doctor Khalil that. Because what he needs right now, more than anything, is to come home.

'Are you on a hot date with our Barry tonight?' asks Marje later that afternoon, when she catches me looking at my watch again.

'No, and I told you to behave. Our Terry's coming home. Just for a visit, mind. But if it goes well, he's going to do an overnight next Sunday.'

'So what are you bloody doing still here, then?' asks Marje. 'Go and get him. You've been waiting for this long enough.'

'Thanks, Marje,' I say. 'I'll make time up tomorrow.'

'No, you won't. Now bugger off.'

I smile at her and take off my apron. Five minutes later I'm walking down to the hospital, remembering all the times I went to pick Terry up from school. Always worried in case something had happened to him and he'd got in trouble. And all the times I'd lain awake at home when he was little. Scared that he'd be able to hear Mum and Dad fighting and then, a few years later, scared that Mum would get so drunk she'd wake him up coming upstairs. I can still remember lying awake the night after Mum had died too. Feeling guilty for feeling relieved. And scared stiff that they would take him into care or something. They didn't, though. They said I was old enough to look after him at eighteen. Not realising that I'd already been looking after him for years. And here I was now, still caring for him. Still worrying. But with a slither of hope in my heart this time.

When I get to Terry's room in Kingfisher ward, he's all ready, sitting in his chair, waiting.

'Hello, pet. You all set?' I ask.

He nods. 'Bit nervous. I haven't been out since, you know.'

'You'll be fine,' I say. 'That was your illness and you're a lot better now. Doctor Khalil said so. He wouldn't let you out if he thought you weren't well enough.'

'It's weird because it's a new place, too. It doesn't really feel like going home.'

'I know. It'll be fine, once you're there, though. Once you've seen your things.'

'Is there owt left from old place?'

'Only your TV and video and all your tapes.'

'Who lives there now? In our old place, I mean.'

'I don't know, love. I haven't been back. We've got a new home now. A fresh start and all that.'

Terry stands up and picks up his carrier bag.

'Shall we make a move then?'

'Yeah,' he says, as he follows me out of the room.

It is strange seeing Terry standing in the kitchen, looking around the home he has never seen before.

'You've got a new kettle and toaster,' he says.

'Yeah, Martin gave them to me when I moved in. You know, chappie I told you about who's going to represent you at appeal.'

'Finn's dad,' he says.

'That's right,' I say, pleased that he has actually been listening while I've been chatting away on visits.

'He sounds nice, that Finn.'

'He is. You'd like him a lot. I'm sure you'll get to meet him soon.'

'What's this?' Terry asks, pointing to a flyer I have stuck to the fridge.

'Oh, it's an art class that's starting next week. I picked it up in library, thought I might go, although I'm not sure I'll be able to fit it in.'

'You should go,' says Terry. 'You were always right good at art. And I'll be fine. You don't have to worry about me.'

I smile at him. It's not true, of course. But it's so good to hear him actually thinking about other people again.

'Thanks,' I say. 'I might just give it a whirl.'

Terry follows me upstairs into his bedroom and looks around.

'It's big,' he says. 'Bigger than my last room.'

'Yeah. And it's nice and bright.'

When we get back down to the living room, Terry goes straight over to the TV. He looks in the cardboard box to check that all his tapes are there.

He turns and smiles at me. 'Put kettle on then, Sis. We've got time for a couple of episodes.'

I toddle off into the kitchen. When I come back with the teas, he's watching the crappy Freddie Mercury and it's almost like he's never been away.

BEFORE

13

FINN

I lie next to Mum in the tent on Sunday night. I am not sure if she is asleep or is just pretending like me. My legs are tired from the long walk we had earlier, and my tummy is still full after the veggie sausages and baked beans we cooked for tea. But all I can think about now is Dad. He will be worried that we haven't come home and has probably realised that he will be going to the meeting with Mrs Ratcliffe on his own in the morning. That's if he still goes. I expect he will cancel it because there's no point going if I'm not going to be there. And however angry he is about it now, he's going to be even angrier by Thursday when we go home.

I can't help thinking this is all my fault. If I hadn't been sick, Mum might not have thought of taking me away on a camping trip. I wonder what the other kids will say at school tomorrow when I don't turn up. They'll probably think I'm pretending to be ill just to get out of the exams. Lottie will guess, though. I'm pretty sure she'll work out that it's actually a big protest.

If I had a mobile, I could text her and let her know what was happening. I think she'd be very excited. But then maybe she'd get in trouble for not telling on me, so it's probably best that I haven't got one. I understand why Mum didn't bring her mobile now. Dad would have rung one hundred times and we would have ended up going back.

I try to join up the stars into constellations in my head. I still have them kind of imprinted on my eyes, because I was staring at them for so long earlier. It's a very clear night. I wonder if Dad looked out at the stars tonight. Or whether he was too busy being angry to look.

When I wake up in the morning, I have a tummy ache. At first I think it's because I have my SATs today, but then I open my eyes and remember that I am in a tent and that I have a tummy ache because I am not doing my SATs today.

'Morning, sweetheart,' says Mum. She is awake and sitting up in her sleeping bag next to me.

'What time is it?' I ask.

'Just gone seven,' she replies.

I nod. There is still time to go home. We could pack up and leave now and if we got a taxi we could get to school on time. Maybe everything would be OK if we did that. Maybe it would not be as bad as I think.

'Hey, come here,' says Mum as I start to cry. I let her put

her arms round me and rock me to and fro, like she used to do when I was little.

'I'm going to get into really big trouble, aren't I?' I say, my voice cracking.

'No, you won't,' she replies. 'If anyone's going to be in trouble, it will be me. But remember that all we're doing is taking four days' holiday in term time. Olivia Worthington did that when she went to the Maldives, didn't she?'

'Yes, but she asked them first and it wasn't in SATs week. And she brought Mrs Ratcliffe a very expensive present back.'

'Well, you could always take her a tent peg.' Mum is smiling. She is trying to be funny, I know that. It's just that I don't feel like laughing.

'Listen,' continues Mum. 'I'm not going to let you get in trouble for this, OK? I will accept full responsibility. But if you want to go to school today, I'll take you now, there's still time. I don't want you to do anything you're not happy with.'

I hesitate before replying. There's now a tug-of-war going on inside me, instead of in the playground.

'I don't want to go to school but I feel really bad about not being there when I should be and I can't stop thinking about how cross Dad and Mrs Ratcliffe will be.'

'OK,' says Mum, pulling me in closer to her. 'It's nice that you care about other people's feelings, but this is about you and doing what's right for you, not what everyone else wants you to do.'

I nod and wipe my nose on my sleeping bag.

'Let's try to take our minds off it and go for a lovely walk this morning and how about we get you an ice-cream this afternoon?'

I look up at her. I only usually have ice-creams when I am on holiday, but I suppose I am on holiday now, in a funny kind of way.

'Where will we get it from?' I ask.

'There's a shop in the village. We need to get some more food too, we're running low already.'

'Won't they know I'm supposed to be at school?'

'We'll go around three thirty. No one will notice you.'

'OK,' I say, managing a little smile.

My tummy ache has gone by the time we walk into the village later, which is a bit of luck as I don't think Mum would let me have an ice-cream if I still had one. I had too much ice-cream at a party in Pizza Hut once and I was sick in the car park outside and Mum said my tummy wasn't used to rich food like that.

I am still trying to work out which ice-cream to go for. I have had Magnums before, and I like the white ones best, but Soleros are nice too and I like cones with scoops of ice-cream, but I think you only get them at the seaside and I can never decide what flavour to have anyway.

It's definitely hot enough for an ice-cream. Mum asked me to put my legionnaire's hat on and she's got her sun hat and shades on and it really does look and feel like the summer holidays. Which is good, because it helps to take my mind off the fact that it isn't, and I should be in school.

When we get to the shop, I look straight away to see what

sort of ice-creams they have. It is quite a small freezer, but they have Magnums and Soleros, so Mum leaves me to decide while she gets a basket and goes and gets the shopping we need. The song about the dark days that the floaty lady with long red hair sings is playing on the radio and I look up and see Mum dancing a little bit in the tins aisle and it makes me smile, which is a good thing. When the floaty lady finishes the jingle for BBC Radio Leeds comes on. Dad listens to that station sometimes in the car, which is why I know it, but Mum doesn't usually have it on at home because she says 6 Music is better.

A man on the radio says it is four o'clock and starts reading the news and my hands start to feel a bit sweaty because I know school has finished and I should have been there, so I put my palms on the top of the ice-cream freezer to cool them down. And the next thing I know the man on the radio is saying my name and that police are concerned for my welfare because I was taken from my home by my mother two days ago and I didn't turn up at school today and at first I think I must have just imagined that inside my head but then Mum comes up to me and her eyes are wild and scared and she grabs hold of my arm.

'Finn, we have to go,' she says.

'Did they just say my name on the radio?'

'Ssshhh,' she says, putting her finger to her lips.

'Why are the police concerned about me? How do they even know about me not going to school?'

'Not now, Finn,' Mum whispers. 'We have to go.'

I look down and see that she has put the tins back and is carrying an empty basket.

'But what about my ice-cream?'

'We haven't got time for that.'

'You promised,' I say. My voice comes out all high. I am trying hard not to cry.

She bites her lip. 'Well, just grab one,' she says, putting down the basket.

I slide open the freezer door. I hadn't even decided what I was going to choose. My hand hovers between the Magnums and the Soleros.

'Quickly,' hisses Mum. 'And wait here while I pay for it.'

I pick up a white Magnum and hand it to her. I stand there and watch as she takes it up to the till. There is no one in front of her, so the lady serves her straight away. Her hands are shaking as she hands over the money. As soon as she has the change, she heads for the door, glancing round to beckon me to follow her.

'Why –'

'Ssshhh,' says Mum again. 'Not until we're out of sight. And keep your voice down.'

Her eyes are still crazy, and I don't like the way she is talking to me. I follow her round the corner and down the lane to a quiet spot where no one is about.

'Why were they talking about me on the news?' I ask, my voice more like a squeak.

'I don't know,' says Mum, crouching down and holding my shoulders. 'All I can think is that your father must have gone to the police.'

'But you left the note saying we were going camping. Why would he tell the police?'

'I don't know. I need to phone him,' she says. 'I need to get this whole thing to stop.'

'But you haven't got your mobile,' I say.

'I'll use a phone box. I'll call him at work now. I'll get it sorted, Finn. Don't worry.'

I don't know why she is saying that. The man on the news just said the police are concerned about me and she is still shaking, so it seems fair enough that I should be worried about me, too.

Mum takes my hand and heads back in the direction of the main street.

'Where are we going?' I ask.

'To find a phone box. I'm pretty sure there's one in the main road, on the next corner.'

She is right. There is. I have never been in a phone box before and I want to know how it works. And if it's like a Tardis and much bigger inside than it looks.

'You wait outside, Finn. I'll be as quick as I can.'

'But what if the police come looking for me?'

Mum sighs and shuts her eyes for a second, then seems to decide that the police might come looking for me because she holds the door open and I go inside. It is not like a Tardis at all and is actually even smaller inside than it looks from the outside and it has a funny smell, a bit like the smell on the stairs of car parks.

Mum hands the Magnum to me, takes her purse out and rummages around for some coins. She picks up the phone, pushes some numbers and, when someone answers, asks to speak to Martin Carter, then says 'Hannah'.

I tug her sleeve. 'Can I talk to – '

'Ssshhh,' she says.

I hear Dad's voice next. It is loud and angry even though he is at work and I am listening to him on a phone that is pressed to Mum's ear.

'He's fine,' says Mum, when there is a pause at the other end. 'He's here with me.'

Dad says something on the other end.

'It doesn't matter where we are,' Mum replies. 'I want to know why you've got the police looking for us. We've just heard it on the news on the radio. You knew I was taking him camping, I told you that.'

I can't hear what Dad says, I have to try to work it out by the length of the pauses, the looks on Mum's face and what she says in reply.

'In the note,' she says with a frown.

Mum sighs and rolls her eyes as Dad speaks. 'The one on the windowsill by the door with your name on it.'

A pause.

'Well, it was there. I wouldn't just take him without telling you. What sort of person do you think I am?'

There is a very long pause after that while Dad says a lot of words. Mum is crying now.

'You still had no right to go to the police. This is nothing to do with them. You need to tell them it was a misunderstanding. That he's safe and well.'

Dad shouts the next bit and I can hear every word.

'I'll call the police when you fucking bring him home,' is what he shouts. I start crying too.

'It was making him ill, Martin,' says Mum. 'He was sick the night before we left, do you even know that? I needed to get him out of that situation for his own good. I gave him the choice to come home last night and go to school, but he didn't want to. We need to listen to him, Martin, and you'd stopped listening. There was no other way.'

There is another pause. Dad is talking more quietly this time.

'And do you think telling the police is going to help him at school?' Mum asks. 'Having his name on the news and kids and parents thinking I've run off with him without telling you. Do you think that's going to make things better for him when he goes back?'

Mum seems to be trying to do all her crying in the bits when Dad speaks, so that she can talk when it's her turn.

'I'm not the one who stopped talking, Martin. You're the one who refused to carry on with mediation and started communicating by solicitor's letters, threatening to take him away from me.'

I think that must have been a good thing to say because there is a silence on the other end of the phone and then Dad's voice seems to go quieter.

'Well, you need to promise me that you'll be reasonable when we come home, too,' she says. 'And the first thing you can do is to go to the police and tell them it was all a misunderstanding. When you've done that and I know I can bring him home without them being involved, I will. But you have to get them to call off the search for him first.'

She puts the phone down and hugs me tightly, sobbing into my hair.

'I'm so sorry, Finn. I'm so sorry for all of this.'

I let her hold me while I do my own crying. It sounds like we are crying the same song. My music teacher would say we do very good crying harmonies.

'Why did he call the police?' I ask.

'He says he didn't see my note. He thought I'd run away with you. That we weren't coming back.'

I stare at her, imagining how scared Dad must have been.

'It could have blown down when you shut the door,' I say. 'Your shopping list did that once. It fell behind the shoe rack.'

'Did it?'

'Yes, I found it when I was looking for my trainers and put it back on the windowsill.'

Mum screws her eyes up tight. 'Oh God. How could I have been so stupid?' she says.

'Call him back and tell him,' I say.

'Not now. Hopefully he's calling the police.'

'Later then.'

'Maybe.'

'He'll look for it when he goes home, won't he? And he'll find it and read it and know you weren't lying, and everything will be OK, and I won't be in trouble with the police.'

Mum starts crying again. I suddenly remember the Magnum still in my hand.

'Are you allowed to eat ice-creams in telephone boxes?' I ask.

Mum does a sort of half-cry, half-laugh and brushes the tears from her cheeks.

'Yes, but we'll go outside, back round the corner to that quiet spot.'

I try to open the phone box door, but it is very heavy. Mum squeezes past me and pushes it open with her bum. I follow her back to where we were before and peer into the bushes across the road to see if there are any policemen waiting for us.

I unwrap the Magnum. It is a bit melty but if I eat it quickly, I think it will be OK. It doesn't taste as nice as I remember, though. It doesn't taste of being on holiday. It tastes of tears and shouting and feeling bad inside. I look around for a bin but there isn't one, so I put the stick in my trouser pocket.

'Are we going home now then?' I ask Mum.

She shakes her head and does the biting-her-lip thing again.

'I don't know, Finn,' she says, sitting down on the little wall at the side of the road and putting he head in her hands. 'I've made such a mess of this and I don't know what to do any more.'

'I don't want the police to find us,' I say. 'I don't want to be arrested.'

'You won't be arrested,' she says. 'They just want to know that you're safe.'

'So why don't we go to a police station and show them I am?'

Mum sighs and takes hold of my hand. 'Because right now, they think I took you without telling Dad. They think we've run off for good. And that means I could get in big trouble if I just show up.'

'I don't want you to go to prison,' I say, looking down at my feet.

'I won't,' says Mum, giving me another hug. 'But that's why we need to wait for Dad to tell the police that it's all been a big misunderstanding.'

'So, are we still going to camp out tonight?'

'I don't know yet. But we can't stay where we are. The warden or someone who has seen us might have heard it on the news. We need to go somewhere there are no people around until we know it's all been sorted out and it's safe to go home.'

'Like a proper hideout?'

'Something like that. Let's go back to the campsite. We'll pack all our things away super-quick and try to find somewhere.'

I nod, feeling the full tummy ache again now. I hope if we are caught that I am not sick in the police car because Mum might never let me have an ice-cream again.

BEFORE

14

KAZ

Monday morning arrives and I realise bloody Theresa May was right about one thing – there is no magic money tree. Not outside our front door, at any rate.

I have two crackers for breakfast but by midday my stomach is rumbling so much that I'm worried Terry will notice when I go and see him later. And I don't want him worrying about me on top of everything else. Besides, if the only thing between me and a square meal is swallowing my pride, it's got to be done. It's not like I'm the first to go. Everyone knows someone who's been these days. Kerry in the flat next door goes every week. I saw her coming home with a Marks and Spencer carrier bag full of food and asked how the hell she could afford to shop there. That's when she told me: it was the carrier bag she'd been given at the food bank.

When I arrive at the old community centre where they run

it, there's a small queue outside. Like it's the hottest ticket in town. In a few years' time there'll be three of them in every town and kids won't be able to remember what it was like before we had food banks. Food banks and vape shops.

It's only when I get towards the front of the queue that I wonder if I should have brought any proof of identity. Something to show I am in genuine need – apart from my rumbling tummy that is.

I edge inside the front door into the hall. I came here once for someone's wedding reception when I was in my early twenties, can't remember whose now. One of the girls from my class who got married, like pretty much all of them did apart from me. Terry didn't like it though; it was too noisy for him, so we left after half an hour. There were quite a few dos like that. Gave up bothering in the end. And people gave up asking me.

'Hello, pet, have you been before?' an elderly woman asks me.

'No, love. Do you need any ID or owt?'

'Just your name and address on here,' she says, holding out a clipboard. 'It's so we can keep track of who's been.'

I nod and write my details on the piece of paper, all the time hearing Terry saying not to give them our address because they'd pass it on to MI5.

'Right, if you go over there and see Shirley in blue slacks, she'll sort you out.'

I do as I'm told. I suspect Shirley is a churchgoer; she has that air of organisation and an obvious desire to help, coupled with a faint smell of old hymn books.

'Hello, there, what can we get you today?' she says, like I've arrived at the pick and mix section in Woolies.

'Um, just basics, please. I've not been before, so I don't know what you've got.'

'Let's start with breakfast things, then,' she says, picking up a Waitrose carrier bag from a box. 'We've got some cornflakes, Weetabix or porridge.'

The Weetabix she points to includes a pack that is organic; as if the people who donated it thought we'd not eat anything less. I'd eat bloody dog food if you put it in front of me right now.

'Cornflakes would be great, thanks,' I say, knowing that will taste best with cold milk and I need to have the hob on as little as possible. Shirley adds some long-life milk and a box of teabags. I tell her I don't need coffee and follow her to the next shelves, where there are lots of different packets, pots and tins. I ask for beans, soup and noodles; all things that can be cooked without the need to put the oven on. I spot a packet of Waitrose organic wholewheat lasagne sheets. Presumably donated by the organic Weetabix person, who may well have brought them in the Waitrose carrier bag I am holding. I know they meant well, and beggars can't be choosers and all that, but they really haven't got a fucking clue.

Shirley takes me round the corner to some more tins. I take some peaches; I haven't had peaches for years, and tinned potatoes, peas and carrots.

'What about some biscuits?' asks Shirley. I glance behind me, where a young mum has three little girls in tow, all of them noisily clamouring for things. She looks as if she might burst into tears at any moment.

'No, you're all right, thanks,' I reply. 'Let her have my packet for the little ones.'

Shirley nods and pats me on the hand.

'Is it just yourself at home?' she asks.

'Yeah, for now. Me brother's in hospital at moment.'

'Oh, I'm sorry to hear that. Let's hope he's up and about in no time.'

'Thanks,' I say, even though I know he won't be.

It's only as I'm coming out that I spot a familiar face from the café at the front of the queue.

'Hello Joan, love,' I say.

Her face crinkles into a smile. 'Hello pet, I were so sorry to hear you'd lost your job,' she says.

'Aye, I hope our Danny's still looking after you best he can.'

'He's a good lad, does what he can when he hasn't got that dragon breathing down his neck.'

I manage a smile.

'So how are you keeping, Joan?'

'Oh, you know. Mustn't grumble.'

I reach out and squeeze her hand. It feels even bonier than I remember.

'Take care, love,' I say.

I walk home afterwards with my Waitrose carrier bag of food, wondering how long I can make it last. Don't let the bastards get you down, they say. But that's hard when they're the ones making all the rules.

*

Terry is sitting in his chair when I arrive later. He looks up.

'Have you got my torch?' he asks.

I shake my head. 'Have you taken your meds?'

'Yeah. I don't need them, though. There's nowt wrong with me.'

'You'll get home sooner if you take them, though.'

He shrugs.

'I won't have to go back to work, will I?'

'No,' I reply. 'Not there, at any rate. They've let you go.'

'Why? Did I do summat wrong?'

I sigh. 'The girl in toilet, Terry. That's why police arrested you.'

'Am I going to go to prison?'

'Hopefully not. Doctor Khalil has told police that it wasn't your fault. That it happened because you're ill.'

'I'm not ill, though. I shouldn't be here.'

'For Christ's sake, Terry,' I say, walking over to the window before I say anything else I might regret.

I gaze out at the garden outside, trying to blink back the tears. I know he won't be like this much longer. The meds tend to work pretty quickly. And the daft thing is that when this Terry has gone, I'll miss him. I always do. And then I'll have the new Terry to contend with. And he's bloody hard work too. Because he'll sleep most of the time and put on weight and get down because of it and I'll have to deal with all of that. And the truth is that I am tired of all of this. More than fifty years of looking after Terry; trying to protect him from all the shit life's thrown at him. His dad, then his mum;

the people who were supposed to take care of him but who actually caused him harm. And I'm not sure how much longer I can go on doing this, or even whether I should ever have been allowed to try. Because I am clearly not up to it. Mam was right all along.

I ask to see Dr Khalil afterwards. He's with a patient, so I have to wait outside his office for a bit. When he arrives, he smiles and shows me in. If I did piss him off last time, he's very good at not showing it.

'I'm sorry if I were a bit short with you before,' I say. 'I were upset about Terry and I can be a bit of an idiot like that sometimes.'

'Please, no need to apologise. I was simply concerned about you. It's an enormous strain looking after someone with schizophrenia, and I wondered if you may both benefit from him living in a therapeutic community for a time.'

'I get that. I were going to ask you if you could ask them if there might be a place for him, please.'

Dr Khalil looks down for a moment.

'I'm sorry,' he says. 'I hope you don't mind but I took the opportunity of enquiring, in case you changed your mind. Unfortunately, due to the current funding situation, places are only being funded for patients who don't have any family to look after them.'

I stare at him, trying not to show how disappointed I am. How much I'd been hoping for some help.

'Oh, right. Never mind. Thanks for trying for him.'

I stand up, ready to go.

'Please be assured that we will continue to provide your brother with the best possible care and if we can support you in any way when he's ready to go home.'

'Oh, we'll be fine,' I say, managing a hint of a smile. 'We'll just keep plodding along like we always have done.'

Doctor Khalil nods. 'He's lucky to have you,' he says.

I leave the office without replying because I don't want to tell him how wrong he is.

When I get home, the landlord has been. There is a letter for me on the doormat. He hasn't bothered with an envelope. Clearly, I wasn't worth the expense. It's a final demand for the rent. With a warning that if I don't pay within twenty-four hours, I will be evicted.

I knew it was coming, but seeing it written down like that is hard to take. I slump down onto the floor, with my back against the door. I've got nothing to pay it with. It's as simple as that. It's not as if I can ask the landlord for more time, either. He's a heartless bastard and he's not interested in sob stories. I've known him chuck women with kiddies out on the streets before now. Anyway, what's the point of asking for more time? Father fucking Christmas isn't going to turn up tomorrow with my rent money in an envelope, is he? Even if I did ask for this advance on my Universal Credit, it wouldn't cover it. Not without Terry's money too. And it's going to be three months before we get our full benefit now. I'm not going to a loan shark, either. I've seen what they do to people and I'm not going there. But where does that leave me?

I bang my fist down hard on the floor. I've fucked everything up for Terry. He's not going to have a home to come back to. He really would be better off without me. If he didn't have any family, he could get one of those supported housing places Dr Khalil was talking about. It's only me who's stopping him. I hear Mam's voice again: 'You're good for nowt apart from wiping our Terry's arse.'

Well, I'll show her. I won't let Terry down again. I'll put him first this time. Because he deserves better than me. I didn't stop Dad hurting him, or Mum hurting him. I couldn't stop him being forced to work and getting arrested and sectioned. Without me, he'd be properly looked after. By people who actually know what they're doing and can at least provide him with a roof over his head. Unlike me.

He'll be so much better off without me. He might not realise it at first, but he will later on. This is the best gift I can give him. And I'm going to make sure I don't mess this up, like I've messed everything else up. I look around me, trying to work out the best way of doing this. I can't bear to be here when they come to kick me out. I know that much. I'm not going to give them that satisfaction. I'll give them something to remember instead.

I go through to the bathroom and open the cabinet. I find them in the back corner on the top shelf. Hidden out of sight, where I put them five years ago. Just in case of an emergency. Well, this is an emergency. Although not the sort

I was thinking of at the time. There are ten left in the packet. I hope that's enough. I hope it won't matter that they're out of date.

Perhaps I need alcohol too, just to make sure. Strong stuff. Only unfortunately, Mam didn't leave any of that behind. I suddenly remember the one thing she did leave, though. It's been hidden away for years and is the only thing I've got left of her. But maybe she can finally do some good.

I hurry through to my bedroom and pull open the bottom drawer of the chest. I rummage around in the corner and find it under a jumper, still wrapped in tissue paper. A plain gold wedding ring. Not much to show for twelve years of being beaten black and blue, but there you go. I pick it up and look more closely. It's thin and light. Probably the cheapest thing Dad could get at the time. I can't imagine it will be worth much, but maybe it could still get me enough for what I need.

I can't help thinking Mam would approve. Selling her ring for booze. It's a wonder she didn't do it herself. I steel myself to place it on my ring finger. And as I do so I can see her clearly, standing there in her nightshirt next to the cooker, her dark hair dishevelled and tied back loosely with a white band. A bottle in one hand, the saucepan handle in the other.

Terry is in front of her, playing with his cars on the kitchen floor. I see her stumble, the pan of boiling water still in her hand. She is falling forwards. I try to move, to dart forward and lift him up out of her way, but my limbs are frozen in terror. All I can do is stand there and watch as the saucepan's contents fall on his arm. I hear his scream, a sound that goes straight through me and pierces my heart. Because I was supposed to be looking after him. To be protecting him from her. And I failed him.

I take the ring off. I failed him then, but I will not fail him now. I put it in my pocket and head out of the door.

It's a fifteen-minute walk back into town to the pawnbroker. I don't think I've ever been inside. Terry asked once what it sold, when he walked past it as a kid. I remember telling him then what my father had once told me: that it was 'hope that things would get better'.

The bell rings as I push the door. It's one of those old-fashioned shops that's been here donkey's years. Not one of those bright new chains that have come along, like vultures, now that there are more desperate people to go round.

'Hello, how can I help you?' asks the middle-aged man behind the counter.

'I wonder how much you can give me for this?' I say, passing him Mum's ring.

'To buy or pawn?'

'Buy,' I reply.

He unwraps it carefully, holds it up to the light, looks at it more closely through a magnifying glass, then pops it on the little scales next to him before shaking his head and looking up at me.

'It's only nine carat, I'm afraid. And very thin, which isn't fashionable nowadays. I can maybe go to twenty but no more.'

It's not much, although he has an honest face and I believe him that that's all it's worth. It's enough for what I need, and that's all that matters.

'OK,' I say.

'Is it yours?' he asks.

'No,' I say. 'It belonged to my mother.'

'Always hard to part with something of sentimental value, isn't it? Are you sure you don't want to pawn it?'

I shake my head. 'No, thanks. I won't be needing it where I'm going.'

When I get back to the flat, I start tidying and cleaning. I'm not having anyone saying that I didn't have standards. I may not have been able to pay my rent, but that doesn't mean I'm some lowlife, living in squalor.

A strange sense of relief settles on me as I clean. I haven't got to worry any more. I am past caring. And caring is pretty much all I have ever done.

When I am satisfied that everything is in order, that I have left nothing that will make anyone think badly of me, I put on my shoes, pick up my bag, containing the twenty-pound note, and leave the flat. It is only once I get outside that I realise I haven't even thought about where I am going to buy it from. Not being a drinker, I don't even know where the nearest offie is. The supermarket is too far away, and I don't want to walk along busy roads or be around lots of people anyway. I want to be somewhere quiet. I remember the petrol station on the way out of town towards Sowerby. There won't be many people there and it's a nice walk down by the woods. I turn and set off in that direction.

It is dark by the time I arrive. I cross the forecourt and go in. The lad behind the counter doesn't even look up. It feels wrong to go straight up and ask him for the bottle of vodka I can see there. That is the sort of thing my mother would have done and, more than anything, I don't want to become my mother. I may be choosing the same method of death as her, but it doesn't mean I have to be blatant about it. I go down one of the food aisles and pretend to look at things without really seeing. I think about Terry instead. About how he will take the news. At least the meds will help to take the edge off. He will probably hate me for it, for leaving him like that. He won't understand that it is for his own good. That without me he will get the support he really needs. Because I was never good enough to be his mam. I did my best, but I was a kid too. I needed a mam as much as he did. In the end, I let him down like everyone else did. This is going to be the hardest thing I have ever done but I am doing it for him. Because I know he can have a better life without me. The life he always deserved.

AFTER

13

FINN

I wake up with a tummy ache, as I do pretty much every day now. Dad is still doing the 'it will get better when you settle in and make friends' thing. He wants it to be true, but it doesn't matter how much he wants it, it is not going to happen. If anything, it is getting worse. It's not just Harrison now, although he's still the worst. It's Jacob and Toby, and most of the other boys and two girls called Ava and Sophie, who laugh at what the boys say and egg them on. That's what I have to look forward to every day. That's why I always wake up with a tummy ache.

I get up and go downstairs. Dad and I do our usual thing of not saying much over breakfast. He asks me what lessons I have, and I tell him, and neither of us mention the fact that I hate it or that breakfasts were always much better when Mum was here.

As soon as I arrive at school, it starts. It's like they have been lying in wait for me. I go and sit in the refectory until the bell goes, hoping that they will leave me alone in there. But they don't. Harrison and Toby and Jacob follow me and sit on the table next to me. They don't talk to me, but they talk about me and they do it loud enough that they know I can hear them.

'What we need,' says Harrison, 'is a campaign to get him out of school. He's the wrong sort of boy and we don't want him here. So what we have to do is make his life so bad that he has to leave.'

'Yeah,' says Jacob. 'Let's get him out by Christmas. We can get rid of him that way.'

'We need to get everyone in the class to do it,' says Toby. 'Make it something that they all join in with.'

'Yeah,' says Harrison, looking up and smiling over at me. 'That's what we'll do. Oh, hi Finnona, didn't see you there.'

They throw back their heads and laugh, big silly laughs. I am trying so hard not to cry that I can't actually open my mouth and say anything back. So I sit there and stare at the table and pretend I don't know they were talking about me, but I do and they know I do and everything is horrible and I wish I was back at our garden club with Kaz and my Alan Titchmarsh rose.

By break time, I'm pretty sure that everyone knows. Some of them hold their noses when I walk past. When I go to squeeze past Ava and Sophie to get to my seat they scream.

'Urgh, don't let him touch you, he's got Finn Disease,' says Ava. 'If he touches you, you'll die.'

Some of the other girls start laughing. I miss Lottie. Lottie would have something to say to them. I can't say anything because Mum told me to always be nice to girls. I think she thought other girls were like Lottie, but they're not.

I go and sit next to Mustafa. I wonder if they have told him to be mean to me too, but if they have, he doesn't do or say anything.

'Hi,' he says. 'Are you going to music club after school?'

Mustafa plays the violin. Music club is where I first talked to him.

'Yeah,' I say. 'My ukulele's in my locker. I don't like carrying it about because, you know.'

He nods, like he does know. I think he keeps quiet about his playing, too.

'How long have you been playing?' he asks.

'Four years. My mum got me it for a birthday present.'

He nods. 'Are you going to play it in the Christmas concert?' he asks.

'I don't know,' I say with a shrug. 'It depends if I last that long.'

Mustafa looks at me. 'There are always mean boys,' he says. 'There were mean boys at my last school. They made jokes about where I come from.'

'It's not funny, is it?'

'No,' he says. 'It's not.'

I sit next to Mustafa in science. It is my favourite lesson apart from music and Miss Cahill is nice. I think she is my favourite teacher. About halfway through, she has to leave the class-room because one of the technicians has forgotten to put out something we need for an experiment.

The second after she goes, Harrison turns to me and says, 'You spoil the class.'

He says it in a loud voice, so that everyone can hear.

'We don't want gay boys at Ickfield.'

'I'm not gay,' I say.

'You either like sport, or you're gay.'

'Yeah,' says Jacob. 'So don't deny it, Gay Lord.'

Lots of the other kids laugh. I can feel my face flushing. I stand up. I don't know what I am going to do, but I know I need to stand up. The others start calling out. I can't make out everything they are saying but none of them are nice things. Miss Cahill comes back into the classroom. The kids instantly go silent, leaving me standing there.

'Is everything OK, Finn?' she asks.

I nod and sit back down again.

They surround me the moment I get my ukulele from my locker. They must have been waiting for me. They must have planned it.

'Where you off to, Gay Lord?' says Harrison.

'Music club,' I say.

'What is it you play?'

I don't want to answer but I think that if I don't, he might make me get the ukulele out of its case, and I don't want to do that.

'Ukulele.'

'What the fuck's that?'

'It's like a little guitar,' I say.

'Show me.'

'I haven't got time,' I reply. 'I'll be late for music club.'

'I said, show me.'

He steps closer to me. Jacob and Toby are standing at either side. There is no way I can escape. There are no other kids or teachers around because my locker is in a quiet area, away from the main corridor. I have no choice. Slowly, I unzip the case and get out my ukulele.

The laughter starts straight away.

'Look at that stupid smiley face,' says Harrison. 'That's a little kid's thing.' He grabs it from my hand.

'Give it back,' I say.

'What, and let people think boys at Ickfield are big babies? I don't think so.'

He drops it on the floor.

'Oops, butter fingers,' he says, smirking at me. He lifts up his knee and stands there on one leg with his other foot hovering over it.

'No, please don't,' I say.

'What's the matter? Scared you're going to cry if I break it?'

'My mum got it for me — ' My voice breaks as I say it. Harrison brings his foot down heavily on the ukulele. It makes a horrible splitting, creaking sound and then it is silent. It is dead now. And the music has died with it..

'Well, Mummy's going to have to get you a new one, isn't

she?' They all laugh and walk off together. The tears are pouring down my face. I kneel down on the floor and pick up my ukulele and cradle it in my arms, like it is a dead animal. Mum would cry too if she could see it. I know that.

'And this Harrison did it on purpose?' asks Dad, when I show it to him later.

'Yeah. He's trying to make me leave the school.'

'Why do you say that?'

'Because I heard him say it this morning. He said he was starting a campaign to make me leave school because I'm the wrong sort of boy.'

'What does he mean by that?' asks Dad.

I sigh. I hadn't wanted to tell him, but I am so mad about the ukulele that I am going to, now.

'He calls me Gay Lord. He says I must be gay because I don't like sport.'

'When did this start?' Dad is asking a lot of questions suddenly. It's like he hasn't listened to anything I've been saying and he's hearing about it for the first time.

'On the first day of school.'

'Why didn't you tell me?'

'I told you I hated it.'

'Yeah, but not why.'

'You wouldn't have listened. You were too busy telling me I'd settle in and make friends.'

Dad blows out and puts his head in his hands.

'I'm sorry,' he says. 'I just want you to be happy there.'

'Well, I'm not. I hate it.'

'I'll call the head teacher tomorrow. He shouldn't be allowed to get away with this.'

'That'll only make it worse,' I say.

'Well, what else can I do?'

'Let me leave, like I want to.'

'Finn, we've been through all this. It's an excellent school. Let's get this lad sorted out and maybe that'll help calm things down a bit.'

I shake my head and walk off, because I know it's going to make it a whole lot worse.

Mrs Goodfellow's office is at the far corner of the school, looking over the fields at the back. It's like she wants to be head teacher, but she doesn't really want to see or hear what's going on.

It is a funny name for a lady too, Goodfellow. Dad is standing next to me. Apparently, she'd said she wanted me to be at the meeting too so she could 'reassure me'. I can't think of anything she can say to reassure me, apart from telling me I can leave.

'Remember what I said,' says Dad. 'We'll keep it polite and we're only here to talk about this incident. I don't want you saying you hate the school.'

I shrug. I wouldn't tell her I hate it anyway. I don't want to tell her anything. I just want to leave and never come back.

Dad knocks the door. She calls out, 'Enter,' in a bright, high voice and we go in.

Mrs Goodfellow stands up behind her desk and comes out to greet us. She is tall and thin and has her long hair piled on her head, which makes her look even taller. I think she must like being tall.

'Hello Mr Carter,' she says, shaking his hand, 'delighted to see you again.' I had forgotten that she would have met them when they came to look around. She must have met Mum too. I wonder what Mum thought of her.

'And Finn, thank you for coming. I won't keep you from your lessons for too long, but I wanted to offer you some reassurance. Please, do take a seat,' she says to both of us.

I look around as we sit down. The walls are covered in floral wallpaper and there are paintings of birds hanging on them. There are dainty ornaments of ballerinas on a shelf and a vase of flowers on her desk. It looks more like that posh tea-room Mum took me to in Ilkley once than a head teacher's office.

'Now,' says Mrs Goodfellow, looking at me as she sits back down behind her desk. 'I was so sorry to hear about the accident with your ukulele on Wednesday.'

I look at Dad. If he isn't going to say something, I will.

'Er, Finn was quite clear that his instrument was broken deliberately.'

Mrs Goodfellow smiles. 'I understand that, but I have spoken to the young man involved and he has assured me that it was a highly unfortunate accident. When Finn dropped his ukulele, he was walking past, and in trying to jump out of the way, he overbalanced and stepped on it. He really is very sorry.'

'No,' I say. 'That's not what happened. He did it on purpose and he laughed as he did it and said mean things to me.'

Mrs Goodfellow shakes her head. 'I do understand that you're very upset, Finn. Your father tells me the instrument was of sentimental value, but I can assure you that the young man in question would not lie about such a thing. His father is Chair of Governors here, so he comes from a highly reputable family.'

'I hope you're not suggesting that Finn's lying,' says Dad.

'Not at all. But I do think he may have got confused about what happened, due to the emotional nature of the incident.'

'No,' says Dad. 'He doesn't get confused and I can assure you he also comes from a highly reputable family, although, of course, sadly, not one that is represented on your governing body.'

For the first time since we entered, the smile disappears from Mrs Goodfellow's face.

'Mr Carter,' she say, 'I do not like what you are insinuating. What we have here is two contrasting versions of events. I have spoken to all the young men involved and the two witnesses have confirmed that it was entirely accidental.'

'They were laughing as he did it,' I say, my voice cracking. 'They're his friends. Of course they're going to lie for him.'

'I can see you're getting a little emotional, Finn,' Mrs Goodfellow says. 'And I do understand that you've had a difficult few months, but it is important that we all try to keep calm and resolve this situation. To that end, purely as a gesture of goodwill, Mr Cuthbertson, the father of the young man involved, has kindly offered to pay for a new ukulele to replace the one damaged in this accident.'

Dad looks at me. I shake my head.

'That won't be necessary, thank you,' Dad says. 'I'll be replacing it myself. I have to say that I'm very disappointed that Finn isn't being believed and you aren't taking appropriate action against the boy involved and his friends.'

Dad is talking like a lawyer now. He's quite good when he's like this. Still not as good as Mum, though. She would have stormed out by now.

'I think,' says Mrs Goodfellow, 'the best thing Finn can do now is to try to integrate a little more with his classmates. It has been noted by members of staff that his social skills need a little work.'

Dad looks at her and shakes his head. He opens his mouth to say something, then shuts it again. Mrs Goodfellow stands up.

'Well, thank you for taking the time to come and see me and discuss the matter,' she says. She holds out her hand. Dad shakes it but he doesn't return her smile.

'I do hope that the boys involved will be closely monitored around Finn,' Dad says. 'Perhaps if he wasn't being subjected to hurtful comments and having his property smashed by fellow pupils, he would be able to integrate a little better.'

Dad turns and walks out. For the first time in my life, I feel proud of him.

'I told you she wouldn't listen,' I say, as soon as we get outside.

Dad's eyes are dark. They go like that when he is angry.

'I know. I'm sorry. If this was a court of law, she wouldn't have got away with that. She's clearly protecting him because of who his father is.'

'It's going to get worse now,' I say.

'If he says or does anything to you, you're to tell a teacher straight away.'

'They won't believe me either.'

'Then tell me when you get home. I believe you, OK?'

'So why are you making me stay here?' I ask.

'Because all the other good schools are full now. There's nowhere else you can go. We've just got to try to make the best of it.'

I shake my head. 'Mum wouldn't make me stay,' I reply. 'Mum didn't even want me to come here in the first place. She was right. You should have listened to her. Why did you never listen to her?'

I turn round and run off in the direction of my classroom, ignoring Dad's calls. When I go in and sit down, Harrison has a big, smug grin on his face.

AFTER

14

KAZ

Finn looks completely broken when I arrive. I step inside and give him a hug.

'Hello, love. I'm so sorry about your ukulele.'

He'd phoned me to tell me about it. Martin had said he could because Finn had explained that I've got an old phone and fat fingers, so am rubbish at texting.

'I hate him,' Finn says. 'I never really hated the kids at my old school, but I hate Harrison.'

'I know, pet. I hate him too and I've never even met little blighter. Has your dad done owt?'

'He's still mad at Mrs Goodfellow, like I am, but he says I still have to carry on going to the school.'

'I see. Is he still mad at me, too?'

'I don't know,' says Finn. 'Why don't you go and find out? He's making tea.'

I go through to the kitchen. I'm aware I should try to make peace with Martin. He's taking a day off work to do Terry's tribunal on Monday, which is pretty decent of him. The least I can do is apologise.

Martin looks up from the chopping board.

'I'm sorry,' we both say at once.

Martin smiles. 'Well, that's all sorted then,' he says.

'No, really. I didn't mean to have a go at you,' I say. 'And I don't think I'd be a better parent than you. Not judging by mess I've made with our Terry. It's just I have a habit of opening my gob first and regretting it later.'

'You had every right to have a go,' says Martin.

'Did I?' I hadn't been expecting this response.

'Yeah. And I should have bloody listened to you. Sometimes, you don't want to hear the truth though, do you? Not if you've fucked things up big time.'

I sit down at the table.

'Finn told me what happened at school.'

'I know. That Harrison's a nasty, lying little shit but it's not him I'm angry at. It's the head, for trying to cover it up because his dad is the Chair of Governors.'

'Finn said she didn't believe him.'

'She believed him all right. She just doesn't want to upset Harrison's father. He's got two other kids at the school, apparently. And his money is quite clearly more important than my bursary kid.'

'What you going to do about it then?'

Martin shrugs. 'I don't know.'

'You can pull him out.'

'Come on, Kaz. I've had all this with Finn. We've got to be sensible about this.'

'Sensible's overrated,' I say.

Martin manages a smile.

'What?' I ask.

'Hannah always used to say that.'

'Maybe she had a point.'

'She always had a point but it was usually different from mine.'

'Aye, well, they say opposites attract.'

Martin shakes his head.

'It wasn't like that. Not at first, when we met at uni. We had a lot in common then.'

'So what happened?'

'Life, growing up, parenthood. Hannah just remained the same idealistic, wonderful but entirely impractical person she was as a student. So, I figured one of us had to be a bit more responsible. Which is why I became the boring person who did the nine-to-five, paid the mortgage and reminded Finn about his homework.'

'I could have done with someone like that.'

'I don't think Hannah saw it the same way, though. She thought I'd sold out, lost all my idealism. She said I took issue with everything she said and did.'

'And was she right?'

'Probably. We both had very different upbringings. Sometimes that only comes out when you have a kid of your own. She was adopted. Her parents were older and were very laid-back hippy types. My parents were uptight, so I was always wanting to play it safe, do the conventional thing. I think it was my way of making sure I didn't screw up as a dad. Didn't exactly work out.'

He turns away from me for a moment. Maybe I did judge him too harshly at first. At the end of the day, we're all trying to do our best. We just have different ways of going about it.

'You've got a chance to do things differently now.'

'Have I? I can't see how, to be honest. I know Hannah was right. This isn't the school for him, but I don't see what I can do about it now. Even if I did pull him out, who's to say the same thing wouldn't happen in the next one we tried? I can't keep pulling him out of schools forever.'

'Well, there might be summat out there he'd like. You need to find a school that's right for him.'

'Yeah, and that's easier said than done,' says Martin. He walks over to the oven and checks the dinner.

'Be ready in five minutes.'

'Right,' I say, seeing that I'm not going to get any further with him. 'I'll go and get Finn.'

I fetch Terry home on Sunday evening. I've made us a nice fish pie for tea, to celebrate his first overnight. He comes straight in and sits down on the sofa with his feet up.

'Make yoursen at home then,' I say with a smile.

'I'll be home soon,' he says.

'Let's not get our hopes up too much.'

'No, Doctor Khalil said. Reckons I can do two nights next weekend and he'll see about letting me come home week after.'

'Really?'

'Yeah. Said he were going to talk to you when I go back tomorrow.'

'Better hope I say yes, then,' I reply.

'Cheeky bugger,' he says with a smile.

He sits for a moment, looking around him, as if familiarising himself with the place again.

'It's all right here.'

'Yeah,' I say. 'It is.'

'Better than other place.'

'Aye.'

He starts fiddling with his buttons.

'Are you fretting about tomorrow?'

'A bit. Feels like I'm on trial. I'll have to tell them about that wee girl. God knows what they'll think of me.'

'It's them who are on trial, Terry. They're ones who messed it up. You should never have been found fit for work. It's their fault that happened. Doctor Khalil has told them that in his statement. Martin reckons you've got a good case.'

Terry nods. 'I'm just worried about losing. I can't go through all that again, Kaz. If I have to work, I'll end up straight back inside and who knows how long it'll take me to get out next time.'

'I know. We'll do our best, eh? I can't make any promises, not after last time.'

'OK. Fancy a bit of *Mr & Mrs*? Can't beat a beat of Derek Batey to take your mind off stuff.'

'Go on, then,' I say.

'I'll be all right if they ask questions like that tomorrow. So I can choose my answers from sometimes, always, never or occasionally.'

Martin arrives promptly at nine the next morning.

'Did Finn get off OK?' I ask.

'Yeah. Not at all keen, but he went.'

'Poor mite. Let's hope he has a better week.'

Terry comes to the door behind me.

'This is Martin, Finn's dad,' I say to him. 'Martin, our Terry.'

'Hello,' says Terry, stepping forward to shake Martin's hand. 'Thanks for doing this. Our Kaz says you've been a right help.'

'You're welcome. It should never have happened. It's time we got it put right. Are you ready to go?'

'Aye,' I say. 'Let's get it over with.'

There are three of them sitting behind the bench when we go in. Two middle-aged bald men in suits and a woman with silver hair and wearing a pearl necklace.

'Fucking hell, Kaz,' whispers Terry. 'I don't think we've got a hope.'

'Come on,' I say. 'Remember what Martin just said. All you've got to do is tell truth.'

He nods and we all sit down. The woman in the pearl necklace introduces them and explains what will be happening.

Martin looks at me and nods. A few minutes later, he's standing up, going through the case, reading things out from the big file he's holding. I had no idea he'd done this much work on it. I passed on the papers they sent, but then I left him to it. He reads the bit out he'd told me about from Doctor Khalil's statement. The bit where he said that he didn't feel sufficient weight had been given to the previous instances where Terry had been sectioned after starting work.

I give Terry's hand a squeeze before it's his turn to go up.

'Just remember, if you're stuck, sometimes, always, never or occasionally.'

Terry manages a smile. He fidgets a bit while he stands there but once they start asking questions, he's fine. He tells them exactly what happened. How he could hear the rats scrabbling around the toilet. I catch the look on the woman's face. I just can't work out if she's horrified at him, or them for sending him out there.

We wait outside in the corridor while the panel make their decision. Terry is walking up and down, fiddling with his buttons again.

'What do you reckon?' I whisper to Martin.

'He's got a very strong case. Just depends if they're the sort who'll be prepared to overturn it.'

We get a call to go back in, fifteen minutes later. The woman in the pearl necklace smiles at us as we go in. She starts talking; I can't work out some of what she's on about, but Martin is nodding as she talks. And then I hear it. The bit where she says the original decision was wrong and they're putting him back on Employment Support Allowance. I grab Terry's hand.

'You've won,' I tell him. 'You've won case.'

Terry is quiet when we come out. Quieter than I imagined he'd be. He sits down on the chairs outside, puts his head down and I see his shoulders start to shake. I sit down next to him and put my arm round his shoulder.

'It's OK,' I say. 'It's over now.'

'I know,' he says. 'But it should never have fucking happened, should it? Not to me, or you or that wee girl. None of it should ever have happened.'

'No,' I reply, relieved he doesn't know the full extent of the toll it took on me. 'None of it should ever have happened.'

BEFORE

15

FINN

The warden isn't around when we get back to the campsite and the only other tent apart from ours has gone too. Mum gets all the stuff out of our tent and puts it in a pile with our rucksacks. She is doing everything very quickly.

'If you can try to pack our rucksacks the best you can, Finn,' she says, 'I'll get to work on the tent.'

I look down. I can't see how all those things actually fitted in, but I suppose they must have. I pack my bee rucksack first because that is easy. Then I start rolling up the sleeping bags like Mum has shown me and stuffing them into the rucksack, putting our toiletries in the side pockets and tying our cooking things on the outside. I have managed to get most of it in by the time Mum has finished the tent.

'Great job, Finn,' she says, 'can you pop and fill our water bottles while I get this attached to the rucksack?'

I run over to the shower and toilet block, where there is a drinking-water tap. When I tell Lottie about this bit, I will tell her I was excited, even though I am actually scared. I don't want Mum to go to prison. From what I have seen on TV, prisons are horrible big, dark, scary places and Mum is soft and gentle and likes dancing and baking and I don't think they would let her do those things in there. I thought they only put murderers and robbers in prison. I didn't think they sent mums who take their child camping there – even if they didn't tell their husbands about it.

When I get back to Mum, she has already hoisted her rucksack onto her back. I clip the water bottles on.

'Right, let's be off, then,' she says, although she doesn't look or sound very sure about it. She looks completely different from when we arrived at the campsite. Kind of like all the fun and hope has been squeezed out of her.

'Where are we going?'

'Not far,' she replies. 'Somewhere I remember that should be a nice, quiet spot.'

'What if the police find us before we get there?'

Mum gives me the best hug she can manage with a huge rucksack on her back. 'Try not to worry, Finn. We're going to get this all sorted out. Everything will be fine.'

'OK,' I say, although I don't see how and judging by the look on her face, I don't think she believes it any more than I do.

We walk for a long way. Down through the woods to some country lanes and then along the river. It's still hot and we stop every now and again to have a drink of water. Mum doesn't put the rucksack down even though I know it is super-heavy and I can see the dents the straps are making on her shoulders. She doesn't say much either. She has her sun hat and her shades on, but she still looks sad, even though I can't really see her face. Even the way she is walking is sad.

I wish I could do something to cheer her up, but I have never been good at telling jokes and I don't think doing the crazy chicken dance and making chicken noises would be a good idea right now.

My legs are tired and I'm hot and bothered but I know I mustn't complain because that will make her even sadder. Eventually, the river leads into some more woods. It is cooler under the trees and Mum stops for a moment for another drink.

'Where are we?' I ask.

'Copley Woods,' she replies.

'But that's not far from home.'

'I know. It means we're halfway there already.'

'When are we going home?'

'As soon as Dad's told the police and it's all been sorted out.'

'Do you think he'll have told them yet?'

'I don't know,' she replies. 'We can listen to the news on my wind-up radio later.'

'Everyone at school will know by now, won't they? About the police looking for us, I mean.'

Mum looks down at the ground. 'I suppose so,' she says.

'They'll all be talking about it when I go back to school.

Asking loads of questions. Saying that I was scared of the tests and ran away. It will be worse than it was before.'

Mum sinks down on to her knees and starts crying. Sad crying, not the sort of crying you do when you graze your knee. I stand there, not knowing what to do. I kneel down next to her.

'Sorry Mum,' I say.

She shakes her head and cries even more. 'I'm the one who should be sorry,' she sobs. 'I'm the one who's messed all this up. I was trying to help but I've made things worse and I'm so, so sorry.'

She does some more crying. She is almost bent in half and she still has the heavy rucksack on. I worry she is going to get completely squashed under it.

'Take it off, Mum,' I say. 'It'll hurt you. Take it off.'

She sits up and eases the straps off her shoulders. The rucksack falls to the ground with a clatter as the frying pan bashes against the water bottles. The marks the straps have left on her shoulders look sore. I feel bad that I have made her do this. I should have kept quiet about all the stuff at school.

'Let's go home now,' I say. 'Maybe we won't get into as much trouble as we think.'

'You won't, Finn, but I will,' she says, reaching out for my hand. 'I should have realised it was a stupid idea, but I panicked and now look what I've done.'

She is crying again now. Big, soggy tears that stream down her cheeks from underneath her shades. She is squeezing my hand and it is like she is squeezing the tears out because I am crying too.

She leans over and hugs me to her.

'You'll be OK. I know it's not going to be easy for you, but Dad will take good care of you.'

'What do you mean?' I ask.

'They won't let you live with me after the divorce,' she says. 'Not now the police have been involved. They'll say you have to live with Dad, but we'll still see each other as much as possible and do lots of fun things together.'

'No,' I say, shaking my head in the hope that I may shake the words out of my ears and pretend I never heard them. 'I want to live with you.'

'I know,' she says, 'but I've messed things up, love. They'll say I'm an unfit mother because of this.'

'But you said Dad's solicitor was going to say that anyway.'

'He was but we could have argued he was wrong. Not now the police have been involved – there's no way they'll let you live with me.'

I stare at her, trying very hard not to burst into tears again.

'But it's not your fault the note blew down. I'll tell them that. I'll tell them that it happened to your shopping list too. They'll see that it was just a mistake.'

Mum is shaking her head and squeezing both my hands harder.

'It doesn't work like that, Finn. I've messed up big time and they're not going to let me forget it. When you're a kid, it's OK to make a mistake and learn from it. Even when you're an adult, you might be given a second chance, but when you're a parent . . .'

Her voice trails off and she just sits there on the ground. I wish I knew what to say but I don't because I am a kid and no one at school teaches you what to say when your mum is upset, only how to multiply fractions and label a Viking longboat.

'Don't get divorced then,' I hear myself saying. 'You and Dad can just carry on in separate rooms like you are now and we can still be together, and I don't mind about the arguing.'

Mum hangs her head.

'I'm sorry, Finn,' she says, 'we can't stop it now, we've gone too far down that road. I have tried, honestly, but there's no going back.'

All I can think of is how much I will hate it not living with Mum. I don't even see how Dad can possibly look after me when he doesn't know where anything is or what I like in my sandwiches. He will have to phone Mum up all the time and ask her stuff. And she won't be there when I need a cuddle. And I might still need a cuddle, even when I'm eleven. I feel the tears rolling down my cheeks and the trees around me go blurry. It's all gone horribly wrong and I don't know what to do about it.

'Then why don't we actually run away?' I ask. 'If that's what they think we've done, we should do it. We've got the stuff we need with us. We could go to the Isle of Mull, that place where they filmed *Balamory*, with all the different-coloured houses. I liked it there. They had a really good chocolate shop and if it's like *Balamory*, they will only have one policeman and if he's like PC Plum, he'll be nice and won't arrest you or tell anyone we're there.'

I was hoping it was a good idea, but Mum is crying even more now.

'We can't do that, Finn. Not in the real world. I'm your parent and Dad's right, I need to do the responsible thing and take you home.'

'But being with you is all I want. You can teach me stuff, like you always said you wanted to. We can make a school in the tent and study flowers and things.'

Mum has her arms wrapped round me now. She is crying softly into my hair and squeezing me so tightly it is getting difficult to breathe.

'I'm sorry, Finn,' she says again. 'I'd like that more than anything in the world, but it just can't happen.'

'Can we pretend then?' I ask. 'Just for tonight. I don't want to think about going back and not being with you, so can we pretend that we have run away and that we live in a tent now and I go to school in a tent?'

Mum hesitates and wipes my tears away with her fingers. 'OK,' she says, 'we can. Just for tonight, though. I'll take you home first thing tomorrow.'

'Can it be after breakfast?' I ask. 'I want to have veggie sausages on the campfire one more time.'

She nods and smiles. 'We're out of sausages so we'll have to pop to a shop and see what we can get.'

'But what if the police see us?'

'We'll go later, when it's dark. There's a shop at the petrol station not far from here. They won't be looking for us by then, anyway. Dad will have phoned them.'

'OK,' I say. 'Can we find somewhere to set up the tent now? I want to build my school.'

The hiding den and school we make is a good one. Mum finds a spot right in among the trees where no one can see us from the path. There is only just enough room to put the tent up, but I like being away from everything and everyone. It's like we are the only two people left in the world and that's what I want to believe right now.

We lie down for a bit in the tent and read, then we go and collect some nature things and I draw them in a notebook Mum has brought with her and label the parts of the leaves. If we had some crayons or chalk with us, I would do some leaf rubbings. I love seeing the veins in leaves coming through onto paper. If you try to do a rubbing of your leg, none of the veins come out. I know that because I have tried. Trees are cleverer than humans, really. Trees and squirrels.

'I liked school today,' I say as I sit and watch Mum cook the spaghetti hoops later.

She turns and smiles at me. It is a sad smile.

'It was good, wasn't it?' she says.

'Better than normal school. We don't do anything outside at school apart from play football and that's a complete waste of being outdoors.'

Mum smiles again. It's a better smile this time. 'I know teachers shouldn't say this, but you're my favourite pupil.'

I smile and the smile turns into a little laugh. Mum's does too. For a moment she has sparkly eyes and a sparkly voice. I think if we lived in the tent all the time there would be a lot more sparkliness.

Mum shares the spaghetti hoops out between our tin bowls. She gives me more than she's got. I look up with a little frown.

'It's OK, you're a growing lad,' she says. 'I'll have a big breakfast in the morning.'

We wait until it is starting to get dark before we set off for the shop. I have my bee rucksack on, and Mum has a little bag clipped on her belt that pulls out to become a shopping bag. It has got bees on too because she says they remind her of me.

'What time is it?' I ask, as we walk through the trees.

'About half past nine.'

'We forgot to listen to the news on your radio,' I say.

'I know. It was nice just sitting and talking with you. I didn't want to spoil it.'

'But we don't know if Dad has told the police now.'

'I'm sure he has,' says Mum softly.

'We could put it on when we get back, just to make sure.'

'It'll be a bit late, Finn.'

'Well, we haven't got to worry about neighbours, and we can find some music afterwards so you can have a dance. The floaty lady might be on singing about the dark days again.'

'The dog days,' says Mum, with a smile.

'What?'

'Florence, the floaty lady. She sings about the dog days being over.'

'Does she? I thought it was about spring and the dark days being over. What are dog days? Are they good or bad?'

'I'm not sure,' says Mum. 'I read a thing online about it and people couldn't agree whether they were good or bad.'

'When that dog bit me when I was five, that was definitely a bad dog day.'

'Yes,' says Mum, as she takes my hand, 'It was.'

'Maybe it just depends if you like dogs or not.'

By the time we reach the main road, it is dark. We have our head torches with us for going back through the trees and I am looking forward to that bit. It will be like a proper adventure.

We walk for about ten minutes before I see the petrol station ahead. As we get nearer my tummy starts to feel a bit funny.

'What if the person in the shop heard the news on the radio and calls the police,' I say.

'I really don't think they will,' replies Mum. 'It'll probably be some student who's got more important things to worry about.'

'Like what?' I ask, wondering what students who work in petrol stations worry about.

'Oh, maybe what time they're finishing, if they've forgotten to do their essay and whether they'll have enough money to go out next weekend.'

I shrug. They don't seem like very important worries to me, not compared to being hunted by the police and not being able to live with your mum any more. We walk on in silence.

There is only one car in the petrol station when we arrive. The driver is filling it up with the hose thing that looks like an elephant trunk.

As we walk into the shop I look over and see that there is a young man at the till with short, sticky-up hair. Mum is right, he is probably a student and he doesn't seem interested in us at all. I glance around but I can only see one other person in the shop; an older lady in a grey cardigan, and she's not looking at us either. She's wandering around as if she can't decide what to buy. My tummy doesn't feel as bad now. We go over to the aisle where the cold things are. I can see meat sausages but no veggie ones.

'We might have to find something else for breakfast, I'm afraid,' says Mum. I try to hide how disappointed I am, then crouch down and spot them on the bottom shelf.

'There,' I say, pointing to a pack of four sausages with the little green tick on the front.

'Fantastic, well spotted,' she says, picking them up. 'How about I get one of those bottles of smoothie you like too?'

I nod and smile at her. I love that she's making a special breakfast for me. I am trying not to think about what will happen when we go back home and imagining that we will have breakfast outside our tent every day for the rest of our lives.

Mum picks up a mango and pineapple smoothie and we go up to the till. The man who was filling up his car is paying for his petrol. The grey-cardigan lady is standing in front of us, but she still doesn't have any shopping and there wasn't another car outside, so I don't understand why she is in the queue. She is staring into space like I do sometimes. She looks a bit sad. Even her plaits are droopy. The man in front goes and it is her turn. She asks for a bottle of something on the shelf behind the counter. It is when I hear her voice that I remember that I have seen her plaits before.

'Mum,' I whisper, tugging her sleeve. 'It's the sheep apron lady from the café.'

'Is it?' she says.

'Yes, but she hasn't got her sheep apron on. What if she recognises us and phones the police?'

'She won't do, love. She'll have seen hundreds of people in that café, she won't remember everyone.'

She might not remember everyone, but I think she will remember me because of my hair and because I made a big scene. I am not the sort of kid who people forget.

I watch as the probably-a-student man serving puts her bottle on the counter. It has see-through liquid in it. I think it is alcohol because there is a big sign saying alcohol and cigarettes cannot be sold to those under 18 above the shelf that he got it from. The sheep apron lady hands him some money. I notice that her hand is shaking as she takes the change. She picks up the bottle, turns round and sees me. I can tell that she remembers me straight away.

'Hello, pet,' she says, her voice not as sing-songy as I remember it. 'You came in for your breakfast, didn't you?'

I nod. I wonder if she is going to mention that I also ran out before we got it, but she doesn't say anything. . She glances down at the bottle in her hand and tries to put it under her cardigan. I don't know what to say and she doesn't seem to know what to say and Mum is keeping quiet even if she does know.

'Take care, then,' sheep apron lady says and starts to walk away. I hear the door open behind us; I look round in case sheep apron lady spotted us earlier and called the police. It isn't the police, though. It's two men. A big one and a smaller one, and both of them are dressed in black and they have their hoods up and scarves wrapped round their faces and they're wearing gloves, which is weird because even though it is night-time, it is still warm and I don't even know where my scarf and gloves are because they have been put away until next winter.

The smaller man runs to the counter and the big man stays by the door and shouts something and points his rolled-up carrier bag at us and the sheep apron lady. It takes me a second to work out that he shouted, 'Get down,' but Mum is already grabbing me and pulling me to the floor. I think we are being arrested and he is one of those undercover detectives I have seen in films.

'Are they policemen?' I whisper.

'No,' Mum says in a tiny voice. I hear the smaller man shouting at the probably-a-student man behind the counter. He is telling him to open the till. And that is when I realise what is happening. It is also when I scream.

'Shut the kid up,' the big robber shouts. Mum is holding me very tightly. I can feel her arm shaking on my back. All the time I was worried about the police and I should have been worried about robbers.

The smaller robber is yelling at probably-a-student man to go faster. My face is pressed against Mum's chest, so I can't see anything, but I hope he is giving him the money. As soon as he has the money he will run away. Only then the police will come, and they will see us, and we will be arrested anyway. I burst into tears.

'Fucking shut him up,' the big robber shouts. I try to stop crying but I can't, and it gets louder; screams and sobs and huge gasps of air, all somehow rolled into one. I hear footsteps approaching. I lift my head up for a second and see the big robber's boot kick Mum hard in the back. She screws her face up, lets go of my hand for a second and gives a little yelp, like the noise a dog makes if you step on its tail. He's hurt her. He's hurt my mum who would never hurt anyone. I feel something rising up inside me. It is hot, and in a hurry to get out. I scramble to my feet and kick the big robber in the shin as hard as I can.

I can hear lots of noise, like I could in the playground that time. Everybody yelling at me. Mum screams, 'Finn, no,' and her hand is on my arm and she is pulling me back down, but the big robber turns and grabs me too. He is holding up his hand with the rolled-up carrier bag in and pushing me to the floor and as I land, Mum rolls over on top of me and then I hear Mum scream and I have never heard anyone scream like that before. It is so horrible it stops all the other noise. For a second, I think maybe it was a bad dream and I have just woken up and am lying in the tent next to Mum. But then someone shouts, 'No!' and I think it is the sheep apron lady and I know it wasn't a bad dream at all. The noise starts again, and other people are shouting and moving, but Mum is not doing either of those things. She is lying completely still on top of me. Someone is dragging me out from underneath her. The first thing I see is the robber's carrier bag stuck in Mum's side and I do not understand how it could do that and then I see blood coming out from under it and Mum's head falling back on the floor.

I look up to see if the robbers are still here, but I think they have gone. When I look back down again the probably-a-student man is kneeling next to Mum, holding her wrist and shaking his head. He gets his phone out of his pocket and stands up and walks away. I sit up a bit and see there is a black handle sticking out of the carrier bag and lots more blood and I know then that it is a knife he was carrying and he has stabbed Mum; my soft, gentle mum who loves dancing and baking and doing the chicken dance.

I shut my eyes and scream and the person who dragged me out from under Mum puts their arms round me and hugs me and a plait falls in my face, so I know it is the sheep apron lady and she is crying and telling me it's over now but it is not over, Mum is lying on the floor next to me and the pool of blood is getting bigger and it reaches the veggie sausages, which Mum must have dropped.

I start crying and sheep apron lady tries to lift me up and pull me away from Mum but I am not going to leave her and

I am kicking and screaming so she lets go and I lie down and curl myself round Mum's head and put my head on her chest but it is not moving up and down because she is not breathing and I know we will never sit outside our tent eating sausages for breakfast. Not tomorrow and not ever again.

Sheep apron lady sits next to me stroking my head while I cry until an ambulance man comes in and kneels down next to Mum. He looks up and shakes his head too and then I see there are two policemen behind him and I think they have come to arrest Mum and take her away and I start screaming at them and telling them to leave her alone because she is my mum and she was only trying to help and that the note fell down behind the shoe rack and none of it is her fault; she was only trying to do her best.

Everybody starts talking at once and I feel sheep apron lady's arms lifts me up gently and she is crying almost as much as I am. She holds me very tightly and keeps whispering that she's got me. I see the bottle she bought lying on the floor. It isn't smashed but she doesn't stop to pick it up, just takes me out through the door. I feel the fresh air get stuck in my throat as I gulp back the tears. I can hear one of the policemen talking into his radio and another police siren somewhere in the distance. She takes me round the corner away from the ambulance and we sit down on the ground and she puts her arms round me and rocks me back and forth and strokes my hair and it feels like I have known her forever.

'I've got you,' she whispers over and over again. 'I've got you, Terry.'

BEFORE

16

KAZ

I hold him for what seems like a long time but may only be a matter of minutes. Rocking him softly to and fro. Like I used to do with Terry, when he was little. I don't know what else to do. His mam has just been murdered in front of him. His life will never be the same again. And for some reason I am the one holding him. I am not even supposed to be here. I was on my way home to chuck some vodka and pills down my throat. That is what I am supposed to be doing. But instead I'm here, holding a little boy whose mam has been killed in front of him. And I know already that I will not take my own life now. Not tonight or any other night. Not when I have seen a life snuffed out in front of me like that.

As I look down at the boy's tear-stained face, all I can think of is that it should have been me. The robber should have taken my life, not hers. That would have been fine. It would have saved me the hassle of doing it myself. I should have got up and confronted him. I mean, I had nothing to lose, did I? I couldn't move, though. The woman who was supposed to be topping herself tonight froze, just like she had once before.

I am aware of footsteps approaching. I look up and see a woman paramedic who I hadn't even noticed was here.

'Can I give the lad a check-over, please?' she says quietly. 'I need to make sure he wasn't injured at all.'

I nod. Though what's it's got to do with me, I don't know.

'What's his name?' she asks.

I realise I don't know. I haven't asked him that. I'm really not much use at all.

'I don't know,' I say.

'Sorry. I thought you were related.'

'No. I met him once before in the café where I used to work, but I don't know his name.'

The boy raises his head. Squints a bit in the light coming from the shop behind her.

'Hello,' she says, bending down to him. 'My name's Shagufta and I'm a paramedic. What's your name?'

'Finn,' he whispers.

'Finn, can I have a quick look at you to make sure you haven't been hurt, please?'

Finn looks at me. I give a little nod. The paramedic gently unfolds one of his arms. He is hanging on to me with his other hand, though. I give it a squeeze. The paramedic gradually works her way across his arms and torso.

'Can we get you to stand up, just for a moment?' she asks.

We hold one arm each and lift him to his feet. It's only as he stands up that I notice the blood on his rucksack. For a second, I think he must have been stabbed too.

'Let's just slip this off you,' the paramedic says. She takes it and passes it to me. I am relieved to see that there is no blood on him underneath. It's not his blood at all. It's his mam's. I exchange glances with the paramedic. She was obviously thinking the same thing.

Finn is shivering now. It must be the shock setting in. The paramedic asks if it hurts anywhere. He shakes his head. She checks over every inch of him anyway.

'Thank you, Finn,' she says eventually. 'Looks like you're fine. I do want to keep you warm, though.' She takes out a foil blanket from her bag and wraps it round him. I notice that he is looking across at me and realise too late that he has seen the blood on the rucksack. He starts crying again. I pass the rucksack quickly to the paramedic and wrap my arms round him, the foil blanket rustling as I do so.

'Are you OK?' the paramedic asks, turning to me. 'Were you hurt in any way?'

'No,' I say, quietly, unable to look her in the eye as I remember the ambulance man who came to our kitchen to see to Terry after I dialled 999. The ambulance man who I'd lied to and told it was an accident; that my little brother had pulled the saucepan down on himself while I was taking up a cup of tea to my mum who was ill in bed. It was what she had told me to say. The shock seemed to have turned her sober enough to think straight and she always was a good actress.

'No, I'm fine, thanks.'

'I'd better give this to the police,' she says, gesturing to the rucksack. She goes back into the petrol station shop and I am alone with the boy again. It is only now that I wonder just how alone he is in the world. I've only ever seen him with his mum. He might not have a dad. Not one that lives with him, anyway.

A policeman comes out and walks over to us. His radio crackles, causing Finn to look up. The policeman crouches down to his height.

'Hello, there. It's Finn, isn't it?'

The boy nods.

'Finn Rook-Carter?'

He nods again. I can't understand how they have found out his surname for a second, then I realise they must have checked for ID on his mum.

'Are you going to arrest me?' Finn asks. 'Are you going to put me in prison because Mum said you wouldn't. She said Dad would phone you and sort it all out.'

I hold him tight. I have no idea what he's talking about.

'No,' says the policeman. 'No one's going to arrest you. You're not in trouble, Finn. We're here to help you. Your dad is on his way. He'll be here very soon. A lady police officer is bringing him. She's going to help look after you, too.'

Finn starts crying again. The policeman turns to me as I hug him.

'I'm sorry,' he says, 'I don't know your name.'

'Kaz Allen. I'm not family. We were just in shop together when it happened.'

He nods. 'Thank you for looking after him. I'm afraid we will need you to come down to the station so we can take a statement. The young man who works here will be coming too. We need as much information as possible.'

'Right, OK,' I say.

'Have you got a phone?' he asks. 'Is there anyone you'd like us to call?'

'No,' I say. 'No one, thanks.'

A few minutes later a police car pulls up in the forecourt. The woman driving gets out. So does a tall man with flecks of grey in his hair and beard. He looks pretty much how anyone would look if they had just been told their wife had been murdered. As soon as Finn sees him, he breaks away from me and runs over to him, throwing himself at him and pummelling his little fists against his chest.

'You shouldn't have called the police,' Finn screams. 'The note fell down behind the shoe rack. We were coming home in the morning but now Mum's dead and we can't have sausages on the campfire and it's all your fault.'

Finn's dad crumples and starts crying too. Huge, big, man sobs. I stand there, not knowing what to say or do. The policewoman looks about as uncomfortable as I feel. She walks over to me and speaks in a quiet voice.

'Hello, are you the lady who's been looking after Finn?'

I nod.

'I'm the police family liaison officer. I wonder if you would be kind enough to look after him for a few more minutes. I need to take his father inside to do a formal ID. I don't want Finn to go in there.'

'Of course,' I say. She goes back to Finn's dad and puts her hand on his shoulder. Says something into his ear. He looks up and looks across at me. Wipes his eyes with the back of his hand. A few moments later he walks towards me, Finn still attached to him, half clinging, half pummelling.

'Thanks,' he says, prising Finn's arms away from his body and letting him reattach himself to me.

'I'm so sorry,' I say. It sounds pathetic but I don't know what else to say. He walks off into the shop, the policewoman holding his arm. I look down at Finn and pull him closer to me as I hear the anguished cry of his father from inside.

I only see Finn once more, when we arrive at the police station. He went in a different car to me, with his dad and the policewoman. His face is pale, his eyes scared. He reminds me of Prince Harry walking behind his mother's coffin at her funeral. Red hair, sad face, looking tiny and absolutely lost without his mam. He stops as they go to walk past me. I step forward and bend down to him, giving him another hug.

'You're being so brave,' I say. 'Your mam would be really proud of you.'

He walks off solemnly. Like he is following the coffin. And I bow my head because I know, in some ways, he always will be.

AFTER

15

FINN

I stand there in the changing rooms in my shorts and rugby shirt, knowing that I am going to hate this more than I have ever hated any PE lesson in my life, and that is saying something. We are playing a game of rugby. It's not going to be tag rugby, like we played for half a term at school and was just running about and kids pulling a coloured tag you tucked into your shorts. This is proper rugby. We did passing last week (I am no good at it) and today we are going to do tackling and play our first game. I have never played proper rugby and I have only seen a couple of bits on TV, when I went into the living room and Dad was watching it. From what I could work out, it is played by big men with beards who like head-butting and jumping on top of each other. I cannot think of anything I would rather do less, but although Mr Makin said about my long hair meaning I could go and play netball with the girls, apparently that is not an option now. I knew I shouldn't have had my hair cut.

'Hey, Gay Lord, ready to play a man's game?' says Harrison. He has been worse since. He knows he can do whatever he wants to me now and they will let him get away with it. Jacob and Toby stand behind him smiling. They are like the Crabbe and Goyle to Harrison's Malfoy. If I was Harry Potter, at least I could cast a spell on him. But I'm not. I look like Ron Weasley. And my friend Hermione goes to a different school. So, I stand there and say nothing. That doesn't make it stop, though.

'Never played proper rugby before, have you?' says Harrison. 'That's because you went to a school for thickos, not a prep school like us.'

'I've played tag rugby.'

'That's for girls. You don't get hurt in tag rugby.'

I try not to show him that this comment scares me.

'Let's go and line up, Finn,' says Mustafa. He is even smaller than me, so he must be really scared about proper rugby too. I follow him outside. It is just starting to rain. Mr Makin is standing there in his rugby kit with a ball under his arm.

'Look lively, lads,' he says. 'You're about to play the finest sport on earth.'

He blows his whistle and all the boys line up, before he marches us off to the sports field. When we get there, the first thing I notice is how muddy it is. I wish I could wear my gardening gloves and my waterproof dungarees that Mum got me when I was nine, but which still fit.

I am wearing boots with studs in that Dad had to buy

specially and they rub my ankle bones and make me walk weirdly. I would have been happier with a pair of wellies, but they weren't on the sports kit list.

Mr Makin blows his whistle and says we are going to learn how to tackle safely. He gets two boys to come out and demonstrate. By the end of it, they are both covered with mud. I don't see what is safe about falling into a big patch of mud without waterproof clothing on.

He tells us to go away and practise with our partner. Me and Mustafa look at each other and shrug. He has the ball, so he starts to run away very slowly. I go up to him and put my hands on his waist and he drops the ball, which I then pick up.

'Look at Gay Lord. He doesn't want to get his hair messed up,' says Harrison, loud enough for me and most of the other boys to hear, but not Mr Makin. It doesn't matter that I've had my hair cut. They are still going to tease me about it anyway.

'Or get a ladder in his tights,' says Toby.

The other boys laugh. We swap over. I run with the ball and Mustafa chases me half-heartedly. As soon as he gets to me and touches my waist, I just hand him the ball.

I hear Mr Makin's whistle blow. 'Rook-Carter and Ali, you are an embarrassment to the game of rugby,' shouts Mr Makin. 'Carry on like that and you can go and join Miss Hambleton's netball practice.'

The other boys howl with laughter. 'Right,' continues Mr Makin, 'Rook-Carter, you can work with Cuthbertson, Ali, you go with Johnson. Perhaps that will buck your ideas up a bit.'

I stare at Harrison, who has a smug grin on his face. Toby

is also laughing as Mustafa starts to walk over to him. What I really want to do is to run away and never come back. Instead, I go over to where Harrison is standing.

'I bet you wish you never grassed on me now,' he says. 'This is payback time.'

The sound of the other boys laughing almost drowns out the rain. Harrison throws the ball hard into my face, so that it stings.

'Ladies first,' he says.

I start to run away. I want to run all the way home. To never come back to this stupid school. I cannot run fast enough, though. I can hear Harrison as he comes up behind me. I know he is going to get to me any second. I feel a bit sick inside. A second later I feel his hands grab the top of my legs and pull them away from me. I put my hands out to save myself, but it is too late. I fall flat in the mud. I feel the full weight of Harrison as he lands on top of me with a grunt. His knee comes up and connects with my balls. For a moment, I think that I am going to be sick. I am struggling to breathe. I can't work out whether my eyes are shut, or it is just the darkness of the mud. What I do know is that I don't want to be down here, on the ground. I try to get up but the weight stops me. I am shaking and my back is wet. It is blood. I know it is blood. I can feel it seeping onto my back. It will be there when I stand up. Her blood all over me.

I start screaming. I am not sure if they are still here or they have gone now, but I cannot help it. The screams keep coming. I am screaming for her. Screaming 'Mummy,' over and over and over again. The weight lifts. I do not dare get up though, because if I do, I will see her lying there. I will see the carrier bag and the knife and the sausages on the floor. I would rather lie here forever covered in her blood than see that again.

Someone is pulling my arms. Hauling me up off the floor. I keep my eyes tightly shut and cling on to them. It must be Kaz. I try to wrap my arms round her, but then I realise it is not Kaz. It is a man's voice calling my name. I open my eyes a fraction, just enough so that I can see who it is. The first thing I see is Mr Makin's whistle, swinging in front of my eyes.

Mr Makin asks Mustafa to come back to the changing rooms with us. I think he is scared I might start screaming again, and he doesn't know what to do if I do.

'Do you need a doctor, Finn?' he asks.

I am not sure if he means a doctor who gives you medicine or the sort of doctor Dad took me to see after it happened, one who wants you to talk about how you feel. Whichever it is, I don't want to see one.

'No,' I say. 'I just want to wash the mud off my face.'

He tells Mustafa to stay in the changing rooms with me. For us to wait here until he comes back with the other boys. When he goes, I look at Mustafa. I don't know what to say, so I don't say anything. I just walk slowly into the toilets with my head down.

They are still laughing at me when they come back into the changing rooms. Mustafa and I have got changed back into our uniforms and are sitting on the benches.

'Finnona wants her mummy,' says Harrison. 'Finnona's been crying for her mummy.'

'Leave him alone,' says Mustafa.

'Yeah? What you gonna do about it? Get your family to make a bomb to blow us all up? That's what your lot do, isn't it?'

I don't even say anything to stick up for Mustafa, because I still cannot speak. I don't know what happened. Why it all came back like that. All the stuff that I have tried to force out of my head for so long. The stuff I only see or hear in nightmares. But it felt like I was back there. Like it was happening all over again.

I sit down and tie up the laces on my school shoes.

'Never knew you were such a mummy's girl,' says Harrison. 'Does she still read you bedtime stories? Does she tuck you in bed at night? Give you a goodnight kiss?'

They are all laughing. Every one of them except Mustafa. I pick up my school bag, leaving my muddy PE kit behind, and walk out of the changing room. Mr Makin is in his little office. The door is open, but I don't see him as I creep past. The sports block is separate from the rest of the school, so I don't have to sneak past anyone else. I carry on walking, past the main entrance and out of the gates. As soon as I get to the other side, I start running. I may not be very fast on a rugby pitch, but it turns out I am much faster when I am running away from school. I don't know if they are going to come after me, but I am not going to take that chance. I keep running until I get to the bus stop. I have no idea what times the buses are, but I am lucky. I only have to wait two or three minutes before one comes along. I get on, still trying to get my breath back, and show my pass. I think for a second the driver is going to say something. Ask if I'm bunking off. Shut the doors and drive me straight back to school. He doesn't though. He just nods and pulls away from the bus stop.

I sit in the corner at the back of the bus, like I have done something naughty, and stare out of the window. I know exactly where I am going. The last place I was happy. The place I wish I was every day when I am at school.

It feels strange going past our house and not getting off. I do not want to be there, though. I want to be at the place I feel closest to her. It is quite a long walk from the bus stop. Down the main road and then cutting off into the woods. It looks different from the last time I was here. There are no bluebells like there were back in May. Some of the leaves are starting to turn yellow and orange. And there is no Mum singing or dancing or helping collect things for my nature tray. Just the emptiness in the air where her breath used to be.

I start to worry I will not be able to find it. That I will be walking around for hours and every bit of the woods will look the same. But even though I am coming from the opposite direction, I recognise it as soon as I get there. The spot where we camped. Our tent isn't there any more, of course. Dad came to get it and the rest of our stuff a few days after, while the police family liaison officer lady looked after me. I had to tell him where it was and draw a map for him. I didn't want to see it when he brought it back. I didn't want to look at any of our stuff. All I wanted was the one thing he couldn't bring back to me. Mum.

The ground is still wet, but I don't care; I want to get as close as possible to where she was. I sit down and shuffle around until I think I am in the exact spot where we sat while she cooked breakfast. I shut my eyes and try to imagine the smell of our sausages, try to remember what she was wearing on the last day I saw her, because for some reason she changes in my head every time I try to picture her.

I feel close to her here. Dad has offered to take me to visit her grave, but I do not want to be where she is dead. I want to be where I was with her when she was alive. That is the her I want to remember.

They will be looking for me now, I know that. I wonder if Dad will report me as missing to the police again. I hope not. I do not want to be chased or arrested. I do not want to feel scared. I came here to try to stop feeling scared. I take my mobile phone out of my school bag. I always have it on silent when I am in school. There are seven missed calls; all from Dad. They must have phoned him at work. He has texted me too. His message says: '*Finn, please let me know you are safe. Tell me where you are and I'll come and pick you up. You are not in trouble.*'

I hold the phone in my hand while I try to decide what to do. I don't want to go back to school but I don't want the police coming looking for me either. I don't want to be on the news again.

I press to return the call. Dad answers straight away.

'Finn, are you OK?'

'Are the police looking for me?'

'No. I haven't called them yet. I've only just got home and I wanted to check here first.'

'Will I have to go back to school?'

'No. I'll bring you straight home. I promise. Where are you?'

'Where me and Mum had our tent.'

There is a sound on Dad's end of the phone. I think he might be crying. It is a moment before he says anything.

'Don't go anywhere. I'll come and get you now,' he says.

It's not that long before he arrives. He must have come in the car and then run from the road because he is out of breath. He sinks down onto his knees and hugs me. He is definitely crying now because his tears are making my forehead wet.

'I was so worried,' he says. 'School said you'd been screaming and crying out for Mum.'

'Harrison tackled me in rugby and he fell on top of me. I couldn't breathe. It was like I was in the petrol station again.'

Dad screws his eyes up tight and strokes my hair.

'And then he was teasing me in the changing rooms; calling me a girl and saying Mum still kissed me goodnight.'

'Did you tell a teacher?'

'No, because they wouldn't listen to me. And Mr Makin hates me anyway because I don't like rugby.'

I am crying now too. I remember crying like this when I was on my way here with Mum when she told me I wouldn't be able to live with her any more. I have never heard Dad do noisy crying like this though. He cried at the police station, but it was quiet crying. I don't think he even did noisy crying at the funeral, although maybe I just couldn't hear him because I was crying so much. I hated the funeral because it was sad, and in a church and everyone wore black, apart from Rachel who came in purple, and Mum wouldn't have liked it one little bit. It was the wrong kind of funeral for Mum. They didn't even play the song about the dog days being over and I told Dad that was her favourite.

'I'm sorry, Finn,' says Dad eventually.

'What for?' There are lots of things he could be sorry about and I'm not sure which one he means.

'For calling the police. I was so worried about you that I messed it all up. When I went home after your mum phoned and found the note on the floor, I felt so stupid. I rang the police straight away, but they couldn't call off the search without seeing you for themselves. I know it's my fault and I understand that you're still mad at me for that. I'm mad at myself too. I always will be.'

We cry some more, and I wipe the snot from my nose. 'I should have kept quiet,' I say. 'If I'd stopped crying and screaming at the petrol station and kept quiet, the robber wouldn't have kicked Mum and I wouldn't have kicked him back and none of it would have happened.'

Dad is shaking his head. 'It's not your fault. You must never think it's your fault. You were scared. You were incredibly brave. Remember how I cried when you told the police lady you'd kicked the robber? It was because I was so proud of you.'

'But I made him kill her.'

'You didn't, Finn. He killed her, it's his fault, not yours. That's why he's going to go to prison.'

'I thought you said he's in prison already?'

'He is, but after the trial he'll be sent there for good.'

'I wish I could kick him again,' I say. Dad does a little laugh in among the crying.

'She'd be so proud of you, Finn. She loved you so much.'

'Did you love her?' I ask. 'Because you never say so.'

Dad puts his head down and does some more crying.

'I never stopped loving her,' he says. 'Not even for a minute.'

'Not even when you were arguing?'

He shakes his head. 'I know I wasn't very good at showing it. Sometimes, you can love someone but find it really difficult to live with them.'

'Because she liked doing the crazy chicken dance and you didn't know how to do it?'

'Yeah,' says Dad. 'Exactly that.'

AFTER

16

KAZ

'*Finn's safe. I've got him. We're on our way home.*' I close my eyes and let go of a long, deep breath as I read the text from Martin. He'd called me earlier to tell me Finn had run away from school. Wanted me to know, in case he got in touch or headed for my house. I put down the scouring pad I'm holding and take off my Marigolds. I've been cleaning place top to bottom ever since. Only thing I could think of to try to stop me fretting about him. Surprised I didn't take the steel off the sink, I scrubbed it that hard.

I don't know what's going to happen now. I can't bear to think of him going back to that school. Not even for a day. Hannah wouldn't have let it happen, I know that much. She laid down her life for that boy. Like I was going to lay down mine for Terry. It would break her heart to see him suffering like this. I need to pay her back for saving my life too. I need to find some answers.

I pick up my bag and leave the house. I head straight to the library. They have books and computers and librarians. They have answers.

When I turn up at Finn's house later, Martin opens the door looking almost as bad as he did that night.

'He's in bed,' he says. 'He's not asleep, though. Go up. He says he wants to see you.'

I put my bag down in the hall and go upstairs. The curtains are drawn in Finn's room but there is still enough daylight to see him clearly. His face is very pale, paler even than usual, or maybe it's just that his shorter hair makes it seem that way.

I sit down on the bed and lean over to give him a hug.

'I'm so glad you're OK,' I say. 'You scared life out of me.'

'I had to go. I couldn't stay there a moment longer. I couldn't breathe, Kaz. It was like it was all happening again.'

'I know, love,' I say, stroking his arm. 'Your dad told me everything.'

'Do you still think about what happened that night?' Finn asks.

I nod. 'Pretty much every day. I have nightmares about it sometimes, too.'

'So do I,' says Finn, brushing away his tears. 'I have this nightmare where when I stand up, I've got her blood all over me and I look down and it's even on my hands.'

'It wasn't your fault,' I say. 'You were so brave. The police lady said that afterwards, didn't she?'

Finn nods. 'Dad says the trial's next month. You'll be there too, won't you?'

'Yep. And I know we're not really allowed to talk about what happened until then, but I want you to know I shall tell them exactly how brave you were. Because I was there. And you were a damn sight braver than me. I know that much.'

We both cry for a bit.

'I'm so glad you were there,' says Finn. 'I wouldn't have had anyone to look after me otherwise.'

'I know,' I reply, 'me too.'

He falls asleep in my arms, eventually. I creep out of the room and go back downstairs. Martin is in the kitchen, sitting staring into a mug of coffee. I sit down opposite him.

'You know Hannah saved Finn's life, that night; what you don't know, is that she saved mine too.'

He looks up at me, frowning.

'You've never asked why I was there,' I say.

'I thought you were just getting some bits of shopping in.'

I shake my head.

'I were buying vodka. I had a bottle of it in my hand when the robbers came in. I were going to go back to my flat and use it to wash down some of our Terry's old antipsychosis tablets. I had them out on table waiting for me. I thought he'd be better off without me, see. Thought I'd messed up so badly, that were best way out.

'I kept hearing me mam's voice taunting me, see. Saying it were my fault Terry had been hurt when he were a kid, when actually she'd been blind drunk and that's how he'd ended up being scalded. I'd blamed mesen for it for all those years and I'd worked out that Terry would be better off without me.

'Only I were there when your wife gave her life to save your son. And I held your son when he were crying his heart out because he'd lost person he loved most in world, and that's when I knew I couldn't do that to our Terry.'

Martin reaches out his hand across the table to take my shaking one.

'I'm sorry,' he says. 'I had no idea.'

'When police dropped me off back home in early hours, those tablets were still on table. I put them straight in bin. I lay on bed for a bit, trying to work out what to do. Landlord were coming to evict me later that day but I knew I had to hang on in there, for Terry's sake.'

'So that's how you ended up in the hostel,' says Martin.

'Yeah. Sometimes you have to grab on to nearest tree branch when you fall, even if it's a very low one. And I had three people not to let down after that night. Terry and Finn and Hannah.'

Martin nods as his eyes cloud with tears.

'Do you think Finn's going to be OK?' he asks.

'Yeah, I hope so. He'll find trial hard, mind.'

'I know,' says Martin. 'I'm going to try to get him some more counselling. I think he'll need it.'

'What about you?' I ask. 'Perhaps you could do with some too.'

'Maybe. I feel so guilty being alive,' he says. 'Finn loved her so much more than me and she was so much better than me in every way.'

'Then honour her memory,' I say. 'And show Finn how much you loved her by doing what she would have done.'

I go to my bag, get out the computer printout the librarian ran off for me and put it on the table in front of Martin.

'He needs you now,' I say. 'And he loves you way more than you realise.'

Doctor Khalil smiles at me as I pass him in the corridor.

'He's had his bag packed since seven o'clock this morning,' he says.

'It'll be right nice,' I say. 'Three nights at home together.'

'Have you got anything planned?'

'Just telly tonight. He's still catching up with his old videos. And we're going to a friend's house tomorrow for tea.'

'That'll be good for him.'

'Yeah,' I say. 'I think he's looking forward to it. Someone I've been wanting him to meet for ages.'

'Well, if all goes well, he can go home for good next Friday.'

'Thanks,' I say. 'For everything, I mean.'

We stand on the doorstep outside Finn's house, Terry with a bottle of wine in his hand. He bought it himself out of his benefit money. We had no idea what to get, of course. Had to ask the chappie in Lidl.

Martin opens the door.

'Hello,' says Terry, holding out the bottle, 'this is for you. To say thank you for tribunal, like.'

Martin takes it.

'Thank you,' he says. 'That's very kind. I'm just glad I could help. Your sister's done so much for our family.'

'Aye, she's good, our Kaz. Not a bad old stick for her age.'

'Cheeky sod,' I say, giving him a dig with my elbow.

'Anyway, come through,' says Martin. 'Finn's in the garden. There's something he wants to show you.'

We follow Martin through the house and out into the back garden.

'Hello Kaz,' Finn says, running up to give me a hug. He turns to Terry, 'Hello Our Terry, I'm glad you're feeling better now and I'm glad Kaz got you some new school shoes when the kids at school were mean to you. They're mean to me too sometimes, so I know what it's like.'

Terry smiles at him and nods. I always knew they'd understand each other if they ever got to meet. I'm just so bloody glad they did. Finn turns back to face me.

'Come and see what we've got,' he continues. 'It's not as big as the one at Castle Howard but it's solar-powered, and Mum would have liked that and it's got LED lights that go different colours, so I can see it from my room at night.'

He grabs my hand and pulls me towards a small stone fountain. The word 'Mum' is written in little stones around the bottom.

'It's beautiful,' I say, 'what a lovely way to remember her.'

'Yes, Alan always does something to remember people that have been lost when he does *Love Your Garden*. A little quiet spot, he calls it. And I've got something to tell you,' says Finn. He runs back into the kitchen and comes back clutching the computer printout I gave Martin. 'I've got a new school. We went yesterday to have a look around. It's in Hebden Bridge and it's not like a normal school, it's only small and you don't have to wear uniform or play rugby and I can grow my hair back like it was before. They do lots of things outside in the woods and they have a beehive and there's a boy there who knows Lottie and I think Mum would like it because it's not like a normal school, it's weird, like me, but good weird.'

'That's fantastic,' I say, looking up at Martin and giving him a wink. 'That sounds just like your sort of school.'

'It is,' says Martin, 'but they only open four days a week, which leaves Monday free. What we're looking for, is someone to help Finn with gardening club on a Monday. If you know anyone who's free . . .'

'Will you, will you, will you!' screams Finn, jumping up and down. I nod.

'I'd be delighted to.'

Finn launches himself at me.

'Thank you,' he says, giving me a huge hug.

'That's fantastic,' says Martin. 'Normal rates will apply and if you could start on Monday, that would be great. And if you would ever like to come too, Terry, you're very welcome.'

'I might just do that,' says Terry. 'Doctor said it would be good for me to get outside a bit more.'

'There you go then,' says Martin.

'And you can bring Barry too sometimes,' Finn says. 'If he's your boyfriend now.'

'Cheeky monkey,' I say, unable to contain my laughter. 'You don't have boyfriends at my age.'

'But you are going out with him next week,' says Terry.

'Only because it's his birthday and he were going to be on his own. I thought it would be nice for him to have some company.'

They are all looking at me. I expect they have noticed the colour in my cheeks.

'I'm sure it will be,' says Martin. 'And just so you know, he's also welcome here anytime.'

'I think I'll call him Barry-not-Kaz's-boyfriend, from now on,' says Finn.

'And you, young man, had better start behaving yoursen. Else I'll be calling you Finn-the-cheeky-monkey.'

He laughs. We all do. It feels good.

'Would you like me to show you around the garden, Terry?' asks Finn. 'We used Alan Titchmarsh's "Create Your Dream Garden in Just 4 Weeks", because that's all we thought we had, but we can do more to it now. I've got some ideas already. You can come up to my room and meet Alan Titchmarsh later, if you like. He's only cardboard, not the real one, but he's very good. My best friend Lottie got him for me. And if we go down here,' he says, steering Terry towards the bottom of the garden, 'I'll show you the Alan Titchmarsh rose Kaz got me for my birthday.'

I turn to Martin and smile. 'Don't worry,' I say, 'Terry'll get his own back when you come to our place and he makes you watch *Stars In Your Eyes* videos all night.'

'I'm quite looking forward to it,' says Martin.

'So am I,' I reply.

'Thank you,' says Martin, holding up the piece of paper that Finn has given back to him. 'I never even knew it existed.'

'The librarian said they've only just started taking older kids. They'd been in to use the library a couple of times. That's how she knew about it when I asked.'

'They can still do their exams, too,' says Martin. 'But they just do things their own way. Finn's way. Hannah would have loved it.'

'Good,' I say. 'Because we both owed her big time.'

I look up as I hear strange noises coming from the bottom of the garden and see Finn flapping his arms around.

'What's he doing?' I ask.

Martin smiles. It's a moment before he seems able to answer. 'He's showing Terry the crazy chicken dance.'

AUTHOR'S NOTE

This is my tenth novel and is therefore a bit special to me. I've always wanted to write a novel from the point of view of a child; some of my favourite novels (*To Kill a Mockingbird*, *The Boy in the Striped Pyjamas*, *The Lovely Bones*, *Room*, *Life of Pi*) are told though the eyes of a child. I think we have much to learn from children and so often the innocence and simplicity with which they see things, helps to illuminate complex issues.

As the mother of a son, one of my biggest concerns is the way boys are increasingly being pressurised to conform to an ever-narrowing gender stereotype which restricts their emotional development, their future ambitions and their ability to simply be themselves. My own son has managed to stay true to himself in the face of hurtful comments and bullying (the worst of which occurred when he was just eight years old), but so many children, particularly those without parental support, end up conforming to the 'norm' simply as a survival strategy. The fact that so many children continue to be bullied at school and many do not receive the support they should is a national scandal.

In Finn, I wanted to create a character who was having a

tough time at home and school to see how he would cope when the world was particularly cruel to him (although I love him to bits and hated doing it to him!). At a time of crisis, Finn needed a friend and in Kaz, I like to think he found one of the best.

I have also wanted to tell the story of someone like Kaz for a long time. Too often the voices of marginalised people in our society are not heard in fiction. The inequalities in our country have deepened over the last ten years and the poorest and most vulnerable people in our society have had to bear the brunt of swinging cuts and austerity. People suffering with mental health issues have been particularly badly hit. The voices of people like Kaz and her brother Terry deserve to be heard. I wish that I could say their experiences are not typical. Sadly, many of the cases I read about during my research were far worse than theirs.

I'll be making donations from the royalties of this book to the mental health charity Mind www.mind.org.uk; the Anti-Bullying Alliance www.anti-bullyingalliance.org.uk, and the Trussell Trust www.trusselltrust.org who run many of the UK's foodbanks. If you're able to make a donation too, however small, I'd be hugely grateful. Thank you.

ACKNOWLEDGEMENTS

While writing a novel is a largely solitary pursuit, there is a huge support team who help along the way. Therefore, I give thanks to the following people: My three editors; Emily Yau, for being there at the beginning and letting me write something 'a bit different', Cassie Browne, who took up the baton and offered much support (and huge patience), and Emma Capron, who doubled-up for the last leg and cheered me across the finishing line. Your top editorial skills and feedback are much appreciated. Everyone at Quercus, especially Milly Reid, Hannah Robinson, Hannah Winter and Bethan Ferguson, for their hard work and tireless championing of my books; my agent, Anthony Goff, whose expertise, advice and support continue to be invaluable, and all at David Higham Associates, particularly the translation rights team who ensure my books find new readers across the globe.

Jacqui Lewis for her copy-editing skills and Patrick Carpenter for the cover design; my website designer Lance Little; Rebecca Bradley for her police fact-checking service and all those who helped me with questions about the benefits system and mental health. Special thanks to Max (provided by Articulate Speech,

Drama and Casting) for being my 'Finn' in both the paperback cover and the book trailer. You are a complete star!

A number of charities/rights organisations were also invaluable for research purposes, especially Mind, John Pring's Disability News Service, the Mental Health Foundation, Rethink Mental Illness, Disability Rights UK, Mental Health and Money Advice, Young Minds, Anti-Bullying Alliance and Citizen's Advice. Nathan Filer's book *The Heartland* was also extremely helpful.

Thanks to my family and friends for their ongoing support, to my husband Ian, who has excelled himself this time by donning waders to take the cover photograph and for filming and editing the fantastic book trailer, and to my amazing son Rohan, who, as well as helping edit the book trailer, has taught me so much about the strength it takes for a boy to be different in the face of bullying and abuse and who I am so proud to see growing into such a wonderful, unique and talented young man.

Thanks, as always to the fantastic booksellers out there, especially the excellent independent bookshops The Book Case in Hebden Bridge, The Book Corner in Halifax and The Grove in Ilkley, who are so supportive of my work. And to the librarians, bookbloggers, book clubs and fellow authors for sharing the book love and helping to spread the word.

And finally, to my readers, for buying, borrowing, recommending and reviewing. I know I say it every time, but the messages and feedback you send me really are the best part of being an author. I hope you enjoy this book too and please do get in touch via Twitter @lindagreenisms, Facebook Author Linda Green and my website www.linda-green.com. I look forward to hearing from you!

READING GROUP GUIDE

1) How did you respond to the story being told in the Before and After sections?

2) The bullying Finn suffered at school highlighted how hard it can be for children who are perceived as 'different'. What did you think of the way the adults in the story responded to this?

3) What were your first impressions of Kaz and how did they change as the novel progressed?

4) Terry had a very different childhood to Finn's, but they also have lots in common. How did the author explore the similarities and differences between them?

5) How do you feel Finn's relationships with his mother and father were developed during the novel?

6) Did you find yourself siding with either of Finn's parents? How do you feel the author tackled the issue of the difficulties of being a good parent?

7) Finn and Kaz have an unusual friendship. In what ways did they help each other as their friendship deepened?

8) How do you feel Hannah would have responded to what happened to Finn in the 'After' sections of the novel?

9) Kaz's role as a carer to Terry has shaped her life. Do you feel it will continue to do so in the same way?

10) Has the novel changed how you feel about the way the most vulnerable people in our society are treated?

the
last thing
she told
me

**Even the deepest-buried secrets
can find their way to the surface . . .**

Moments before she dies, Nicola's grandmother Betty whispers
to her that there are babies at the bottom of the garden.

Nicola's mother claims she was talking nonsense. However,
when Nicola's daughter finds a bone while playing in Betty's
garden, it's clear that something sinister has taken place.

But will unearthing painful family secrets end up
tearing Nicola's family apart?

**The emotionally charged suspense novel from
Linda Green, the bestselling author of
While My Eyes Were Closed and *After I've Gone*.**

Available now in paperback, eBook and audio.

Quercus

After I've
GONE

You have 18 months left to live . . .

On a wet Monday in January, Jess Mount checks Facebook and discovers her timeline appears to have skipped forward 18 months, to a day when shocked family and friends are posting heartbreaking tributes following her death in an accident. Jess is left scared and confused: is she the target of a cruel online prank or is this a terrifying glimpse of her true fate?

Amongst the posts are photos of a gorgeous son she has not yet conceived. But when new posts suggest her death was deliberate, Jess realises that if she changes the future to save her own life, the baby boy she has fallen in love with may never exist.

'The story was authentic, absorbing and unputdownable. I fell in love with Jess and although I raced through the pages I didn't want the story to finish. And it really was the perfect ending . . .'
Louise Jensen, bestselling author of *The Sister*

Available now in paperback, eBook and audio.

Quercus